Praise for the Ben Pecos series by Susan Slater

"Take a great plot idea and Susan Slater's skill with language, combine them with her understanding of the religion and culture of a proud and ancient people, and you have a gripping novel."
—Tony Hillerman on *The Pumpkin Seed Massacre*

"...an appealing mix of new and existing characters; beautiful, even mystical, descriptions of New Mexico; dry humor; crackling suspense; and a surprise ending."
—*Booklist* on *Yellow Lies*

Praise for the Sam McCain series by Ed Gorman

"Gorman's delightful series...provoke[s] a bracing nostalgia for a time that was neither as innocent nor as dull as is sometimes said."
—*Wall Street Journal*

"Gorman's successful capturing of time and place...sharply evokes the twilight of the '50s."
—*Los Angeles Times*

"Gorman seems to have hit a mother lode with this series."
—*Publishers Weekly*

SUSAN SLATER   ED GORMAN
IRENE MARCUSE   MICHAEL JAHN

CROOKS, CRIMES AND CHRISTMAS

W✸RLDWIDE.

TORONTO • NEW YORK • LONDON
AMSTERDAM • PARIS • SYDNEY • HAMBURG
STOCKHOLM • ATHENS • TOKYO • MILAN
MADRID • WARSAW • BUDAPEST • AUCKLAND

CROOKS, CRIMES & CHRISTMAS

A Worldwide Mystery/November 2003

ISBN 0-373-26473-9

A WAY TO THE MANGER Copyright © 2003 by by Susan Slater.

THE SANTA CLAUS MURDERS Copyright © 2003 by Ed Gorman.

WHAT CHILD IS THIS Copyright © 2003 by Irene Marcuse.

THE GOLD BAND Copyright © 2003 by Michael Jahn.

Printed in U.S.A.

CONTENTS

A WAY TO THE MANGER
by Susan Slater

ONE

SHE BANGED THE stall door shut, pushed the latch in place, then listened. No one had followed her. But she could only choke back the waves of nausea so long. The game was tied. She was expected back on the floor. Her team, Valley 26, Chama, 26. She was the center—the star center, Coach Leonard would say. Well, wouldn't everyone just think she was a star if they could see her now? She put her forehead against the cold tile wall and tried to block out the roar of the crowd. Valley must have scored. She pulled up her jersey and slipped the elastic waistband of her shorts down to rest on her hips—shorts from her freshman year that were now baggy, but becoming increasingly uncomfortable. She unpinned a long strip of Ace bandage from around her stomach, working her hand down between skin and tan textured fabric—holding the confining material away from her body. She took a deep breath. How much longer could she hide what was happening?

CHRISTMAS VACATION started today. This was the last game before break. Maybe by the time they came back to school, she wouldn't have to worry anymore.

"Charlene, you in there?" The door to the bathroom banged against the wall.

She took another deep breath. "Yeah, I was just a little dizzy."

"You fell pretty hard, but me and Chantelle got even. That bitch won't trip you again."

Charlene smiled. She had friends, good ones. But ones who wouldn't understand what she was thinking of doing. She quickly tightened the bandage, slipped the safety pin in place and closed it. A pause, she exhaled. She pulled her shorts up and settled her jersey in place. Number twenty-one was ready to return to the hoop wars.

"Hey, you got the truck?" Jeni had to yell to be heard, but dumped a stack of damp towels on the gym floor to make room for her on the bench.

"Yeah." Charlene sank down, elbows on knees, chin in her palms and watched Valley score the last ten points—pull away and keep their lead. Then it was over. A hundred excited fans swarmed the floor.

"Let's get out of here." Jeni grabbed Charlene by the hand and ducked under the bleachers, heading for the back door. "Where you parked?"

"Outside the gate." They were both running now—beat the crowd or be thirty minutes caught in traffic. The cold air took her breath away. She was glad she had stuffed a pair of jeans behind the truck's seat. She now wore them unzipped, but with an oversize sweatshirt pulled almost to her knees, nobody guessed her secret. She hoped there was a sweatshirt somewhere among the fast-food wrappers on the floor of the truck. Thank goodness it was Friday night and she was staying over with Jeni; she could borrow what she needed. Stupid, but she'd forgotten her gym bag.

"I'm starved." Jeni was hopping along on one leg at a time pulling on sweatpants, then hooded top.

"You're always hungry." Charlene beeped the truck open and clambered behind the wheel. Would her brothers ever forgive her for buying a Toyota? Probably not. But the money had been hers, left to her by her grandfather. A truck to take her into Albuquerque for school next year and home on weekends. Only now, plans had changed. Would there even be college? Ever?

"Pizza?" Jeni rolled down the window and leaned out.

"Huh?" Charlene accelerated backward, then pulled forward and fell in line behind three other cars trying to beat the rush.

"Pizza. Do you want to go into Bernalillo?"

"Sure. Why not?"

"Charlene, quick, there he is. Oh, he's sooo cute."

"Jeni. Not now."

"He's looking this way."

Charlene floored the accelerator and spun out around the other cars in the loose gravel before her tires bit into the pavement that led uphill to the highway.

"What's wrong with you? He could have gone with us."

"Jason Arnold doesn't want to go with us anywhere."

"Hey, you're the one who used to drool all over him."

"Well, that's past tense." She cut the steering wheel and bounced the Tacoma onto the pavement.

"Be careful."

"Wear a seat belt."

"Why are you in such a bad mood?"

"Sorry. I'm just hungry, too."

She could feel Jeni eyeing her, but kept her own eyes on the road. Jason Arnold was already represented in the cab of the truck—only Jeni didn't know it. For that matter, neither did Jason. She had been stupid. She wasn't going to risk humiliation by telling him that their one night by the river last spring resulted in something that could only cause heartache. She felt the baby kick. In protest? Maybe it didn't like being called heartache. Maybe it knew already that its mother hated it, didn't want it, considered her life ruined because of it.

"Charlene. You just passed Pizza Hut. What is *wrong* with you?"

" Sorry." Charlene slowed, made a U-turn and had barely rolled to a stop before Jeni jumped out to join a group of girls standing by the door.

"Come on." Jeni turned back to wave.

"You go on. I just remembered I need to pick up a prescription at Walgreens. I'll meet you back here, unless I find something more interesting to do." She laughed. She and Jeni talked at length about how as firm as their friendship was, a date could change all that in a heartbeat. One time they'd planned to go to the movies in Albuquerque, but Jason had asked her out. Jeni understood. There was no question but that the date came first. Charlene rolled up her window and couldn't hear what Jeni yelled back. It sounded like "Good luck." She must think that Charlene was meeting someone. Jeni was popular; she wouldn't lack for rides home if Charlene was late. What she was about to do couldn't be put off.

The stretch of I-25 between Bernalillo and Albuquerque would take about fifteen minutes. She had the address of where she wanted to go on a slip of paper in her billfold, which was still in her gym bag, but she had it memorized. How many times had she stood in front of a pay phone at the edge of the Pueblo's recreational center and couldn't reach for the numbers, couldn't lift the receiver? Why? Because she didn't know what she would say.

Almost eight months pregnant—or was it past eight months? She never could figure out stuff like trimesters. But she'd put a star around the date when "it" happened. What had been the first words out of his mouth when his body had finished the spasmodic bucking? "Don't tell." And then he had felt it necessary to say he wondered how many others she'd "lured" to the river, how many others she'd professed to love. Had she said that she loved him? She didn't think so. But there in the dampness of the riverbank, her own coming-of-age trickling down her leg to mingle with the sand and moss, she knew before any end-of-the-month would come, her body had betrayed her.

She'd lain motionless long after his hurried footsteps took him to the road and his car. She heard the engine turn over…once…twice…then roar to life. There was a squeal of tires and he was gone. Jason Arnold, class president, son of the superintendent of schools, liar, cheat and so good-looking he made her heart ache. Even now.

She'd let things go too long to have an abortion. But she couldn't have done that. Adoption, that would be perfect. If her timing was right, she might even deliver and be back at school before anyone would be the wiser. She'd read about agencies that helped. Ones that placed children with families who picked up the expenses. And from what she'd read, she'd have a choice. She could pick which Mr. and Mrs. Right she wanted. It all seemed too easy, too contrived. But what else was there? What else could she do? Her father would be livid and she knew she couldn't stop him from confronting the Arnolds. Father *and* son.

She slowed when she neared the outskirts of town. It was already dark. She knew the agency would be closed, but she'd brought the letter to slip through the mail slot. The letter that gave the number of the pay phone in front of the recreational center. Four o'clock tomorrow. Her instructions were that they call her at exactly four and ask for Persi. That was her mother's nickname. She asked that someone try three days in a row before giving up in case she couldn't make it tomorrow. She couldn't go into town during the day and cut mandatory weekend practice; so, maybe someone could meet with her in the evening. But first they needed to talk.

The agency was on Central, past Nob Hill about two blocks west of San Mateo Boulevard. She'd have to drive right by the University of New Mexico. The school she hoped to attend. Coach Flanagan had already scouted her and had talked with Leonard. She'd tried to get Leonard to tell her what had been said, but he just smiled and said she'd know soon enough. Would there be a full scholarship? Would she start in the fall?

With a jolt she admonished herself for false hopes; no pregnant girl would be given a scholarship. Not now and maybe not after the baby was born. Could she keep it a secret and get back on the court and back in shape? She'd beg her parents to let her go to camp next summer. She'd be ready by fall; she had to be.

The low single-story building was set back from the road with a parking lot in front. Deciduous trees lined the drive on the right and several sprawling arborvitaes crowded the entryway. Charlene pulled into the drive, parked a couple spaces from the door, turned off the engine and just sat there. There was one other car in the lot, a white Honda sedan closer to the street. She could see the mail slot to the right of the door. It was big enough for packages.

Her note was in the glove compartment. She drew it out and quickly looked it over one last time. That would do it. It would have to. She'd only given the phone number of the pay phone and said that she needed to talk to someone—no mention of the problem, and, of course, not her real name.

She slipped out from behind the wheel and closed the door behind her. The night was raw compared to the warm cocoon of the truck's cab. She shivered and pulled the hood of her sweatshirt over her still-damp hair. When she caught a glimpse of her silhouette in the plate glass of the building's front door, she almost laughed. She looked like someone caught by those secret cameras in banks. Men with hoods pulled low, holding a bag.

She lifted the brass flap of the mail slot, hesitated, then let the envelope slip from her fingers to disappear from view. It was done. She had just made an important decision. Maybe the most important one of her life.

"Turn around and keep walking. I have a gun."

Suddenly the entryway was bathed in light. Charlene hadn't noticed the door ajar or the smallish woman with hair tucked behind each ear who stood stiff-armed, holding a gun pointed at Charlene's chest. Charlene opened her mouth to protest as the woman stepped across the threshold, the gun now dangerously close. Close enough that Charlene could see its owner's hands tremble. A gust of wind pulled the woman's long skirt back against her ankles, ankles made thick by ribbed wool socks.

"We don't keep money here and we don't have drugs."

"No. Wait. I just left a letter. All I want to do is talk to someone."

"It could be a bomb for all I know. Or maybe anthrax."

"I don't know who you think I am, but I'm Charlene Toya. I live in the Tewa pueblo." Charlene paused. "I'm pregnant. I need your help." She waited and watched the eyes of the woman in the doorway as they swept over her. She thought the hand holding the gun relaxed a bit.

"What do you want?"

"To talk."

"Why don't you come back in the morning?"

"Can't. I have practice—basketball."

"How far along are you?"

"Seven, eight months."

A sigh. "How do you think we can help?"

"Do you have time to talk now?" Charlene pulled the hood back and let her hair escape to curl over her shoulders. She was taller than this diminutive woman in the doorway. Taller by six inches at least. Charlene was proud of her six foot, almost six-feet-one-inch frame. A long-torso frame that tucked a baby up under her rib cage. With loose shirts it hid a pregnancy even from her parents.

"Come with me." The gun was now tucked in a pocket and out of sight. "We can meet in here. I'm Molly. I'm the physician's assistant here at the clinic. Have you been here before?"

"No."

The woman turned once to look at Charlene and this time she smiled and laid a reassuring hand on her arm. "I'm sorry about the gun. We've been broken into three times since last summer and probably have three bomb scares a week. We're not in a popular business."

Charlene nodded and followed her down a short hallway

to a brightly lit corner that held an examining table, a desk and two chairs. The walls were covered with prenatal posters outlining the body's changes and growth of the fetus at various stages.

"Who's your regular doctor?"

Charlene shrugged.

"Does that mean there isn't one?"

"Guess so."

"Have you been seen at all?"

Charlene shook her head. Who could she have told who wouldn't have told? Seeing a doctor had been out of the question.

"Why don't we start with an examination now? Here's a gown. I'm going to double-check the front door. I think I locked it but I'm so paranoid." The woman pulled the door shut behind her.

It was difficult not to trust this smallish woman with graying hair and large, bright-green-rimmed glasses. Or was Charlene just desperate enough to grasp at anything? Any bit of friendly authority who might help? She shrugged, slipped out of sweatshirt, pants and underwear, taking time to hide the Ace bandage under the pile; then, she tossed the bundle onto the closest chair and grabbed the paper gown. The table wasn't built for a tall person. Her long legs dangled far enough over the side to touch the floor—flatfooted. Million-dollar legs. Isn't that what Coach Leonard called them? She could step over, squat under, outtwist, outturn any foe…or at least that's what the *Albuquerque Journal* had said.

A quick staccato knock and the door opened a crack.

"Ready to go in here?"

"Yeah." As ready as she'd ever be.

The door pushed open and Molly entered, her denim shirt now covered by a white lab smock.

"I want you to ask questions. If I say something that you don't understand or if I go too fast, let me know."

"Okay."

"First, I'll start with a couple questions of my own. What is the father's position in this?" Molly stopped arranging the drape over Charlene's stomach. "Does he know?"

"No."

"Do you think there would be a problem?"

Charlene nodded.

"How about your parents? Do they know?"

"No."

"Do you have a close relationship with them?"

"Does this mean you have to tell them?"

"No, not at all. I'd like to establish your help-group. Because of your age, because what is about to happen to you—giving birth—can sometimes require the help of others—"

"How?"

"Just getting to the hospital on time might be challenging if you don't live close to one. Is there a clinic or hospital close to your home? Or are you thinking of using a midwife?"

"I live on the reservation. Tewa. I can't have the baby there."

"But you're at least an hour from town. Had you thought of what you might do?"

"I thought I'd say that I was going to basketball camp and just go away somewhere and then go back home after the baby was born."

Molly stopped her examination and pulled up a chair. "Where would this camp be?"

"It could be here, in Albuquerque."

"Who was going to arrange this?"

"I hoped you would."

Molly sighed and leaned back in her chair. "It's not what we do here. Most of the time we terminate pregnancies. Young women who, for whatever reason, do not want a child. I'm sure you know it must be done within the first trimester."

"And adoption?"

"Charlene, I may not be able to help you even with a

referral. As a Native American your child is protected—shielded by law from adoption outside the reservation—outside your tribe.''

"No way."

"I can't quote you the name of the Act that prohibits non-Native American adoption of Indian children, but we had a case about a year ago. A Navajo woman—''

"What happened?"

"She kept her baby."

"But I can't."

"Charlene—''

"I can't."

"Let's talk about this. There's a solution, I know there is. Lots of times parents are willing—''

"No." Charlene hadn't meant to raise her voice, but this was getting her nowhere. She'd have to rethink. "I need to leave."

"Let me finish the examination."

"I really need to go. I have to pick up a friend in Bernalillo."

"This is important. We need to talk about what's going to happen—to your body. How to recognize when your baby wants to be born. There are vitamins I need to start you on—''

"No."

Molly paused and looked at her. "All right. I'll be outside."

Charlene waited until the door closed firmly, then got up. What would she do? What could she do? If she told Jason, would he loan her the money to go away? No, he'd just deny it. And where would she go? She'd planned to leave the day Christmas vacation started. That was Monday. They had a month off. She didn't have to be back until the sixteenth of January. She wound the Ace bandage tightly around her middle. There would be an answer—there had to be an answer.

Molly looked up from a nurse's station in the hall when

Charlene came out. "I wish I could be of help. I want to help. I want you to trust me."

"Thank you. I'll call if I think there's anything you can do."

"What about my calling you? Staying in touch? Is this the phone where I can reach you?" Molly held up the letter that Charlene had pushed through the mail slot.

"Yeah, that's the number." What would it hurt to lie at this point? She'd never see this woman again.

"Listen, I know this is going to sound like more adult platitudes, but this is not the catastrophe you think it is. Someday you'll look back on this and—"

"Don't. You don't know how I feel. You don't know anything about me. It was a mistake to come here. I'll figure out something. I don't need your help." Charlene didn't stop until she'd pushed out the front door after snapping back the dead bolt. She stood in the parking lot. The cold settled around her and was oddly calming. She couldn't believe her rotten luck; being a Native American meant sacrifice and now that she had a chance at a life no one in her family had ever had, she couldn't even get rid of the one thing that could ruin it.

She walked across the parking lot and pushed the security button to open the truck. Strange. No welcoming lights blinked on. Could she have been in such a hurry that she left it unlocked? She always tried to be careful. Oh, no. Not only had she left it unlocked; she'd left the door ajar. But why were the interior lights out? She needed to be more careful. And check the bulbs or maybe the fuses.

It wasn't until she was almost behind the steering wheel that the hand snaked out from the passenger's side and grabbed her arm.

"No screaming. Just continue to get in the truck nice and easy."

The man was all in black and he was big; his head brushed the cab's overhead liner. There were no lights in the parking lot and his face was in shadow but she could smell him—peanuts, recently he'd been eating peanuts. And judging from the crunch when he shifted his feet to turn toward her, peanuts in the shell. Did that make him any less menacing? She didn't think so.

"What do you want?" Charlene didn't know where she'd found her voice.

"To talk. We need each other."

"Sure." So, was he going to rape her? She squared around in the seat and reached for the interior light. Swiftly and roughly he knocked her hand away.

"I wouldn't do that."

"I'm pregnant." Would that be the turnoff? Keep her safe?

"I know."

She felt the barrel of the gun press into her neck.

TWO

BEN PECOS STOOD on the clinic steps and adjusted the poncho over the thin shoulders of the man in front of him. The wind was icy. Sure sign that there would be an early winter. He patted Lorenzo Loretto on the arm and noticed that his grand-daughter had recently given him a haircut, not without its challenges if the chunk of hair missing above his left ear told the story. Lorenzo was almost a hundred. And a village hero. But always knowing what he was trying to convey was tough if not impossible. Ben thought the granddaughter did a good job at interpretation and was patient far beyond what most would be. Lorenzo had lost the ability to speak but commu-nicated by drawing or miming his needs.

Ben rolled down the sleeves of his flannel shirt and stayed on the steps long enough to watch Lorenzo take the first turn that would lead him to the church. He'll be warm, Ben as-sured himself; Father Emerson would see to that. There might be some leftover from the priest's breakfast, a bagel or a cup of hot chocolate. Lorenzo had turned into a sort of good luck charm. Everyone wanted to be a part of his well-being.

But wasn't that what a small community was all about? Helping hands when they were needed? And after all, a pueblo was the best example of the extended family. Ben looked out over the squat, flat-roofed adobe cubes, many joined back-to-back or side-to-side separated in clumps by winding dirt roads, evidence of families expanding, adding rooms for the next generations. But living together, sharing rituals—keeping their history alive in the oral tradition.

He was so much a part of all this he saw in front of him and so very little. When his mother had died of alcoholism, his grandmother had chosen to send him away to what she thought was a better life, an easier one with opportunities that would have eluded him had he stayed. And hadn't she been right? He was preparing to go for a Ph.D. in psychology and come back to help. The Mormon family who raised him had provided well. But what had he missed? His chance to belong. Even though his father had probably been Anglo, his mother, his grandmother, his uncles all were a part of this network bound by language, a religion that was filled with symbols of the earth but also embraced Catholicism.

He'd divide his time between the clinic in Tewa and the Albuquerque Indian Hospital until after the Christmas holidays. Then he would be uprooted again. This time to start on the last phase of his education—schooling, whose cost would need to be paid back to Indian Health Services by returning to his roots. A sudden gust of wind whipped across his face. His thoughts turned again to Lorenzo. Would the old man get out of the cold? Maybe he should have walked with him to his granddaughter's house. It was difficult to know what to do, what would be accepted as help. It took a long time to gain the trust of these people, his people yet not his people.

Ben sighed, opened the door and stepped into a string of Christmas lights snaking down the hall. It was Saturday morning and he'd thought he'd have the place to himself. Tough to get paperwork done in a crowd.

"I think these need to be placed above ground level," Ben said to no one in particular but loud enough to be heard in the back. "Hello? This could be a dangerous situation out here. Who's on light patrol?"

"Me." A thin, brown-skinned woman peeked around the door of the first office on his right, then stepped out into full view. "I'm so sorry, Doctor, but there were just too many twists. I want to put them on the roof and they have to be perfectly flat."

Ben wondered who would pull roof detail and was afraid he already knew. Christmas was just two weeks away. Wasn't all this decorating a little late? Maybe they left everything up until July; in some places that seemed to be a New Mexico tradition.

"Are you sure you want to put up lights now?"

"Have to."

"Have to?"

"Too many docs going on vacation over Christmas. No one will enjoy them."

So that's who the lights were for. Interesting. Two of the docs were Jewish, one an out-and-out agnostic and the fourth? He wasn't sure what she was unless the Green Party could also be a religion.

"Miss Thompson thought you might help."

Yep. Putting the lights up was going to be his detail.

"Are there outlets on the porch?" Ben couldn't remember seeing any.

"We run an extension cord through the window."

"Oh." Somehow meeting code wasn't a consideration.

"Last year we had all red lights. But Miss Thompson wants them mixed this year. She bought blue and green and white, see?" The Indian woman—he thought her name was Persingula—held up a stack of small boxes. "She thought it would be nice to outline the windows and the door. These icicle lights are for over the door."

Things had just gotten complicated.

"Persingula—"

"Please, Doc, call me Persi."

"Persi, this will take hours."

"It's Saturday."

An unspoken question seemed to hang in the air; what could he possibly have to do on a Saturday that could supersede putting up Christmas lights? He was beginning to wonder himself. He knew it would get him brownie points. And he needed all the help he could get.

"You're right." He smiled and noticed how beautiful the woman in front of him was when she returned his smile.

"I saw you at the game last night."

"Hey, best game yet. Nobody can stop us as long as we have Charlene Toya."

"She's my daughter." Persi looked down, but Ben sensed her pleasure at his remark.

"She's a natural. Is she being scouted?"

Persi looked puzzled.

"Are colleges trying to get her to sign with them? Promise to play ball and come to their schools on scholarship?"

"Oh, yes. The University of New Mexico has sent—" she paused "—scouts."

"They have a terrific program. That would be wonderful. She'd be close to home, but just far enough away to feel like she was on her own."

"That's important, isn't it?"

"Feeling a sense of independence? Most children need to break away from the family." But this was a pueblo. Children stayed home, helped at home, married, had children and never left. They had done so for centuries. The need to get away was Anglo, not Indian. So many Western ways intruded upon daily life here.

"My husband and I have encouraged her to give UNM a chance."

"Is there another school that she's interested in?"

"Coach Leonard told us that two big schools from—" she searched for the term "—back East had called him. Would that be a long ways?"

"Might be. But something in the Midwest—Kansas, Nebraska—wouldn't be."

"I asked her to stop by and help me with the lights, but I guess she's forgotten. She's tall." Persi stopped and looked up at Ben's six-foot-two-inch frame. "But I guess she won't be needed."

"I'd like to meet her. She's a tremendously talented young athlete."

"I'll go call her. She stayed the night with a friend." Persi walked back into the office on his right.

"Meet you outside."

BEN LOOPED THE STRINGS of lights around his arm and backed out the front door. He'd need a ladder and some hardware, which meant foraging in the garage. He thought he remembered a ladder, but that had been a few months back. The garage held maintenance vehicles for the pueblo and odds and ends of extra parts, new batteries, oil, various fluids.

"Dr. Pecos?"

"What is it?"

"I don't know what to do. Charlene never went to Jeni's house last night. She dropped her at the Pizza Hut and went into Albuquerque. No one has seen her since."

"Is there a boyfriend? Someone else she might be with?"

"No. Charlene only cared about sports—basketball, I should say. There weren't any boyfriends."

"I'm sure there's an explanation, but let's be on the safe side. I'll call the Pueblo police and have them check around here. Let's go to my office." Ben didn't add that it might be a good idea to involve the Albuquerque police. He'd ask Elmore Waquie, the local chief of police first.

THREE

LORENZO NEEDED a new walking stick. He didn't like the smooth cane with its curved handle that Dr. Pecos had given him. There was no spirit in the wood. He couldn't even tell what kind of tree it had come from. A tree with no voice, that was what kind. And to top it off there had been a rubber tip on the end. That was the first thing he took off but kept the little rubber cup in his room with other treasures under his bed. A real stick would talk to him, tell him of its life. Maybe it had floated down the river or had been carried by beaver and jammed with others to dam a stream and become part of the beaver's house. He listened to this "stick" holding the shiny perfect roundness to his ear, but shook his head. He tapped the cane on the ground and didn't like the thump it made—a flat sound that was empty. But he couldn't tell that nice Dr. Pecos that someone had robbed the wood of its life.

He'd look for another today down by the river but first he needed to find his teeth. His granddaughter made him wear them everywhere now, said people would want to talk to him and he needed to look presentable. So she laid out fresh washed jeans every morning and a starched shirt. She even had his poncho cleaned. And all because he had helped that Dr. Pecos's girlfriend. People in the village called him a hero. He wasn't sure about that, but he liked the attention and extra goodies. Every morning he got a free Krispy Kreme at the store up by the road. Big boxes were brought in from Albuquerque. For that treat he always took his teeth out and let the doughnut's sugary goodness become a lump on his tongue. Then he'd push it against the roof of his mouth and click his tongue against his palate as the lump dissolved. Maybe his teeth were at the store.

Lorenzo thought he might be almost one hundred years old. Any proof had been destroyed. He lived behind his granddaughter's house in an adobe addition built by his great-grandsons. Speech was difficult nowadays but his eyes and ears were sharp as ever. He adjusted the rolled bandanna tied around his forehead and tugged the poncho up around his neck. It was cold. The wind whispered a promise of snow. He'd have to hurry if he wanted to get to the river and back by afternoon.

He hurried past the old graveyard in front of the church. This was Lorenzo's favorite time of year. Already red plastic poinsettias dotted the wooden crosses that perched, some leaning precariously close to the ground, at the head of each grave. Soon lights would outline the old church and the bells would be cleaned in preparation for Christmas Eve. Every year a family was honored by being chosen to give lodging, *la posada,* to the Christ child. A manger was prepared and the family awaited Christmas Eve when they would find a lifelike baby doll wrapped in swaddling clothes snuggled in the straw. Lorenzo liked to go to mass on Christmas Eve and afterward in the early morning follow the priest through the village as he led the worshippers to the chosen house. There would be good things to eat and sometimes presents.

A short blast of northerly wind cut through his reverie and whipped open his poncho. He needed to move faster. The houses lining the dirt road that would take him across the fields to the river marked his way. There was never a question of getting lost. Only Anglos got lost. They would follow a road and take the wrong fork. They expected house numbers and different-colored roofs—not cluster after cluster of brown mud homes joined side-to-side or front-to-back without distinguishing characteristics unless you knew the make of automobile the family drove. And Lorenzo liked it this way. There were no tours through his village with people pointing out of bus windows. At feast days groups came from miles away, but they were respectful. No one was turned away at a feast day.

Anyone could eat with a family whether they were known to that family or not.

In the old days, his mother would speak of having to feed the Navajos—the group of Indians who would raid the pueblos and take their corn and livestock. But if they came on a feast day, they would be invited into the homes and fed. One time his grandmother put meat from a black bear into her stew. *Shush,* or black bear, was sacred to the Navajo. Everyone believed that those Navajo who ate the stew would die. Lorenzo couldn't remember how the story ended, but he didn't think there had been any fatalities. Mostly everyone told the story over and over and got a good laugh.

FOUR

FOR THE LIFE OF HER Charlene couldn't have told someone where she was, where the man who ate peanuts and held a gun to her head made her drive, then stopped, blindfolded her and drove another fifteen minutes himself. But now she was in a room cuffed at the wrist to another girl and both of them were very pregnant and very scared. They had scooted the two twin beds close enough to touch and talk without projecting their whispers too far into the room. The room was barely more than a cubicle and by the whimpers and muffled conversations around them, this living arrangement repeated itself up and down a long hallway.

There seemed to be only the two captors: the man and a strange, squat heavyset woman with short spiked gray hair who met them in the kitchen. Her florid face folded into three distinct chins one on top of the other until the last settled on her chest. The man called the woman Serena and she called him Jerry. Not their real names, Charlene would bet on that. When they had first come into the brightness of the cheery yellow room, Jerry supported her weight and directed her up the three narrow steps from what must have been a garage, a blindfold securely in place. Then he had turned her to face the woman and with a flourish pulled the soiled bandanna down to her neck. The woman had looked disgusted and spoke to the man in a language Charlene didn't recognize. From the woman's tone, she wasn't pleased. But not pleased with her? Charlene wondered. What kind of victim was he supposed to bring to her?

It was Serena who pulled the blindfold back into place. Then she instructed Charlene to hold out her hands and balance the two towels, bar of soap, tube of toothpaste and brush before being led to the cubicle. Only when she was seated on the cot-size bed did Serena slip the blindfold off, stuff the bandanna into her pocket and take the toiletries from her and put them on a box in the corner. Then Serena motioned for Charlene to stand.

"I will take your clothes, now. You will be more comfortable in a little smock." Serena picked up a checked gingham nightshirt from the foot of the cot. "Here, this is for you."

The girl next to her appeared struck dumb. Her slim frame with oversize tummy made her look like a daddy longlegs. But her eyes were haunting. She turned to Charlene and silently implored her to help. Instinctively, Charlene knew this girl was younger. Much younger than she. This child next to her looked maybe fourteen. At seventeen Charlene might be the oldest girl there. That was a sobering thought. But help? How?

"They call me Beanie," the girl said and held out her hand.

"Charlene." It wasn't really a handshake, more of a desperate holding on, but only for a moment before Beanie dropped her hand and moved away.

"Now, Beanie, my darling, you know what we do here." Serena's English was heavily accented. "Yes, yes, your arm, please." Reluctantly, Beanie held out her arm. "Now, Charlene, the same." The cuffs came as a surprise. Snapped into place there was no leaving, not without trailing this spiderized girl with her.

"I leave now. You get acquainted. Beanie, you tell her how things are. I rely on you."

The door closed but there wasn't the silence that Charlene had expected. Up and down what must be a hallway, there were murmurs, excited whispers but no one called out.

"Where are we?" Charlene could just make out Beanie's profile in the darkness. Dark hair pulled back from her face was tied with a ribbon. The short checked gown barely came to her knees. The covers on Beanie's cot had a mussed, slept-in look and Charlene realized that she must have awakened her.

"I don't know where we are. We never see outside. You'll see in the morning, the windows are boarded over." Beanie's voice seemed resigned. "I lost my last roommate, you know."

"Lost?"

"Yeah, I think she had her baby."

"Then she went home?" Charlene figured that these people only wanted her baby. And wasn't that what she wanted? To give her baby to someone who would love it and raise it and she could go back to school and sports.

A short harsh laugh. "Home?" Beanie paused, then added, "There is no going home. They kill us."

Charlene felt a chill, a finger of ice that skipped down her spine. "No, you're wrong. They only want our babies. When they have what they want, why would they kill us?"

"Because we know about them." Beanie inferred by Charlene's tone that she was being dumb.

"I just don't believe you."

"Okay. Have it your way. But when these girls have their babies, they never come back. And—" Beanie leaned in close "—I've heard screaming, not labor, but scared stuff, like someone was threatening and they were fighting to stay alive."

There wasn't much for Charlene to say. She'd wait until morning and see what she thought.

"How long have you been here?" She decided to take another tactic.

"Maybe a month. I tried keeping track by making marks on the wall, but Serena got really mad."

"What's Jerry like?"

"We don't see much of him. I don't think he's allowed up here."

"Is there a clinic? Where do they take everyone when it's time?"

"There's a doctor, or some old man in a white coat. He gives us exams. And there's a room at the end of the hall. I think that's where we deliver."

"Have you seen it?"

"No. But others have."

"How many of us are there?"

"Hard to say, maybe five, maybe ten. But somebody leaves almost every day."

"Leaves?"

"Has her baby and disappears."

"Where do they feed us?"

"Here. We only get out to go to the clinic, or what passes for one."

"How often?"

"Maybe once a week."

"How close are you?" Charlene wondered if she should get so personal, but this girl was tied to her.

"Maybe a week. I don't know. But I heard the doctor say it was close."

Charlene sat back on the cot being careful not to jerk Beanie's hand and arm.

"And you?"

Charlene honestly didn't know. Was it two weeks? Six weeks? Or closer to a month? She shrugged, but realized that it was so dark that any movement couldn't be easily seen.

"I really don't know."

"Will there be someone to miss you?"

"Yeah, I hope so." She thought of Jeni and the pacts they had made about how it was okay to stand up the other if a boy was involved. Would Jeni think something was wrong or would she think Charlene was meeting someone? They were supposed to spend the night together. Please, please

Charlene silently begged, tell someone, go get help. "What about you?"

"No. I don't think so. I ran away and maybe my mom wonders where I am, but that's about all."

Runaways. Could that be why Serena was so angry at Jerry? Charlene had a truck; she was not a runaway. If this place was filled with girls off the street, then it could be a safe little operation. And deadly. Babies could be born and the mothers never missed. Was Beanie right? The mothers were murdered?

"Where's the bathroom?" Charlene was suddenly tired and didn't want to keep Beanie up any longer.

"I have to go, too. I mean whether or not I have to really go. That closet is the bathroom."

Charlene noticed a door ajar in the corner. "How are we going to do this?"

"I'll stand up and come around."

The maneuvers were cumbersome, at best. But soon Charlene was lying on her back in her underwear, their cuffed wrists flat between them.

The scream at first seemed to come from everywhere. It tore at the walls, then bounced all around them.

"Who is that?" Charlene sat bolt upright, forgetting about her tether.

"Someone's time. Maybe you'll get used to it. You know, most babies are born at night. Why do you think that is?"

Charlene didn't have the foggiest. But she needed to think. She would not give up her baby to these people and she would not die. If she was certain of one thing, that was it. She would not die.

FIVE

JULIE REALLY DIDN'T expect to find Ben at the clinic on a Saturday. But as she nosed the Miata down the short incline into the parking lot, she saw his pickup by the side door. She hadn't thought of an excuse. Would she need a reason for being here? Surely, just wanting to see him would be enough. They would be going to Illinois in January. Ben would begin school and she would start a new job as rookie anchor for Channel 3 in Chicago. Not a very auspicious start to a relationship. They could both be buried with work. But she felt the bond was strong. It was just coming back to a place like this that would be difficult. Not much call for an anchor in places like Pawnee, Oklahoma or Rosebud, South Dakota. And Ben would have to repay Indian Health for his education. This pueblo an hour from Albuquerque was a mecca compared to some of the out-of-the-way places he might be asked to serve.

She pulled in beside the pickup, then flipped down the visor and checked her image in the vanity mirror. Freckles, freckles and then more freckles. She sighed and pushed a strand of red-gold hair back behind her ear and studied her reflection. Good eyes, sort of hazel with thick black lashes, all natural, a gift from her father's side of the family. Her hair, a mass of curls that defied hair spray as well as gravity softly framed her face. Not bad if she did say so herself. A little lipstick and she'd be ready.

The siren caught her off guard. It was well-known, however, that any official business demanded activating the light bar and turning up the volume, even if the trip entailed a jaunt of less than a mile. So it could be anything, a murder, or time to get a flu shot. Yet, this was a Saturday. She paused as she watched the white Bronco with tribal insignia pull up in front of the clinic and a man in a brown uniform hurry inside. Now curiosity kicked in and Julie hurried up the steps herself.

"Julie." Ben was standing just inside the door with the officer. If the tone of his voice told her anything it was that she didn't need an excuse to be there. "Have you met Elmore Waquie?"

"No, I haven't. I'm Julie Conlin." Julie held out her hand.

"You're Lorenzo's friend." The grin was wide and accepting.

"Yes. I guess I am." Julie laughed. Everyone in the village knew she'd given him her poncho and then how he'd scared off her would-be murderer. "I'm much indebted to his quick thinking."

"And this is Persi, Charlene Toya's mother." Ben turned to include the shy Indian woman standing in the office door and quickly filled Julie in on why they were all there.

"This isn't like Charlene. She always calls, especially if there was a change of plans."

"I've alerted APD in Albuquerque. But I'll need a better description of her truck, license plate, that sort of thing. I think I'll run by Jeni's house next. Take a statement. My crew will check the river and outlying fields."

"You don't think—" Persi couldn't finish.

"Never know what to think. Just can't leave anything to chance." Elmore nodded, but respectfully looked away. "I'll let you know what we find. Dr. Pecos, Miss Conlin, let's stay in touch." They stood and watched Elmore climb into the Bronco and drive back the way he came. No one seemed able to move.

"I need to go home." Persi broke their silence. She walked

to the row of hooks by the door and took down a thick navy parka. "But I don't know what to do."

She was dangerously close to tears, Julie thought. And what could she do? What could anyone do?

"Stay by the phone," Ben said.

SIX

FINDING A WALKING STICK proved to be more of a challenge than he'd thought. Every one he picked up had some flaw. There was one that had a handle that looked like a dog, but it split from tip to first gnarled bump when he put weight on it. Another didn't feel right, all twisted and rough, it hurt his hand to hold it. Maybe if he went closer to the river. The fields had given way to sparse woods and just beyond was the river, twisty and sluggish on this winter day.

Lorenzo stepped out of the protection of the stand of scrub oak and cottonwood. The wind buffeted him, then whistled away to rustle through a short-cropped patch of grasses. He didn't exactly like the bitter air that he could see with every breath, but the new year was almost upon the village and these last days of the sun bustled with activity. There were rules to follow and penalties for forgetting them. Houses must be cleaned, debts paid, trash hauled away. In the old days prayer feathers were prepared in a bundle to tie underneath their horses' tails. But who had horses now? Lorenzo couldn't think of one family that kept the creatures for work. Some turned them out in the fields or let them run wild along the mesa, ignoring Bureau of Land Management regulations. But no one plowed their fields or rode to town.

The winter solstice was just part of the cycle of the year, a time that ebbed and flowed to nature's rhythm. And the new year was not marked as the Spaniards had intended, but was observed in mid-December. Special dances to honor the buffalo, the deer and eagle would soon be presented. The plaza would be crowded. Spectators would line the roofs and the edges of the hard mud-packed open area, the navel of the village or its true center.

Lorenzo believed there was a tubelike hole that stretched from this navel to the center of the earth itself. And it was this hole that the medicine men filled with seeds, all the seeds of the crops that the village grew and used to depend upon for food. If the medicine men weren't careful, they could slip down the hole when they placed the seeds deep within the earth. This was done in late winter when the snows covered the fields and all was sleeping. But in spring if the medicine men had been careful and thorough, wisps of green sprouted up in the fields and corn and melons and squash would again be plentiful.

And side by side with the ways of his ancestors was the mark of the other world; a world that sent unmarried men in long cloaks to build buildings to gather in and pray to one God and his son. A son that had a beard and whose mother had never been with a man—Lorenzo shook his head. How could that be?

Yet, his people accepted these new deities, didn't question as they built their houses decorated with crossed sticks and observed their holidays. The birthday of Christ would soon be honored. All the village would participate, rejoice and give thanks unto the child's father who lives in the sky; and later that same day the village would perform a dance and honor their own spiritual guides. It was a puzzle, but the religions seemed to exist side by side. In all of Lorenzo's life he'd never known there to be conflict between the Church and the ways of his village.

If he hadn't been looking at the path, he might have missed the stick—a stick with the head of a fox. The pointy nose with rounded ears laid back against its head atop a thick, smooth branch of weathered tan wood. It was perfect. Lorenzo tried it for size. Again, perfect. It bore his weight and fit his cupped hand and felt warm and tingling. He held it to

his ear and smiled as he closed his eyes and saw the fox, a
vixen, trotting across an open field.

"Yiii!" Lorenzo jumped as a hand landed solidly on his
shoulder.

"Sorry, old man. I didn't mean to scare you." Elmore truly
looked chagrined. But Lorenzo waved his new cane in the
air and tried to tell the man that he'd better be careful; sneaking up on someone could have dire consequences. But the
words didn't quite form correctly without his new teeth. He
watched as Elmore leaned close to try and catch his words,
but finally shook his head.

"Lorenzo, I want you to listen carefully. We're looking
for a young girl, Charlene Toya. She could have driven her
truck down this way. Do you know Charlene?" Elmore was
peering at him. "Charlene plays basketball for Valley. She's
the star. Basketball. Do you know what basketball is?"

Elmore faked a dribble, his hand patting the air around
Lorenzo as he sprinted in a circle and then squarely in front
of the old man leaped in the air and pushed the imaginary
ball upward toward a basket in his mind's eye somewhere
above the cottonwood's second tier of branches.

"Air ball. You lost your momentum there at the top of the
key."

Elmore turned to give his second in command a dirty look
as the man hugged himself in laughter. "If you think you
can get a point across any better, you try." Elmore turned
back to face Lorenzo squarely.

Elmore sounded snappish and out of sorts, but Lorenzo
slowly nodded. Charlene. Sometimes he'd go to the games
and sit under the bleachers to get warm. Charlene was a big
one. Too tall for an Indian girl, Lorenzo thought. But he knew
her parents, nice people who often gave him food. And Charlene, she put that ball in the round circle time after time and
the crowd would roar its approval. He always thought her
mother had seen a bounding deer when she was carrying
Charlene. She could have watched an agile doe clearing the

fences that laced the fields together behind the village. When a woman was pregnant she needed to be careful not to let images imprint upon her newborn child. There was a child in the village with a birthmark along his scalp line shaped like a wolf's head. Already this boy had great powers. But Charlene? Was she lost? Hadn't he seen her last night?

"Have you seen Charlene Toya?" Elmore spoke overly loud and right in his face.

Lorenzo shook his head.

"She drives a red Toyota."

"He's not going to know the difference between a Toyota and a turtle." The man in uniform shook his head in disgust. "This is a waste of time, if you ask me."

"Oh, yeah? Look." Elmore stepped aside.

Lorenzo drew an elongated circle with the tip of his cane in the river sand, then an inner circle shaped more like an egg. The final tracing of the cane connected the two circles above the center line with curved handlebars.

"Tell me that ain't the Toyota emblem."

Lorenzo thought Elmore looked smug. But he knew the truck. Charlene always drove too fast. Lorenzo pointed at the symbol and shook his head. He hadn't seen Charlene since the game last night.

"Thanks, old man." Elmore patted him on the shoulder. "We better get going." Leaning close to Lorenzo's right ear, "We're going to check up river. If you see anything, you tell that granddaughter of yours. Okay? Do you understand me?"

Lorenzo nodded. Anything to make Elmore stop yelling in his ear.

SEVEN

"WHAT DO YOU THINK could have happened?" Julie turned away from the window in Ben's office. "It's been three days."

"I honestly thought that the Albuquerque police would have come up with a lead by now, or maybe the truck."

"I've offered to follow up the story for the *Journal*. They'd like some safety-of-the-pueblo-gone-bad angle."

"Would it do any good to remind them that the last time she was seen, she was heading toward Albuquerque?" Ben had a problem with sensationalism in the press. *But at least Julie will be sympathetic to our Indian ways.* Funny that he would be including himself, thinking the word *our*. Was he feeling more connected? More a part of this village? His uncles had invited him to dance on Christmas day. Take him into the kiva and prepare him to represent his clan—

"Did I lose you?" Julie was watching him.

"Sorry. Guess I was wondering where you were going to begin."

"First, I'd like to talk to Charlene's best friend. I think her mother called her Jeni. There just might be something she would tell me that she hadn't shared with the police."

Ben didn't doubt that. Julie had an uncanny way of getting at the truth whether or not the person was ready to share.

"Need some backup?"

"I thought you'd never ask."

CHRISTMASTIME WAS SLOW for the clinic. Too many things happening for people to get depressed. Ben had seen two people needing med refills only that he referred to the physician on call, and made a third appointment to meet with a newly married couple but not until after January first, and that was it. Slow didn't really capture it. Persi hadn't come in that morning and the clinic director said she was on leave for an undetermined length of time. Ben didn't know why, but that sounded ominous. He truly wished there was something he could do. Maybe tagging along with Julie would turn something up.

Ben expertly turned the truck into a space between two adobe houses about five blocks from the clinic. Charlene's friend, Jeni, was Jennifer Tafoya who, with five brothers, lived with her mother and grandmother close to the center of the village. Jeni asked if they could talk at the recreational center, saying she'd rather have some privacy. She nodded over her shoulder where behind her the yelling drowned out all conversation. If he didn't know better, Ben thought loss of life might be imminent. Being the oldest sister to five brothers would be a challenge.

They all squeezed into the cab and drove the two short blocks to the center. It would be warm inside and there were soft drinks. The gym was always open during the day and often used by NBA aspirants when winter weather made outdoor hoops impossible.

There were several boys, maybe middle schoolers, Ben thought, taking turns playing "horse." The sound of one ball bouncing was a hundred times better than whatever it was that was happening at Jeni's house. There was privacy in the bleachers and the three of them settled four rows above the floor on the hard wooden planking.

"I know what you're going to ask me. And I've thought and thought and I don't think I know anything that I didn't tell Elmore." Jeni's voice shook.

"I really appreciate your talking with me. Sometimes in talking, something rings a bell, is triggered by what is said.

Often you don't even think it's pertinent." Julie had a small notebook, but after flipping it open to a clean page, left it lying in her lap.

"Let's start by your telling me exactly what Charlene said to you before she took off for Albuquerque."

"Well, she dropped me off at the Pizza Hut. She said she had to pick up a prescription at Walgreen's."

"Which store?" Julie made a notation.

"That's just it. She didn't say. It was the first I'd heard of it."

"What time was it when she left you?"

"The game was out about 6:30, so, a little after seven maybe."

"All Walgreens are open until ten, I think," Julie added. "How long did you wait at the Hut—until you realized that Charlene wasn't coming back?"

"Like I told the Albuquerque police, I didn't think anything of Charlene not coming back. We had this deal that if we had a chance for a date or something…you know, with a guy, well, we'd know the other would understand."

"So, there's a boyfriend?"

"Uh, no."

Oh, yeah, Julie thought. Jeni's eyes shifted away and she began to fidget with the beaded fringe on her jacket.

"But there has been a boyfriend?"

"Well, not recently."

"How long ago?"

"Almost a year."

"Was it serious?"

Jeni shrugged.

"Did they see a lot of each other?" Julie tried another tactic.

"Not a lot."

This was beginning to fall into the pulling teeth category, Julie mused. But it could be a really important lead.

The ringing of the phone under the bleachers to their right shrilly interrupted.

"I'll get it. It's probably for one of the kids." Jeni motioned toward the floor and bounded down the four planks and ducked under the bleachers. Julie silently cursed. She was struggling to build some momentum, but the phone put her back to zero.

"I'm *not* Charlene Toya." Jeni's raised voice caught their attention. Ben and Julie exchanged quick looks before Ben rushed to the end of the row and swung down to land solidly on the floor beside Jeni.

"Let me talk." He almost roughly took the phone.

"I'm Ben Pecos, counselor at the Tewa clinic. How can I help you?" He held the receiver from his ear and motioned both Julie and Jeni to listen in.

"Clinic? I seem to have gotten the wrong number. It was my understanding that I could reach a Charlene Toya at this number or, at least, leave a message with someone named Persi."

"Persi is her mother."

"Mother?" The woman on the other end of the line sounded surprised, Ben thought.

"What is this concerning? How do you know Charlene?"

"I'm not at liberty to say."

"Charlene Toya is missing. No one has seen her in three days. Now, if you have information that would help with the investigation, you need to come forward."

"Missing? I don't understand."

"She didn't return home two nights ago and she didn't tell anyone where she was going. Please, if you have information—"

The abrupt click startled him. Should he have pushed? Demanded? Reluctantly he placed the receiver back in its wall holder.

"What did the woman say when you answered?"

"She thought I was Charlene."

"Did she identify herself?"

"Uh, yeah, her name is Molly."

"Just Molly?" Ben hoped against hope there would be a last name.

"Only Molly."

"No other identification? Where she works? How she knows Charlene?"

Jeni shook her head.

"How old did she sound?" Ben smiled as Julie entered in. Good question.

"Not young. Like my mom's age, maybe."

"From the time you said 'hello,' what was said?" Julie had her notepad.

"Uh, stuff like—"

"Jeni, please be exact. I know it might not make sense to you, but anything could be of help."

"Okay. I said hello and she said 'Charlene, I think I have an answer'—no, she said, 'I think I've solved your problem....' Yes, she said *problem*."

"What else?" Julie prompted.

"That was pretty much it. I told her twice that I wasn't Charlene. Oh, yes, she asked me if I was Persi."

"How would someone older know Charlene's mother's name? And why?"

"Maybe it was someone from UNM—representing a scout." Ben offered.

"And calling a pay phone under the bleachers at the recreational center? How would anyone even get this number unless Charlene gave it to them?"

Ben admitted that Julie had a point. This made no sense and the abrupt hang up was worrisome. "I don't know what else we can do."

"I probably need to get back. I'm supposed to be watching the boys."

"I think we need to get you back then." Ben could only hope there was a house left standing. They'd been gone fifteen minutes, more than enough time for that demolition team to raze it.

"One more thing, Jeni, what's the name of the boyfriend from last year?"

"That was really a long time ago."

"It might be helpful."

"I don't think Charlene would want me to say."

"Jeni, if Charlene's life is in danger, she'd want you to help." Ben almost regretted his words when he saw Jeni's eyes widen.

"You think someone might hurt her?"

"I hope not. But we can't be sure until we find her."

Jeni looked at the ground and for a minute Ben thought she wouldn't tell them.

"Jason Arnold." Then she was gone, bolting out the double doors not waiting for a ride.

"The name Arnold is familiar," Julie said.

Ben and Julie sat back down on the bleachers closer to the phone this time. Waiting for it to ring a second time? Ben thought so, but knew they would wait in vain.

"Jasper Arnold, Jason's father, is superintendent of schools for the valley. Jason's a really good-looking kid if you like spoiled brats."

"How do you know so much about the family?"

"Had to interview with good ol' dad when I wanted to set up that teen counseling program at the high school. Basically he told me there were no problems at his school that would require counseling—no drugs, no drinking, no drunken parties, no teen pregnancies—his school was exemplary."

"Do you believe that?"

"No. I think the high school is made up of normal kids who are just as likely to get in trouble as students in any other school. The Arnolds are from Tennessee. The first question he asked me was what side of the Mason-Dixon line I was born on."

"That doesn't make sense."

''I think he was trying to figure out my ethnicity. It wasn't my imagination that after I explained my roots, he was decidedly cool. Ended our little conversation soon after that.''

''I wonder how Jason managed to date an Indian girl?''

''Who says his parents knew anything about it? Persi didn't. She told me there had never been boyfriends, only sports for Charlene. Aren't parents usually the last to know?''

EIGHT

THERE WEREN'T ANY windows. Well, a window above the bed, but it had been boarded up. Charlene looked the room over carefully. It was small but in the dim light emanating from one shadeless fifteen-watt bulb in a lamp on the floor by the door, there was only one way out, the padlocked exit-entrance leading to the hall. Charlene had gone over and over the hall from memory, the number of steps to the bedroom, the stairs down to the kitchen, the number of steps on the stairs, the door to the garage. Then going in reverse where the door would be that she'd originally come through. She'd made herself memorize everything, not just the steps or distances, but what she'd touched, what she'd heard. There was a fridge or an upright freezer by the door in the garage. Its compressor had whirred on as they climbed the steps leading to the kitchen. She'd touched the appliance; she had been that close. There had been no handrail on her left, on the right going back down.

If she had to find her way out in the dark, she could do it—not stumble but go directly to the exits. And it was her only chance. Speed. No guesswork. And she'd have to be ready to fight, catch Jerry or Serena off guard. They wouldn't expect her to put up a fight and they wouldn't want to hurt the baby. She'd have a chance. She had to believe that she could get away.

Every morning before they were served the bowl of watery Malt-O-Meal, one piece of dry toast, one paper carton of whole milk, and one piece of fruit, Charlene would have

Beanie stretch out on the floor, tethered wrist next to hers while she did push-ups. The key would be strength. Someone in condition would have the element of surprise on her side. Until last week she had run four miles a day.

Her chance could come any time now. Her one chance to escape could not be lost. When Beanie went into labor, they would come to get her, and Charlene would escape. She must be ready to do whatever would be necessary to save herself…to save her baby. She'd started sleeping in her sweatshirt, feigning being cold. When she left, she wouldn't have shoes or sweatpants. Survival would mean swift, direct action and brains.

NINE

BEN KNEW she would meddle. But wasn't writing the story her excuse? She was disappointed that Charlene's disappearance had been a tiny two-inch chunk of a column in Monday morning's paper. Not even any names. Just the fact that a young girl was missing and thought possibly to have been in Albuquerque the night of her disappearance. The make and model of the Toyota were given and that was about it. Lame. Albuquerque police seemed to be dragging their feet. When she'd questioned the detective handling the case, he'd fairly snapped at her, saying that the reservation needed to take care of their own. In short, until someone could prove that a crime had been committed and committed in Albuquerque to boot, then none had taken place. Frustrating. Julie felt she was at a dead end.

Unless…the boyfriend could provide a lead. But she didn't even know if the relationship had lasted long enough or had been strong enough to qualify for that term. He needed to be questioned. Of that she was certain.

The Arnolds lived in school housing provided by the district about five miles above the high school. Ben had given her directions and suggested she take his truck because the road into the neighborhood wasn't paved. The modest brick bungalows had a down-at-the-heels look. All needed their trim painted and most could have used new front doors or screens. An assortment of dogs roamed freely, much as they did in the pueblo. Ground cover was at a minimum. Even in winter the ground was splotchy. Where grass had been planted, the lawns were worn through and balding spots of dirt dotted the front yards—too many go-carts, skateboards, or in-line skates, Julie thought. These homes had a distinct rental appearance. The homes of educators, but transients nonetheless.

The super's house was at the far end and was bigger by a two-car garage, a screened-in back porch and front patio—that was automatic clout. She saw a Jeep Cherokee in the front drive and the garage doors were open. That was promising. She'd wondered if the family would even be home during the Christmas vacation.

She edged the truck into the drive, paved, she noticed along with a half mile of sidewalks that wound through the houses, but the streets were pounded-smooth dirt. Wonder what the holdup was? Why hadn't the streets been blacktopped? This neighborhood had to be fifteen years old.

Before she could get out of the car, a teenage boy walked out of the garage, looked at her, then continued to carry a garbage bag around to the back. Not very sociable, but he was cute. Julie probably had eight years on him but that didn't mean she couldn't remember what a budding heart-throb looked like. Blond hair cut short, but long enough in front to spike upward a couple of inches. Broad shoulders accentuated by the black lambskin jacket, a pretty pricey one at that from what she could see; opaque sunglasses like those favored by jocks—narrow, wraparound and again, very expensive. Maybe Mr. Wonderful had a job. He'd have to, she decided as her eyes strayed down to his leather biker boots, or mom and dad had an expensive project on their hands.

Julie got out of the car and walked toward the open garage. With any luck, he'd have to come back this way. It was her intention to talk to him, not engage the parents in conversation.

"Who are you?" He didn't seem to want to waste time with amenities. He just walked around the corner of the garage and straight up to her. She willed herself to not step backward. She innately knew that doing so would give him an edge, and she hated bullies.

"Julie Conlin, reporter for the *Albuquerque Journal.*"

"My dad's busy."

"I'm not here to see your dad. I'm here to see you."

She liked the way she'd caught him off balance. Even if she couldn't clearly see his eyes, he paused, pouty lower lip opening a fraction of an inch.

"Why me?"

"I'm investigating the disappearance of Charlene Toya."

"What does that have to do with me?"

At least he didn't waste time with faking that he didn't know she was missing.

"I've been told that the two of you were close—boyfriend-girlfriend."

"Oh, yeah? Well, you were told wrong."

Julie wished she could wipe that derisive smirk off his face.

"I don't think so."

"Well, I do. So, what are you going to do about it?"

"Ask you some questions anyway."

"Sorry, I'm busy." He turned to go, dismissing her as if she weren't there.

"How many times did you sleep with her?" Julie had no idea where she was going with that but it caught his attention and made him turn around to confront her squarely.

"Listen, bitch, your information is fucked." Again, a step forward to back her up.

No, it isn't, Julie said to herself. His reaction was speaking louder than truth serum. All her senses went on alert. She'd bet a paycheck that one Jason Arnold *had* indeed slept with Charlene Toya.

"I think my informant was telling the truth."

"Get out of here."

"You talk to me or you'll see your name in print tomorrow—*Albuquerque Journal.* Jason Arnold last to see Charlene Toya alive and rumored to have been intimately involved—''

''You can't do that.''

''Try me.''

He was studying her; the pout, gone now, had given way to chewing on his lower lip.

''There's nothing I can tell you.''

''Think. Anything. Jeni said you were at the Pizza Hut Friday after the game but left early.'' Was he there? Julie was fishing.

''I didn't see Charlene there.''

''Did you meet her somewhere?''

''Like I told you, we weren't together.''

''And last spring? More than one person say the two of you went out.''

''A couple times. That's all. Twice.''

''And since then?''

''*Nada.*''

''Do you know if she's dating anyone now?'' And the way he paused, feigned giving it some thought, she knew he'd give her a name. A wrong name.

''Yeah. I think she's with Steve Pecos.''

Ben's nephew? That would be easy to trace.

''Thanks for your help.''

She turned to go just as he called out, ''Hey, no problem.'' Sure, she thought, I can count on you anytime. Not.

TEN

BEN AWOKE to the clear coldness of an early morning after a night of snow. He stepped out of his grandmother's house to enjoy the cottony world around him. He strained to hear cars on the highway about two miles above, but the whiteness cast a blanket over all sound. Six inches frosted the parapets of the cluster of houses with walls adjoining his grandmother's. The mud-brown adobes looked like gingerbread structures made by children. These were not the squared, code-driven adobes of perfection that one found in Albuquerque. These were lovingly built of mud cut from the river's edge—rectangles of clay and sand that were left to dry, becoming the sturdy building blocks used to construct homes.

This would be the first Christmas without his grandmother. One of the first to succumb to the mystery disease last summer, she had been a stabilizing part of his life. And he struggled with wanting to do what she would have thought was right. Continuing his education would have met with approval and returning in four years to apply his learning here to his own people—that would have pleased her. But the decision was bittersweet. She wouldn't know. She wouldn't be a part of his graduation.

His uncles had offered to let him stay in their mother's house until it was time to leave. He appreciated all the kindnesses. But he was just as much an outsider as he always was, a half-white kid coming back from Utah for summers in a pueblo. The first year or two after the Mormon family had adopted him, coming home was painful. Children teased him because he was different and he couldn't speak their language. He didn't look like them; his hair was cut different and he wore crisp new jeans that screamed "outsider."

The summer he was seven, he took all three pairs of new jeans and scrubbed them on rocks by the river and left them to dry in the sun. The result wasn't exactly what he'd wanted but he felt there was great improvement. He bore holes in the legs and scraped the denim almost white along the seams of the pockets in front. When he proudly took them home, his grandmother wisely pretended not to notice. She had borrowed some striped T-shirts from his cousins and had put away his long-sleeved pressed dress shirts. She even had found a baseball cap, just his size with the Los Angeles Dodgers insignia. He always wondered how she'd managed that. When he went out to play that afternoon, he looked like everyone else. Well, almost.

Christmas was one week away. And Charlene Toya had been gone one week. Ben fought a tightness in his chest, a foreboding. Time was never on the side of the victim. And there were no clues. The Albuquerque police were treating it like a runaway. The truck hadn't been found. It seemed obvious to them that she had just taken off. "Happens every day," a detective named Salazar had commented. But to a child from the pueblo? And why? Why would a young woman, a basketball star, her life ahead of her with scholarships and awards, run away? It made no sense.

Ben was convinced of foul play. Would the spring thaw uncover a body, human remains on the mesa that a couple of dirt bikers would notice and call the police far too late for anything besides mourning and burial? He shook his head as if to dispel such thinking. He needed to stay positive. He wanted to support Persi who was a zombie. He'd insisted that she stay home. The clinic doc had prescribed tranquilizers, but shouldn't they be doing something else?

Thanks to Julie there had been print space in the *Albu-*

querque Journal. She had even talked her supervisor into a series on troubled teens—the runaways who took to the streets. Thursday was the first installment. She didn't believe that it had anything to do with Charlene, but it kept her name in front of people. And Ben agreed that was important.

He doubted that anyone would be at the clinic but he decided to walk in. The first big snow of the winter would ground a number of patients, even if they did live less than five miles away. Actually, he welcomed a slow day. He could tackle some paperwork in the quiet.

As he opened the door, the ringing of the phone shattered any quiet he'd hoped for. And it was his phone. Julie. He stamped his feet, scattering specks of snow across the rubber mat by the front door, tossed his jacket on a peg in the wall and rushed to his office.

"Tewa clinic, this is Ben Pecos." For a moment he thought the line had gone dead. Could be the snow. Utilities were never a given in the mountains. "Hello?"

"I'm sorry. Mr. Pecos, this is Dr. Creighton. Molly Creighton. We spoke last Saturday."

"Yes, of course." A doctor. She hadn't identified herself as such last week. Did this mean that Charlene was all right? Or had there been an accident?

"First let me say I have mixed feelings about calling you, but I saw the article in the newspaper and thought I had to. I'm sure I don't need to tell you about patient confidentiality. I gave my word that I wouldn't share information entrusted to me in good faith."

"I understand, but Charlene's life might be in danger." Probably an understatement, Ben thought.

"That's exactly why I'm calling. I don't think I realized at the time that she was desperate to do something on her own. May I be open with you? I'm assuming that you're in a position of authority?"

"I'm an intern here, a counselor. I wish you would be candid. I work with Persi Toya, Charlene's mother. We're all deeply concerned." Another understatement, Ben thought. Scared shitless was closer to the truth.

"Are you a member of the tribe? Of the pueblo?"

"Yes. I'm Tewa." Was this important? It seemed to be.

He heard a sigh and then again the exhalation of a deep breath. Would she share? And what could be so secretive?

"Let me preface what I'm about to say by sharing with you that I'm the patient advisor at the Planned Parenthood clinic in Albuquerque. Charlene came to see me on the night that she disappeared. She chose the clinic because she thought we could help. But as I explained to her at the time, we see more women in the first trimester who need counseling about termination. We're not set up to place babies."

"I'm lost. Are you saying that Charlene was, uh, is pregnant?" She must be talking about another Indian girl. Hadn't Charlene scored fourteen points for Valley just a week ago?

"Very pregnant. My guess is at least eight months. I was unable to complete my examination but from what she said, term wasn't far off."

"No one knew. I watched her play basketball last week, the day she saw you."

"She's a big girl and my guess is that the baby is not that large. At this point I'd say five, maybe five and a half pounds. She was using Ace bandages to hold the baby up and tucked back into her body cavity. A loose fitting shirt and it's no surprise that the pregnancy wasn't detected."

"But her parents, her mother, surely she would have noted something different?"

"Not necessarily. When a parent isn't looking for something like that, it's easy not to see."

Ben was quiet. Pregnant and no one knew. Seeks out an abortion clinic— "Why did you say she contacted you?"

"She had hoped that we would be able to place the child. In fact, she thought we might be able to find a place for her to have the baby over Christmas break and then go back to school with no one the wiser. I, first of all, had to tell her that we didn't do that but secondly, a Native American baby is protected by all sorts of adoption laws.''

Ben felt a twinge of sadness. He hadn't been protected. Almost thirty years was a lot of time—new legislation, new rights—he just hadn't quite been born at the ''right'' time. Had his mother been like Charlene? Alone and frightened at the prospect of a family without support? But his mother had come home. And his grandmother had raised her baby until she felt it was better to sacrifice—send him into the Anglo world so that he would prosper. Had it been the right thing? Most would say yes.

''Mr. Pecos?''

''Sorry, I was just thinking of Charlene and how distraught she must be. Did she say anything about her parents?''

''Only that they didn't know. The same for the boyfriend.''

Boyfriend. Shit. Jason Arnold. Wouldn't his father be pleased to know that his only son had gotten a local girl pregnant. Ben was beginning to see how Charlene might be desperate.

''How did you leave it with her? I mean, did you encourage her at all to tell her mother?''

''Of course. I insisted that she tell her parents. But she was adamant. She felt she had ruined her life and no one would understand. She left me the number that I called last week, the recreational center, wasn't it? Mr. Pecos, I think Charlene took off on her own and might be in trouble. I can't imagine a young girl having a baby without support, let alone a hospital.''

A runaway. So the police were right. It certainly didn't alleviate the worry but it did rule out foul play. Somehow, Ben didn't feel comforted.

''What will you do with this information?''

Ben noted that suddenly the sharing of it had become his concern.

''I don't know. I think the family needs to know.''

"Yes, I do, too. I think Charlene's taking off under the circumstances counters any promise of silence."

"You don't seem to think she'll come home."

"Probably not until after the baby is born."

"And the baby?" Ben was recalling headlines of newborns found abandoned, no, discarded by young mothers who feared they had everything to lose.

"I wish I knew."

Ben felt she was thinking the same thing he was. A teenager having a baby was an unknown commodity.

ELEVEN

"I THINK IT'S THE dumbest idea I've heard yet." Ben wasn't trying to mask his anger. She was being impossible. Irresponsible. Putting her life in danger and maybe Charlene's.

"Ben, listen to me. The paper will support me. They want me to do this."

"Anything for a story? Is that the mentality? No concern for your safety, no way to monitor your safety, just take your chances. Is this ego or a chance to help Charlene?"

"I think that stinks. You should know how I think by now."

And, in fact, Ben thought he did, but to go undercover, pretend she was a runaway teen just to see if there was any information on Charlene... Well, that was just too risky. He'd shared Molly's information. Perhaps he shouldn't have. But Julie was a confidant, someone he hoped would be a lot more someday. And he valued her opinion. But not this, not putting her life in danger. Wasn't his biggest concern that he wouldn't be there to help?

"Did I lose you?" Julie was in Albuquerque sitting out the slick roads in her apartment.

"Sorry. I was just thinking."

"That could be dangerous."

Even her attempt at humor didn't lighten his mood.

"I won't stay out at night unless I have to." She paused and he knew she wished she could take back that last part.

"What will you be looking for?"

"Anyone who has seen Charlene or knows where pregnant teens can go for help."

"What are you going to wear?"

"Ben, I'm going to look like I'm sixteen."

"I'm thinking of bad pop singers, more skin than should be exposed at puberty."

"Ben, you're not my mother."

Not your mother and not someone who has been in your life long enough to give orders. He needed to back off. But, damn it, he cared about this woman and didn't want her to put herself in danger.

"I appreciate the caring. Honest. I'll be careful."

"Do you have your cell phone?"

"I'm not sure that's what all the chic down-an'-outs own."

"If you get in trouble, what will you do?"

"I don't plan on getting in trouble."

Famous last words, Ben thought, but said, "A person always needs an escape route."

"I just don't know exactly what I'll be doing. I thought I'd try the clinic for the homeless first."

"Good choice. Will you let someone know who you are?"

"No. I'm going to be a pregnant teen."

"Julie—"

"Ben, please, let's just see what happens. Do you have a better idea?"

And, of course, he didn't. Would pregnancy have forced Charlene to run? Maybe. But he just didn't have a good feeling about finding her safe and now Julie…

TWELVE

SO, NOW WHAT? Julie never admitted she was wrong, well, not unless it was so obvious that she couldn't help it. And this plan had seemed so foolproof. Land on the streets as a runaway, pregnant, no past, no future and see who would come forth to help.

Was that what Charlene had done? But there was no reason to think that she'd stopped in Albuquerque. Still, it seemed unlikely she would have strayed that far from home. And money. What would she have done for money? Was she living in her truck? And how close was she to delivery?

Julie leaned into the bathroom mirror and studied what she hoped was a replica of the latest teen makeup. A teen rag sporting Britney Spears on the cover lay on the counter. Julie just felt overdone, lips too big outlined in cocoa, smudged in with mahogany; severe, barely curved brown lines for eyebrows and tons of mascara. Tons. Her lashes felt gooped together. And the hair parted in the middle pulled away from her face with barrettes, little pink flowers with yellow centers, the pink matching the tube top that pulled above the jeans that rested below her navel.

She checked the image in her bedroom's full-length mirror. She really needed a belly button ring. Might be too much, though. And pain wasn't something she sought out. She idly wondered what Ben would think of the outfit, then smiled. There would be a couple of things he'd like. And would probably like to keep the showing private. He could be so old-fashioned. But she liked that.

She thought she'd make her appearance on Central then wander toward downtown. The homeless clinic run by Saint Joseph's Health Care was off Second. She pulled a ragged sweatshirt over her head and slipped an arm into a stained parka, a two-dollar find at a local thrift shop and just funky enough to say "street," but the fake fur trim hinted of better days. She'd found a much-used backpack and stuffed an extra sweatshirt, some T-shirts, one pair of sweatpants into one side and then a plastic bag full of cosmetics and toothbrush into the other.

It had been three days since the snow. Albuquerque was famous for its bright sunlight that melted even the most persistent white stuff and cleared streets by the following noon. She would leave her car in the apartment's carport and walk. Late afternoon already meant almost total darkness. Luckily, her apartment was close to downtown. She had absolutely no plan. Loiter came to mind, and she idly wondered if there was a knack to all this. And knew there was—some pecking order that reached beyond first come, first served when it came to jockeying for space or food or whatever. And who would be her competition? What fellow runaways would befriend her, if any? She didn't dwell on possibilities. She just tucked a folded fifty-dollar bill in her jeans watch pocket, thrust her feet into warm socks and Mary-Jane-style clogs. Done. One more check in the mirror and she was out of there.

She approached Central from the north, walking up Fifth past the county building, law offices and the public library. Fake luminarias lined the tops of territorial-style flat roofs. The make-believe candles in bags of sand were actually plastic look-alikes that could be switched on and off from inside the warmth of an office. The real thing would be in place just four days from then, thousands of small bags filled with sand and a votive candle would line the sidewalks of Central and Old Town. Rooftops, the square, the gazebo, the church, the community would be ablaze with light. All done on Christmas Eve to guide the spirit of the Christ child. There would be bus tours of gawkers and for twenty-five dollars, one could view decorations in some of the pricey neighborhoods, all from the comfort of a city bus.

In some parts of town, they were called *farolitos* or little lanterns. Others honored the tradition of digging small pits and lighting diminutive bonfires. It was a tradition she would never tire of. So many other towns were decorated in plastic and tinsel, not that Albuquerque didn't have its share, but candles in bags of sand seemed like the real thing. She pulled the parka up around her neck; even after sundown, there was still a wind. She could always duck into the library and get warm.

She looked in through the glass doors. Not a lot of people. Maybe she wouldn't be noticed. She lowered the backpack to the ground. Could she walk over to the computerized card catalogue and pretend to look something up? Yeah, right. Great for a street person—research. Just what a down-and-out teen would do. She hesitated with her hand on the door. A drink of water? Rest room? She hoisted her backpack into place.

"They ain't too keen on us folks going in there."

Julie whirled and barely stifled the impulse to run. She hadn't seen the man sitting on a bench in what appeared to be an arbor of intertwined brown twigs and stems just to the right of the wide sidewalk.

"Where you from, missy? Can't say that I've seen you before." The man was leaning forward and wore so much clothing his head poked out of the mound like a tortoise. The stocking cap was old and looked hand-knit. "Come now, you can talk, can't you? Cat ain't got your tongue now, has it?"

Julie felt paralyzed. Where was she from? Stupid. A simple question and she was stumped—hadn't thought out in advance any plausible story. But her wide-eyed stare made raccoonlike by her outlined lids must be believable because he patted a place beside him on the bench and smiled, crooked brown-stained teeth and all.

She shook her head and took a step toward the street.

"I ain't a-going to hurt you. You out here all alone is a bad idea. You gotta home to go to?"

Again, she shook her head, but she faced him squarely and, with far more courage than she felt, she said, "I'm fine."

"Oh, sure you are. Come here and tell Uncle Skipper all about yourself."

If she didn't talk to him, she'd be passing up a contact, maybe a valuable one. And she had to start somewhere. Wasn't this why she was out here? She hesitated, but then sat on the edge of the bench.

"I'm looking for a friend. We left together—well, at the same time anyway. And we were going to meet in Albuquerque. But she was going to call me when she got here and she did and that was two weeks ago. I can't find her." Hadn't she put Kleenex in her pocket? Miraculously, she pulled one out and blew her nose. Skipper patted her knee.

"Your friend got a name, honey?"

"Charlene."

He thought a minute and then shook his head. "No, nobody by that name in any of the shelters I been to. Would she have been using another name?"

That was something Julie hadn't thought of. Again, she was feeling a little ill-prepared. "My friend is going to have a baby."

"That's not good news. And she's living on the streets?"

Julie nodded.

"Look, you see that van coming down the street?"

Julie nodded. The white twelve-passenger van looked full as it pulled to the curb.

"That there's transportation to a shelter. Must be the Junction. Come on. Can't leave a young thing like you out here."

Go? He wanted her to spend the night in a shelter? He must be referring to Joy Junction. Well, why shouldn't she go? This might be the best and safest time to question people. On cold nights various shelters and churches sent vans out to scour the downtown area for those needing shelter. There would be blankets and a hot breakfast and maybe answers.

Julie wasn't prepared for the rows and rows of people who had staked out a portion of the warehouse floor. She had been given two blankets and waved toward the general direction of a recreational room that seemed to house only women. At first, she didn't see anyone under thirty or forty. She hung back by the door, surveying the room. Every one of the approximately twenty women seemed to know each other. There was even a fight starting over a blanket in one corner until the raised voices brought in a man who seemed to act as bouncer. Things got quiet after that.

Julie eased down in a corner to the right of the door and folded one blanket inside the other so that she had a home-made sleeping bag.

"This here's Dottie's spot. She don't come till later, but I make sure she has her spot."

Julie stood. "I'm sorry. Where should I go?" Julie could tell that the woman had expected her to put up a fight.

"Well, there might be room for both of you right here. You gonna have to ask Dot, though. I can't tell you whether there is or not. She comes on the last van."

Julie had no idea what time that might be. It was already after eight according to the clock on the wall. She was hungry and tired and already feeling that Ben might have been right about her trying to get information this way. So far, it smacked of a dead end.

"You hungry?" The woman had turned back to gesture toward the door. "We got some good sandwiches in there on the table."

Someone had provided food in a room they called the kitchen even though a fridge and a table were the only qualifications. The food consisted of leftovers from a Chamber of Commerce luncheon. Since it was after eight in the evening, Julie idly wondered where the sandwiches had been for the last six hours or so. But they looked okay, maybe the bread was a little dry on the ones on top. Julie pulled a ham and Swiss on rye from under the top layer and took a canned soft drink from the counter. Apparently, more Chamber of Commerce fare. Must not have had a very good RSVP system working to have this much food left over.

"Skipper said you was looking for a friend."

The woman who had warned her about being in Dot's territory was wrapping three sandwich halves in a paper towel.

"Her name is Charlene. She's really tall and she's Indian. Have you seen her?"

"No, can't say that I have." Suddenly, she stuck out her hand. "Name's Sue."

"Julie."

"I hear your friend's pregnant."

Julie nodded.

"I had a little friend for a while. Her name was Beanie and she was pregnant."

"What happened?"

"Don't know. I wouldn't have thought she'd leave without saying goodbye. But she didn't come back one night."

"Maybe she went home."

"Nah. Didn't have one of those to go to. Dad was dead and Mom was in jail. She ran away from the foster home. She was so young. Maybe fourteen. How old is your friend?"

"Seventeen." Julie couldn't even imagine what it would be like to be fourteen, alone, pregnant and on the streets. "How long ago did she disappear?"

"Not long back. Maybe three weeks. She should be having her baby 'bout now."

"Tell her about the others." Julie hadn't realized that the woman leaning against the side of the fridge had been listening in.

"What others?" Julie thought Sue sounded irritated.

"The ones who disappeared right before Beanie. The ones I told you to report—"

"And I told you to go report yourself, if you were so smart."

"I think they was murdered. And you coulda saved Beanie. Beanie depended on you and you let her down."

Sue lunged, taking half a table of sandwiches with her as she grabbed the woman's arm and pushed her against the wall. "Beanie's just fine. Nothing happened to her."

"You don't know that, do you? You know she was talking to the Peanut Man and you didn't stop her."

Suddenly the ubiquitous bouncer rounded the corner and both women stepped back. The fight was over as quickly as it had begun.

"Who's the Peanut Man?" Julie asked Sue.

"Some say he tries to get girls to go into prostitution."

"You don't think so?"

"All the girls he ever talks with, I know for a fact are pregnant. And none of them ever want anything to do with him."

"But a bunch of girls disappeared?"

"Yeah. Maybe three or four over the summer."

"Where would I find the Peanut Man?"

Sue shrugged. "Everywhere and nowhere. I don't know. He just comes around."

It was obvious that Sue was done talking. Julie walked back into the big room now filling up with women. There was no sign of Dottie so Julie left her blankets where they were and, slipping out of her jeans, crawled between the layers. They even smelled fresh as if someone hung them out in the sun and fresh air every day.

As much as she was positive that she wouldn't sleep, the next thing she knew, someone was shaking her shoulder.

"Sue? What time is it?"

"Five. You'll miss the vans 'cause you're still waiting on the bathroom if you don't get going now."

Julie would take her word for it. She slipped on her jeans, grabbed her backpack and rolled the blankets.

''You can just leave 'em there. They'll collect 'em later.''

Julie had no idea who *they* were, but she dropped the roll back on the floor and followed Sue down the hall. The smell of coffee floated toward them from the kitchen.

''Got doughnuts today.''

Julie was more interested in a shower. By the time she was cleaned up with a new layer of makeup in place, the doughnuts were almost gone.

''Here, I got you one. I figured you'd like chocolate.'' Sue held out the confection on half of a paper towel.

''Thanks.''

''Listen. I want you to stay with me today. I got territory off of downtown and I need to go check on it.''

Julie was somewhat relieved and a little apprehensive. She needed to find out more about Peanut Man and she supposed this would be as good a way as any. But she'd just about made up her mind that another night in a shelter wasn't going to happen.

The day was promising to be warm as she watched Sue retrieve her shopping cart from a holding area behind the clinic for the homeless. Sue seemed to know everyone and Julie took advantage of introductions to ask about Charlene. No one had seen her. Would Charlene have left the area? It would seem so, but Julie found that hard to believe. Pregnant or not, her plans seemed to include finishing her senior year and going on to college.

Two more days until Christmas. Julie thought of Persi and Charlene's family. How unbearably sad; the not knowing was the worst. Sue didn't seem to want to talk so Julie trotted along beside her, helping with the cart when they needed to maneuver over curbs.

''That one there's mine. Been mine since I can remember.'' Sue pointed to a large blue Dumpster that seemed full to overflowing. ''Ain't been by in a while and sure looks like she's full.''

Julie looked around. The Dumpster was parked behind a

series of stores in a strip mall with a liquor store on the end; a Chinese restaurant called The Jade Garden; a thrift store; Dollar store; cubbyhole for a State Farm rep; and a bingo parlor.

"You know where the best stuff comes from? Right there." Sue pointed to the bingo parlor to her right. "They never save things. Find a sweater? It goes in the trash. I found a billfold with fifty dollars one time. Sometimes the dollar store throws out some good stuff, but not very often."

Julie surveyed the blue container whose lip was at least two feet above her head and vaguely wondered how Sue got in and out of something so seemingly people-unfriendly.

"This here will give you a step up." Julie watched as Sue dragged up a wooden crate that had been secreted in back of the container. "My arthritis is bad when it's cold."

So this was the price for learning the street ropes, or protection, or whatever it was that Sue had to offer. Dumpster diving was going to be her activity for the morning.

Julie was quickly thankful that temperatures had been below freezing at night. The odor from the sack of fish heads would have knocked her off her perch. As it was, she just moved them aside.

"What am I looking for?"

"Anything. You let me be the judge as to whether it's a keeper."

Julie promptly tossed down a frayed extension cord, box of water-damaged crepe paper, a sack of fortune cookies— open with mouse droppings in the bottom—a piece of aluminum weather stripping, a box of printed envelopes that indicated the State Farm guy had recently moved, and curtain rods—some with the end brackets missing—and two boxes of Christmas lights that looked like they hadn't been opened. She was amazed how Sue went over each treasure and started keep-no keep piles. Julie was dismayed to see the fortune cookies go into the keep pile.

She had just turned back to uncover the next armload of

goodies when a white Honda sedan slowly approached from the west. Julie saw it first coming up the alley off Twelfth Street and turned to tell Sue, but she had already put down the latest find and was walking toward the alley.

The driver stopped and waited for Sue, but left the engine running. They seemed to know each other. And only when a handful of peanut shells hit the asphalt did it dawn on her. Peanut Man. Julie pretended to be busy, but watched as Sue seemed to indicate her with a nod of the head and Peanut Man leaned over the steering wheel to peer in her direction. The man looked big, muscular arms and shoulders in a short-sleeved T-shirt and the bull neck of someone who works out a lot.

There wouldn't be any getting away if he didn't want you to. Could this man have plucked Charlene off the street? It was possible. She saw Sue take something from the man—a palmed bill? Probably. It was possible that Sue pimped for the guy and then set up her newfound friends. Beanie probably hadn't had a chance. And wasn't it possible that she had just been sold, too? Suddenly she realized that the car wasn't running. She glanced in that direction in time to see the Peanut Man unfold from behind the wheel. Run. Every instinct screamed run.

Julie scrambled out of the Dumpster, one foot springboarding her forward so that she hit the parking lot running. Would he chase her? No. Because directly in front of her, slowing rounding the corner of the last of the row's businesses was a security cop in a wanna-be car complete with light bar and, she'd bet her life, a siren. If she could have taken the time to kiss him, she would have. Instead, she sprinted, cursing the Mary Janes every step of the way, up the sidewalk in front of the businesses, pausing only after she'd reached the end of the row and could look back down the alley from a safe distance.

Great. The wanna-be was talking to Sue and Peanut Man. This would give her time to double back and get a license plate number. *Crazy.* She heard the word in her head. Even sounded like Ben was saying it. But this was as close as she would get to someone who might have abducted Charlene. And the police could handle the rest. The tag number was key. She ducked across the alley and through a broken piece of fencing. Albuquerque was a city of walls and fences; it had been written into the town charter way back when because the tumbleweeds would blow in off the mesas and fill yards with rounded stick vegetation blocking driveways and doorways. But now boundaries would be a pain.

There was only one wall to scale and then she'd be behind the car. She could hear talking and once again quietly blew a kiss in the direction of the wanna-be. Dropping to her knees, she crawled forward. When she was twenty feet beyond the car, she inched toward the edge of the fence that bordered the alley and lifting her head, paused. The sound of an engine starting gave her coverage and she rolled to a sitting position, still hidden by a clump of desert papyrus. DMP 871— The car suddenly turned away from her and sped back the way it came. She was missing one number. But surely the cops could trace it with what she would give them.

She stayed hidden until Sue started to walk back to the Dumpster. The wanna-be continued on down the alley. Did Sue even know she was gone? Julie wasn't waiting to see. She scrambled upright and jogged down a driveway between two houses. She'd cut over to Indian School and call a cab from the Pueblo Indian Cultural Center. Home. Another bath, clean clothes, a call to Ben and a call to the police.

THIRTEEN

SOMETHING WAS WRONG. It was late, or early. Charlene didn't know which. She had just fallen asleep when she had turned over on her right side, dragging Beanie's arm with her. Beanie's lifeless arm. Immediately, she sat up.

"Beanie." She kept her voice to a stage whisper. "Beanie, wake up." Again, Charlene gently shook her arm. Nothing. She felt for a pulse. Faint. Wait. Did it fade? She searched Beanie's wrist, then pressed four stiff fingers against her neck. Had she been mistaken? There was no pulse. Something was terribly, terribly wrong. But this was her chance. She had to be ready. She had to be able to elude Jerry. She wasn't afraid of Serena. Lean muscle could win over fat. But how could she leave Beanie?

"Serena!" The yell seemed to bounce off the walls. Instantly, she heard murmuring from the room next door. Again, Charlene called out. And when the door opened, Serena was alone. What did this mean? Where was Jerry? Was he in the kitchen? And then Serena was gone. To get him? Did she forget her keys? She left the door open.

"Go."

"Beanie?" Charlene couldn't believe it. Was she okay? Had she suspected all along what the push-ups meant? That she was planning her escape? "Are you okay?" She put a hand on Beanie's forehead and felt the coolness of perspiring skin.

"I'll be fine. You have to go. I'll help." Charlene didn't

have time to ask how because Serena bustled through the door.

"Now, now no need to get excited. Babies are born all the time." This time she had a ring of keys in her hand. But still no Jerry. Where was he? They were never apart.

But this was it. She would just have to trust that Beanie would be all right. But none of them would survive unless someone escaped.

The cuff had barely swung free when Beanie threw herself forward into Serena's arms. At the same time Charlene bolted through the door. From the angry outburst, she envisioned that Beanie was holding on to Serena, forcing the older woman to drag her weight as well.

Charlene took the back steps two at a time. She felt for the fridge and counted two, four, six; she was on the garage level, her bare feet smacking the cement floor. There was a weak yard light over the back entrance.

The door was locked. Damn. She felt along the frame. Would they be stupid enough to leave a key? No. Then she turned. She had never counted on them keeping the truck. But it made sense. They wouldn't want it picked up. And there it was.

She opened the driver's side door. Jerry had left the interior light off, but she quickly felt the keys dangling from the ignition. Now for the door. Had she felt a garage door opener by the back door? Up the steps, on her right. Yes. Press. Back to the truck. Behind the wheel. Pump once, twice. Where was Serena? Would she leave Beanie and come after her? Probably. "C'mon baby, turn over. So, you haven't been driven in a while, don't be bitchy." The door was jerking upward. Shit. A flicker of headlights at the head of the lane—some one hundred yards straight behind her. "Now." As if in answer, the truck roared to life.

Slamming it into reverse, Charlene peeled backward, spun to the left and turned squarely into the lane accelerating, shifting to second, then third. She wouldn't need her headlights until the last second—the moment before she would ram the oncoming car unless it swerved. If it wasn't Jerry, then it might be the doctor. Either one would try to stop her.

"Got any guts?" Charlene screamed as she aimed for the headlights and watched the car swerve into a ditch, but not before she caught the surprised look on Jerry's face as he realized what was happening. She mashed the gas pedal, turned on her headlights and negotiated a sharp right turn that put her on a paved county road. Where was she? She could see lights in the distance. Head toward them, that would be safe even at ten o'clock at night if the clock in the dash was correct. Then she'd go home. There was such a feeling of relief that she didn't need to wonder whether it was the right thing. She knew it was..Whatever was going to happen with her child, the baby would be alive and safe. And she would lead the police back to the houseful of young girls.

She hated the snowmen and Santas and reindeer with red noses that pranced across roofs of the subdivision. But it was civilization and she knew where she was; she could excuse Rio Rancho anything, even its preoccupation with plastic. She was just a few miles from the turnoff that would put her on Highway 44 and home. As she passed a twenty-four-hour gas station, she knew what she had to do—call the police and direct them to the house. She owed Beanie. She owed all of them, all the faceless cries in the night.

She pulled around to the back of the station and pulled a crumpled pair of sweats from behind the seat along with a pair of running shoes. Thank God she hadn't cleaned her truck out when her mother wanted her to. Pulling on her clothes, she got a handful of quarters out of the ashtray and headed toward the pay phone on the side.

He saw her first. She had just removed the receiver when she saw the white Honda coasting to a stop at pump number one. And Jerry was looking straight at her. Would he chase her? He must guess that her truck was in back. She wouldn't wait to find out. She'd left the truck running. Bounding out of the booth, she saw an SUV pull in front of him and stop at pump number two. He'd have to back up to get out. Couldn't happen to a nicer guy.

Again, she circled the back of the station and floorboarded the truck to round the building just as Jerry was pulling out from the pump, heading in the opposite direction. She had an advantage, not a big one, but an edge before he could turn and come after her. She darted out between two transports and wedged the truck into the flow of traffic—eighteen wheeler after eighteen wheeler. A lot of rigs ran at night and if she could just stay close for a while, Jerry wouldn't be able to pull something on the highway.

She kept an eye on the rearview and saw the Honda get socked in by traffic that kept it sidelined. Charlene pulled into an open lane and kept her foot on the gas—sixty, seventy, eighty—still keeping a buffer of big trucks around her. Did he know the road like she did? The way into the pueblo? It would be a help if he didn't. She knew it well enough to run without lights. By the bridge outside San Ysidro she couldn't see him any longer and she'd lost her big rig escorts on the road to Farmington. But she wasn't going to relax; she couldn't. She needed to get home. The pueblo was just beyond the next curve. Three more miles. She'd made it.

The first sputter didn't register. A second sputter and the truck coughed and went dead. Gas. She hadn't even thought to check. Yep, the needle was way beyond the last mark. Quickly she cut the lights and aimed the truck down a cow path off the highway to her left. She was on Indian land now. Her land. Land she rode across as a child on a mustang tamed by her uncle. She bounced to a stop and didn't hesitate even to lock. She just took off running across the rough sand dodging cacti by the light of a moon playing hide-and-seek with a high-flying bank of clouds. She saw a community horse tank up ahead and allowed herself the luxury of stopping and looking back.

Nothing. She scanned the highway. Could he also be driving without lights? The moon hid, then popped into view. Her eyes weren't playing tricks. There were no cars coming this way.

Suddenly she grabbed the edge of the horse tank. The pain was so swift and severe, radiating out and up from her navel, that she gasped and staggered almost to her knees.

"No. Not now. Please baby, wait. Be safe." As if in defiance, another pain shot up her left side and seemed to circle. "Breathe, breathe," she admonished herself. She was rocking now, begging the pain to go away. Just as suddenly as it had come, it disappeared. At the exact moment she saw the car. She couldn't wait to see if he saw the truck. She hadn't been able to get very far off the highway. He would see it and try to track her.

Thinking was wasting time. Charlene started to run, willing the pains to not come back. She held her side when another pain threatened to overtake her and kept on. How long could she last? Three miles along the river and she'd be home. But would the baby wait?

FOURTEEN

LORENZO COULDN'T SLEEP. His granddaughter fixed him warm milk and opened a package of Oreo cookies. But he wasn't hungry. He filled his pockets with the little chocolate sandwiches and waited until the house was quiet. Then he slipped his poncho over his head, took his foxhead cane and left by the door in the back of his room. The night was clear and cold with a playful moon that peeked out from a thick bank of clouds. It was a good night for the baby Jesus to come. He would be able to see his way. But this was a time of sorrow and the baby Jesus would only see the sadness of the village. There could be no rejoicing as long as Charlene remained lost.

Lorenzo had thought that perhaps witches had taken Charlene. There would be many who would have been envious of her height and swiftness. But they wouldn't have taken her truck. He was sure of that. So, her disappearance hinted of worldly mischief. But her parents had sought the help of a medicine man who began a witch hunt anyway around the village by first achieving a clairvoyant state induced by herbs and secret potions of which only he knew the origins. Then with a fetish in hand to ward off the evil, he held it up to the cardinal directions, asking the spirits to lead him to the witches. But it didn't work. There were no witches to be found around the community. Lorenzo knew for a fact that the medicine man tried the ceremony twice.

Early in the summer a witch had died and two days later a terrible dust storm followed by hail had flattened the early corn plants and shredded the leaves on the squash and pumpkin. His people believed that the witch had been refused entry into the underworld and had come back to wreak havoc. But when the storm had passed the witch returned to dust and was forgotten.

Now it was the time of the weasel. A symbol for winter because the sharp-nosed little animal would change the color of his coat from brown to white and wear this symbolic snow until the spring. Then when new life would need to appear, there would be ceremonies to thaw the ground and melt the snow and bring the trees to blossom.

Lorenzo sighed. There were so many rituals of his people that were now forgotten. Young people watched television. They didn't listen to their elders. Was that why Charlene had disappeared? She had not followed the teachings of her elders? Sometimes the teachings were strict, but he'd never known the punishment for not following them to be obliteration. But that's what had happened. Charlene had disappeared. Not a trace.

In nature's rhythm the loss of a child was upsetting. At this time of year during the "days of the sun," the sun deity would report to other deities the happenings of the village. At this time also, those who would die in the upcoming year were marked in some way. Lorenzo had watched Charlene from under the bleachers go up and back, up and back sometimes carrying a ball, sometimes just catching it, but always jumping, twisting, ducking and putting the ball in the metal circle. There was no mark. Charlene had not been marked for death. Lorenzo was certain of that.

What could she have done that was so bad? Bad enough to remove her from her home? In the summer she had worn silver jewelry during a ritual. Silver is cool and meant to be worn only during the winter months. If worn in the summer it will bring on cold weather. One must wear black beads of obsidian or jet. Even stones are classified as "warm" or "cool." Could that have angered the deities?

Tonight the river called to him. Maybe it was this that had awakened him. He felt pulled by the river's flow. It wanted to talk to him. What secrets were in its depth? What must he learn? The ground was frozen and crusty, not comfortable for his moccasined feet. But he hurried on, drawn by an urgency he could only imagine.

Stepping through the brush he didn't hear the car and only saw it when it switched its lights on and swerved to miss him by inches. He raised his cane and yelled at the white man behind the wheel. No man should drive by the river in delicate sand, squashing new growth that only slept now but would push up green and golden unless it was killed.

Lorenzo hated cars and he told this man so. He'd forgotten his teeth and the sounds he heard weren't the words in his head.

The man stepped from the car, glanced in his direction, but was more interested in the front wheel of the car, which appeared to be doubled back under the car's body. This wheel wouldn't roll anywhere. The driver must have agreed with him because he kicked the wheel several times and then turned back to confront Lorenzo. There was a gun in his hand. But the man only waved it in his direction, threatening, Lorenzo thought. Then he bolted into the brush and was gone.

Lorenzo looked in the car. Empty except for an ashtray overflowing with peanut shells.

FIFTEEN

SHE HADN'T SEEN the lights of his car for some time now. Could she relax? Slow the pace? Or had he abandoned the car and was coming on foot? Her heart raced. Would he do that? She slowed and then bent double, clutching her side. No, no, no. By sheer will she tried to keep the baby from wanting to come into the world. She gasped, clung to the trunk of a tree to keep upright and waited for the contraction to subside. She was counting now—two minutes apart, less even. Wasn't that a sign that she could wish for all she was worth, but if the baby wanted to be born, it would come into this world in its own time?

She wouldn't have heard the crack of dry wood had she been running. But there it was. Clear and followed by another and another. Someone was coming toward her and wasn't trying to cover the sound. Quickly she stepped behind the tree and squatted in the cattails. She almost gasped when she saw Jerry, gun in hand, looking up and down the river's bank. He stood listening for what seemed an hour before taking off upstream. Toward the pueblo.

Now what? He was effectively cutting off her escape route. Should she follow him? Trail him to the village outskirts and hope she could get help? Another pain rippled through her body. This one left her panting, wanting to scream out so badly that she could taste the metallic salty residue of blood where she had bitten her finger. Her sweatpants were soaked from her body's fluids. She slipped them down to relieve the pressure on her stomach. It wouldn't be long. She started to rise, but fell back to her knees, then instinctively squatted and pressed forward and down huffing and breathing in great gulps until her child slipped from her body.

And as it filled its lungs with cold night air, it yowled. Charlene tore off her sweatshirt and wrapped the small body, cradling it close, severing the umbilical as her ancestors had done. She wasn't even cold in the thin cotton T-shirt she wore underneath.

"Shh." The crying lessened. But had he heard? She must find out. There was no doubt that he would kill her. She knew too much. Maybe if she could lead him away from the baby. At least one of them would live. She would never let him have her baby. She would act as decoy until she could get someone's attention. Feverishly, she dug a hole in the soft bank and lined it with reeds and placed the swaddled baby in the little cave. "I'll be back, baby. You'll be safe here. Don't cry, now." And then Charlene took off forcing her body to jog forward up the bank toward home.

SIXTEEN

LORENZO WAS too upset to go home. He'd walk along the riverbank to quiet his nerves. His home was private. This land where he lived. Strangers shouldn't come onto his land, not threatening strangers, ones with guns. What had the man wanted? He needed to follow the man. His path was clear and he was headed toward the village. Lorenzo would try to tell somebody, if only he could get someone's attention. But at least he would see where the man went. This man was no spirit. And he meant harm.

Lorenzo would never be able to tell anyone how he found the baby. Was it a cry that his ears picked up? Would anyone believe that his walking stick began to vibrate and planted itself in the soft sand of the riverbank, the little fox refusing to move? Standing as if on alert. But that's exactly what happened. Lorenzo tugged and it dug in deeper; then, he saw the flattened reeds and the cleverly concealed mouth of the little cave. He reached in, withdrew the tiny bundle and saw the O-shaped puckered mouth and flailing arms and legs. He took off his poncho and put a layer of this blanket cloth around the baby, securing its arms and legs. It quieted and he held it close to his chest.

But now what to do? The baby needed warmth and food and cleaning. He picked up a handful of wet leaves and gently wiped the baby's tiny face. He would take it to his grand-daughter. She would know what to do. Lorenzo couldn't hold this bundle clutching it to him with both hands and carry his walking cane so he left the little fox and promised that he would be back in the morning. But the going was slow. Lorenzo needed the cane for balance.

He was maybe two miles from the village, but if he kept the little bundle warm, wouldn't the baby be all right until he could reach safety? He prayed for guidance and listened as the answer played in his head. At the edge of the village he would know what to do. At the edge of the village he would know what to do. It played over and over but he knew to trust this voice.

JULIE HADN'T GOTTEN to Ben's until after nine on Christmas Eve. She had phoned the police the day before, then filled out a report at the station nearest her in the morning. She hadn't held out hope that they would find him, the man in the dirty white Honda. But they did. One of the young detectives had called her that evening, hoping to get favorable press? Maybe. More likely, he'd call back and ask her out. But at least she knew what had happened. They had detained the man for questioning, but eventually had to release him. There was simply not enough evidence and living on the street like Beanie and her friends did made them practically invisible.

The police had also brought in Sue. The young detective said he thought she knew a lot more than she was saying, but was afraid to share. He promised to keep an eye on her. Julie thought he meant harass her, put the kind of pressure on her so that she'd finally tell them whatever she knew. But for now it was another dead end. At least the man had a name. Jerry Burges, a transplant from New York who worked as a night security guard for a chip maker in Rio Rancho. Not a high-paying job. Did he supplement it somehow?

She couldn't think of a time that Christmas had seemed so empty. She had failed to find Charlene. Even this Jerry didn't seem to be an answer. No one seemed any closer to solving Charlene's disappearance. Her foolproof plan had proved futile. Even Ben was withdrawn. He had kissed her, but instead

of intimacy, it screamed of preoccupation. She had driven to
the pueblo for midnight mass. Christmas Eve was special and
attended by most of the village. Ben had talked of the baby
doll that would be left at the home of the family honored to
have the crèche. And flanked by luminaries, the parishioners
would follow the path of light to the baby and then celebrate.

SEVENTEEN

AT THE EDGE of the village, Lorenzo stopped, out of breath, his right arm aching from holding the baby, his breath coming in short gasps. But he saw what the voice was trying to tell him. Ahead at the edge of the village, the first street on his right was lined with light. Candles in paper bags of sand flickered and glowed, beckoning to him to follow. He stumbled toward the road and followed the light to the end. And there a house was surrounded in light. Luminaries lined the edge of the flat roof, the porch, the open door. More candles lined the window and glowed from a dining room table.

But what caught Lorenzo's attention was the cradle. Not exactly a cradle but a wooden trough formed by two *Y*s with wooden slats in between like his nephew's goats ate from. Only this one was lined with silken, golden straw. And he knew that this was where he would put the baby. But when he got near, there was already a baby in the straw. Then quickly Lorenzo felt relief. This was a plastic baby. It didn't need a nice bed. He would take the plastic baby away and put a real baby in its place. Then with his baby safe, he would go to the church and find his granddaughter.

CHARLENE STARTED AFTER Jerry, but quickly felt her body go from the feverish heat of having given birth to the aftershock of sweat freezing on her skin, robbing her of all energy. She must keep going. What would he do if he found her? Found the baby? It would not be good. She was sure of that. She couldn't stop her teeth from chattering and couldn't seem to make her feet work. One foot didn't seem to want to lift up and go ahead of the other.

She tripped and sprawled flat and couldn't keep from crying out. Then she held her breath. Someone was crashing through the underbrush, coming toward her, not being careful about making noise—not having to be careful about noise because when he found her, he would—do what? Kill her and escape? With an effort she didn't know she had, she scrambled up and began to run around him, making him the pursuer as she headed toward the village. He didn't know she had had her baby. She'd have to count on that. He'd think that he was getting the two of them. Would that keep him from shooting her? She didn't know.

She left the road to run along the river, hoping the sound would cover her steps. But her breath was labored, coming in short gulps and she couldn't seem to fill her lungs. She tripped over the gnarled roots of a giant cottonwood and couldn't get up. She didn't know how much time she had. Had Jerry seen her sprint toward the river? She'd have to hide; she couldn't go on. Clawing her way between the protruding roots, she burrowed in the wet leaves, mounding them over her body before losing consciousness.

JULIE SLIPPED HER HAND into Ben's. He looked down and smiled, then put his arm around her. They were in a pew at the back of the very crowded church. It seemed as if everyone was seeking some relief, an answer to the sadness that enveloped the village. The congregation was somber. There had been very little conversation before the priest came forward to begin mass. Even the acolytes, often a possibility for comic relief, lighted the fifty or so candles that banked the sides and back of the dais without incident, then retired to sit in straight-backed chairs to the side of the small stage.

Someone had brought in pine boughs and poinsettias. The star-shaped bracts in red and white were bunched together at the base of the altar and along the front of the stage. Even the life-size statue of the Virgin was knee-deep in greenery interspersed with bright-red petals. There were fresh pine boughs above each station of the cross along both walls and huge red bows fixed to the ends of the pews. Julie breathed in the fresh pine scent with overtones of melting paraffin, and heavy wool coats that had been in storage. Not a scent a perfume maker would want to bottle, but then, why not? Next to the scents of a roasting turkey and pies baking, didn't pine, candle wax and mothballs just scream holiday gathering?

From the back someone started a tape of Christmas music and the nervous shuffling of the crowd was muffled as the words of old favorites drifted through the church. "'Away in the manger no crib for his bed, the little Lord Jesus laid down his sweet head…'"

"'We three kings of Orient are…'"

"'Silent night, holy night all is calm, all is bright…'"

"'O come all ye faithful…'"

Julie snuggled into Ben's side and felt his arm tighten. The setting, the mood, all was perfect except for the overpowering sadness Julie felt.

The priest chose to deliver a short sermon, a talk on keeping faith even when that faith was challenged. He encouraged everyone to pray for Charlene's welfare and to renew hope by welcoming the Christ child into their lives this very evening and to always trust that God could perform miracles. And at this time of the new year, they should rejoice in knowing that their God would protect and lead them. When the time came, the line to receive sacraments—already four deep—stretched nearly out the door.

After another round of taped music, the service was over. The priest asked everyone to follow him to celebrate the miracle of birth and pledge themselves to living in the image of God's son. With that the priest walked down the aisle and began the trek to the chosen house. Julie and Ben fell in behind the priest. The walk was not a long one, but led back behind the church toward the river, then veered to the right.

The lighted path glittered in the distance and acted as a beacon to lead the villagers to their destination.

Charlene's parents, Persingula and Patrick, had been chosen. Was this done before Charlene had disappeared? Or did the priest think it would bring good fortune and a celebration in their home might lessen their grief? Julie hoped it worked. Persi and her husband deserved something good.

The priest had fallen back from the lead to allow the crowd to surge forward but the first screams brought him running back to the head of the group, Julie and Ben close behind.

"Look. Father, it's a miracle."

The crowd parted, forming a semi-circle around the manger where tiny arms and legs waved in the air and lusty lungs howled disapproval of the entire situation.

"It's the Christ child!" a woman shouted.

"Well, if that's the Christ child, then God has a sense of humor. That baby's a girl." The man who spoke was closest to the manger.

There was almost total silence as everyone pushed forward to see. And, yes, Julie noted, the baby had kicked off its covering and there was no mistaking the child was a girl. Didn't someone say that God worked in mysterious ways? Would the villagers think that God had given Persingula and Patrick a baby girl to replace Charlene? She'd bet some would be thinking that way. Wherever this child had come from, it had already worked the miracle of helping some renew their faith.

"Let me through." Persi was pushing her way to the front. "Oh, the poor little thing is freezing." She lifted the baby and smoothed the blanket underneath before placing the child in the center, wrapping it and then lifting the bundle to cradle it in her arms. "Who has fresh goats?" There were a couple of nods from those in the front row. "Well, bring some milk, then." There was shuffling as two people pushed back through the crowd to leave hurriedly.

Julie noted how efficient Persi was as she checked the arms

and legs of the baby and bent to listen to its breathing. But it also dawned on Julie that the baby was wrapped in her old poncho, the one she'd given Lorenzo. And, yes, there he was at the edge of the crowd, shivering but looking as smug as he could without teeth. She tugged on Ben's sleeve and whispered her suspicions. This was Charlene's baby. She'd bet her life on it. But where was Charlene? Could Lorenzo tell them? Had Charlene brought it here? Or had Lorenzo?

"We've got to talk to him," Julie whispered.

Ben nodded, and, taking her elbow, turned to weave their way back through the crowd to where Lorenzo was standing. Ben slipped off his jacket and draped it around the old man's shoulders.

"He's getting a little expensive to keep clothed," Ben said as Lorenzo gathered the jacket around him, pulling the leather to his nose and breathing deeply. "Maybe he needs this, too." Ben pulled off his plaid wool muffler and wound it around Lorenzo's neck. This met with nodding and a mouthful of nonsensical sounds as Lorenzo patted the scarf and ran his hands down the sleek front of the leather.

"Seems pleased," Julie noted. "A little more masculine image than the poncho." But I know what I'll buy Ben for a late Christmas present, she promised herself. Because she had a feeling the jacket wasn't coming off.

"Let's go out on the porch." Ben took Lorenzo's arm and motioned to the door.

Lorenzo followed, then stood expectantly as Julie faced him. "Where is Charlene?"

Lorenzo immediately shuffled his feet as if running, then lifted his arm and aimed an imaginary pistol formed by crooked index finger and cocked thumb.

"Oh, my God." Julie looked quickly at Ben. "Someone is chasing her—trying to kill her."

"We may be too late. It's hard to say how long the baby has been here or how long it took Lorenzo to bring it here."

Julie knew Ben was warning her not to get her hopes up of finding Charlene alive.

"But where did he find the baby?"

"We may never know."

"Fox...river...go."

"What?" Julie and Ben turned in unison.

"Fox...river...go." Lorenzo was pointing beyond the porch to the river.

Ben was already shivering in a wool turtleneck sweater, but he grabbed Julie's hand. "Let's go. If we head to the river and look for a trail we can trace his steps here."

"But I thought he said *fox*. Is that what you heard?"

Ben nodded, but was already off the porch.

"Yeah, but who knows." He shrugged. "Maybe we'll see a fox."

"Ben, I'm afraid Charlene's in trouble."

"Me, too."

Wearing slacks to church hadn't been her first idea of correct attire for Christmas Eve, but Ben had convinced her that as drafty as the church was and unpredictable as the heating system was, slacks came under the heading of survival. And now she was thankful she'd listened.

They completed the first mile at a brisk jog, stopping to search clumps of vegetation and thickets of scrub oak. Occasionally they would pick up Lorenzo's footprints in the soft riverbank. He had stopped often, probably to shift the baby's weight before starting out again, Julie thought. It was a miracle that he'd been able to carry the baby so far.

They must have been close to two miles from the village when they saw it—both at once.

"There's our fox."

The stick was planted firmly upright and the head pointed toward a large cottonwood. They both scrambled over its roots and stopped when they saw the tiny cave.

"He led us to where he found the baby, but not to Charlene." Ben couldn't hide his disappointment.

"I feel she's out here somewhere. Probably not in very good shape," Julie added. "Maybe if we fan out and cover the distance between here and the village, we'll pick up her trail."

"Julie, over here."

She followed the sound of Ben's voice and found him standing by the white Honda with a crumpled front wheel.

"Ben, that's Jerry's car." She hurriedly filled him in on Jerry Burges and what the police had told her. "I don't think Lorenzo was lying. If Jerry was after Charlene, he might kill her."

"And you might be right." The man who spoke stepped out of the shadows of the cottonwood's trunk. "I'll thank you both to step this way." He was motioning away from the car.

The moonlight obscured the man's expression, but not his sheer bulk. Julie's first thought was that the man was a giant—enormous arms, chest, legs like posts. But it was the revolver that kept her attention riveted to his outstretched hand.

"I think we'll leave you here and then the two of us will take a little walk."

The one being left behind was going to be her, Julie thought and wasn't surprised when he handed her a gag and told her to put the soiled rag in her mouth and tie it behind her head. There was little left to the imagination as to what he'd do if she didn't follow directions.

"Now, get in here." Jerry opened the back door of the Honda and shoved her behind the driver's seat but not until after he'd pulled a slip knot tight around her wrists, pinning her arms behind her back. Then he repeated the maneuver around her ankles. Seeing her trussed up and sprawled across the Honda's back seat seemed to satisfy him and he slammed the door shut.

"The two of us are going to go hunting." This was obviously said to Ben. Julie couldn't see, but she prayed that

Ben wouldn't do anything foolish. And then she waited. Hoped that Jerry wasn't watching the car as she jackknifed her body, rolled to a sitting position and wiggled over the front seat to plop unceremoniously facedown trussed feet bent back. Then squirming onto her back, she wedged herself behind the steering wheel and leaned both heels against the center of the wheel and pushed with all her weight. The horn didn't disappoint her, but sounded loud and beckoning.

EIGHTEEN

"DIDJA HEAR THAT?" The deputy stopped. The car horn sounded insistent in the distance, its shrillness blasting into the clear night like a pesky alarm gone wrong.

"I'd have to be deaf not to." Elmore wasn't in the best of moods. He still had to put together that kid's swing set before morning. Playing Santa wasn't in his job description, not as sheriff and not as a father. Whoever heard of a Native American Santa? And walking around in the cold and damp wasn't his idea of a great evening.

"Kids?"

"Huh?"

"The car horn. Someone in trouble or just kids horsing around?"

"Check it out. I'll continue north along the river."

There was no way that Elmore was going to do his deputy's job. It probably was kids celebrating Christmas Eve. Elmore had been called to the house of Persingula and Patrick Toya. What a Christmas Eve it was turning out to be. Usually it meant a couple of drunks, not miracles and babies left in mangers. Lorenzo, bless the old man's heart, tried to tell them about something down by the river. *River* was the only word he understood other than something that sounded like "ox." But that made no sense. It was his decision to scour the river's edge a couple of miles out from the village. The doctor had called in to check on the baby and thought it was less than two hours old. And that meant a mother nearby and maybe a mother in trouble. Unless hoping to abandon the child, she left it in the manger herself.

Elmore shook his head. Used to be babies were taken care of. Families wanted children. Already there was talk about the baby being a gift to replace Charlene. He didn't believe that way. There was probably an explanation, a very human one and he would find it.

He clicked off his flashlight. The moon was light enough. Suddenly he realized that the night was quiet, no horn. But the explosion of gunfire caught him off guard. Three quick blasts, in the air no doubt because that was the signal of trouble. Pulling his weapon, Elmore started down the riverbank following his deputy's tracks.

SO HOW HEROIC DID HE FEEL? Not very, Ben decided. At least Julie was all right, judging from the sound of the horn. Jerry hadn't expected that and had cursed and threatened to kill him on the spot. In fact, Ben wasn't sure why he didn't until Jerry asked him to show him where Charlene lived. And that's where they were headed when the shooting began. More like warning shots. And it was comforting to know that there was help. But it seemed to rattle Jerry. Not the brightest bulb, Ben decided.

So when Jerry stumbled over a mound of dirt between the exposed roots of a cottonwood, only to have the entire center of the pile sit upright and begin to scream, Ben kicked the gun from his grasp, dived for it and then chose not to shoot as Jerry struggled upright and scrambled out of range. Let him run. He wouldn't get that far and Ben's attention needed to be on Charlene because that's who had emerged from the shallow grave—feverish, delirious and screaming her lungs out.

IT WAS 3:00 a.m. before the doctor walked back into the Toya living room, accepted a cup of coffee and gave everyone the news they had hoped to hear: mother and child were doing well. A few days of bed rest and Charlene would be on her feet, good as new. She had suffered from exposure and had been in shock from loss of blood but as the doctor insisted, young people were resilient and Charlene was in superior shape.

Persi was still holding the baby, sleeping now in fluffy pink blankets brought over by neighbors. The stocking cap on her head was pulled almost to her eyebrows. Lorenzo sat at the kitchen table sipping a cup of hot chocolate, his favorite according to the granddaughter who had tried to return the leather jacket but to no avail.

Based on Charlene's description and hastily drawn map of how to get to where she had been held, the police raided the dormitory and took everyone into custody. Even Beanie and her new baby. Elmore and his deputy had found Jerry hiding near the water tank up by the highway.

Ben and Julie were just saying their goodbyes when Coach Leonard walked in. It seemed like most of the village was still out and about.

"I was going to bring this by in the morning, but I thought you'd want to tell her first thing yourself." He handed an envelope to Persi.

"Tell me what?"

Everyone turned to see Charlene in the doorway to the bedroom, looking pale and grasping the doorjamb.

"You got your offer. Full scholarship to UNM," Leonard said.

"Wow. That's great." Then she paused. "Do you think they'll still want me?"

"I imagine you'll find some help with your daughter." Leonard glanced at Persi. "The university don't care about your private life, they just want a basketball player. And you've got eight months to get into top-notch shape and give 'em what they want. We'll see, but I've got a summer camp in mind that will get you ready in no time."

Everyone cheered and hugged Charlene. Lorenzo looked up startled, but then went back to his cocoa. It was a pretty good Christmas after all, he thought as he patted the soft lamb's leather sleeve of his new jacket.

THE SANTA CLAUS
MURDERS
by Ed Gorman

ONE

I DON'T KNOW about you, but I've got pretty good sales resistance when it comes to any kind of class reunion. I don't mean the big summer three-day specials. I mean in the more impromptu sort you get when you live in a town of twenty-eight thousand and most of your classmates are still around.

Before I say "Yes, I'll go," I always haul out the old high school yearbook to run a kind of checklist.

I want to see how many of the good-looking girls are still unmarried and-or divorced. But the thing is, some of the good-looking girls aren't so good-looking anymore, and this is only eight years after graduating; and girls you didn't pay much attention to have bloomed into beauties.

You see the dilemma of relying on your high school annual.

Of course, I make other kinds of checklists, too, when I'm flipping through those slick yearbook pages: who has made a lot of money, who has gone somewhere and really distinguished himself or herself, and, of course, given some of my friends from the Hills, who is taking an extended tour of our prison system. You can say one thing for my old friends of an illegal bent—none of them are on death row. I think that's something to be proud of.

Maybe if it hadn't been snowing, and maybe if snow didn't make me feel lonely, and maybe if loneliness didn't inspire in me a rhapsody of truly sickening self-pity…maybe I wouldn't have gone that Friday night.

And if I hadn't gone, maybe I wouldn't have gotten involved in one of Chief Clifford—''Cliffie'' to those who know him and hate him—Sykes, Jr.'s bungled murder investigations.

There's a Bob Nugent in every class—at least there was back in the fifties when I was in high school.

The popular term then was brownnose. The nuns and the priests always relied on him to be the exemplary student and the kid who'd help them move desks or deliver groceries to the poor after school. He was the kid they always pointed to when they were on our ass about some crime within the prison walls—why can't you be more like etc., etc.

You know the kind I'm talking about. Not blessed athletically, not good-looking, too corny for the popular crowd and too popular for the corny crowd. He wasn't even an A student. Bs, mostly, and he had to work hard to get those.

He was class president; he was the student the bishop sent to welcome the governor to our school; he was the altar boy that all the seminaries scouted, the problem there being that he was just as girl crazy as the rest of us.

What he mostly was was a glad-hander, and I suppose that's why we all figured he'd be the most successful kid in our class. But you're probably getting ahead of me. You know what I know—that the kid who promises to be the most successful never is. God or fate or sheer random bad luck steps in and blights him somehow.

With Nugent it was the jeep accident the summer of my junior year in college. We'd been at the sand pits swimming and drinking beer well into the night. That was the summer the Twist was so popular. Even gorillas and Republicans could do the Twist, so between diving into the water, gurgling down 3.2 beer, and trying to get Trojan wrappers undone before it was too late, a lot of people danced.

We all left by nine-thirty, the least drunken person in each car driving. Nugent's girlfriend, Sandy Beaumont, had her brother's jeep. It was a WWII relic that was pretty much rusted out. All I can remember is that they didn't leave the sand pits until after everybody else did, so I didn't hear about the accident until I came down to breakfast the next morning. I'd passed out on my bed the night before, and my folks, who didn't appreciate my drinking, let me lie there in the same funky clothes I'd worn all day at the sand pits.

It being a Sunday, my dad was at the table. "We tried to wake you up last night to tell you about it, but you were too far gone to wake up. I sure hope you weren't driving last night."

"No, Mary Ann was," I said.

"Thank God for Mary Ann. She's the only sensible one in your whole class."

I didn't want to spoil my mom's vision of such decorum and purity and tell her that Mary Ann was the first one who'd stripped down and jumped in the water last night. Or the one who brought two marijuana joints to the party yesterday, these thanks to the same older brother who'd provided the 1951 Hudson convertible she was driving.

"You better get him some coffee, hon," Dad said. "And you might also put a shot of bourbon in it, too, sweetheart. He'll need it."

Dad had sure been right about that. Needing the bourbon, I mean. This was August 3, 1957.

IT IS NOW December 21, 1961. I'm the least successful attorney in my hometown of Black River Falls, Iowa. I'm twenty-four years old, I own a 1951 red Ford ragtop, which is customized just enough to pass itself off as a half-assed street rod. I am unmarried despite proposing somewhere around 4,632 times to the beautiful Pamela Forrest, and I'm trying to figure out a way of easing myself out of this house.

It's a very nice house, a large white Colonial-style place in that section of town where the wealthy people live, a new Buick Roadmaster and a new Lincoln in the garage and virtually my entire high-school graduating class of twenty-seven people filling the elegantly appointed first-floor rooms of the place. The falling snow lent the scene a prairie kind of nostalgia.

The home is the property of Don Lillis. Don inherited this place—and a large steel manufacturing plant—when his father passed a few years ago. Don imported a wife from Chicago, which is about five hours due east of here, telling us she was a model. She is pretty and bright and very pleasant and always blushes when Don brags about her modeling days.

One night, with too many drinks in her, Sara confessed to a bunch of us that she'd been a "Junior Miss" model for Marshall Field's in high school. But Don is one of those guys who has to have the best of everything. And so it was he imported not just a wife but a model. Even if she was only a high-school model.

There were three kinds of people there that night: the braggarts, the just-plain-folks folks and the potential arsonists-assassins-atomic-bomb-droppers who should never have even a whiff of alcohol but who spend their lives wading through vats of it.

I spent time with all three.

The braggarts were the loudest of the groups. In a town this size, success is having your own Ford franchise or a couple of those new McDonald's hamburger places or owning both drive-in theaters or being the doctor to the gentry. Or being an associate in the town's oldest law firm. This group included all of them and none of me.

I'd been just a few feet from them for a time, occasionally eavesdropping. To hear them tell it, they were on the verge of taking over the world very soon now. Yep, business was so good they had to find other places to invest all this cash that was flooding the banks that held their accounts.

I don't like to brag but... Each of them began at least one sentence that way. And then of course they'd start bragging without shame. And with no little exaggeration.

"Hey, if it isn't Perry Mason," said the drive-in-owning

Pete Foley. Hands of various sizes and strengths stabbed at me. I shook them all. Next I'd be kissing babies.

"How's the law business?" said the McDonald's man, Larry Garrigan. Meaning how much money was I making.

"You probably get some kind of combat pay for working with Judge Whitney, don't you?" said Ford franchisee Todd Wayman.

Pete Foley nudged me. "She's actually a good-looking gal, McCain. For somebody her age, I mean. You gettin' any of that stuff?"

Knowing male chortles.

Actually, Judge Esme Anne Whitney is a good-looking fifty-year-old woman. Her particular section of her Eastern old-money family had to flee out here after a financial scandal. They ran Black River Falls for nearly a hundred years until, right after WWII, the Clifford Sykes family, a hillbilly tribe up from the Ozarks, which made a lot of questionable money from the government, building airstrips and such for training camps, took over the town for themselves.

The only power left in the family resided in the courtroom of Judge Whitney.

I work for her as a court investigator. I took night-school classes at the University of Iowa so I could get licensed as a private investigator. She's my only client.

After we spoke of how all of them would like to get into Judge Whitney's knickers despite her age; after we spoke of how every person in this group except me would soon put away his first million; after we spoke of how the Hawkeye basketball team was falling apart this year; after we spoke of which of our former classmates—here the voices dropped to a stage whisper pitch—still looked sexy or which had put on weight or which was on her second marriage or which was a single mother with two kids who probably would appreciate a man who gave her some good loving—they each had themselves in mind, of course—and which guy had burned out quickly, after all that Peter Foley said, "God, did you hear what Bob Nugent did tonight?"

We all wanted to hear, of course. Me included. Hearing stories of lives in decline inevitably make you feel pretty good about your own life. Even if your life is forlorn, it isn't nearly as forlorn as that guy's, for God's sake.

"He had that pathetic Santa Claus suit on," Foley said, "and then he got it all over himself. Puked in his beard and all over the red jacket." He shook his head. "It never ends with that guy. All the stories you hear."

And there were plenty of Bob Nugent stories to tell, each one sadder than the last: Bob, who was supposed to be the most successful of all of us, including the kings-of-the-world in my little group, drinking too much and dropping out of college after only a year; Bob enlisting in the army but getting kicked out for drinking; Bob managing the carpet store out on Duncan Road after he came back to town, and getting fired for drinking on the job.

Then there was the assistant manager job at the supermarket—drinking. And the job selling new Plymouth cars—drinking. There had been a marriage, several tries at clinics for alcoholics, more jobs ending because of drinking, and finally his becoming the handyman for the nuns at the school and convent. Bob rarely sober but the nuns never losing patience or judging him. Just praying for him. Giving him a tiny basement room to call home, hot meals three times a day, Mass and communion every morning.

"He's upstairs passed out," Peter Foley said. "He called up today and asked if he could play Santa Claus. You remember how he always played Santa Claus in high school?"

"Good way to cop a lot of cheap feels from girls," Todd Wayman said. "He always conned them into sitting on his lap." He shook his head. "The poor bastard. What the hell ever happened to him, anyway? He just all of a sudden went to hell."

"You ask me, I think it was when he got kicked out of

the service," Larry Garrigan said. "Everybody knew why he got kicked out. He didn't have any self-respect left."

"The Plymouth sales gig," Foley said. "Renner treated him pretty bad. Used to chew him out right in front of customers. You know, for being drunk."

"It's funny," Wayman said. "I used to really dislike him. Such a damned brownnose and everything. The nuns always bragging on him and using him as an example to the rest of us. I didn't really want him to be successful, you know what I mean? I mean, it was petty. But that's how I thought when we were still in high school. I thought it'd serve him right if he fell on his face when he got out into the world. But when I heard he got kicked out of the service, and then he came back here to face everybody, I couldn't help it. I felt sorry for him tonight. And then when I saw him puke on himself, everybody standing around and watching him—"

"Sorry I missed it," I said.

I drifted away.

The house was big enough to have two fireplaces, one of which was downstairs in the basement, which had been decorated like a lavish Chicago department store Christmas window. Huge tree, its bulbs of gold and red and blue and green the only light except the fireplace. From somewhere, they'd imported mannequins dressed in turn-of-the-century holiday carolers garb, complete with top hats for the men and boys and long, elegant scarves for the women and girls. The conversation here was soft and friendly. No bragging. No Bob Nugent stories. Everybody down here was under the sway of the soft glow of the holiday tree. I spent some time with a few old classmates. Even though I might never have been tight friends with them, there's a bond I feel with the people I went through school with. They're kind of shirttail kinfolk as far as I'm concerned. It was good to see all of them.

Since everybody was in couples, I decided after a time that I'd drift back upstairs. Maybe my luck would be better there.

There had to be at least one girl who wasn't attached to somebody.

That was when I made the mistake of going to the kitchen to swipe a Pepsi.

THE BELLIGERENT ONES—all six of them—were out in the kitchen. Two of them were arm wrestling; one of them—the former gymnast—was standing on his hands; and the other three were hovering near a Texas fifth of Jack Daniel's black. They sure wouldn't want to run out. They were arguing in loud hayseed voices about the prospect of a Negro coach in the Big Ten. They were doing the KKK proud. I guess I didn't want these guys to be my kin, shirttail or otherwise.

None of them seemed to notice me as I grabbed a Pepsi from the refrigerator. As a man who towers five-five and weighs 125 pounds, I don't pack enough flesh to absorb more than a drink or two, after which point I get very silly or very belligerent. It's always as much of a surprise to me as it is to everybody else. So I was drinking Pepsi. I got my can, inserted the church key and cleared out before the white robes and the burning cross appeared.

I spent the next half hour in the company of the regular folk. The good, quiet workers: the dads who took an extra job if necessary; the moms who took in wash or sewing or peddled Avon if needed; the wall-eyed girl and the guy with the limp who probably had the best marriage of anybody in the house; the serious little guy who'd lost his wife in a car accident and was now raising their daughter alone; the frightened little woman who'd evoked many imperious smirks when she tried out one year for the cheerleading team; the boy who'd grown up without benefit of indoor plumbing and consequently didn't always smell the best. But here they were tonight, having survived the cruelty of high school, smiling, scrubbed, friendly, but segregated, as always, with themselves.

For the first time since walking through the door, I felt

comfortable. These were my people. The ones I'd mostly hung out with in grade and high school both. No bragging here, no boozy belligerence, just good people having a good time at the end of a hard workweek.

Tom Sizemore, with whom I'd shared a tent at Boy Scout camp two years running, was there with new wife, Patty, a farm girl from near Shellsburg. Tom had been and still was one of the quietest people I'd ever known. He spoke when there was a good reason to.

Tom, a heavyset guy, had been a damned good tackle on the high-school team. He'd gone to the U of I where he took up agriculture. After graduation, he went to work on his father's farm. The markets had been more erratic than usual in the past few years.

"I didn't get much of a chance to say hello at the wedding," Patty said to me, shaking my hand. "Tom always tells me what a wonderful guy you are." She had merry brown eyes and a smile that just made you smile right back.

Tom smiled. "I don't ever remember saying that in my life."

"I hypnotize him," Patty said. She was one of those slender, sun-browned farm women who seem to love the hardship of begging the ground and the bank to help them survive at least one more year. She ran the farm pretty much by herself. She knew how to make you feel comfortable.

But nobody was to stay comfortable for very long because somebody upstairs began to shriek with such ferocity that every face in the house turned up to the second floor and tried to imagine what sort of horror could have possibly inspired such a sound.

I was about five feet from the staircase, so I went up first. The screams continued.

When I reached the second-floor hall, which was as carefully decorated as the rest of the house, I saw Connie Bryce stagger from a door down the hall. She clamped her hand over her mouth and tottered toward what I assumed was the bathroom.

Just as I reached the door she'd come out of, I heard her start to throw up in the john.

The room she'd been in was a bedroom done in various shades of blue from what I could see from the hallway spill light. I flipped on the light. Double bed, walk-in closet, dark blue wall-to-wall carpeting, framed Norman Rockwell prints. The room was sexually neutral. Male or female could reside here. I decided this was probably a guest room.

The present guest was beyond appreciating the decor. He was the saddest Santa Claus I'd ever seen, even sadder than the drunken ones the Salvation Army occasionally puts on the street corners.

It wasn't just that he'd puked all over his white beard or that he had food stains all over his merry red Santa coat or even that he was wearing thin cheap white tennis shoes instead of festive black boots—at any other time, these little things might have spoiled the Santa Claus fantasy. But now there was something much more dire spoiling the illusion, that being the hunting knife somebody had plunged deep into his throat.

The room stank of the human machine shutting down for a final time. The kidney function turning off for a final time. The bowels emptying. The lividity settling in.

Thunder on the staircase. Sounded as if hundreds were trampling up here.

I clipped off the light, hurried to the door, blocking the entrance.

"I'm sorry, folks. Something's happened to Bob Nugent. Right now I need to see Don and Sara. And I need to ask you all to go back downstairs and wait until the police get here."

The group of twelve—not hundreds after all—were working through their boozy fog, realizing that something here was seriously wrong indeed.

"He's dead, isn't he?" one of the women said.

"Yes, I'm afraid he is."

"My Lord, did somebody kill him, Sam?"

"I wish I could say more, Betty. I know it sounds awful stuffy, but the police have to handle it from here. So please everybody, please go back downstairs."

"Cliffie's a fool," one of the men said. "He'll screw this up the way he usually does."

"You and the judge'll have to step in the way you always do," said one of the women.

"Cliffie may not be a brain trust," I said, "but at least he finally broke down and hired two good men, Grimes and Manners. They know what to do even if Cliffie doesn't."

Don and Sara were there, then. They started for the bedroom door, but I stopped them.

"This is *my* house," Don snapped. "Now get the hell out of the way, McCain."

Sara put a temporizing hand on his arm. "Please, Don. He's a detective."

Don scowled. "Private detective. Mike Hammer and all that nonsense."

"People, please," I said, "I can't let Don and Sara in until you go downstairs. Please."

This was the best show of the evening. I didn't blame them for wanting to stay. But they left, one couple, then another, then another, all of them getting a last good gape at the darkened bedroom doorway.

When Connie Bryce came out of the john, I said, "Connie, I need you to wait up here."

"He's dead."

"Yes."

"Somebody murdered him." She had the fuzzy voice of a person in shock.

"What the hell is she talking about, McCain?" Don said. "Somebody was murdered in there?"

"Go in and see for yourself," I said, standing aside.

When it came down to it, though, angry Don seemed reluctant to rush in. So did Sara.

But after glancing at each other, and then glancing at me, they started walking slowly through the doorway.

The overhead light was flipped on. No screams. No outbursts of any kind.

I took Connie Bryce, a pleasant girl who used to let me crib from her algebra assignments, into a small den, sat her down, poured her some brandy. While she was starting to sip that, I called the police. Harry Daly, the dispatcher, said they'd be right out. He sounded excited. The prospect of a murder at the home of a wealthy person like Don Lillis— now that was the kind of excitement you just didn't get all that often.

From the doorway, a gray-faced Don said, "I'll send everybody home, Sam."

"No. You can't. The police'll want everybody here. Please go downstairs and make sure nobody leaves."

"Who would want to kill Bob Nugent?" Connie said.

"I guess that's what we need to find out," I replied.

TWO

CHIEF CLIFFIE SYKES, JR. would have been a Nazi, but he couldn't master the art of clicking his heels together, which isn't as easy as it looks. Or to put it another way, Cliffie Sykes, Jr. never gets invited to Albert Einstein's birthday parties.

"All right, everybody, stand back, stand back."

It was with these cordial words that Cliffie made his entrance. The two men behind him, new men, Grimes and Manners, were actually competent law-enforcement officers but they had to pretend to be just as dumb as Cliffie—no easy task—or he'd fire them. That I know of, Cliffie has taken only some law enforcement classes: "Losing the Evidence Bag," "Bullying the Elderly," and "Insulting His Betters," which would include every living thing on this planet, including cockroaches.

Cliffie and his men were in the familiar khaki uniforms Cliffie saw Glenn Ford wear in a western movie years ago, a uniform complete with a campaign hat like the one Smokey The Bear wears. Cliffie secretly thinks he's Glenn Ford. Wears his service revolver slung low on his hip; wears pointed cowboy boots of the kind known as Texas boots; and tries to look boyish when he gives the ladies a smile with those urine-yellow teeth of his. Of course, I can't begrudge him his fantasy. I secretly think I'm Robert Ryan.

"Stand back, stand back," Cliffie kept saying all that way into the living room with the beamed ceilings and the open fireplace. "Nobody leave until we get done with Santy Claus."

"Everybody's sitting down, Cliffie," I said. "So you can stop saying 'Stand back,' all right?"

A couple people tittered.

Cliffie glowered. "My men are going to get all your names and ask you some questions. You can go when they're done with you." He gave us a look at those teeth again. Big Cliffie smile. "Unless you're the killer, of course."

At this point, fortunately for all humankind, Grimes and Manners took over. They set up a small interrogation room in the kitchen, and one by one they began interviewing the guests.

The guests, meanwhile, had the pleasure of sitting in the living room listening to Cliffie talk about his recent trip to Dallas where he'd appeared on the same stage as Roy Rogers in celebrating some lawman's association. Much to his delight, Rogers's famous horse Trigger had taken a number two right on the stage in front of everybody. Cliffie actually slapped his knee when he told that one. And he'd be telling that one right up until he went to that big lawman's association in the sky.

Most of the guests talked among themselves about Bob Nugent. The people who got sentimental about him, which was most of them, called him "Bobby," his name until he'd been late into high school. One more of us was gone. From such a small graduating class, a good number had already been called. We were facing our own mortality, too. The Irish say that when you mourn somebody at a funeral, you're really mourning yourself. I wouldn't argue with that at all.

Grimes and Manners passed people through quickly. Since there was a bathroom on the main floor and a bathroom in the basement, there'd been little if any reason for any of the guests to go upstairs. Why Bobby Nugent had been up there was still unknown. But anybody who had gone up there was likely to receive special attention from Grimes and Manners.

Finally, it was my turn.

Grimes was a big man in his midthirties. He'd had a minor boxing career over in the Quad Cities but gave it up after he learned that the only way he could start fighting in Chicago was to take several dives the Mob wanted for fighters they owned. He did what three generations of Grimes men had—become a cop. He was taking courses at the U of I in criminology.

Manners was a towhead who looked a lot more Southern California beach than Iowa cornfield. He was here strictly for romance. His fiancée lived here. I expected he'd be moving on after their wedding. He was a serious lawman, too. He'd spent five years on the Cedar Rapids force and become one hell of a crime scene man.

The ambulance came and then the medical examiner. By that time the press was here, too, the press in Black River Falls consisting of a creaky old man with a bad head cold, no patience and a flash camera that wouldn't flash when it was supposed to.

The name gathering and the questioning took two hours. Everybody left as soon as possible.

For the most part, I sat in the kitchen with the hosts, Don and Sara Lillis.

Don kept pouring himself shots of J&B and shaking his head. "We'll have to move."

"Let's wait and see," Sara said. She wore an expensive suede jumper that flattered the mahogany color of her pageboy and the dazzle of her mahogany-colored eyes. She had a beauty mark a few inches to the right of her upper lip. It fit in perfectly with the poised, cool manner she always projected. "We could always just close it off."

Don was anything but cool and poised. He had dark, angry good looks. He was as hairy as anything you'd find at the zoo and always wore his clothes—tonight it was a wine-colored suit with a blue shirt and wine-colored necktie—so tight you sensed he could rip out of them any time he wanted to. He troubled the air. There was a menace about him—just a hint of it—that never left him, even when he was telling a joke. He'd beat me up pretty badly in sixth grade. But there hadn't been any girls around so I was able to forgive him. The menace was electric tonight. "When's that stupid bastard going to be done, anyway?"

"If you mean Cliffie," I said, "he's just wrapping things up now."

"He practically accused me of killing Nugent, didn't he, sweetheart?"

Sara nodded, but her gaze on him was skeptical. She frowned every time he freshened his drink, every time he made a crack about Cliffie, every time he said that they'd have to move now that a murder had taken place in their home. She didn't look happy, and I had a sense it wasn't just about tonight.

"He'd better be careful or I'll sue him for character defamation," Don said.

She looked at me and smiled with great dramatic unpleasantness. "He thinks people don't know about him, our little Donny does. He thinks he's very crafty."

"That's all I need," Don said. "You turning bitch on me tonight." His jaw muscle bunched. He took a couple steps closer to her. His air of menace was no longer subdued. "Do you want people going around whispering that your husband's a murderer?"

"Well, they certainly whisper other things about you. True things."

"Thank you for all your wifely support, dear. I have some shit-kicker cop on my back, and now you're starting in on me."

She touched long, elegant fingers to her head. "I'm getting one of my headaches."

"Sure you are," Don snapped. "It's because that dumb bastard Cliffie's upsetting everybody. McCain, I'm hiring you as of here and now."

"As what?"

"As what? What the hell do you think as what? My attorney! If he starts bothering me again, I want you to take over."

"He's going to think it looks funny if you bring me in at this point, Don."

"I don't care what he thinks. It's a disgrace that Cliffie is the law in this town."

Cliffie came in two seconds too late to hear his name taken in vain.

"There you are," he said to Don.

"Where else would I be?" Don said.

"Your living room is empty. Couple of my men'll be here for a while longer. I'm taking off."

"Gee, and just when I was starting to like you."

"Don't get too smart for your own good, Don. Somebody saw you punch Nugent earlier tonight, right before he got into his Santy Claus getup. You're the only one who had a motive to kill him." Somehow I knew that Cliffie saying "Santy Claus" would have me in a mental hospital by dawn. "An eyewitness, Lillis. Ned Tomlin."

I would have bet he couldn't do it. Too full of himself for anything like blushing. But that's exactly what Don Lillis did when Cliffie told him about the eyewitness.

"I was mad he showed up drunk was all," Don said, sounding defensive and resentful. "That's all there was to it. You think I'd kill somebody over that?"

"Yeah, well, we'll talk about it tomorrow," Cliffie said and turned toward the back door.

"Just a minute," I said.

Everybody looked surprised that I'd said anything at all.

"You can't just leave him hanging like that," I said.

"Oh, yeah," Cliffie said, "who says I can't?"

"You're implying he killed Nugent."

"I am?"

"Of course you are."

"All I said was that I wanted to talk to him in the morning."

"No, that isn't all you said. You said that he was the only one who had a motive to kill Cliffie. Now how the hell would you know something like that?"

"Don't start with your lawyer bullshit, Counselor. A guy slugs somebody, there's something going on. And it's a lot more than for just showing up drunk in a Santy Claus outfit."

"He didn't kill Nugent."

"Yeah? Now how would you know that, Counselor? Were you here when Nugent got here?"

"Well, no."

"And were you with your good friend Don here every single moment tonight?"

"You know I wasn't."

"You're damned right I know it. And that's why I'm not going to take any of your lawyer B.S., Counselor. If you want to bring Don here into my office tomorrow at ten, fine. Otherwise, shut your trap."

Cliffie gave the living room a sweeping look, as if there might be more corpses stashed beneath the couch or stuffed behind a chair. "Fancy house like this, hard to sell, buyers know there was a murder in here. That place in Des Moines, they still haven't sold."

"I wonder if that could be because there were six corpses jammed into a closet for seven months before anybody found them?" I said.

"Dead people are dead people, Counselor. Would you want to live in a house where somebody'd been murdered?"

"I would," Don said, "if the corpse was yours."

I grabbed his arm.

"Kinda funny, isn't it?" Cliffie said. "All three of us classmates. And Don growing up and thinking he was so high and mighty. He'd barely speak to me in the hall, Counselor. Didn't want to be seen around Ozark hill trash like me. And now look. He don't have no choice but to do what I tell him to now, does he, Counselor?''

"That's enough, Cliff," I said. "This is supposed to be an impartial police investigation, remember?''

"Always so high and mighty, weren't you, Don?" Cliffie couldn't resist one last jab. Then he looked at me. "You better tell your client here that I won't tolerate any back talk. And the next time he says he wants to see me dead, I'm gonna make him sorry he ever said it. You understand?''

"I'll take care of it."

He glared at Don, then beamed at me.

"You'd better take care of it, Counselor. You sure as hell'd better."

He gave a jaunty little salute to Sara and then walked out the back door.

"That son of a bitch," Don said. "He's really going to hang this thing on me."

"You'll go with him tomorrow won't you, Sam?" Sara said.

I shook my head. "Look, you're very well regarded in this community. You belong to all the right clubs and go to all the right places."

"I forgot you were a Commie," Don said. "In high school, honey, he was always giving speeches about the common man. All that crap."

"Please, Don," she said.

"All I'm saying is that you need a lot higher-powered lawyer than I am. Somebody who can spook Cliffie a little."

"I'd prefer you," Sara said.

"So would I," Don said.

"Then it's settled. Don'll pick you up at your office right before eight tomorrow morning."

"Eight? We don't need to be there before ten," he said.

"We need to talk, get our story straight. I need to know why you hit him tonight for one thing. If you don't want to do it in the morning, let's do it now."

He sighed. "I'm too tired to do it now. I need to relax or I'll never get to sleep."

Sara stood and said, "C'mon, Sam. I'll walk you to your car. He won't change his mind. He'll meet you at ten at the police station."

She slid her arm through mine. Don wasn't real keen on it apparently.

"What the hell's this all about?" Don said. "Why don't I walk him to his car?"

"Because you're drunk and in a bad mood. And because I want to tell Sam how he should handle you tomorrow. You're going to have a very bad hangover, and you're twice as hard to handle when you're like that. Sam'll need some advice."

"Fine with me if Don walks with us," I said. I probably would have felt as excluded as Don did. And curious about why my wife wouldn't let me join them.

She walked over and kissed him on the mouth. A beautiful sliver of tongue ran across her upper lip. "God, I love the taste of J&B."

Outside I said, "You sure this is smart, not letting him come with us?"

"He'll get over it. Besides, it's good for him to not get his way. Builds character. Almost nobody ever says no to him, and that started way back with his parents."

She'd thrown on a long, dark coat. We stood on the drive watching our breath in relief against the front porch lights. The county medical examiner's car was still here, but otherwise the driveway was empty. We both shivered a little, but the air was so clean on Midwestern winter nights, a true intoxicant.

"I was reading a piece the other day that said that most people make decisions between twenty and twenty-five that they can never undo. You think that's true, Sam?"

"I guess I'd have to think about it."

"I married Don when I was twenty-three."

She said no more on the subject. She didn't need to. Her face had changed. There was usually a kind of obstinate goodwill about it. The good and dutiful suburban housewife, I suppose. Everything is fine and orderly, no matter how empty or desperate or lonely you feel inside. Everything had damned well better be fine and orderly, anyway. But there was a sorrow on her face now, one that made latent age lines more severe, but oddly lent her features a truer beauty than the perky mask of domestic bliss.

"Do you ever forget who you are? I don't mean your identity, but who you are inside." We walked slowly. Her arm was still through mine. The moonlit parking area looked huge and empty with only my ragtop on it. "I don't know who I am anymore. I don't know what I want. I don't even know if I'm happy or sad. I'm not sure I feel much at all, either way, as a matter of fact. It's like I'm this train on this track and I can never get off. I'm just pulled along by inertia."

"You ever think of analysis?"

"I see a shrink in Iowa City twice a week. Don hates him. He thinks Dr. Nussbaum will try and put the make on me."

I laughed. "From what I know of shrinks, maybe he will."

She laughed in return.

"Dr. Nussbaum is sixty years old, bald, fat and has arthritis in his knees so bad that he can barely stand up without help. I think if he ever tried anything I could escape his clutches."

She turned and looked up at the chimney. Gray curling smoke played against the low and heavy field of stars and the icy beauty of the quarter moon. "Every few minutes it hits me."

"What does?"

"That a man—an actual human being—was murdered in my house tonight. It's unreal. This is Black River Falls. Stuff like this isn't supposed to happen here. That's one reason I was happy to get out of Chicago."

"Yeah," I said, "isn't supposed to but does."

"Maybe Don's right about moving," she said, still staring

at the house. "Maybe Bob's ghost'll haunt us or something. People move out of murder houses all the time."

"I guess." I hesitated before I spoke again. "Between us, Sara. The argument Don had with Nugent tonight. Was that really because Bob was drunk?"

She hesitated, too, but by the time she opened her mouth to speak, the front door opened. Don was silhouetted, cigarette and drink, filling the doorway and saying, "You two about ready to wrap it up?"

"We sure are, Don. I'm just heading out now. I'll see you at ten—but I wish you'd change your mind and meet earlier."

"I need my sleep. I'll see you at ten," he said. "Now why don't you haul that expensive ass of yours in here, Sara?"

An entire history of marital problems could be heard in that surly command.

As she started to walk toward the front door, she turned abruptly and said to me, in barely a whisper, "Nugent was blackmailing Don. That's why they were fighting."

And then she was gone.

THREE

MRS. NUGENT WAS one of those Irish women you saw at Mass every single day of the week. She was holy but not pious nor even particularly judgmental. She had her faith, and she just hoped that you had yours. She wore the kind of frayed and faded coat that most immigrant women don as if they were uniforms, and her gray finger-waved hair was mostly hidden beneath a dark blue flannel scarf with little tendrils of fibers waving in the wind like seaweed.

I'd tried her house first. The woman who answered said that Mrs. Nugent had driven herself to the morgue. I leaned against my ragtop, finishing off a Lucky, waiting for her to come out of the front door of the building that houses the morgue as well as the driver's license bureau. A pretty strange combination, even for a small town.

I kept thinking about Don being blackmailed by Bob Nugent. What could Nugent have on Don? And Don sure didn't strike me as the kind who'd pay a blackmailer, either.

Don and Sara's marriage was something else I hadn't known about. Don loved to show off Sara. That seemed to be one of the few ties they had left. He seemed to like showing her off the way he would a car or an expensive watch. I had to say that she didn't seem to mind it all that much.

The exterior morgue door opened, and a faint shadow shape emerged. Moonlight picked out the drab colors the woman was wearing. The headscarf, the Russian-winter coat, the purposeful steps...all I could think of was the nightly news footage you saw of middle-aged women in Hungary and Poland. They existed, but they seemed dead to pleasures of any kind, good food or music or even a pleasant night in front of the tube. Grubbing for warmth and food and a moment of joy here and there. That would be her life.

She actually seemed to shrink the closer she got to me. I didn't know how that was possible. I could smell the cabbage in the tumbledown kitchen of her rotted old house. I used to go there once in a while to swap comics with Bobby. One day I asked him what the smell was, and he said "Cabbage. People always ask about it." And I could see he was embarrassed by my question.

She wore Oxfords as sturdy as vaults. She wasn't crying. She made her way efficiently to her 1949 Nash, the kind you always see cops drive in crime movies.

I moved away from the ragtop and said, "Mrs. Nugent, there's a café up the street. I'd like to buy you a cup of coffee."

"Oh, it's you, Sam," she said. "I don't see too well in the dark like this." Actually, the street we were on was well lit. She raised her thick eyeglasses to me. "Did you hear what happened to my poor Bobby?"

I took her in my arms and let her cry. I imagined it wasn't the first time she'd wept tonight nor would it be the last.

After ten minutes or so, during which she kept apologizing, we walked up the street to the café. The place was smoky even though it was empty. It had that Edward Hopper feeling, like the transit station between Earth and death.

We took a booth that was more tape than fake leather. It looked like somebody had worked it over with a switchblade. She went to the bathroom. I ordered us coffee and pumpkin pie. The waitress wrote with great care. Maybe her tickets would be displayed someday in the Museum of Café Tickets.

We talked around it for five minutes. When the pie came, Audrey Nugent said, "Oh, no, Sam, I couldn't eat. It wouldn't be right."

"What wouldn't be right?"

"You know, poor Bobby dead and me eating. Especially pumpkin pie."

We all have neurotic reactions to death. Some people worry about being buried alive, even though the embalming process pretty much makes that impossible. Not to mention the autopsy. Other people worry about having a proper—i.e., expensive—funeral so everybody will know how important they were. Now Audrey Nugent was telling me that it wasn't right to eat, especially pumpkin pie, after your son dies.

"What if he's up there watching us?" she said.

"He probably hasn't been up there long enough to start watching yet. I'm sure there's some kind of indoctrination they have to go to. You know, so they know what they're supposed to do and stuff like that."

"I guess I never thought of that," she said. "But I think you're right. He's probably not watching yet." She picked up her fork. Her eyes looked like huge marbles in the thick lenses of her glasses. "You sure this is all right, Sam?"

"I'm sure, Mrs. Nugent. But I'd eat it fast before he *does* start laughing."

She smiled. "You're pulling my leg now, aren't you, Sam? Were you pulling my leg about that indoctrination thing?"

"Well, doesn't it stand to reason that it'd be a little bit like going into the army? They tell you which barracks you're in, where to put your clothes and what all the rules are?"

"You always were a joker, Sam." She had a forkful of pumpkin pie in her mouth. Then she pushed the pie saucer away. "It's not right, Sam. It's blasphemous."

"If you say so. Now I need you to tell me about Bob."

"I'll start crying again."

"There's nobody else here except the waitress, and she's pretty much asleep. So cry all you want. But I want to know about Bob these last few years."

"How come, Sam? I mean, you and Bobby weren't close or anything. Forgive me for saying that."

"Because I want to head off Cliffie Sykes before he starts arresting people at random the way he usually does."

She started crying again. A lot. The waitress brought over a box of Kleenex.

"I'll tell you what," I said as tears became mere sniffles. "Why don't I give you a call tomorrow. Give you time to think things through. I know I'm pushing you too hard tonight, and I apologize."

"That's probably a good idea," she said. "Poor Bobby. I just never thought his life would turn out this way. And he was just starting to get back on his feet, too."

I paid our bill and we went back out into the frosty night. Electric Christmas decorations were in every store window. A variety of Santas stood in the same windows.

Nothing's lonelier than a winter's night. If you're out and about, you have to feel jealous of all the married folks nuzzling in their beds; or all the kids dreaming space patrol dreams; or the young lovers still at that point in their relationship when everything about the other person is ridiculously dear. I used to keep things the beautiful Pamela Forrest would leave behind: napkins, a crushed cigarette pack, a comb with strands of that golden hair making it holy. Later, I could hold these objects up the way a psychic does a piece of clothing from a kidnap victim, and I could recreate her perfectly in my mind. I would feel joy and pain in equal measure, an exact emotional replica of the relationship we'd had since fourth grade.

As we walked along, Mrs. Nugent looked stooped and elderly. She was only in her middle forties. I scraped her car windows for her, accumulating balls of frost and snow in my wake. A couple of times, I had to stand on tiptoe to reach all the way across the hood.

I finished her windshield and said, "Now, do you have somebody at your house tonight?"

"My sister."

I remembered the woman who'd answered the phone. "Good. Be careful on the roads. They're slick."

"You sound just like my sister." A wan smile. "She thinks I'll never come back alive from the grocery store when I go."

I got her in the car. She overthrottled it but finally got it running smoothly. She turned on the defroster. Between my scraping and warm air being blown on the windshield, she'd be able to see all the way home.

She pulled away, her U-joints making ghoulish sounds, fishtailing a little. When she reached the first patch of ice, she corrected, then began her fifteen-mile-per-hour trip home.

I went home. Tasha, Crystal and Tess—the cats I'd inherited when a girl I knew headed west to become the next Sandra Dee—all greeted me at the back door of my second-story apartment. The only time they greet me like this is when their food bowl is empty. Other times, they mostly yawn, or don't even wake up.

I had a bologna sandwich and half a glass of 7UP. I watched the last ten minutes of Jack Paar and then went into the bathroom to get ready for bed.

Images of Bob Nugent's corpse kept flickering across my mental screen. The vomit in the fake beard bothered me more than the real blood did, but somehow it symbolized his whole life. Out of control. Messy. Comic in a sorrowful way.

In the bathroom, I did my business, brushed my teeth, did twenty push-ups and then went to bed.

When the phone rang, it scared me. I'd just settled in with a John D. MacDonald paperback. The phone sound was so unexpected and shrill that goose bumps coarsened the back of my neck and my arms. The ringing was somehow obscene, too. The silence had been perfect. And now the phone had defiled it.

"Katy Barry," a woman's voice said.

So that's how the long night ended. Me lying in bed trying to remember Katy Barry, who had been the femme fatale of the high school class ahead of mine. She'd also been captain of the cheerleaders, homecoming queen, girlfriend of the star quarterback, inspirer of at least half a dozen legendary fist-fights among the high school gods. A fetching redhead, she was known for dumping every boy she ever dated for any length of time, including her star quarterback.

That was about all I knew. You even lose track of the immortal beauties. I had no idea if she lived in town; what sort of life she'd turned out to have; and why somebody like her would call me. Especially at this time of night.

"How are you, Katy?"

"I need to see you tomorrow." She was about half drunk. Maybe a little better than half.

"Any special reason?"

"I may know who killed Bobby Nugent."

"And how would you know that?"

"Bob used to stay in our motel sometimes."

"You own a motel?"

"Me'n the old man do."

"Where is it?"

"Iowa City. The Palms Motor Court."

"Been a long time since I've seen you."

"You know why I'll always remember you, Sam?"

"Why?"

"Because I stood right behind you the day we had to make our first confession and you told me how scared you were God was going to strike you dead as soon as you told the priest how bad you were."

"God must've taken the day off or something."

"I'm sorry I was such a bitch in high school."

And a bitch she'd been.

"Really, Katy? I guess I don't remember that."

"You're pulling my leg."

"Maybe a little."

"I can't go to the cops, Sam. My old man, he was in the slammer for a while. He's on parole. He don't want to know nothin' about nothin' as they say in stir. You know what I mean?''

My old man. Parole. Stir. This was the femme fatale of the high school class ahead of mine?

''Yeah. Nothin' about nothin'. You really think you know something, Katy?''

''You think I don't. You think I'm just some lush callin' because I'm drunk?''

''I just asked a question.''

''Every couple weeks, he stayed here, Sam. And we talked. My old man hated him. He thought maybe I was rollin' over for Bobby, if you know what I'm sayin'. Can you imagine that? For Bobby? But Bobby talked.''

''I see.''

''I know all kinds of things about Bobby. And that ain't the bourbon talkin'.''

''I didn't think it was.''

''The old man's got some business to do tomorrow—he's done roofing and he's got to crowd in a lot of work before the snow starts—so if you want to stop over in the afternoon, we could have a talk.''

''That sounds nice. Give me the address, will you?''

She gave me the address and directions.

''About two?''

''Unless you hear otherwise,'' I said, ''I'll see you at two tomorrow afternoon.''

THE CATS AND I wrestled for position in the big double bed, I picked up my John D. paperback again. The phone was nice enough to remain silent the rest of the night.

FOUR

THE MORNING WAS sunny with the temperature in the forties, which meant that last night's snow was vanishing quickly. Most folks wanted a white Christmas. I suppose I did, too, but it was nice walking around downtown without freezing. I managed to squeeze in an hour of Christmas shopping before meeting Don at the police station. I'm pretty sure that somebody in the Iowa legislature had shoved through a secret bill dictating that only Perry Como, Bing Crosby and Johnny Mathis were allowed to sing through our public address systems.

In the town square, the Jaycees were sponsoring a snowman-building contest. Tots through eighth graders. Moms were allowed to give the wee ones a bit of help. As usual, some of the snowmen were masterpieces, top hats, corncob pipes, brilliant red scarves.

One of the schools had set up a hot chocolate stand. They probably would have done better if it had been twenty degrees colder. But I did my bit, anyway. Certain smells and sounds can momentarily transport you back to your childhood. Hot chocolate is one of the things that can do that for me again. I'm six years old and just in from an hour of sliding down Sullivan Hill. My face is frozen numb, as are my fingers, despite the heavy mittens I wore. And as soon as I can kick off my buckle boots and snow clothes, there's my mom with a steaming mug of hot chocolate. I guess that's why I read so much science fiction, despite the disapproval of most folks who hate that "flying saucer stuff," even though Robert

Heinlein and Isaac Asimov have as much in common with flying saucer nuts as the Pope does with prostitution. It's just the idea of parallel worlds I guess—that nothing ever really dies. That there are multiple Earths. And that on one of them at this very moment a six-year-old named Sam McCain is drinking his mom's hot chocolate. And yes, there's a marshmallow in it.

Cliffie was in a suit. That was the first surprise. The second was that he had Henry Fickens sitting in the interrogation room. Fickens is from the county attorney's office, one of those austere, arrogant middle-aged men who probably wanted to be an executioner when he grew up. He wore a gray suit, a blue tie, rimless glasses that gave his eyes a reptilian look. He keeps threatening to run for state office but his postwar flirtation with the KKK—which was trying to establish its prewar footing in Iowa and Missouri—would undo him.

"Where's Mr. Lillis?" Fickens said.

"He'll be along," I said. "It's only five of."

Fickens grimaced. "You'd think he'd want to get on our good side."

"Gosh," I said, "and here I was under the impression that all that matters is the truth. I guess brownnosing counts, too, huh?"

Fickens sighed. He has a Ph.D. in sighing. "Here comes one of McCain's self-righteous speeches about truth and justice."

"The game starts at noon," Cliffie said, "that's all I give a shit about."

The Hawkeyes played somebody on the road. I wasn't a big sports fan. I guess I'm a rebel. You know, like in all those songs in which Annette Funicello sings about her boyfriend being a rebel.

"They don't have sports in Russia," he said to Cliffie. "He'd probably be more comfortable living with the Commies, don't you think?"

"You two knock off the bullshit," Cliffie said, looking uncomfortable in his stiff blue suit and white shirt and frayed blue necktie. "I wanna be outta here by eleven. I gotta pick up beer and chips and crap before I go home. And I plan to see the tip. So you two want to gnaw on each other, it's fine by me. But do it after we nail Don Lillis's ass to the wall."

"Another thorough, open-minded investigation by Chief Clifford Sykes, Jr."

"Pick on Fickens," Cliffie said, "but leave me the hell alone. I don't like workin' on a Saturday morning as it is."

There were at least 3,624 smart-mouth responses to Cliffie's last remark, but I dared not speak any of them.

So we sat and waited. I was ready to give Fickens an Academy Award for sighing. This guy was the Laurence Olivier of sighing.

For his part, Cliffie read *Confidential* magazine. Or what was left of it. Liberace and a few others had basically sued them out of business. When he came to one page, he said, "It says here that Marilyn Monroe has bigger knockers than Jayne Mansfield."

This earned a disapproving sigh from Fickens and a smile from me.

"You know, I woulda said Jayne's was bigger," Cliffie said. "I mean, just looking at them. You know?"

I'm sure you'd agree with me that there was no better way to spend an hour or two than sitting in a room with Cliffie and Fickens listening to Cliffie read his magazine aloud, the way my dad used to read us kids the Sunday funnies. Oh, yes.

DON DID three things wrong.

One, he showed up fifteen minutes late. Two, he drove his new white Jaguar sedan. And three, he wore a suede car coat that was worth three times the amount of petty graft Cliffie took in over a month's time.

Men like Fickens do not take kindly to men like Don Lillis.

Nor do men who think that men with Jags should be ticketed at every possibility and instruct all their officers to go forth and just do exactly that.

I'll spare you the 10:12 to 10:43 segment of this.

All they did was badger Don. A: He was seen arguing with Bob Nugent. B: He was seen going upstairs several times during the party. And C: He was known to have a pretty bad temper, especially when he was drinking, and he was seen to be drinking heavily by everybody at the party. Even his wife reluctantly admitted that he was drinking heavily last night.

After they'd gone through the same three points twenty or thirty times, varying the phrasing slightly so as to not induce sleep, Fickens said, "We don't know what you and Nugent were arguing about, Don. And it really doesn't matter. All that matters is that we all want to spare your family—you've got a name to protect in this community, Don—all that matters is that we spare your family the embarrassment of a trial. I mean, what'd he do? Try and kill you? Get yourself a lawyer, Don. You can afford the best." He scowled at me. "A first-rate one, Don. And then you can go manslaughter at worst. At worst, Don. And at best, you go free. Self-defense. No prison time at all."

"So this is what you've got on him?" I said. "This is your whole case?"

"You wish it was our whole case, Counselor," Cliffie said, checking his watch. "Show him, Fickens."

He picked up a manila envelope and withdrew a black-and-white photograph of a hunting knife. The hilt was special. It was wood and had been carved into the shape of an eagle's wings.

"Look familiar, Don?" Fickens said.

It sure looked familiar to me. The last time I'd seen it, it was sticking out of Bob Nugent's throat.

As usual, Cliffie had given me exactly zero information last night. He could argue, and correctly, that Don didn't officially become my client until Cliffie was ready to leave last night. And therefore, this morning was the only time he needed to share what he had. By his rights, he had no duty to be helpful to me.

"You know whose it is, Fickens," Don said.

"I'd like you to give me the name out loud so our esteemed counselor can hear it."

"Gee," I said, "haven't I heard this particular ploy on TV cop shows about six million times? Obviously, it's Don's or you wouldn't ask him to say it out loud."

"Hard to put one over on you," Fickens said. "An important lawyer like you."

"Damned right it's his," Cliffie said. "So you figure it out, Counselor. We have his knife and the body in his bedroom. Now what do you make of that?"

"That there were a lot of people at the party and that they were going up and down all night to the bathroom, that's what I make of it."

"So our friend Don here is innocent?" Fickens said.

I wasn't sure of that, but I had to reply as if I were. "Damned right he is. It wouldn't be a whole lot of trouble for somebody to take his knife and stab Nugent with it. Tell them where you kept the knife, Don."

Don hesitated.

"Yes, Don, please tell us where you kept the knife," Fickens said. He obviously knew the answer or he wouldn't have said it.

"In my desk," Don said.

"Home or office desk?" Fickens said.

"Home."

"Was there anything special about the desk?"

"You know there was, Fickens, or you wouldn't have asked me."

"I'm just trying to get everything down on tape here, Don. Now tell us what was special about the desk."

"The bottom drawer on the right—it's where I keep a lot of valuables. You know, gifts and things. Not anything terribly expensive. But things that are valuable to me in a personal way.''

''Like the hunting knife your wife had made special for you.''

''Yes.''

''Now tell us about the desk. What made it special.''

''It locks.''

''I see. And was it locked last night?''

''Yes.''

''And who had the key?''

''I did.''

''Did you ever have a copy of the key made?''

''No.''

Fickens looked up at me with his evil baby face and smirked. ''So we have a body in your bedroom that was stabbed to death with a knife your wife had made specially for you as a gift. And the knife was locked away last night, and you were the only one who had a key. Is that what you've told me?''

''Yes.'' For the first time, Don looked miserable. His arrogance was gone. His face was slick with sweat. And he'd taken to biting the stray fingernail.

''Have anything to say, Counselor?'' Cliffie said.

''Yeah,'' I said, ''it's time we wrap this up.''

It was 10:58.

''I'm going to ask for a million dollars bail,'' Cliffie said.

''That's ridiculous,'' I said.

''Flight risk.''

''Flight risk? What the hell're you talking about?'' I said.

''He owns his own plane, don't he?''

''Yes.''

''Well, there's the first part of it, and he's risky as far as I'm concerned. I stabbed a guy to death, you can bet I'd be thinkin' of headin' to the border.''

All sorts of choice words came, but I wouldn't be doing my client a favor by expressing any of them. And much as I hated to, I had to concede that a locked-away weapon made the only man with the key at least a promising suspect. And Cliffie rarely spent longer than six hours following a homicide before arresting somebody. So he was now sure that he had his man and you could rubber stamp that manila file folder Case Closed.

That was the little game we played in Black River Falls. Cliffie arrested them, and then Judge Whitney, who reveled in humiliating him, hired me to find the real killer. Cliffie had been right only twice in the past three years. We had a comfortable lead. Judge Whitney would want to make it even more comfortable.

She'd go along with the bail request because she'd see that at least superficially, Cliffie had two good reasons to arrest him and charge him.

"What's her home number, anyway, Fickens?" Cliffie said.

The evil child looked at me and smiled. "I don't know it offhand, but I'm sure the counselor here does. I'm told he and the judge are very good friends. *Very* good friends." The only things he didn't do were wink and nudge Cliffie in the ribs. *Very good friend, Chief. Get it? Having sex together?*

The sound was sharp and disturbing. A sob. Don, the ever cool Jaguar Don, had his head in his arms on the table and was crying.

Fickens smirked at me and said, "Pleasure doing business with you, Counselor."

"This is total bullshit," Don said when Cliffie allowed us to be alone in the room.

"First of all, just assume this room is bugged."

"That's illegal."

"So's murder."

"What's that supposed to mean?"

"It means that for a guy who's been charged with murder, you're not exactly helping me out here."

"I'm innocent. That's all you need to know."

"Why did you hit Bob Nugent?"

"He was drunk."

"I don't believe that."

"Well, exactly what the hell can I do about you not believing me?"

"Somebody told me he was blackmailing you."

He froze. Not for long. And not in any dramatic way. But just for a moment, mind and body virtually shut down as the information I imparted was absorbed.

"Sure, some deadbeat like Nugent was blackmailing me."

"What did he have on you?"

He made frustrated fists of his hands.

"Where the hell'd you get this crazy story, anyway?"

"That doesn't matter."

"It sure as hell matters to me. If I find out who told you something like this, I'll sue them. And don't think I don't mean it." The eyelids narrowed. "And the more I think about it, the more I think maybe Fickens was right. Maybe I need a lot better lawyer than you."

I stood.

"Frankly, I'm relieved. You're not anybody I'd want to work with, anyway."

"Pretty damned high hat for a guy who can't make a living at his law practice."

I started to walk to the door.

"Come back here," he said.

"For what?"

"I want you to work with me."

"You'll have to tell me the truth this time."

He sighed. He wasn't in Fickens's class at sighing, but he was pretty damned good.

"All right, I'll tell you the truth."

"Was he blackmailing you?"

"Yes. Now will you get the hell back here and sit down?"

FIVE

My OFFICE PHONE RANG just as I was dumping the presents I'd bought on a table.

"I trust Cliffie made an utter fool of himself as usual," said Judge Esme Anne Whitney without saying hello or good morning. Friend of presidents—golf with Ike many times; celebrities—Leonard Bernstein takes her to dinner on her frequent trips back to "civilization," i.e., as if you really need an i.e., here, New York City; even the occasional movie director—"I'm always after him to go on a diet but you know, of course, he never will," that being—who else?—Alfred of Hitchcock, Esme is a rather harsh judge of lesser beings, i.e.—excuse me for overdoing these—the likes of Cliffie. And me.

"Not as foolish as I'd hoped, I'm sorry to say."

"A little cryptic this morning, aren't we?" The sharpness of her response told me that she was running ahead of schedule for a Saturday morning, meaning she'd done her fifteen-minute yoga, showered, had her breakfast and first snifter of brandy and was now enjoying her fourth or fifth Gauloises cigarette of the day. In other words, in tiptop fighting shape.

"Bob Nugent was stabbed with Don Lillis's handmade knife his wife gave him two years ago. He kept it in a locked desk drawer, and he was the only one who had a key."

"My Lord," she said. "You mean Cliffie's actually got a case?"

"Not only does he have a case, Fickens is helping him out with it."

"Fickens—I even hate saying his stupid name—is an idiot."

"Which makes him twice as smart as our Cliffie."

A blast of smoke was exhaled against her phone. Gauloises are so strong I could smell the smoke even down the phone lines.

"You know I don't like this Lillis very much," she said.

"I know."

"Nouveau riche."

"I know."

"Not that I'm a snob."

"Heavens, no."

"It's just that they're always wanting to tear things down and put up new things, and the new things are invariably inferior to the old things."

"Plus there's always the chance that he's guilty," I said.

"Are you giving up already? I don't want Cliffie to win this one. It's Christmastime, and that would ruin my entire holiday."

"What if he's guilty?"

"Then it's up to you to prove he's not."

"He sure isn't making it easy. I practically had to torture him to get him to admit that Nugent was blackmailing him. Nugent snapped some pictures of Lillis with a woman who wasn't his wife."

"Blackmail? That sounds like TV or movies or something. Do people really do that sort of thing, McCain?"

"All the time."

"Well, yes, I suppose in your world they do."

Every once in a while she says stuff like that. Every once in a while I get this abrupt headache that feels as if somebody has cleaved my head in two with an ax. Someday I'll have a successful law practice and won't have to be her investigator.

The conversation was taking place with my back to the door of my tiny one-room office. Only now did I become aware of a presence behind me. I do not always get my clients off, sad to say; and even sadder to say, they or some of their kin occasionally sneak into my office and try to shoot me or set me on fire or something equally unpleasant.

I decided it would be a good thing to turn and see who was there.

I hadn't seen Mary Travers in six months. Just as I had wasted a good share of my life uselessly loving the beautiful Pamela Forrest, Mary had wasted a good share of *her* life loving me.

But over two years ago she'd married Wes Lindstrom, a rather severe young man whose father owned the pharmacy where Mary had worked. She'd wanted to go on to college, but her father got throat cancer right after we graduated and there just wasn't money enough. Mary and I had come from the Knolls, that hybrid of ghetto and backwater that the proper people of the town don't even like to acknowledge.

She had one of those sweet, vulnerable faces that accurately depicted her soul, which was also sweet and vulnerable. She was lovely and erotic in her quiet way, her dark hair and dark eyes vivid in a movie star way.

She was dressed, as always, in good, simple clothes—a camel hair coat, brown kneesocks, cordovan penny loafers— but she'd also added something new to her ensemble. I'd never seen her sport a black eye before.

I held up a just-a-minute finger then decided a sit-down-over-there finger was better. She nodded and took the least uncomfortable chair in my office.

"Are you still there, McCain?"

"Yes, Judge."

"I want you to start on this one right away. The honor of my family is at stake."

She takes this family thing seriously. But then her family *had* been deposed by a sobering group of misfits that made Ma and Pa Kettle look sophisticated. I imagine that would be hard to forgive or forget.

"Right away," I said.

"And I'd appreciate updates every few hours."

"And updates you shall have."

Another blast of cigarette smoke. "I know you don't understand how I feel about Cliffie, McCain. Or what family honor means."

"No, you're right, my family has no honor."

I looked over at Mary. She smiled. I'd told her many Judge Whitney stories over the years.

"You know that isn't what I meant. It's just—well, people of my station—I'm trying not to sound like a snob here, McCain."

"Updates you shall have, Judge. Every few hours." I wanted to talk to Mary. I hung up. I would pay later for my abruptness.

"Hi, Sam."

"Hi."

"I'm sorry."

"For what?"

"For not wearing sunglasses."

"It really makes me mad you're not wearing sunglasses. In fact, I feel a psychotic episode coming on now. I may just leap across this desk and give you a noogie."

"Covering up my black eye, is what I mean. Maybe I need the sunglasses."

"I would've seen it eventually."

"I wanted you to see it right away. And feel sorry for me."

"I do feel sorry for you. And besides, unveiling it would have been much more 'dramatic' as you say. Walking around with it open, there's no drama."

"I wear my sunglasses on the street." She took them out, slipped them on. "I call them my Audrey Hepburns. This was the kind she wore in *Sabrina.*"

"I thought all the girls today wanted to be Marilyn Monroe or Sophia Loren."

"I'll stick with Audrey." She laughed. "Gosh, here I am

almost twenty-five years old and there's a part of me—in my mind—that still wants to cut out paper dolls.''

"The good part of you," I said, sentimental about her suddenly. "The innocent part of you. Don't ever lose it."

That smile again. Oh, Lord, may heaven be half as sweet and nurturing as that smile of hers. "I'll buy some paper dolls on the way home."

I sat down before I got foolish and kissed her. I wanted to kiss her. We'd kissed maybe 2,831 times since starting Catholic school together back in kindergarten. We'd come very close to making love many times. And one time not so long ago, we actually did make love. But the black eye presumably meant that she was here to see me as a lawyer, and lawyers don't generally kiss clients. Not this lawyer, anyway, though admittedly the fact that my clients are mostly grizzled males who tend to get violent and pound upon people right before relieving them of their money and other valuables... Well, that may have something to do with why I don't kiss clients.

I wiggled and waggled myself into position in the chair. I put my elbows on the desk and put a sincere look on my face, like those slick guys on TV who sell cigarettes and nasal decongestant sprays. I said, "Looks like Wes gave you an early Christmas present."

"I'm not sure what to do."

"You know the signs of a concussion?"

"I'm all right."

"Might not hurt, seeing a doctor."

"Really, Sam. I'm fine."

"Ever happen before?"

"Several times. Not black eyes. But bruised ribs and lumps on my head. And once he tried to strangle me."

"The son of a bitch'll be lucky I don't go over there and kill him." The anger surprised me as much as her. I'd never liked the imperious Wes anyway.

"That's why I wondered about coming here, Sam. Because all this could get very personal. You and me and Wes. I know where I stand with Wes. But I never could quite figure out where I stood with you.''

''I'm sorry for not treating you better.''

''I always felt like the second fiddle to Pamela Forrest.''

''I tried not to make you feel that way, Mary. That's why I didn't call you as much as I wanted to. Because I knew that's how you'd see it.''

She put a finger to her exquisite nose. I thought she was going to cry. Maybe she did, too. She closed her eyes a moment, leaving the finger on her nose. I could almost feel her make the conscious decision not to cry.

She sneezed.

''Boy, that's all I need right now is a head cold.'' Then she continued, ''This started right after we got married.''

''What started?''

''How jealous he is.''

''You give him reason to be jealous?''

''Gee, Sam, you know me. I take my wedding vows seriously. There's no reason at all for him to be suspicious.''

''I had to ask. If I'm going to help you, I need to know everything.''

She started playing with a brown button on her camel hair coat.

''There's really nothing to know. We—don't have much in common. And sometimes he's out a lot. He says he has to belong to all the social clubs for the sake of the pharmacy. I don't complain. I'm home with Debbie.''

''Wow. How old is she now?''

''Almost a year.''

''Man,'' I said. ''Almost a year.''

You might think that twenty-four is pretty young to feel the years starting to race by. But lately I've been aware of how we're all changing, all the people I grew up with. You have to grow up eventually. But along with the virtues of adulthood, you lose a few of the precious vices of youth, the creative vices that make you aware of the world as only youth can appreciate it.

"Sometimes he hits me because of you," she said.

"Me?"

"He thinks I'm still in love with you. It makes him crazy. And then sometimes he accuses me of having an affair with our neighbor up the hill. Do you know Don Lillis?"

Just in case you thought that this was going to be one of those stories where the Don thing doesn't tie in with the Mary thing, that's what you get for trying to jump ahead.

"I'm representing Don," I said. "At least until he can contact a high-powered lawyer in Des Moines."

"Representing him?"

"You didn't hear about Bob Nugent being murdered at Lillis's house last?"

"I was just so caught up in arguing with Wes— And then, I grabbed Debbie and took her over to my mom's. That's where I took a shower and everything. I've got this real old skirt and blouse on. I think I wore them in high school."

"You've got a daughter and you can still wear your high-school clothes? A lot of women would envy you."

"They wouldn't envy the way I keep my weight off, though. I just never know when Wes is going to explode at me. I'm so nervous I barely think of food. I think it's affecting Debbie, too. She's started crying for no good reason. I think she's becoming aware of the tension."

"Does Wes drink?"

"Not much. But when he does…" She shook her head. "That's usually when I get punched or kicked or strangled."

"You sure you won't go and see Cliffie?"

"I don't want to destroy Wes. He's basically a good man. He's not as cold as people think he is. It's just his jealousy. He's so insecure about me."

"Are you considering a divorce?"

"A trial separation is what I thought we could talk about. That would save face for him. But I'd be living on my own."

She frowned. "The other night, he had some drinks and went down to the Lillises'. They weren't home. He got into a fight with some guy who was snooping around their house."

"Did he recognize the guy?"

"Said he looked like a hobo. Didn't see him real well. Must've been a strong guy, though."

"Oh, why's that?"

"He knocked Wes out for a few minutes. There's this huge goose egg on the right side of Wes's head."

I shifted in my chair. "This is kind of awkward, Mary."

"Handling my separation for me, you mean?"

"Well, that, but after what you've told me, I'll need to talk to Wes about what happened with the hobo."

"Oh? Why? Will that help Don Lillis?"

"It sure may. Somebody in or around his home a few nights before the murder."

She gave a tiny shrug. "Well, that won't bother me. Two separate cases."

"For now, anyway, they are," I said. "Your husband could end up as my key witness. Right before I tell him you want a trial separation."

"Maybe you should tell him on the phone."

"I'm not afraid of him."

"He's a lot bigger than you are. And he was a star basketball player, remember."

"So you're saying that he's in better shape than I am?"

She smiled that soft, slow, sweet smile.

"I guess you're right, Sam," she said. "But just in case, be sure and tell your mom the number of your hospital room so I can come visit you."

SIX

SATURDAYS the lunch counter is packed at Lindstrom's Rexall Drugstore. Saturdays near Christmas you can barely get in the door for all the shoppers. You can't get near the lunch counter unless you get there for breakfast and keep your seat until the lunch menu goes up on the small blackboard behind the counter.

There was a guy walking around dressed up as Santa. There were a couple of chunky elves who could be seen smoking cigarettes on a break and peering out from behind a curtain at the mass of humanity. There was maybe the most spoiled five-year-old I'd ever seen throwing some kind of tantrum at the head of an aisle and then—obviously filled with the holiday spirit—spitting at his mother when she took him by the wrist and yanked him closer to her. Where was Dr. Spock when you needed him?

The perfume counter was crowded with working-class men buying scents for their wives. My dad had probably been among their ranks earlier in the day. Children of the Depression and then of the war, they'd measure everything by size. Bigger was always better. They wanted bigger houses, bigger cars, and so, it stood to reason, when they bought perfume, they wanted bigger perfume. They didn't care about the scent itself so much—though the voluptuous middle-aged woman wearing the bright-green sweater would gladly spritz them with a sample—they wanted the biggest bottle they could get of the stuff, and all they had to spend was three or four bucks. It was funny and sad at the same time. That's how it struck me anyway. The funny part I understood. The sad part I didn't understand, but I felt it nonetheless.

Wes Lindstrom is a rangy man with a handsome but cold face. He's a pharmacist and store manager. You'd think that between the two he would have picked up at least a couple of social skills. He hasn't.

In his white medical jacket, he looked something like a young doctor on a soap opera. He was just getting down from a stepladder. He'd been fixing a large Christmas bulb that was hanging from a string of such bulbs strung across the ceiling.

He'd watched me walk up to him with a mixture of annoyance and disbelief. "I'm not sure I want to talk to you, McCain." Because we stood in a river rush of customers— old ladies can be deadly with those arthritic elbows, let me tell you—he kept his voice low so that only I could understand him. "She spent the night with you, did she?"

"Yes. Mostly we spent it running up and down Main Street in the nude."

"The way she's been behaving lately, I wouldn't be at all surprised. I should've known better than to marry a girl from her background."

Meaning the Knolls. You could become the richest man in town, and if you'd grown up in the Knolls, you'd still never quite be respectable.

"I didn't come here to talk about Mary."

"Then I can't imagine what else we'd have to talk about."

"You have some coffee in your office?"

"So what if I do?"

"How about selling me a cup?"

"What if I say no?"

"Then I start talking very loudly about Mary's black eye."

GETTING TO HIS OFFICE took ten minutes. You had to wiggle, push, sidle and angle your way to get through the crowds. Cash registers rang every few minutes, and harried clerks ran back and forth seeing if they had this gift in that color or that size or that pattern. Wes should have been happy. He was making a lot of money. He looked almost as bad as Mary.

His office was large, orderly, well furnished, just what I would expect of Wes. He had enough Hawkeye paraphernalia—hats, pennants, thermoses, stadium blankets—to satisfy a stadium. Like most people from around here, he was a graduate of the University of Iowa.

Not only didn't he offer me coffee, he didn't even offer me a chair. What he did was pour himself a cup and park his ass behind his desk. We were back in ninth grade again. I have coffee and you don't. And I was perfectly happy with that. Dealing with people on a ninth-grade level makes me feel right at home.

"I just want you to know that I don't care that you didn't offer me any coffee, Wes."

"Good, because I don't care that you don't care."

"Who was the guy who hit you the other night at Don Lillis's house?"

"So, she told you about that, did she?" He leaned forward, glaring. "If she let you do anything to her, I'll tear you apart, you crooked little shyster."

"Who was he?"

"Did you hear what I said?"

"I heard what you said. Did you hear what I said?"

"How the hell would I know who he was?" Wes said. "He was just some hobo. And anyway, it was dark."

"We don't have a lot of hobos around here. Cliffie runs them off. You ever think he might have *disguised* himself?"

"That's your world, you little shyster bastard. Not mine. The only time people in my world wear disguises is to costume parties."

"Afraid I'll have to correct you there, Wes. You disguise yourself all the time as the nice, caring pharmacist who enjoys helping people. They'd never know you're a wife beater."

"Look, you—"

"I'm here about Don Lillis. Next time it'll be about Mary."

"I sure hope for your sake you don't try and take advantage of her when she's so upset."

"Forget how much you hate me for the moment, Wes. You need to concentrate. Was there anything you can remember about this hobo?"

"He clubbed me with something. Isn't that enough?"

"Anything odd about him, I mean? Something that didn't fit with the whole hobo bit?"

He swallowed a large amount of irritation and said, "The eyeglasses, I guess."

"What about them?"

"They were new and expensive. Black and horn-rimmed. They didn't go with the rest of the outfit. Now that I think about it, I guess maybe you're right. About the disguise, I mean. A hobo couldn't have afforded anything else."

"Now was that so hard?"

The scowl again. "I can't stop thinking about you and Mary."

"There's nothing to think about, Wes. She came to my office a while ago. Broad daylight. Well-bundled up. And we talked about what happened. What you should be thinking about is why you're always slapping her around."

"Because she cheats on me."

"I don't believe that."

"Oh? You seem to have this image of Mary as this pure, honest woman. She's not."

"You have evidence?"

"A guy can tell."

"That's your evidence, 'A guy can tell'?"

"Damned right a guy can tell."

Nobody wears jealousy well. Even when it's understandable, it's ugly to behold. It always demeans the person who expresses it far more than it does the object of his ire. Wes wasn't worth a damn at jealousy. It agitated him so badly that a tiny tic appeared in the corner of his right eye, his face got flushed and his voice kept breaking when he spoke. He was caged by his own suspicions, the most miserable prison a man can know. Your most merciless tormenter is yourself.

I had to say this just right. Not for his sake, just mine. I knew he'd laugh me off, so it was important that I hold the moment the way I needed to.

"You ever lay a hand on her again, Wes, I'm going to break you in half."

He laughed. "I'll loan you my stepladder so you can hit me."

"It isn't funny, Wes. Aaron Wylie slapped my sister because she broke off with him. You remember Aaron? Running back for the Black River Bisons? Champion high school wrestler, too? I broke his nose and knocked out two teeth. I used a sap to sort of even things up. I paid a $350 fine and was on bench parole for a year. And you know what, Wes? It was worth it. And it'd be worth it if you ever hurt Mary again. We understand each other?"

SEVEN

"How about 'Her breasts were like melons,' McCain?"

"It's kinda overused, Kenny."

"All right. How about 'Her breasts were like ripe fruit'?"

"Doesn't tell me anything. They could look like mangos or plums."

"Good point. I'll just say she had nice breasts."

"Yeah, let your reader *imagine* what *nice* means."

"Good enough for me. Say, McCain, you could write this stuff, you know?"

"Yes, just what I've always wanted to be, a pornographer."

"There you go again."

"Excuse me. You're not a pornographer, you're an eroticist."

"Thank you."

Kenny Lattimore was our town's resident beatnik. He lived in a tiny, tinny house trailer inside a copse of oaks and elms and birches. The small encampment was clean and tidy. The river was about twenty yards from his place. You could almost imagine Indians floating by in canoes. If they did, they'd probably give Kenny an idea for a porno series about horny Indian studs and princesses. *Tepee Temptress* or something like that.

You mostly find Kenny in chinos, a black T-shirt or black sweater, no socks and dirty white Keds. He spends half his time traveling, his favorite places being San Francisco and

Seattle. He stood next to Jack Kerouac one night in a North Beach bar but had been too afraid to introduce himself.

Kenny supports himself by writing sex novels or, if you prefer, erotica. He generally writes one a month, which is enough to support him for a month. He had an agent once, but the guy committed suicide. Kenny is pretty sure it didn't have anything to with the guy having Kenny for a client. I'm not all that sure myself. I heard Kenny on the phone with him several times. Kenny's got an angry, paranoid side. But then, don't we all, Dick Nixon?

He writes for several different houses under at least a dozen different names. He once told me he had no idea how many sex novels he'd written, and I believed him. All I know is that he has four large cardboard boxes crammed with examples of his literary art. The thing is, some of them are pretty funny. And on purpose, too. He is able to spoof what his publishers want as long as he has at least one sex scene every two chapters. Themes come and go, you'll pardon the expression. Lesbian books will be hot for a while; and then orgies will be hot; and then three-ways will be hot. There is even a small market for books with Negro men and white girls having sex. These are sold only up North. In the South the Klan has taken to burning down any store that sells such trash, on the counter or below it. You know, the Klan likes to keep the moral standards pretty high.

Erotica isn't Kenny's only occupation. He is a snoop. Nobody I know has ever been able to figure out how he does it, but you can throw out the name of virtually any townsperson and Kenny can give you five to ten minutes on the person, some very salacious secrets included. The cops should have a file like Kenny's mind.

"I take it you want me to play snitch, McCain."

"I'd appreciate it."

"I should charge for it."

"You'll get to heaven for helping me."

"You still believe in that stuff?"

"I try to believe in it, Kenny."

"There's this beat poet. W. P. Miller. You ever heard of him?"

"No," I said, "but then he's probably never heard of me, either."

"He says you can reduce all life to eating, going to the bathroom, making love and rotting in your grave."

"Oh, yeah, I read that. I think it was in *Reader's Digest.*"

"Very funny. I mean it gives you something to think about."

"Yeah, I love being depressed." I tamped a Lucky from my pack, offered him one and got us both lit with my Ronson. "Don Lillis."

"Affairs."

"Plural?"

"Plural to the highest power."

"Anybody in particular?"

"Seems to prefer lonely wives."

"He should stay home, then. His wife looks pretty lonely. Him running around all the time."

"Guys like Lillis would never see the irony in that, McCain."

"Anybody in particular he's been seeing lately?"

"Pete Foley's old lady, for one."

I whistled. "My banker Pete Foley?"

"Your banker Pete Foley. Dotty's a lot of woman."

"If you like the type."

"What type?"

"Country club. Junior League."

"You ever see her in a bikini, McCain?"

"I wouldn't be able to appreciate her. One of my mom's friends was Dotty Foley's cleaning woman for a year. A real bitch." I flicked ash into the Hamm's beer can he was using as an ashtray. "This a steady thing?"

"Six, seven months, maybe."

"He was there Friday. Foley, I mean. You hear anything about Bob Nugent?"

"Buys his mom a lot of stuff."

"Wait a minute. Bob Nugent? He hadn't held a job for two or three years."

"I'm just telling you what I picked up. He was always buying his mom stuff. TV. Appliances. Paid for a new roof for her place last fall. Same with his sister. Always buying her stuff, too, even though her husband was always throwing him out for swearing around the kids."

"Kenny, this is impossible."

"Impossible but true."

"He didn't have any money."

"Then he had one hell of a line of credit," Kenny said. He snapped his fingers. "You know what fruit I hadn't thought of, for the girl's knockers, I mean?"

"What?"

"Pears. If you look at them a certain way, they look just like knockers."

"No, they don't."

"Well, they sort of do."

"Stick with 'She had nice breasts.'"

"It's just too plain. I read a sentence like that, I think this is one lazy writer. I need an adjective."

"But you haven't heard anything about where he got all this money?" I said.

"Nope." He paused, thoughtful. "How about 'magnificent'?"

"I thought we were talking about Nugent."

"We are." He turned and faced the typewriter. He speed typed a single word. "There. Now I can get on with the story." He turned back to me. "Sorry I can't help you there, McCain. I know for a fact that he bought all this stuff. But I don't have any idea where he got the money for it."

I stood and dropped my cigarette into the hole in the top of the Hamm's can. I looked at the paper in his typewriter.

"You got any of that white goop you use to cover up typing mistakes?"

"Yeah, why?"

"I'd take out *magnificent* and put in *haughty*."

"Hey, I like that, McCain. I've heard of haughty mouths and haughty hips. But I've never heard of haughty breasts before. You think they really exist?"

"I know they do. I've personally seen them."

"Really? Where?"

"Dubuque one sunny spring afternoon. The most haughty breasts I've ever seen. So haughty they were insolent."

"Wow, now that I dig. 'So haughty they were insolent.'"

He turned back to his machine again and took out the white liquid, rolled up the carriage and began covering up the word *magnificent.* Without looking at me, he said, "See, McCain, I told you you could write this stuff."

EIGHT

THE HOBOS, such as they are, generally sleep in one of two abandoned houses down by what used to be the railroad roundhouse. That's been abandoned now, too. There's a new one, the next town over.

Early dusk—all faint starlight and half moon and gauzy gray evening superimposed on mad slashes of gold and salmon and azure—did the merciful thing and hid in shadow the sorry state of the two abandoned houses. All the windows were stuffed with cardboard. The front stoops lay on their sides. The yards were mined with the broken glass of whiskey and beer bottles. One of the houses didn't even have a front door. The yellow Do Not Enter Condemned signs with the bold black lettering had been left intact on the front of the fence.

I didn't have to go inside for the smell to repulse me. Ten feet away I could smell the garbage, feces, sickness, filth and cheap liquor contained inside.

I walked around back. A three-step wooden stoop had somehow remained standing even though it was no longer connected to the house itself. I guessed what you did was lean forward, push in the back door, and then leap across to the threshold. Pretty soon this sort of avant-garde design will reach the suburbs.

I got up on the wobbly stoop, leaned forward and knocked.

He was jack-in-the-box quick. He was also the nearest thing I'd ever seen to a pirate. Complete with black eye patch and a red bandanna on his witchy gray hair. Gray stubble covered his angular face. When he opened his mouth, I realized he had, at most, four teeth. He was old in the way only true poverty can make you old. He might also have been insane. There was at least a hint of that in the single blue eye and the way drool came down his chin when his lips were still.

He wore a pair of OshKosh overalls that were new about the time of the Haymarket Riots. The overalls were covered with so many colorful spills, splotches, spots, blemishes and spatters that they looked like a walking piece of the kind of modern art the snottiest of critics pretend to love.

"You a cop?"

"Lawyer."

"Just as bad."

"I'm not here for trouble."

He smiled, toothless and sad.

"You want to move in, do ya?"

"Yeah. Just make sure I get to sleep next to somebody who's up puking all night."

"Smart punk, aren't ya?"

"I need to talk about Bob Nugent."

The lone blue eye stopped moving. He focused on me. And then he said, "Bobby was all right. He shared the wealth, man."

"Why'd he do that? If he had so much wealth, why'd he come down here?"

"Because he had the same kind of soul all the guys like us have. He said this was the only place he was comfortable."

All kinds of hobos, many if not most, have police records for everything from petty larceny to pedophilia to murder. There's a sentimental picture of the 'bo in popular culture. But you don't meet many 'bos like that in reality.

In my experience—I've handled six or seven cases involving 'bos—even if they're not crooks, they're pretty sad guys.

A voice from inside. A shout.

"Be there in a minute," the pirate shouted back over his shoulder. He gaped at me again. "I owe him a couple of smokes. So make this fast, man."

"Is there a guy around here with a brand-new pair of black horn-rimmed glasses?"

"Nah. Not that I know of anyway."

He was lying, and I don't think he cared that I knew it.

I love giving bribes. It makes me feel like a private eye in one of those movies with a lot of shapely blondes. I gave him two dollars.

He held them and said, "These're pretty wrinkled, man."

"Yeah? So?"

"I like newer ones. Crisper. The feel of them, man. These feel like old dry washcloths."

I hauled out my wallet again and dug around inside. Now there was only faint moonlight. I found two more dollar bills. They were newer.

He plucked them with criminal aplomb from my innocent fingers.

"I get the other two back?"

"Hell, no, man. You give 'em to me, didn't you?"

"I thought we were swapping. New for old."

"Where'd you get that idea, man?"

"All right. Just tell me where I can find this guy?"

He glanced back over his shoulder. When his eyes found me again, he looked tense.

"I shouldn't be snitchin', man."

"Just tell me, and I'll go."

The shout from inside again.

"I tole ya," the pirate shouted back, "just a sec. Don't get your balls in an uproar." To me, he said, "I'm into Zen, that's why I don't get all uptight like he does."

"Good for you. Now where do I find this guy?"

I THINK ANY KID who grows up poor lives in terror of dying alone in a place like this. Little boxes of rooms. Prison cells without bars. Without visible bars, anyway. Little furnished rooms with a toilet down the hall shared by four or five other shambling old men broke and on the dole, spending their hours reading the shared newspaper or maybe an adventure magazine. Or listening to the radio because nobody in the house can afford a TV set except the landlady, and she sure ain't about to let you sit in her apartment and watch it. Most species of animals crawl off to die alone. That's how it is when these men pass, alone in their little boxes.

The house was two-storied and in reasonably good repair given its proximity to the Knolls. It had brown, bricklike siding, none of the windows were held together with tape, no drunks were puking on the lawn, and there weren't any cops here leading somebody away in handcuffs. That put this house on the map of the elites.

Even the landlady was a little better than I would have guessed. When she opened her door, I smelled the friendly aroma of cookies baking. She was a tiny, pretty lady of sixty or so, her white hair done in a tight, flattering permanent. She wore dark slacks, a crisp white blouse and a ruffled pink apron that looked as clean and crisp as her blouse.

"Hi, Mr. McCain. I'm Ellen Weiderman."

"I'm sorry," I said. "I guess I don't remember you."

"No reason you should. My nephew got into a legal situation with his neighbor—a property line sort of thing—and you were his lawyer. He pointed you out to me one day."

"I hope I won for him."

She smiled. "You did." She indicated the lit hall, the stairs running up the west wall. Everything was clean and orderly. "I doubt you're here to take a room."

"I'm actually here to check out Bob Nugent's room, if that's possible."

"Poor Bob."

"Did you know him well?"

"He lived here for four years, and I talked to him just

about every day. I guess you get to know a man pretty well in that period of time.''

''How about a man named Len Welch?''

''Len? He was probably Bob's best friend. Len was a rail-road man till he had some troubles.'' She tapped her head. ''He hears things sometimes—people talking to him. God talks to him sometimes, he says. I believe in God, but I'm not sure He speaks to us directly like that. You know, like He calls us on the phone or anything. Poor Bob was always real patient with him. Len's all right as long as he keeps taking the medication they give him. When he doesn't is when he hears those voices. But he isn't dangerous or any-thing. The neighborhood children treat him like the boogey-man. He gets scared when they follow him and call him names. Sometimes he just comes back here to his room and cries like a little kid.'' She glanced at the stairs. ''In fact, Len's up there right now. Would you like to go up and see him?''

LEN WELCH HAD THE KIND of acne that makes you wince. At least I think it was acne. I felt bad that it shocked me. As if I were blaming him. He didn't offer to shake hands, and I was relieved. The hypochondriac in me was at its irrational worst. If I shook hands with him, maybe I'd get his skin disease…

He'd fixed up his sleeping room to resemble a miniature apartment. In addition to the inevitable bureau drawers, the single bed, the three-shelf bookcase and the cheap faded throw rug, he had a rocking chair with a lamp behind it for reading, and the tiniest TV I'd ever seen. The screen was maybe eight inches. The room smelled of sleep, medicine, whiskey and cigarette smoke.

The landlady made the introductions and then excused her-self.

He sat in the rocking chair. I parked myself on an ottoman that a bath towel had been thrown over.

This is where he would die. If he was lucky, he'd go in his sleep. Probably nobody but the landlady would take note of his passing. I looked at him, his scarred and raw old face, his ears that heard directly from God, his battered railroad hands. On the tiny TV screen, Perry Como was singing "Silent Night" with a chorus of festively dressed support singers. I wanted to say something to Len, but I didn't know how to express it. Just that I was sorry for his life and for his loneliness here. It might have been patronizing of me—what the hell was so great about my life; and anyway, maybe he really enjoyed his life—but I couldn't speak. He'd just die in this room as I would someday die in a room probably not a whole lot different—as millions and millions of people die every year.

Then I laughed.

He looked at me.

"I'm sorry. I just thought of something that struck me as funny."

And I had. It was a tradition in my family to let me ruin at least a portion of every Christmas dinner. Most of the time I wasn't even aware I was doing it.

Everybody'd be just starting in on their food and somebody'd ask me how I was doing, and I'd just start in. It usually started about my clients. This one got his arm caught in a baling machine, that one had terminal cancer, this one had suffered her third miscarriage, and I was pretty sure that this was the year the Russkies would drop the big one on us.

Then my mom would always say, "Dad, you're closest to Sam. Kick him real hard in the leg." And Dad would.

And then the subject would change to happier things.

"He was blackmailing people," I said.

There wasn't any point in a formal inquisition. He had a pretty good idea why I was here.

"You gonna tell the cops?"

"They'll find out anyway, eventually."

He put a Camel cigarette in his mouth, thumb-lit a stick

match, got the smoke going and said, "He got a good share of money from Don Lillis."

"He had pictures of Lillis with another woman."

The blue of the eyes had long ago been washed away. They were almost colorless now. But they were not without shrewdness. When I mentioned the other woman, the eyes narrowed. A smile parted his lips. He had a pair of store-boughts that clacked like castanets whenever he spoke more than three syllables running.

"Who told you that?"

"About pictures of the woman and Lillis?"

"Yeah."

"Lillis himself did," I said.

"I'd dig a little deeper if I was you, Mr. McCain."

"Then that wasn't why he was blackmailing him?"

He kept the volume up just at the threshold of human hearing. He'd steal a look at it, too, every few seconds.

"I love them old Christmas songs," he said.

"Me, too."

"I grew up on a farm. Christmas Eve we'd all climb into the old Model-T and go to midnight mass. Then we'd come home and Ma'd make pancakes, and we'd open presents. We always got clothes—practical stuff, you know—but I didn't care as much about the presents as I did it just being Christmas Day. Those were the best days of my life, them Christmases back on the farm."

Maybe what I'd wanted to say to him he'd just said to himself. He bound his own body and soul up in the succor of good memories. There were tears in his eyes as he sat there staring at Perry Como. And he was right. It'd be nice to be six again and in my pajamas and having a cup of hot chocolate and waiting for Dad and Mom to say we could start opening the presents now.

"You don't seem hard or mean, Mr. McCain," he said.

"Please just call me Sam. I'm not a 'Mr.' kind of guy."

"You don't seem hard or mean, Sam."

"Thank you. I try not to be either of those things." I smiled. "Especially around Christmastime."

"So I'm going to give you a present, Sam."

"That's not necessary," I said, thinking he was going to give me something he couldn't afford.

"Oh, damn," he said. And suddenly the face was even harder to observe. It reflected pain in addition to the ugliness. "I got this prostate infection. The doc give me some medicine for it, but it don't seem to be helping much. I got to hit the john."

He stood, grabbed at the small of his back, right around the area of his kidney, and hobbled over to the door. He left it half-opened as he slipper-flapped his way to the john.

He was gone longer than I would have expected. I got up and walked around the small room. I hadn't realized until then that he had not a single photograph on display. Everybody's got folks and sisters and brothers and nieces and nephews. Even men like Len. But none was to be seen. All I saw was a piece of paste that was a very good replica of a gold brooch. I wondered why he kept it.

I found the bank savings book on top of the bureau. I suppose I could rationalize here and say that I opened it up and looked inside because that's my job as an investigator. The thing is, I'm a nosy bastard. I *shouldn't* be a nosy bastard. A nosy bastard isn't a nice thing to be. But a nosy bastard I am.

I don't know what I was expecting the figure to be. Couple hundred, I suppose; maybe a thousand even if he'd gotten a pension from the railroad, the poor old guy.

Poor old Len Welch had a little over twenty-seven thousand dollars in his savings account.

When he came back, I was sitting on the ottoman smoking a Lucky and listening to Perry Como sing "Rockin' Around The Christmas Tree," the kind of song the nonword *Xmas* was created to describe.

Len sat down again. Made a satisfied sound.

"There, that's better. A *lot* better. It's hell getting old. It really is." He leaned his head back and closed his eyes. I wondered if he was going to sleep on me. He kept them closed when he said, "You know that present I was gonna give you, Sam?"

"I told you, there's no need—" Of course, I'd told him there was no need for a present before I sneaked a peek into his savings book.

"Now that Bob's dead, don't make no difference to me what happens to him anyway."

"Him?"

"Don Lillis."

"What about him?"

"That story he tole ya about why Bob was blackmailing him?"

"Yeah?"

"Wasn't true."

He rocked. I wondered if he was enjoying the pause, creating the tension.

"Then why was Bob blackmailing him?"

"The jeep accident back in high school. Sandy Beaumont died."

"I remember. Bob and Don were in the back seat."

He opened his eyes, as he sat forward.

"Don was driving. Not Sandy. You know how accidents are. Sometimes you can't ever guess who's gonna die in them. He was driving and didn't die. Bob was in the passenger seat, and he didn't die either. But Sandy—she was in back and she died."

"But the cops said Sandy was driving."

"Oh, she was behind the wheel all right. But that's because Don and Bob planted her there. Don was pretty drunk. He was worried he could be charged with something, with Sandy dead and all. So he convinced Bob to help him move her body. He also got Bob to tell the police Sandy was driving. So she got blamed for the whole thing."

You come to believe certain things and after a certain point you never question them. It was part of town history that Sandy Beaumont got drunk one hot August afternoon and killed herself by running her brother's jeep off the road. But it wasn't true. Len's story sounded more plausible.

"But how could Bob blackmail Don if Bob was part of the whole thing?"

"The blackmail didn't start till several years later. By that time, Bob's life was takin' on water. He was really sinkin'. I wasn't around here, then, but a lot of people told me Bobby went from being a well-liked guy to a pretty pathetic drunk. Couldn't hold a job, passed out on the sidewalk sometimes, even did a little shoplifting. Then all of a sudden, he comes into money. Takes care of his mom and her house. Sends his sis some money. Hell, he used to give me money every once in a while, too."

"And the money came from Lillis?"

"That's what Bob told me, Sam. Lillis had a lot to lose, the way Bob explained it. Big house, big car, beautiful wife. Bob didn't have nothin' to lose. That's what made him dangerous to Lillis. Ole Bob, he tole me all about it. He'd get whiffed and tell me everything. He wasn't one who could keep a secret very well."

Now it was my turn to pause. And make him nervous the way he had me.

"I just thought of something, Len."

"Oh?" He sat up even straighter in the rocker. His colorless gaze was apprehensive.

"Somebody saw you out at the Lillis house a couple of nights before Bob got killed."

"Hell, Sam, it wasn't me."

"I think it was."

His expression changed quickly. He suddenly looked as if he were going to start crying.

"Yeah, it was me," he said.

"What were you doin' out there?"

"I was gonna rob it."

"Well, somebody spotted you."

"Yeah. I know."

"You ever burglarize a place before?"

"Nope. I just figured it wouldn't be all that tough."

"You get anything?"

"Not diddly squat. Couldn't even get inside. They have pretty good locks."

"Why all of a sudden rob the place?"

He shrugged. "Bob kept tellin' me about how well-off they are. The Lillises."

"Yeah."

He shrugged again.

"You see these hands?"

I had, in fact, seen his hands. Swollen and misshapen hands. Big hands. Hands that weren't supposed to look like that.

"Damned arthritis is killin' me. I have a reaction to cortisone so I can't take that. I was thinkin' of headin' to California."

"The Iowan's fondest dream." And it was. The state paper frequently ran articles about how many Iowans moved to California every year.

"I needed a stake. Figured I could get it from the Lillis house."

"But no luck."

"No luck at all."

I didn't believe any of this. Why would he break into a house when he had all that money in his savings account?

"So I guess I'm stuck in Iowa for a while," he said.

"The county attorney's going to come around."

"For what?" he said.

"After Cliffie's talked to you, I mean."

"That dumb chief of police, you mean?"

"Yeah."

"He's already talked to me. He's somethin', isn't he?"

"You tell him Bob was blackmailing Lillis?"

"Uh-uh."

"Why not?"

"He can find out on his own. He was always hasslin' Bob. I mean, I admit Bob was a pretty bad drunk, and he'd pass out on the sidewalks and stuff. But that stupid hick cop didn't have to treat him as bad as he did."

I kept thinking about his bank book. No matter what we talked about, I always came back to that.

"You said Bob gave you money, Len."

"Yessir, he did. He was a generous fellow."

"How much did he give you?"

"Oh, couple hundred here, couple hundred there. Like that, I guess."

The idea was pretty simple. What if somebody knew that a blackmailer was getting a nice easy ride from a certain prominent person? So what if this person decided to take over the whole enterprise himself? What if he killed the blackmailer, stole some money the blackmailer had stashed away, and then went to the prominent person and said, "I'm taking over now and by the way, your payment just doubled."

But I needed a lot more evidence than I had at the moment. Maybe he'd come by that twenty-seven thousand from an inheritance of some kind. Maybe it represented his life savings. Maybe he saved up all those "couple hundreds" that Bob Nugent had given—but that was the least likely prospect. It would take an awful lot of "couple hundreds" to equal twenty-seven thousand.

I stood.

"I need to be going."

"Lillis killed him."

All I said was goodbye.

NINE

I PARKED THE RAGTOP in the driveway. Mrs. Goldman, my landlady, had gone to visit some of her friends for the holidays. She's a recent widow who looks a lot like Lauren Bacall even though her calendar age has to be approaching fifty. With her gone, the house, upstairs and down, was dark.

I walked around back. The snow was silver in the moonlight. There were dog prints and rabbit prints on the surface. The alley was jammed with garages from the time when they built them with just a couple feet between them.

I have my own entrance, stairs going up the back to the second floor. I'd just put my foot on the first step when it happened.

I wish I could tell you it was a gunshot. Gunshots have been noticeably absent in this story, and gunshots are sort of a staple in this kind of tale.

But this wasn't a gunshot; alas, it was a snowball.

It hadn't been packed hard enough to hurt. It disintegrated against the back of my head like dandelion, soft flakes flying everywhere.

The laugh was unmistakable. I remembered it from the time I used to give her rides on the handlebars of my fifth-grade Schwinn.

I started packing my own snowball even before I could find her.

"Hey," I said, "that's cheating."

What she'd done was tuck herself inside the garage. Then

when she got a good clear shot at me, she took it and fell back into the darkness inside.

"Yeah, like you've never cheated, Sam."

"Come out here and fight like a woman."

This time it was more like a giggle than a laugh.

"I always had a better aim than you did, anyway, Sam."

And as if to prove it, she lurched out of the garage and fired another snowball at me.

And got me right in the forehead.

Now it was my turn. But she crouched low and started running up the shoveled walk toward me. I got my shot off, but she didn't have any trouble ducking it.

"Poor Sam," she said merrily.

Then she applied a red mitten to my head, front and back, to wipe away the remaining snow and said, "I'd take a drink if you had one."

I led her up the stairs, got the door unlocked and let us in. She snapped the light on behind me. The three cats sat on the couch.

"Good evening, ladies," Mary Travers said.

She'd changed clothes: brown sweater, jeans, tan desert boots. She'd also managed to cover her black eye pretty well with makeup.

"The makeup artist to the stars," I said.

"I did a pretty good job, don't you think?"

"You sure as hell did."

I made us a couple of light bourbon-and-waters and dispensed them with a flourish. She sat on the couch with the girls, and I sat in the ragged armchair where I do a lot of my reading.

"I'm afraid I'm really going to impose on you tonight, Sam."

"That's why I'm here. I love being imposed on by lovely young women like yourself."

She made a face indicating that the time for jokes was over. She began petting Tasha, and then looked back at me.

"I've decided to give my marriage one last serious try."

"You sure you want to?"

She nodded. Was silent a moment.

"I know he loves me. And in many ways, I love him. He needs professional help."

"Somehow I can't see him agreeing."

"If he doesn't agree, then there's nothing to talk about. It's just over."

"All right."

"Such a beautiful girl," she said, stroking Tasha again. "All my life I've wondered what it would be like to be a cat. Not an outdoors cat. Indoors. Just lie around and sleep and play a little bit and eat and then sleep some more."

"Where do I sign up?"

She looked up at me.

"And not have all these human problems we have."

She sipped her drink.

"This is strong."

I laughed. "There's about a quarter shot in there. You couldn't get a Jehovah's Witness drunk on that."

She hesitated again.

"I'd like to invite him over."

"Who?" I said.

"Wes."

"Here?"

"If you wouldn't mind."

"Boy, you're really a creative thinker."

"I know you're being sarcastic, Sam, but it's the only way I can think of to end his obsession with you. All these crazy ideas he has about us sneaking around together. I'm a faithful woman, Sam."

"I know you are."

"And I know it'll be kind of embarrassing and awkward

at first—the three of us being together and all. But it just might humiliate and shock him into facing his problem.''

"Just as long as one of us doesn't end up getting booked for first-degree murder.''

"I'd really appreciate it if you'd do it, Sam.''

"So what's the deal? You'll call him?''

"He's at home. He just left my mom's, seeing the baby. He broke down and cried and told her how sorry he was about hitting me and pushing me around for so long. That isn't like him at all.''

"No, it sure isn't.''

"That's why I think this might work. When he's open to really listening to me. And then the shock value of you being here, too.''

"I doubt he'll agree to come over.''

"If he doesn't, I'll file for a separation Monday.''

I got up from the armchair and said, "I've only got the one phone. Right over there. Help yourself. I'll be in the john running the water so I won't be able to hear you.''

"I appreciate that, Sam. It'll probably get a little—you know, personal.''

To the john I went. I turned on the cold-water tap. Luckily for me, I had a new Ace double book sitting on top of the toilet tank. This was a science-fiction double, *Vulcan's Hammer* by Philip K. Dick and *The Skynappers* by John Brunner. Two of my favorite writers. I sat on the lid and smoked and read. The Brunner got right to it.

I got about thirty pages read when the knock came.

"You can come out now, Sam.''

I tried to read her mood from her voice. Happy or sad? Mission accomplished or mission scrubbed? I couldn't tell.

"He's on his way,'' she said.

"I sure hope this works out,'' I said. "It could be a disaster.''

"I don't know what else to do.''

"I guess I don't, either."

I'd just started fixing us fresh and very weak new drinks when the phone rang again.

"Would you grab that?" I asked.

"The Sam McCain residence," Mary said on picking up. "Just a moment please."

Why couldn't I have a secretary who sounded that crisp and intelligent? She cupped the phone and said, "It's Sara Lillis. She doesn't sound very good."

I carried over the drinks and set them down, then took the phone.

"Hello, Sara."

"You have to come out here right away."

"What's wrong?"

"It's Don—he's acting crazy. I—I don't want to say anything more over the phone. Just please, please get out here."

"I'll be right out."

"Oh, Lord, Sam," Mary said. "Do you really have to go?"

"It sure sounds like it. I'll be back as soon as I can. This'll give you and Wes a chance to talk."

"I don't know if that's bad or good."

"Talking is always good," I said on my way out the door. But I didn't know if I really believed that.

SARA ANSWERED the door even before I got a chance to ring the bell. "I saw you drive up."

"Where's Don?"

"He just went out. I couldn't stop him. Though I think I've got an idea of where he's gone."

"Where?"

"He has an old fishing cabin. It's kind of his retreat when he needs to be alone. No TV, no phones."

As she led me into the living room, where flames burned with great drama and passion in the native stone fireplace, she said, "He took his gun, too. That was the first thing I checked when he ran out of here."

"Did he actually mention the cabin?"

"No, all he talked about was—"

She stopped speaking abruptly. "I pushed him too hard. I reminded him about the blackmail, and he said that he didn't like it any better than I did. And then he said—"

"Did he say that he killed Bob Nugent?" I asked carefully.

"He didn't actually say those words. But—"

"But he gave that impression?"

She bit her lower lip, hugged herself tight. She needed a mommy or daddy at this point. Then she nodded.

"Where's this cabin?" I said.

"I really appreciate this, Sam," she said, even before she'd given me directions. "Just please tell him that I love him and that I want to work this out. Whatever he did, I'll stand by him."

THE SKELETAL FINGERS of winter trees reached to the sky, as if pleading to the heavens. Frost lent the land a furry silver surface. A lonely hawk was briefly silhouetted against the moon. The tiny cabins and mobile homes and houseboats along the sluggish brown river were dark for the season.

Don's cabin was up on a shelf of rock in the middle of deep forest. Snow had obscured the road. I followed fresh tire tracks. He'd brought his Jag.

The word *cabin* suggests a rustic sort of place where poison ivy substitutes for toilet paper and all sorts of squirmy, writhing, unseen things share your bed with you at night.

The Lillis "cabin" was actually a small tract home. Fresh blue paint, a recent reroofing, and a TV antenna made it look prosperous indeed set against the ragged view of snow-covered pines and huge snowdrifts. All the lights were on, giving the scene a warmth it would otherwise lack.

I knocked several times. No answer. I tried the door.

Locked. I walked around to the back. No back door. I went to the front door and resumed my banging. Very faintly, I could hear a radio playing.

The lock took some playing with. It did not yield to a strip of celluloid. It required several attempts with various burglary picks. I had a client who could not pay me—I have many clients like that—so he offered to introduce me to the wonderful world of burglary and its most essential tools. I have used them many times.

He was on the floor. The way he'd done it was to lie on his belly and put the gun to his temple and pull the trigger. He lay on a massive hook rug. One hairy hand clutched the .45 he'd used.

I checked his vitals, though that was useless, and then I looked for a note. Didn't find one.

I locked the door. I stood on the porch and smoked a cigarette. I wish I'd liked him more. It would be nice to send kind thoughts with him on his journey.

I drove back into town. The drive was silent. I didn't play the radio. I just listened to the sounds of the radio and the sound of the wind through the ragtop.

The first person I called was the judge. "You mean Lillis was the actual killer?"

"I'm afraid Cliffie was right."

"But that's not possible."

"Sure, it's possible. You take an infinite number of monkeys and good stuff'll start up."

"So you take an infinite number of Cliffies—"

"He was bound to guess right. At least one of these days."

"It's a good thing I laid in a lot of brandy."

"I'll talk to you tomorrow."

"No, tonight. After you talk to Cliffie. I want to know if he gloated or anything."

"Cliffie gloat? That's a sure thing."

"Call me, anyway."

"It may be late."

"I'm a grown woman, McCain. My parents let me stay up past nine o'clock and everything."

THIS WAS ONE of those moments that could—or should— happen only in a dream. Or nightmare. I was riding shotgun in the police vehicle of one Clifford Sykes, Jr.

You mean aside from the wailing country music on the radio that drowned out the police calls? You mean aside from all the garlic Cliffie'd had on his "Eye-talian" meal at Luigi's earlier that night? You mean aside from the four times he nearly got us killed because he was talking to me instead of watching the road? You mean aside from these and myriad other irritants how was the ride with Cliffie to Don Lillis's cabin? It was ducky; just ducky.

"Well," Cliffie said, walking through the cabin door. "You got one thing right, Counselor."

"Yeah, what's that?"

"He sure looks dead."

Such are the powers of Cliffie's observations.

Grimes and Manners pulled in just behind us and took over the crime scene. Thank God.

Cliffie and I stood on the porch for a time.

"I tole ya, Counselor. He killed Nugent and then he killed himself."

"I guess you were right."

"You guess? Hell, c'mon and admit. You and the judge lost your asses on this one."

At which point, Grimes appeared and said, "Chief?"

"Uh-huh."

"This probably wasn't a suicide."

"What the hell're you talking about?"

"They'll have to check it again at autopsy, but from what we can see there's no gunpowder residue on his gun hand."

"So what?"

Grimes gave me one of his long-suffering looks.

"Chief, if he'd fired the gun, then there'd be some evidence of gunpowder residue."

"The crap they teach you at that police school. Of course, he killed himself."

"All right, Chief. I just thought I'd point that out."

He went back inside.

"Gunpowder residue," Cliffie said. "The crap I have to put up with these days."

THE CORONER'S CAR CAME. Then the county ambulance. Then a lone reporter's car. Cliffie gave a statement claiming that Don Lillis had committed suicide because he'd been feeling guilty over killing Bob Nugent who had been blackmailing him with photos of Don and another woman.

The thing was, Cliffie probably believed every piece of misinformation he'd just dispensed. That's the nice thing about Cliffie. He knows an inner peace that few of us enjoy.

ELLEN WEIDERMAN, Len Welch's landlady, was a lot more curious about my second appearance than she had been about my first.

"Did something happen?" she asked. She was in a royal-blue cotton robe with her hair caught up in a pink scarf and small curlers.

"I just need to talk to Len."

She glanced up the stairs.

"It's nearly eleven o'clock. He's usually asleep by now."

"Mind if I check on him?"

Her face reflected her anxiety.

"Just don't make a lot of noise. The other men are sleeping."

I went up the stairs on tiptoe. She stood at the bottom of the steps, watching me, listening.

The room was empty. The window was open. I walked to

it. The metal fire escape on the back wall made getting in and out easy.

I closed the window, flipped on a light and went to work.

There were the bureau drawers, the closet and a small trunk to check out. The closet and the trunk were pretty much useless.

There was a shoe box in the bottom drawer of the bureau. I took it over to the ottoman and sat down.

I was still worried about catching his skin disease, but I didn't have any choice but to go through his things.

My assumption held up for a time. He'd known that Bob Nugent was blackmailing Don Lillis. He wanted some of it himself. He began to blackmail the blackmailer. Nugent hadn't given him any gifts. Those had been blackmail payments amounting to twenty-seven thousand dollars in the bank.

A nice, easy way to save for a nice, easy future.

The envelope in the bottom of the shoe box changed everything, though. As I sat there looking through it, reading the two letters inside, looking at the photographs, I felt at least some of the sorrow he'd borne all his life.

I didn't like him; I didn't forgive him. He'd killed two people with great and practiced premeditation, but I felt as sorry as hell for him, anyway. I didn't want to but I did.

TEN

THERE WAS A WREATH on the door, which I thought was a nice touch. Not a holiday wreath, a mourning wreath. There was a lone candle in the window. A small-town Midwestern expression of loss. In case the soul of the departed wanted to come back.

I had parked at the far end of the drive, up at the curve, so it was unlikely I'd been seen or heard. I'd worn my tall buckle boots because I knew I'd be walking through snow.

I started on the far side of the large house and went window to window. All the windows but the long mullioned front window and one smaller one on the side were dark.

Through the small one, I could see them. This was a guest room. She wasn't dressed up in anything especially erotic—she would never be so obvious as to play the seductress in any cheap way, no teddy that barely covered her most prized possession; no diaphanous gown as on a Mickey Spillane paperback cover—just a denim shirt and a pair of rather loose jeans.

The guest room was done in various shades of blue. Comforting. There was a walk-in closet with blue sliding doors; a desk with a blue surface, and a blue chair to match; and dark blue carpeting. There was even a blue shade on the table lamp. It was all very *House Beautiful*. The privileged domain of the newly rich who had risen up since the war. He'd probably never stayed in a room like this in his life. He'd be daffy as a kid—scared, true—but all lust and sad dopey feckless love.

I wish I could tell you what she was saying. But there was a car-rocking, shutter-flapping, roof-antenna-snapping wind whipping through the valley at the moment, and so her words, seductive no doubt as a passage in D. H. Lawrence, were lost on me.

I watched the pantomime show, unable to move. He seemed to balk at something she said. She came to his side and sat and touched his face. All those pitted scars. That hideous mask. I wondered if anybody in his life, even his mother, had touched his face so lovingly.

He balked no longer. He took her in his arms and kissed her. All that love he must feel for her—frightened love, knowing deep down but not admitting to himself, what she would do with him eventually—and even more than love. The heady, exhilarating feeling that he had been accepted. That a beautiful, well-born, genteel woman had accepted him.

She pressed him back on the bed, sliding partially on top of him as they continued their kiss.

And it was then I saw the misshapen back left pocket of her jeans. And knew why she'd put on this particular pair of loose-fitting jeans.

The shape was that of a hand gun. Probably a .45.

My realization of what she was doing coincided with her starting to do it.

As she started to slip away from him, find her feet, she began extracting the gun from her back pocket.

I pounded on the window.

They both looked up, startled and scared.

"She has a gun!" I shouted. But with the wind and the heavy glass, I doubted he heard me.

She fired twice. I don't know what I'd expected, but I hadn't expected that.

She didn't hit me but glass sprayed my face, tiny cuts ripping my right cheek.

I dived for the snow just as she fired off another round. Then there were two stark shots aimed inside. Len screamed.

It was coming apart for her, and cool and controlled as she was, she was coming apart, too. She'd likely been planning to have Cliffie find Len's body in the front room. She'd claim she'd been attacked and then killed him.

Finding the body in the guest room, the window shattered, even Cliffie—and Grimes and Manners for sure—would begin to doubt her story very quickly.

I dragged myself to my feet and started running around to the front of the house. There was only one thing she could do, and even now I could hear her firing up the engine in the Jag. It was all hers now—at least for the moment, house, Jag, bank account—all she'd schemed for.

She was backing out of the garage when I, gasping for breath, reached the drive. In reverse, the Jag came howling right at me.

I did the only thing I could. I pitched myself leftward, out of the way, but as the Jag screeched past me, I grabbed the back door handle and managed to yank it open. She had to get out of reverse, which meant turning. And to do that, she had to slow for a few seconds. Which was when I hurled myself into the back seat of the Jag.

She was one inventive lady. While turning, she managed to fire a shot into the back seat. She must have swapped weapons. This one thundered like a cannon. It was probably fully loaded, too.

She must have called me three or four dozen dirty names while careening down the road and firing back at me with a hand flung over her seat. It was a shooting gallery of sorts. Every time I'd get ready to grab her around the neck, she fired again, and I'd have to try to jump out of the way.

She got crazy. The shrieking, the name calling, the pure

ugly terrifying fear of her situation made her almost put the Jag into a ditch four different times.

I had to be careful. I could grab her at any time. But in doing so I'd put the Jag in a ravine, and we'd be going seventy miles per hour. There was a chance I'd be killed.

"There's no place to go," I shouted at her finally. "It's too late to escape. Just pull over here and let's get it over with. You don't want to die this way."

"That stupid Len," she sobbed, "I went over and over it with him. How to set up the suicide. And he didn't do it right."

I thought of the envelope I'd taken from Len's. All those proper photos he had of her. She'd obviously given them to him. Just simple photos, fully clothed. How many, many times he must have studied them and longed for her. And the piece of costume jewelry I'd seen the first time I was in his room. That had been in the envelope now, too. She'd probably convinced him it was the real thing, some precious heirloom of hers that she was giving him for the deep and abiding love she felt for him.

If he'd just kill Bob Nugent so her husband would be blamed…and then kill Don and make it look like a remorseful suicide…they'd be free, Len and Sara, to live out a free and good life, maybe in Europe or South America.

The things we convince ourselves to believe….

The car had fishtailed many times on its sliding-bumping-swerving ride, but this fishtail felt different—ice. A long gleaming patch of headlight-lit ice, and we were sliding right into it and—

Sara lost control of the steering wheel. She cramped the wheels to the right—her first mistake—and then somehow the steering wheel spun right out of her hands as we began to spin around and around on the icy road. I slammed my head so hard against the top of the door that I could feel a geyser of blood spurting from the wound.

She was screaming.
We were still spinning.
I was thrown into the opposite door.
This time the collision brought instant blackness.
Just her screaming...

ELEVEN

AROUND NOON ON Christmas Day, my mom and dad brought me Dad's big lunch bucket stuffed with samples from the family dinner they'd be having later that afternoon.

Dad had been here three times in the past two days. Mom had been here seven.

I ate and they watched me. They took more pleasure from watching me than they would later on from actually eating the turkey and the mashed potatoes and the peas and the gravy and the cranberry sauce and the pumpkin pie with whipped cream topping that Mom had spent all night and all morning making.

"You look a lot better today," Mom said.

"Thanks, Mom."

"You got some color back in your face," Dad said.

"And thirty-nine stitches in my head."

But I was the lucky one. A broken wrist. A broken rib. A concussion. And thirty-nine stitches.

Sara was dead. As was Len. Before he died, he told Cliffie that he'd imitated his friend Bob Nugent, wanting some blackmail action of his own. He started following Sara around. She was sleeping with somebody in Cedar Rapids. He tried to blackmail her. But then she enlisted him in her scheme, giving him nearly thirty thousand dollars over the past year while she worked out all the details.

"I saw Mary and Wes at Mass this morning," Mom said. "Wes said to thank you again for talking to him when he came up to see you. They're back together now. He's going to get counseling, you know, for hitting her, that poor girl. That was very nice of you, dear.''

He'd spent an hour here. I'd finally convinced him that Mary was faithful and really wanted their marriage to work, and that any feelings she might have had for me had been limited to adolescent longings and nothing more.

"Next Christmas we're going to put on a feast for you, you won't believe," Mom said.

"But we need to go now, son," Dad said. "Uncle Mike and the rest'll be getting to our place pretty soon. Uncle Bob wants to watch the Bears game."

"Lord, I hate football," Mom said.

She gave me several dozens kisses, pats, rubs and mom-looks. Then Dad gave me several manly thumps on the shoulder, and they both told me again how good I looked, and then they both said wouldn't it be great that I'd be out of here Tuesday, which was only two more days?

Then I slept.

I'd had enough pain medicine to subdue me pretty well. Plus I always get sleepy when I'm in bed for prolonged periods. It just seems the natural thing to be. Bed, sleep. Makes sense.

I dreamed I was somewhere where they served expensive brandy and people smoked Gauloises cigarettes. Judge Esme Anne Whitney must have been in the dream because this was certainly her MO.

When I woke up, she was there, sitting in a very comfortable leather chair I'd never seen before.

"Don't gawk, McCain. Haven't you ever seen a chair before?"

"How'd that get in here?"

She gave me one of her haughty Eastern looks, took a long drag on her French cigarette, a drink from her snifter of brandy and said, "I had one of my people bring it here for me. Along with a little dry bar and some food I'm having catered here for dinner tonight.''

''You're staying for dinner?''

''Face it, McCain. I'm without a companion tonight and so are you. So we'll just have to make the best of it.''

At which point, she turned on the TV and said, ''Lenny's leading the New York Philharmonic this afternoon. So please be quiet and let's listen.''

Personally, I would've preferred Chuck Berry or Little Richard. But I wasn't about to tell her that. At least not on Christmas Day.

WHAT CHILD IS THIS
by Irene Marcuse

ONE

CHRISTMAS MORNING I found myself standing on the street, holding a baby I'd just traded forty dollars for. I'd come out to buy bagels, lox and the Sunday paper, and here I had a child, just like that, as if a prayer had been answered.

I should've known better. This wasn't the New Testament, after all.

Does every infertile woman have this fantasy? The one where someone abandons a baby on her doorstep, and she gets to keep it? A simple response to a simple desire: I want a baby, and look! I found one!

Because if you're unable to get pregnant, nothing about becoming a parent is easy.

I was pushing forty when my husband and I had to face the reality that we were not going to conceive a child in the usual way. And the plain truth was, we couldn't afford—you'll pardon the expression—assisted reproductive technologies, or most of the myriad and uncertain routes to adoption. No, what we'd done instead, four years before that Christmas morning, was take in a foster child.

It seemed like the perfect solution at the time. A week-old baby girl was delivered to our door a mere five months after we turned in the paperwork. From the moment the social worker placed Clea in my arms, I knew she was meant for me.

Never mind that I'd signed a document affirming my awareness that "The goal of foster care is to reunite the child with the biological family." Or that even when the chances of such a reunion were extremely slim, it could still take years to adopt. Yes, we'd been well warned that our daughter might be in first, second, third grade before anything was finalized. Who could believe such dire predictions?

Not Benno, my feet-on-the-ground husband, totally captivated by the baby. Not me; I had no room for the possibility of loss. In those first few days, when I held Clea against my chest, I had the physical sensation of something growing out of me and wrapping itself around her. An emanation of energy, binding us together. Benno named it right away: bonding. Don't tell me about birth, biological, natural parents— love is thicker than blood, any day.

Four years later, we were no closer to adopting Clea than we'd been on the day she arrived in our living room.

I lived in fear of family court, with its indefensible delays and reliance on the advice of a Child Welfare bureaucracy that cared more for policies than people.

In spite of which, I'd been wanting another child. Talk about irrational—to even think about opening the door to another foster child.

And there I was, with a baby who'd materialized from concrete and fog.

I didn't know much more about him than his name—Jamal. I guessed his age at something under a year. His eyes had a serious, slightly worried expression. I knew exactly how he felt, but I couldn't stop myself—I smiled at him. Jamal smiled back, and that was it.

I felt blessed, the same way I felt when Clea was given to me.

I carried Jamal across the uptown side of Broadway, to the bench in the wide median strip. I needed to get my bearings before I walked in on my family with a new baby.

"Okay, little guy, let's think about all this for a minute." *Wrapped in swaddling clothes,* the verse from the Christmas carol swam into my head. I loosened the blanket so I could have a look at the rest of him.

Jamal helped by kicking free of the heavy wool. It was a full-size blanket, a strange thing to carry a baby around in, I thought. Underneath, he was wearing one-piece blue fleece pajamas with feet and a zipper up the middle. Jamal squirmed around on my lap. There was a definite aroma emanating from his bottom. When I shifted him in order to rewrap the blanket, I noticed some dark stains across the back of his outfit. Round drops, like someone had—spilled a little coffee, Anita. That's all it is.

Already I was uneasy, and putting things out of my mind.

Not just the pajamas and blanket, but also why Jamal's aunt, the woman I'd handed my forty dollars to, had him in the first place, and why she'd chosen me to take him off her hands. Not what she was going to do with the cash, though; I had a pretty good idea about that.

The way I was holding the baby, nursing position in the crook of my arm, seemed to set something off, and he started fussing.

"I bet you're hungry, aren't you, little guy? Well, it looks like we need a few things for you." I could have sworn Jamal nodded in agreement.

We got up and headed for the Love Stores. New York. Eight-thirty on Christmas morning, and there's a twenty-four-hour drugstore two blocks from my apartment.

Jamal seemed surprisingly light compared to Clea, who at four was already too heavy for me to carry more than a block. He rode easily on my hip in spite of his full diaper. Every time I looked at him, I knew I was in trouble. I couldn't keep the grin off my face.

Thinking about that morning brings the smile right back, even a decade later. Even with all that came after that moment.

THIS IS my private ritual, reliving the events that brought Jamal into our lives. I don't do it consciously; it's as if some devoted cluster of memory cells is keeping track. For the past ten Christmas mornings, I've woken up from the same dream.

I am in a room crowded with unsold Christmas trees. Only a few have their branches spread; most are still sheathed in the plastic net that's made them into neat bundles to be shipped south from Vermont. I inhale, expecting the spice of balsam and pine. What I get is a metallic taste on the back of my tongue, a trace of iodine overlaid by a slightly sweet, slightly rotten smell.

Then I see the body. In the dream as in reality, the scene stops me cold. I have no idea how long I stare before I understand what I'm looking at.

As soon as I do, though, I find myself on Broadway. High noon, it must be. The sun casts no shadows behind the people walking past.

"Is that your baby?" someone asks, but doesn't pause for an answer.

I wrap my arms around the infant in the Snugli on my chest and open my mouth to answer. I mean, what did they think? Carrying an infant like that—who else's would she be?

I look down and realize it's not Clea I'm carrying, but Jamal.

Then I'm awake, and profoundly grateful to be where I am rather than in the dream.

THE SKY HAS JUST BEGUN to lighten. My husband is curled away from me. Whatever he's dreaming, it doesn't show in the regular rise and fall of his shoulder. I prop a pillow behind my head so I can look out at the Hudson and watch the water shift from pewter to silver with the sunrise.

"That your baby?" When Clea was little, people asked so often that I referred to it as The Question. Usually they were just curious, although on occasion we were asked by the suspicious and the hostile as well as the friendly.

I never liked it.

Yeah, I know, this is New York, where people feel down-right entitled to butt into the lives of total strangers.

And I did understand why they asked, me being white and Clea being black, but it bothered me all the same. From where I stood, the connection between us was obvious as daylight. The Question, though, brought the insecurity of our situation right back up to the surface.

Benno said I should tell them I was the nanny. That's his sense of humor, but he had a point. The thought of a black family hiring a white woman to take care of their children would knock a whole host of stereotypes on their behinds, and stifle any further inclination to pry.

The best I could usually manage, without snapping, was a nod. If I spoke, it would have come out some variant of "No, I abducted her from the playground, found her on a park bench, rescued her from a trash can," or, more politely, "Of course she's mine. I sent in six box tops and $4.95 for shipping and handling, and here we are!"

Clea's fourteen now. Her adoption was finalized less than a year ago. *Complicated* doesn't begin to tell the story, so maybe you can see why I was sensitive on the subject.

TWO

THE TIDE IN THE Hudson was coming in, making the river appear to flow backward. A finger of new sunlight poked its way between the buildings and pointed out the wavelets heading upstream. I followed the current in the wrong direction, salt water flowing inland from the sea.

The morning Jamal was handed to me began in almost the same way as this one.

Since Benno is Jewish, our Christmas celebration includes his favorite breakfast: bagels and lox. Mama Joy's Deli doesn't open until eight, so I had time to inhale a cup of coffee and wash up the leftover dishes from our annual Christmas Eve party before heading down to the store.

On my way out of the apartment, I always make a withdrawal from the cash pocket of Benno's jeans. I like to have dollar bills rather than quarters for the street people on Christmas morning. Our neighborhood, just north of 110th Street on the upper west side of Manhattan, has what some residents feel is more than our fair share of social service agencies for the homeless and the mentally ill.

Me, I don't begrudge them. New York City is a tough place to get by if you can't afford The Donald's rents. I'm a regular contributor, and not only out of altruism. All those eyes on the street, they know who we are, and they watch out for us. The time three-year-old Clea got away from me and ran to cross the street on her own, it was Marilyn whose grimy, callused hand shot out of nowhere to grab the back of her jacket and stop her. Nothing about Marilyn, from her matted dreadlocks to her limping gait, had given any previous indication of how fast she could move. Or that she'd been pregnant at the time.

Later, when Clea was in junior high at Saint Hilda's and Saint Hugh's, I'd get reports from Leon, who maintained a regular spot on the steps of Broadway Presbyterian Church. "Saw your girl this afternoon," he'd tell me, "with a bunch a her friends. Lot of books in those backpacks, isn't there? She was all bent over. I don't think it's good for their shoulders."

I agreed with him on that. Clea regularly carries twenty-five, thirty pounds to school. They all do; education is serious business already by junior high.

Another time, it was, "Look like your Clea gots herself a boyfriend. I see this red-haired kid, alla time walking with her. You better watch that child."

I never revealed my sources, but Leon's tip prompted a conversation with Clea wherein I learned that she thought the boy had a crush on her, but she didn't like him so much. I had my doubts about his affections being unrequited, and I paid a bit more attention to the social doings at school than I might have without Leon.

The street people are part of the village that's raising my child, and I'm part of the village that feeds them.

THE WEATHER TEN YEARS AGO did not start out sunny, like today. That winter morning was pearl gray, the light luminous and diffuse through low clouds. The buildings, the sidewalks and streets were a monochrome print in shades of stone, concrete, asphalt. The hot pink of a discarded flyer and a yellow potato chip bag in the gutter provided grace notes of color.

Two battered evergreens, abandoned by the Christmas tree vendors who vanished at midnight on the twenty-fourth as mysteriously as they appeared the morning after Thanksgiving, leaned against the shuttered newsstand at 111th. An older couple, the woman in a fur coat, the man carrying a big brown bag from Bloomingdale's, hailed a cab heading downtown. Looking north, I could see all the traffic lights from 111th to 118th switch simultaneously from red to green. Good to go.

I held the shawl collar of my winter coat closed around my neck. The air was heavy with a mist that beaded up on the black wool and curled the strands of hair that escaped my hat. The city smelled lovely, damp and piney from the crushed tree branches, the overtones of exhaust muted by the lack of traffic.

This is my favorite kind of New York moment. The public space as close to deserted as it ever gets, and yet surrounded by buildings full of people living lives I'd never know the details of. In the midst of it, me, another molecule in the flow, slipped for the moment from the tethers of my own particular life.

Leon was asleep in the doorway between a metal-gated Fotorush and a metal-gated Lechter's. I tucked three bills into his blankets so when he woke up he'd be able to afford the breakfast special at Tom's Restaurant, the only brightly lit business in a four-block radius.

Marilyn looked to be up early, stomping her feet in front of Broadway Presbyterian, the hood of her powder-blue down coat pulled up over her head. I took a couple dollars out of my pocket for her and crossed the street.

"Good morning," I called, to catch her attention.

The woman spun and the hood slid back. This wasn't Marilyn, but a stranger with dilated eyes, looking at me like I'd stepped out of her private nightmare. She swayed, unsteady on her feet now that she wasn't moving. I reached out to help her keep her balance. She shivered at my touch, like a wild horse. Or like a person with some kind of drug pulsing in her brain.

"I'm sorry, I didn't mean to startle you. I thought you were Marilyn."

The name seemed to steady her more than my hand on her

arm had. She jerked away and pulled up the hood. "You know Marilyn?"

"Yes." I nodded reassuringly and gestured at the down coat. "I recognized the coat. Are you a friend of hers?"

"I'm her sister. Dolores."

Once she said it, I could see the resemblance. Dolores wasn't quite as tall, but she had the same point to her chin as Marilyn, the same high cheekbones. I'd say Dolores was the younger sister, although that might have been because her skin was without the pockmark scars that marred Marilyn's. Skinnier, too; she had the coat wrapped around her rather than zipped up the front. With her face framed by the light-blue hood, she was beautiful. The Virgin of Guadalupe, I thought, also known as the Black Virgin. My favorite of Mary's incarnations, because she stands in the crescent moon.

"Anita Servi." I held out my gloved right hand.

Dolores looked at me as if I were a fruitcake: who offers to shake with a homeless woman?

On the surface, we were certainly a mismatched pair. I had lined, waterproof leather boots on my feet; Dolores wore once-white Nike sneakers with black laces. I had fur-lined leather gloves, while she kept her hands tucked under her armpits for warmth. Dolores looked to be wearing jeans. Me, I was still in my nightgown. Why get dressed on Christmas morning? Between boots and overcoat, all anyone could see of what I had on was an occasional flash of flowered flannel. New York; your own neighborhood is like an extension of home.

Dolores rose to the occasion, stuck out her hand and tapped mine before withdrawing it back to the shelter of her blue cloak.

Then the bills I had clenched in my left hand registered. A quick dip of the head as she asked, "That for Marilyn, or me?"

Eye on the main chance. "Either or both." I smiled and

gave Dolores the money, but something in the situation worried me. "Is Marilyn all right this morning?"

Dolores shrugged. The money disappeared into a pocket somewhere under the coat. I thought she was going to walk away and that would be that.

But Dolores surprised me with a variant on The Question. "You the white lady with the black baby?"

Well, Clea and I do stand out. I might not have noticed Dolores before, but that didn't mean she hadn't seen us. "That's me," I said.

Some kind of calculation went on behind Dolores's eyes. "You could loan me a little money?"

My first thought was, just what I need, extorted by a crack head on Christmas morning. So much for the romance of deserted Manhattan streets.

Dolores must have read it on my face.

"No, man, all I meant is, maybe you could help me out. Help Marilyn out."

Okay, here came the con. But I was enough of a city girl to just say no. Politely, of course.

"I'm sorry, I was just on my way to the store to get breakfast for my family. You tell Marilyn I said Merry Christmas." I started to walk away.

Dolores grabbed my arm.

I wasn't afraid of her, but I had a New Yorker's alert reaction—the adrenaline of my fight-or-flight response stepped up to the gate, ready to bolt. It was only a block and a half to my destination, where Mrs. Roshan was outside her newsstand, shoring up the stacks of Sunday papers. Unless Dolores had a gun, which was unlikely but not impossible, sprinting to safety would be no problem.

I stood my ground, figuring I'd listen to what she had to say on the chance that Marilyn really was in trouble. If I didn't buy it, well, the encounter would provide me with a story of my own to tell Benno when I got home.

"You know Marilyn had a baby, right? Jamal, he's almost

one year old. He lives over in Staten Island someplace, so Marilyn doesn't get to see him that much. Anyways, Marilyn got herself clean, got herself a room—'' a jerk of the head, indicating it was someplace in the neighborhood ''—where she could have Jamal for the holidays.''

Dolores spoke quickly, anxious to keep me listening. I nodded along. I'd known about Marilyn's pregnancy. She'd been gone from the street for several months, then come back alone.

I'd asked her about the baby. ''A boy,'' was all the answer I got. I wasn't going to pry if she didn't want to talk about it; giving her an occasional handout didn't entitle me to mess in her affairs. I'd assumed the child had gone into foster care. As to Marilyn being clean—maybe, maybe not. What she did with her money was likewise not my business, but I couldn't say I'd noticed any change in her behavior in the past few months.

''I was over to her place last night, you know, Christmas Eve. We had some toys for Jamal, and then we had a little party and Marilyn, she—'' Dolores made an abrupt, sweeping motion with her arm. ''She got all—''

The arm swept back and Dolores came to a full stop, like the momentum of the story had carried her to the edge of a cliff she didn't want to peer over. Her eyes narrowed and the corner of her mouth lifted in a grimace that made her suddenly ugly.

I wanted to get on with my errands, get home to my apartment where presents waited under a tree. I wanted to be there in time to catch the expression on my daughter's face when she saw that the plate of milk and cookies she'd left for ''HoHo'' was empty. I'd had enough of Dolores and her story.

But it was Christmas, and my home would be waiting for me whether I got there in ten minutes or twenty, so I asked, ''Marilyn got a little what? High?''

''Yeah, she— No, she—'' Dolores paused, took a breath,

relaxed her face. "It was just, you know, we—" Now she made scooping motions with her right hand, trying to jump-start what I was beginning to think was her imagination. "Uh, anyways, me and Jamal, we had to...we went..."

The scooping motions again. "Thing is, I got something to do. I have to—"

She's making it up on the spot, I realized. I was in my last semester of social-work school, and was learning how to listen to undercurrents. When it sounds like you're not getting a straight story, there's no point trying to latch on to details; it's better to cut to motivation.

"Why are you telling me this?" I asked.

I suppose Dolores was relieved not to have to go on inventing, and the request spilled out. "I just thought, you already got a kid, maybe you could take Jamal? And I need twenty bucks, you could help me with that, right?" Dolores practically jitterbugged around me on the sidewalk. "Jamal could, you know, play with your kid. Where I gotta go, I can't bring no baby."

Which brought me back to reality with a snap. "Where's Jamal right now?"

The tone of my voice slowed her down. "Hey, man, he's okay. I just left him for a minute so I could...so I could..."

We were back to scooping for words again.

"You left him *where?*" My radar was on, and she knew it.

"I'll go get him, okay? You wait for me, yeah? I'll be right back."

This time it was me who grabbed her arm. "I'll go with you."

"No, uh-uh, no way, no way!"

What I saw on her face was panic.

"Then tell me where he is, Dolores. I'll get him for you."

"No." She stood completely still and met my eyes for the first time in the whole strange encounter.

Not on some drug, but in need of one, I thought. Keep it

normal, Anita. The important thing is the baby, to make sure the baby's safe.

"Okay." I backed down, but not off. "I'm going to the newsstand, then I'll stop at the cash machine and get the money."

"Could you make it forty?"

I hadn't gone higher because I had a feeling Dolores would do it for me.

"Okay, fine. Meet me in front of Mama Joy's?"

"Ten minutes, I be there in ten minutes." She headed south on Broadway.

I started after her. "With Jamal."

Dolores turned and stopped me with a pointing finger. "Don't you be following me!"

So I watched the long blue coat glide along the sidewalk like an erect caterpillar. She looked back once and gave me the admonishing finger again. She threaded her way through a cluster of people outside Tom's, and I lost sight of the blue cocoon.

THREE

I BOUGHT MY PAPER from Mrs. Roshan, then made a quick stop at the ATM. I was willing to part with the money, but no way did I want an edgy and unpredictable street person to watch me withdraw it. I could hear Benno's response to the expense: "So, you agreed to baby-sit for this woman for a few hours, and *you're* paying *her* for the privilege? Nice work if you can get it."

In Mama Joy's, I fretted at how long it took to slice the lox. The whole time I was picking out bagels, I worried that Dolores wouldn't show, that forty bucks wasn't enough of a reason to come back.

But it was.

The blue coat was waiting for me, jiggling a bundle up and down in its arms. I said a quick Hail Mary of thanks.

Madonna and child they weren't. All the beauty in Dolores's face had tightened into worry, need and—fear, I thought, in the moment our eyes met before I looked down at the baby. Practically smothered in a none-too-clean wool blanket, he was neither crying nor asleep. All I could see was his face, poking out from a grown-up's black knit cap. His expression was apprehensive, as if he were braced for the next bounce.

"You got the money? You got it?"

I nodded and held out my arms for the baby.

Dolores got stubborn and held on.

First I tried to hand her the grocery receipt I'd scrawled

my address and phone number on. "Here, you'd better take this, so you know where to come get him."

Dolores didn't want it. "That's okay, all's I need is the money. I got to be going now."

That was the moment hope was born. She was trading her nephew for forty bucks, and she didn't want to know where to get him back?

"Here, just take it."

This time she shoved the receipt into her coat pocket.

I tried again to take the baby.

Dolores kept bouncing him up and down, just out of my reach. Jamal's set face looked as though he were putting all he had into riding out the turbulence.

I believe babies have their own instinct for what's important; it's a survival skill they're born with. Here Jamal was, being schlepped around and passed from stranger to stranger, but he made not a peep.

Dolores held out her hand.

I was reluctant to part with the cash until I'd gotten as much information from her as I could.

"Who's going to pick him up, you or Marilyn?"

"I don't know, man. I got to go *now*."

"Okay, when will you be back?"

"Sooner I get going, the sooner I be back."

Not good enough. "Where will you be? Is there some way I can get hold of Marilyn?"

That got me a moment's focus. "You just— Listen, Jamal's a good baby, he be okay with you for a while."

"A while? How long do you need me to keep him?" What was I getting into?

"Just, just, just… Why you hanging me up? You got the money or not?" Dolores thrust Jamal at me like she couldn't wait to get rid of him.

"Okay, okay." I gave her the cash, and Jamal was mine.

The money disappeared somewhere under the coat, and Dolores was off without so much as a goodbye to the baby.

I called after her. "Hey! What's his last name?"

If she heard me, Dolores didn't look back.

FOUR

JAMAL HAD TURNED OUT to be a delightful child once I got him fed, bathed and dressed in clean clothes. I'd held on to Clea's baby things, so finding a yellow T-shirt and corduroy overalls in the right size was no problem. Seeing the little boy in my daughter's hand-me-downs brought home the feeling that Jamal belonged with us, that he was meant to join our family.

I sat him on the floor, where he immediately rolled onto his knees and crawled full speed for the pile of presents spread under the Christmas tree. I scrambled to clear a path. It wasn't the wrapped packages Jamal was interested in, but the tree itself.

We had it set up on Clea's wooden toy box, out of range of tumbling children. It was a fairly small tree, four feet, wrapped in red chile lights my mother had given me years ago, with a smattering of my grandmother's old glass balls, and the start of my own collection of black angel ornaments. Jamal was fascinated. He pulled himself up on the edge of the wooden chest and batted at the low-risk ornaments I'd hung on the bottom branches. It kept him busy, and us amused, while I told Benno the story of how I'd gotten him.

I had to repeat myself twice before Benno could fully grasp the fact that I'd given a stranger forty dollars in exchange for a baby, and agreed to keep him until some unspecified person came to pick him up at some unspecified time.

"What were you thinking?" Benno said.

I opened my mouth to answer.

"No, don't bother. Forget I even asked." Benno shook his head. "I know exactly how your mind works, Anita."

Clea surprised me by treating Jamal as if I'd gotten him just for her, a live variant on her annual Christmas doll baby. This year it was a fully vocal Baby-Talks, which Benno had bought in defiance of my rule about no toys that required batteries.

The doll could crawl, too. Once around the floor of "Waa-waa-waa" and "I want my blankie" in a high-pitched falsetto, and Benno was ready to shoot the thing. Served him right, I thought.

Jamal's favorite item was the box the doll had come in, especially the plastic window that made a very satisfying crinkly noise when he poked at it.

Clea brought out a jungle's worth of stuffed animals—she preferred tigers to teddy bears—for his amusement. When he got bored with those, she came up with a handful of Benno's old metal Matchbox cars. Once Jamal got a car in each fist, he wouldn't let go.

Benno played Bach concertos on the stereo, and Clea danced around Jamal like a little elf in the tie-dyed leggings and T-shirt my mother had sent from California. Nothing like a hippie grandmother to hit the right note. According to my mother, pastels are for wimps. Dressing Clea in bright colors is one of the few of her child-rearing tenets that I subscribe to.

IT HAD BEEN A LOVELY DAY. We were, as usual, invited to dinner by our elderly neighbors, Catherine and Elizabeth Wilcox. I made a point of going over early to help with setting the table.

Their apartment shares a wall with ours, but other than that, it's a different world. All done in shades of lavender, decorated by dozens of framed, autographed photos of black entertainers Catherine had sung and danced with back in the day, and dominated by a large birdcage that's home to three resident parakeets. Ten years ago, it was still Charlie, Bird and Parker. Blue, green and green, respectively.

I'm on the short side myself, only five-two in stocking feet, but the diminutive sisters make me feel tall and powerful. Elizabeth was dressed for the occasion in a forest-green knit dress with a pleated skirt, and her gray hair neatly braided. Catherine was in her usual color, royal purple, a pantsuit with gold buttons under a bib apron with a poinsettia print.

The children displayed exemplary table manners, to my surprise. The sweet potatoes with melted marshmallow topping were always a hit with Clea. Jamal was totally content with sucking the knobby end of a leg bone and being fed the occasional bite of mashed potato or turkey.

Once we got home, though, things fell apart. First Clea didn't want to share her room, but having Jamal sleep in ours was worse, so she had to give in. Then she didn't want him to use her Portacrib, and we had to insist. Once it was set up at the foot of her big-girl bed, she put up a fuss about going to sleep first. I was trying to delay Jamal's last bottle as long as he'd allow, in the hope that he'd make it through the night.

It was after ten before Benno and I had a moment to ourselves.

THE GLANCE WE EXCHANGED, once the door was closed on the sleeping children, sent Benno to the Metaxa bottle. Pouring two brandies was his only acknowledgment of the pleading I'm sure was in my eyes. We sat on the couch, sipping in silence. It was a rare moment when neither of us wanted to talk.

Or more accurately, when there were so many things we didn't want to talk about.

It was an anxious time for us. Clea was still very much a foster child, with the attempt to terminate the rights of her biological parents stuck in the mire of family court. I wanted another baby; Benno wasn't willing to take the risk until Clea was legally ours.

"You know we can't keep him." Benno broke the silence by saying exactly what I'd known he would. I had no interest in going down that path.

"Marilyn or Dolores will probably ring the buzzer for him at two in the morning," I said in an attempt to end the subject.

"And if they don't?" Benno kept on. "You don't even know who Jamal really belongs to. That woman could've made the whole thing up because she needed money."

It was easy enough to poke my finger through the holes in that argument. "Then where did Dolores get him? And why did she drag Marilyn into it? It's too elaborate a story not to be true. Besides, if she was outright selling a baby, why would she let him go for a lousy forty bucks? I'd've been just as willing to max out the ATM and give her five hundred."

"If no one shows up for Jamal tomorrow, you have to call the agency and hand him over," the voice of reason insisted.

"I can't," I said. Since Christmas had fallen on a Sunday, our agency, Catholic Children's Charities, would be closed on Monday. "They're not open tomorrow."

"Well, you can call the city then. Child Welfare's always open, right?" Benno got stubborn.

"Yes, but I'm not calling them. Dolores trusted me, and I owe her at least another day."

"Who do you think you are, Mother Hale? 'Bring me your babies to take care of while you run around doing drugs, and I promise, whenever you want them back you can have them'?"

"Just let me ask around the neighborhood tomorrow and see if I can find Marilyn. Maybe she and Dolores missed connections, and she doesn't even know where Jamal is." I thought about what I could place on the altar of marital compromise. "If he's still with us on Tuesday, then I'll call Catholic Children's."

"Two days is too long, Anita. You're already way too attached." Benno shook his head, predicting doom as usual.

It was too late to do anything about that.

My conscience refused to yield to the sleep that claimed Benno so quickly once Jamal's fate was settled for the day. For the moment, my desire to keep the baby had won out over the need to be straight with my husband. I hadn't shown the stains on the back of Jamal's fleece pajamas to Benno, and they nagged at me.

It's only a spray of reddish-brown drops, I told myself. Someone spilled a cup of black coffee, that's all, and it splashed onto Jamal's clothing. You have no cause to think it's dried blood.

Except that in one of Dolores's rearrangements of her too-big down coat, I'd caught a glimpse of the same dark drops splattered across her gray sweatshirt.

FIVE

I GUESS OLD PATTERNS die hard; I swear I was awake, alert and out of bed at 3:14 a.m., before Jamal took breath for his second wail. Just as midnight feedings were mine, Benno had early-morning duties. I slept right through whatever noise Clea and Jamal made before Benno got them breakfasted and headed out for the *Times*.

No, what woke me up was Clea plopping a stinky Jamal on the pillow next to my head.

"Get up, Mama!" She rocked my shoulder. "Daddy's not here and this darn baby made a poop."

I sat up and the merciful aroma of coffee overrode the smell of a full diaper.

"How long do we have to keep him?" Clea wanted to know.

I shifted Jamal's bottom away from my face and eyed my lovely daughter. Her recently braided cornrows sported red-and-green beads on their ends; her face wore an unlovely scowl. Sibling rivalry rearing its head; all was as it should be.

"Come here, Bops." I scooped her up into my lap, so I had my arms around her and the baby both. "Jamal isn't as lucky as you, to live with two parents who love him. He's going to stay with us until his mother is ready to take him back."

That qualifier had to be the hardest thing that's ever come out of my mouth. Technically, that was the same condition under which we had Clea, but no way on this round Earth was I going to ever give her back—back! We're the only parents she's ever known; there's no *back* about it.

"Now let's get him cleaned up." I bumped her out of my lap. "What happened to Baby-Whines-a-Lot? Doesn't she need diaper change, too?"

"Mama," Clea objected, "it's Baby-*Talks*."

It's lovely when Christmas falls on a Sunday. A perfect weekend—party on Saturday night, the holiday on a day that feels like one anyway, then the working world takes a day off to laze around the house and recover from it all. Not so my husband. When you're self-employed, there are no paid days off. Even if there were, he'd still have been drawn to work.

Benno's cabinet shop was still down near Canal Street then, an easy half hour on the subway. He liked to go in for part of a day, feed the cat, noodle around with whatever he was working on.

Benno's concession to the holiday was having a second cup of coffee and reading the paper at home. Under ordinary circumstances, neither Clea nor I would have gotten out of our nightgowns all day. But I had a plan.

Clea could go to the shop with Benno; I'd make the rounds of the neighborhood with Jamal and try to find Marilyn or Dolores. Sounded good to me, but neither my husband nor my daughter was happy about it.

I treated them to a little lecture on what another member of the family meant in terms of everyone having increased responsibilities. Most of it went right over Clea's head. Not so with Benno.

"Look, Anita, I said until Tuesday. That doesn't mean I'm going to—"

"Okay, I'll take Clea with me. It'll be an adventure." That got him thinking about me schlepping around the soup kitchens and homeless shelters with a pair of toddlers in tow, and Benno caved.

"All right, all right. Just today, though. I've got work to do."

Jamal was busy pulling himself along the edge of the sofa, practicing how to walk. I felt the dangerous surge of a mother's pride at his persistence. "He's not yours yet, Anita," I whispered.

Clea complained about getting dressed, so I let her stay in the tie-dye outfit. Why not? In exchange for the privilege, she played mama and dressed Jamal in the same overalls with a red T-shirt this time.

It was almost eleven by the time we got out of the house. The Christmas mist had lingered, a damp gray with temperatures stuck in the high forties. Arthritis weather, my mother called it. The kind of weather that swelled fingers and made knees ache.

I headed for Broadway Presbyterian, intending to talk to whoever was waiting for the soup kitchen to open. Marilyn was known there, so it was my best shot at narrowing down what building she might be renting a room in. There were already half a dozen people in line when we got to 114th Street. No one I recognized; these early birds had probably come down from the shelter at the Armory, up on 168th.

I had Jamal in Clea's stroller, and he was fussing at the confinement. I pushed him into the Tamarind Seed and bought a box of graham crackers to pacify him.

When we got back outside, the line had doubled. Still no one I knew, but one of them knew me.

A man about my age, late thirties, in an army fatigue jacket and a black-and-yellow Steelers cap.

"Hey, Missus, you got another one of those babies now?"

Not your usual pair, white woman with black child.

"I'm just baby-sitting for this one," I explained.

"That why you take these kids?" he asked. "You get paid for it?"

"No, I'm doing a favor for a friend. Maybe you know

her—Marilyn? She eats lunch here sometimes, wears a big blue down coat?''

Steelers cap shook his head. The man two ahead of him turned. White guy, sixties, uncombed hair and at least three layers of winter coats.

''She's not here today.''

Tell me something I don't already know.

''No, she isn't,'' I agreed politely. ''She has a room in the neighborhood, though, doesn't she?''

''I don't believe Marilyn was here for Christmas dinner, either.'' Overcoats poked the woman in front of him. ''Excuse me, Sharon, this lady is looking for Marilyn. Do you know where she's been keeping herself lately?''

When the woman, hunched in an oversize plaid men's jacket, turned, I realized I knew her as one of the regulars on my blocks. She was a petite blonde, her hair pulled back in a ponytail, no hat, her ears and nose red from the cold.

''I got nothing to do with Marilyn no more. She has a room in one a them buildings by the cathedral, so she's too good to talk to me. That her kid you got?'' A nod at the stroller.

''His name is Jamal.'' At least here was someone who knew Marilyn well enough to know she had a child. I gestured with my head for her to follow me, and pushed the stroller a few feet away from the line.

''Hold my place, Howard,'' Sharon told Overcoats, and came after me.

''Can you tell me which building she's in? What street it's on?''

Sharon narrowed her eyes. ''What's it worth to ya?''

I shifted my purse around to the front. I hadn't expected to get anywhere for free, but I wasn't about to bargain with her in view of the whole line, or I'd be bankrupt. As it was, I knew Howard of the good diction and the many overcoats was due a buck or two. I offered Sharon a five.

She narrowed her eyes at me, debating how much higher

I'd go. I stared right back at her, letting her know that this was it until I'd heard her information. The cash in hand won.

"Over on 112th, there's some buildings that rent rooms by the week. I seen her go up the block between here and Amsterdam. I don't know which exact one she's in."

It wasn't much, but at least it narrowed down the lobbies I'd have to visit. "Do you know Marilyn's last name? Or anything about Jamal? Like where he lives?"

That stumped Sharon.

"What about her sister, Dolores? Do you know her?"

"Nah, I don't know nothing about her sister. Oh, yeah, wait a minute. I think Marilyn might have someone over on Staten Island. She used to take the ferry over there when she was pregnant, but I don't know who she stayed with. We didn't get too personal." Sharon looked down at Jamal. She rubbed at her belly, an unconscious gesture. I watched her eyes go out of focus. "I got a little boy, too."

I could've asked about her child, his name, how old he was. I could've asked where he was, who took care of him. I didn't. Everyone outside the church had a story, and every one of them would break my heart.

If Sharon had wanted to share, she wouldn't have needed prompting. Her tragedy wasn't my business, and neither of us wanted it to be. I did what I could in that moment.

"Thank you," I said gently. I slipped the folded bill into her hand, and held it for a moment. Her fingers were as red and cold as her face. "If you hear anything else, will you let me know?"

"How'm I supposed to do that?" Sharon snapped back into the present, all her defenses intact.

"You come every day for lunch?" This woman I was not going to give my address to. "I'll be around again tomorrow, the same time."

The program director, an intense man in his forties with a gray goatee, appeared at the door. The line surged forward, and Sharon had to elbow her way back in front of Howard.

I tapped him on the arm and tried to be unobtrusive about handing him a dollar bill.

Steelers cap had sharp eyes, though. "Hey, Missus, how come you didn't say you was offering a reward for information? I could tell you—"

"Ah, stuff it, Half-Back," someone called out from the line. "You know you ain't no more than half-baked!"

"Full of beans, that's him." Another voice.

"Fuller Brush, more like!"

I looked at their faces, mostly shades of brown, mostly male, mostly middle-aged and older, bundled in a miscellany of ill-fitting winter coats and dark hats. It was a crowd that spoke with the same voice, making jokes to pass the time.

"Y'all leave me alone," Steelers cap defended himself. "I'm talking to the lady."

That got another round of commentary, this time aimed at moving the line forward. I wheeled the stroller and walked with Steelers cap. "I thought you didn't know Marilyn."

He shuffled along with the line. "I know I saw a woman in a puffy blue coat like you said up on 125th yesterday. Flashing her some cash to score."

"Where exactly did you see her?"

"Front of Charley's Southern. I axed her for a dollar to get me a biscuit, but she passed on by like she was haunted."

"Do you know who she bought from?"

"Now why I know that?" He glared at me. "Can't do no drugs and eat here!"

We were almost at the steps. "I'll be by again tomorrow. If you see her, will you tell her that?" I pressed a pair of singles into his hand before I backed off with the stroller.

Jamal had covered the front of Clea's too-small red snowsuit with crumbs and was fussing for more. I got a sippy cup of apple juice thinned with water out of the diaper bag and tried that. He slurped it down while the last of the line vanished into the church.

"Hey!" I called out to the director of the lunch program.

He gave me a minute, although he didn't know any more than Howard Overcoats did. Marilyn hadn't been by for lunch in more than a week. A not unusual occurrence, for her or any one of his clientele. People came and went, and no, he had no idea where she might have found a room or how she might have paid for it. If I didn't mind, he was busy?

I could see that.

I considered my options. There weren't many. Staten Island. Dolores had mentioned it, too, but even the least-populated of New York's five boroughs was too big a place to go looking for a man with no name. It was 11:30. Canvassing the SROs on 112th Street seemed like the best I could do.

The buildings I'd be going into weren't the kind that had doormen who knew all the tenants, as well as their relatives and regular visitors. No, the Single Room Occupancy hotels would have managers, and cash would also be required to pry information out of them.

Jamal kicked his legs up and down in the stroller. Now that he'd had crackers and juice, I was getting a "Let's go, what's next?" vibe from him. My kind of kid, ready for anything.

"All right, short stuff," I told him. "Let's see if we can find your mom."

SIX

HALFWAY UP THE BLOCK from Tom's Restaurant on the corner of 112th, I caught sight of the blue down coat. Whichever sister was wearing it had just come out of a building on the south side of the street, at the far end. It was a long diagonal from where we were. I started running, stroller and all. The coat was headed for Amsterdam.

"Dolores!" I yelled. "Yo, Dolores!"

She made a right, and I lost visual contact.

As we got to Amsterdam, a northbound M11 barreled up to the stop on 111th. Sure enough, there was the blue coat, crossing the street to get on. I was closing in, a short block away, but hampered by the stroller.

"Dolores!" I waved at the bus from the wrong side of the street. "Hold the bus!"

Did the driver pause long enough for me to catch it? Hey, this is New York. Buses score extra points by pulling away from the curb just ahead of women pushing baby carriages. There was a green light at 112th; the driver actually nodded to me as he blew past. I swore.

Yeah, if I were independently wealthy, I would've grabbed a cab and followed the damn bus.

But I was an out-of-breath, thirty-something social work student with a frightened toddler whose chubby hands were clenched around the bar across the front of his chariot. A woman easily fifty years my senior, pushing a wire shopping cart along at a philosophical pace, had observed the whole thing. She had a poinsettia in the cart, swathed in white, waxy paper to protect it from the cold.

"That's okay, honey, another one will be along soon," she said.

"Just like men, right?" It was the perfect straight line, but she didn't get the joke.

"Who said anything about them?" the woman snapped. She'd been being kind, and I'd offended her.

"It's okay, I wasn't going anywhere." Buses were no more the object than men.

"You were trying to catch your friend?"

Sharp eyes, these old people we too easily ignore. My new acquaintance was a trim woman in a navy-blue, belted coat with a matching felt hat that had a sprig of plastic holly with two red berries tucked into the band.

"You don't know her, do you?" It didn't hurt to ask.

"The coat I know, but not this one wearing it." She shook her head. "My neighbor donated that coat to the church. She'll be so pleased to know that someone is getting use out of it."

"So you've never seen her before." I was unreasonably disappointed.

"Are you not listening to me? Alice left the coat at the homeless shelter in the Cathedral of Saint John the Divine." The natty woman took a step backward, as if her second opinion of me had been confirmed and I might after all be a bit nuts myself. She raised a gloved hand and pointed. "Here comes your bus now."

Sure enough, another M11 lumbered through a yellow light and right on past the empty stop.

"You'd better get a move on, young woman. You'll never catch a bus if you're not standing at the stop." With that, she was done with me. I watched her push her cart up the walkway to Amsterdam House. I wondered if Alice was the friend she was visiting in the nursing home.

Jamal had let go of the bar across the front of the stroller and popped a thumb into his mouth. Poor guy, so young and already so stoical, I thought. Any other child would have been wailing blue murder, but in a life too full of inexplicable events, chariot races were just one more thing to be endured.

I went into the Hungarian Pastry Shop for a cappuccino to settle my nerves. Even though the place was practically empty, I got my coffee to go. Jamal wasn't looking like the kind of companion who'd be content to cool his heels in the stroller if we weren't moving. I dipped into my purse for one of the toys I'd brought to keep the little boy occupied if he got bored. It was a soft rubber mouse that squeaked when it was squeezed, perfect for getting on my nerves.

Two steps out the door, a man shook a paper cup of coins at me. "I'm soliciting contributions for the United Negro Pizza Fund," he said. "Make your donations right here."

I dropped in my thirty-five cents change. Homeless people are like buses—you miss one, another will be along soon, I thought. It wasn't funny.

Nor was it true that every street person is connected to every other one, but I asked him anyway. "Do you know anyone named Marilyn? Or Dolores? Wears a big blue down coat?"

"No, we don't have any Marilyns or Doloreses registered at this campus." And he was back to rattling the coins in his cup at the next person to walk out of the pastry shop.

SEVEN

BACK ON 112th Street, I had two choices for the building Dolores had come out of, The George or The Martha.

Both buildings had their names carved on their pediments and conical evergreen trees in stone tubs flanking their doors. All resemblance ended there. The George's trees were encircled by tiny white lights. Its door sported a wreath with a red bow and a cluster of pine cones. Through the immaculate glass, I could see gold-flocked wallpaper and a table with a uniformed man sitting behind it. The Martha's trees were tipped in brown, their only decoration a handful of empty Smirnoff minis in the dirt of their pots. Inner and outer doors were wide-open.

It was a no-brainer as to which one was more likely to have welcomed Marilyn as a tenant.

From the moment I stepped into The Martha's lobby, I was sorry I'd brought Jamal with me. It was a grimy place, mustard walls darkened by decades of cigarette smoke and sweat, the tile floor chipped and gray. The high front of what had once been a concierge's desk was now a barricade of wood-grained Formica that supported an open register book and a wilted poinsettia. There was a pathetic swag of tinsel thumb-tacked across its front.

On the desk was a transistor radio tuned to a station playing Spanish Christmas carols, and an antique rotary phone next to a metal spike with a mishmash of papers impaled on it. The back wall was a warren of wooden cubbies with metal numbers tacked to their edges. Most of the pigeonholes were empty, but here and there the regular pattern of dark squares was interrupted by the white diagonal of unclaimed mail.

And where was the doorman to announce visitors and ensure that they signed the guest register? To accept deliveries of dry cleaning and UPS packages?

Yeah, right. The occupants of The Martha weren't exactly the dry-cleaning types. A wrinkled woman with smeary lipstick stepped out of the elevator, followed by a gentleman in a double-breasted overcoat with wide lapels. Neither of them spared me a glance.

Since no one was around to stop me, I flipped through the register, looking for Dolores's name, or any sign that Marilyn might live here.

Nothing.

"Hey, what are you doing there?" A Hispanic woman well on her way past fifty, in a dark red dress with a rhinestone Christmas-tree pin on her well-braced bosom, emerged from a door off an alcove in the back. "You not suppose to touch that."

"Oh, good morning." I did my impersonation of an inoffensive, chipper visitor.

"This here is private property." She scowled at me and leaned forward over the register. Her forearms rested on the open pages in such a way as to block what was written there from my view. Evidently she was one of those people who are unimpressed by a show of innocence.

"I'm sorry." I toned it down. "I'm supposed to be meeting my friend Marilyn, but I don't remember which room she's in. I just saw her sister, Dolores, outside, but I forgot to ask her for the number."

I waited for the woman to either tell me to get lost or give me the information I'd asked for. Jamal, silent except for contributing a squawk from the mouse, kept out of it.

"You don't look like somebody Marilyn knows." There was suspicion in the statement but I thought maybe her expression had softened a bit.

"Does she have a lot of visitors?"

The woman laughed. I seemed to have hit on an icebreaker. "No, Marilyn is not one of the more active ones. She's a good girl. Is that her little one you have there?"

"Yes, this is Jamal." Okay, there was my entree to Marilyn's room. "I'm, actually, I'm baby-sitting for her."

"Baby-sitting?" The woman raised her eyebrows. "You from Child Welfare?"

Stereotypes. But I will say it myself, I look like a social worker. And the pair of us—middle-class white woman with a black baby in a stroller—what are the odds that I'm the nanny?

"No, I really am a friend. I've had Jamal since yesterday. I thought Marilyn would come get him last night but she didn't, so…"

"Marilyn left the baby with you since yesterday?" This surprised her. "She only has him for a few days. I don't understand how come she is leaving him with somebody else."

I didn't, either, but Marilyn had. "Actually, it was Dolores who asked me to look after Jamal. Have you seen either of them today?"

"No, I don't think Marilyn went out since she brought the *niño* on Saturday. Her sister been hanging around. I think she was helping out, back and forth with Marilyn's coat on, but I got a bad feeling from that one. I saw her yesterday morning, in a big hurry when she came in, then she left right away again with something hidden under that coat. She didn't look too good. You said you saw her outside just now?"

"She took the bus uptown, and I couldn't catch her."

"Huh. Now you got me wondering what's up with those two." The woman looked as concerned as I felt.

"If you tell me what room she's in, I'll go up and check on her," I offered.

"Yes, I think you better do that." It must have been my honest face; I didn't even have to ask for what I thought I'd need. She scanned the cubbyholes until she found the right one. "Here, I have an extra key to Marilyn's room, in case she doesn't answer. Six-G."

But suddenly I didn't want Jamal with me when I went upstairs. Based on the holiday touches on her person and her work station, I took a flyer that the woman had a streak of sentimentality that could be mined for sympathy. "Would you mind watching Jamal for a few minutes?"

She looked around the lobby like someone might catch her slacking off, then shrugged. "Sure, he could stay with me."

It was cold in the lobby, but I bent to loosen the neck of Jamal's snowsuit. Mostly I wanted the excuse to whisper a reassurance into his ear. I was well aware of how ironic it was that I in my turn was trusting him to the care of a stranger, with the promise that it would be only a short time.

The woman, who seemed not to notice the chilly wind from the open doors, bent next to me. "You going to stay with Cruz, little man? Maybe you would like to walk around some."

The idea of Jamal crawling around on that floor… "He's not walking yet," I told her.

That didn't stop Cruz. She unbuckled the seat belt and lifted Jamal out of the stroller.

"No? Such a big boy, not walking yet?" she crooned. "Then you can sit on my lap and we will sing songs together."

I left her bouncing the baby on her knees and pushed for the elevator.

I made the sign of the cross as I stepped into it, for protection. The cab was ancient, with enameled metal walls covered in chipping maroon paint, and buttons that tended to stick when you pressed them. It shuddered and wobbled its way up to the sixth floor.

In the hallway, the bulbs in four of the six light fixtures were dead. There was enough light from the window in the stairwell at the back of the building so that I could locate the

G apartment, last on the left. I banged on the door. Judging from the dents, I wasn't the first person in its long history to have done so.

Nor was I likely to be the first to get no response. I did another round of knocking, this time with the key held between the knuckles of my gloved hand for the louder sound of metal on metal. Still no answer, so I used the key for its intended purpose.

The door opened to the right, letting me into a kind of aqueous gloom. A piece of fringed fabric hung over the window, a bedspread or something, that let light leak in around the edges. The material was green, which explained the underwater tint to the air.

A metal bed frame with a rumpled spread was pushed against the left wall. There was an alcove between the bed and the door, with a sink behind a curtain of blue plastic beads. At the head of the bed, a tall dresser, and next to it, a portable playpen with a thin plastic mattress and no sheet. A bright-red Tonka dump truck was its only occupant.

I took in the details as though I were examining a photograph. The way the room as a whole had a disturbed quality to it; nothing seemed quite right. The bed looked sat on rather than slept in. The bureau drawers were closed, but none of them were pushed in all the way. A chair lay on its side. There were a couple of envelopes on the floor, one that looked like a bill, and maybe a Christmas card.

A wooden table stood in the center of the room. What I assumed to be Marilyn's purse, a brown leather sack with a drawstring top, had been dumped out on it. Hairbrush, some makeup stuff, a pack of cigarettes. Also on the table was a pint of Bacardi rum, empty, and three plastic cups. Marilyn and Dolores, partying? And someone else.

At that point, I finally thought to look for a light switch. Sure enough, right beside the door. I flipped it on. The first thing I noticed was a pale yellow diaper bag on the foot of the bed. I let out the breath I hadn't realized I was holding, relieved to have found something that might provide more information about Jamal. I took a step into the room, my hand still on the doorknob, meaning to collect the bag.

That's when I saw the blood.

IT'S THE SAME IMAGE that makes its way into my annual dream, a spray of drops across the wall to the right of the window. The dream, however, jump-cuts me out of the room and onto Broadway. In reality, I was rooted to the spot.

Below the bloodstain was the body of a woman, knees folded under her, bent backward with her head on the floor. Marilyn. There were short slashing wounds on her arms, a larger slash across her chest. I could see the edges of red muscle, framed by the bloodstained fabric of her dress.

No, it was a nightgown. With pink flowers, and the brand-name in flowing script—Lanz of Salzburg. I had a nightgown just like it, except the lace-trimmed yoke on mine was not stained dark as wine.

EIGHT

I STEPPED BACKWARD, out of the room. The door swung closed. I kept backing up until I hit the opposite wall of the corridor and abruptly sat down.

Sank down would be more like it. My knees simply gave out, and I was on the floor.

That was my first experience with finding a dead body.

Back then, I had no inkling that it would be far from the last. As a social worker, what I've learned since is that although you can cope with the sight of death, you never get over how it makes you feel inside. And if someone in my occupation does find herself unaffected, it's time to look for another line of work. Like maybe the fine art of hostile take-overs.

At that moment I knew just enough to identify what was happening to me physiologically: shock. Once I had the word, I remembered how to deal with the symptoms. Breathe. Deep, regular breaths. Elevate the feet. I wasn't dizzy but I figured I should lie down and get the blood flowing back to my head.

I looked at the floor with its unidentifiable sticky spots and abandoned that idea.

I closed my eyes instead, which helped. What I saw was merciful darkness, not the horror of the room. As soon as my oxygenated brain turned over and caught, however, I was back to reality.

I had the diaper bag in my lap, although I had no memory of having snagged its long strap and taking it out to the hall. That's what shock will do for you.

Trauma-induced Alzheimer's, my inner wiseass cracked.

Smarts, I told it. Got me the one essential item in the room.

It was an ordinary pastel plastic diaper bag. I unzipped it. Half a dozen disposable diapers, two jars of baby food, a change of clothes, and— Yes! Written in black waterproof ink, Jamal Walker, with a Staten Island address and phone number.

I had Jamal's last name, and information about where he lived. I should have been glad, but all I felt was the lurch of potential loss. Jamal belonged somewhere, and now I'd have to bring him back.

I started to stand, but my head didn't like the air at that altitude. My legs weren't too happy about the situation either, so I slid back down the wall.

Best to make sure you know what you're doing, Anita, before you go rushing off. Think things through. I figured I might just stay right there on the floor until I came up with something. The hallway was quiet around me, the kind of silence I've come to associate with the presence of death. The absence of life is a palpable thing; it leaves the air around it muted, still.

In contrast to my stunned limbs, my thought processes seemed to be working on overdrive.

Okay, the first thing is, call the cops.

Then the second thing will be the cops turning Jamal over to Child Welfare.

No, they wouldn't, because I wasn't about to let that happen.

My inner Benno had a field day with me, arguing that it was the job of the police not only to handle Marilyn's death and find her killer, but also to take charge of Jamal and locate his relatives.

Not as long as he's in my custody, I told Benno. Not when I've just found a phone number and an address for where he lives.

So you're going to leave poor Marilyn lying in her own blood while you gallivant around Staten Island, Anita?

I don't think so. That was my conscience weighing in.

Conscience, nothing. What I needed to do was find out whether or not Jamal belonged to anyone who was going to fight to keep him. Because the thought that knocked on the back door of my brain was that, with Jamal's mother dead, one obstacle to me becoming his foster mother had been removed.

I know, it was a terrible thing to think. Part of me was aware that I'd ventured into irrational territory.

Not that it stopped me. Maybe I was under the influence of some kind of chemical rush—adrenaline, endorphins, whatever—because I felt I was thinking quite clearly as I came up with the beginnings of a plan. It seemed workable at the time.

In fact, I still think it had its merits.

My first concern was to keep Jamal out of the system, which meant I couldn't report Marilyn's death myself. Okay, I hadn't touched or disturbed anything in the room. With my gloves still on, I wouldn't have left so much as a print on the doorknob.

Really, I couldn't tell the cops any more than anyone else could. If Cruz downstairs was willing to report the death—so far, she'd at least been an ally—then I'd be free to track down Jamal's people. He was my responsibility. I'd told his aunt I would take care of him, and that's what I was doing. But if there was any chance I could keep him, I damn well intended to.

The cops would want to know why there was a crib in the room, and where its occupant was. I thought about what Cruz could say that would be true but not involve Jamal. She didn't have to mention him by name; she could simply say that Marilyn had a child who occasionally visited her. Nothing in the room dated Jamal's presence.

All right. Cruz would just tell the cops she got suspicious

after seeing Dolores leave in Marilyn's coat, went up to check on her and found what I'd found.

The police had no reason to look for the baby. Even if he'd been in the room, he was too young to talk. Wait a minute. I was thinking so fast, I'd gotten ahead of myself.

Had Jamal been in the room when his mother was killed? His diaper bag certainly was. And those stains on his fleece pajamas—

Jamal could have witnessed his mother's murder.

It seemed likely that Dolores had been there, too.

As witness or perpetrator?

Three glasses on the table, Anita. For the sake of my sanity, I had to assume that Dolores hadn't done it, because if she had... No, she couldn't have. Dolores took care of Jamal, brought him to safety.

Not immediately, though; she hadn't had him with her on the street when I first ran into her.

So where *had* he been? Did Dolores leave him with someone else? Had she left him alone in the room with his mother's dead body while she came out and tried to score?

A flash of anger displaced whatever qualms I might have had. One thing I knew: no way was I going to give Jamal back to Dolores. Even if his aunt wanted to take him, her behavior was so irresponsible that not even a family court judge would grant her custody.

I pushed myself to standing against the wall. My knees seemed solid enough to hold me. I took the stairs instead of the elevator. I had the urge to move, to get the circulation going so my body could catch up to my brain.

When, why, who—those were questions only Dolores could answer. It was too tangled for me right then. I was an amateur; what did I know?

That I had a baby to protect. That Cruz could tell the cops as much as I could about Dolores and get them looking for her. A crackhead in a light blue down coat. How long would it take the police to pick her up on the street?

Too long, as it turned out.

NINE

CRUZ PROVED to be a practical woman. When I told her Marilyn was dead, she crossed herself and whispered a prayer. Other than that she didn't act shocked or press for details.

"You see a lot of things in this job. The people who live in this building, they all have hard lives. I pray for them every day." Cruz pushed the phone across the desk so I could reach it. "All we can do now is call the police."

I shook my head and explained that I didn't want to report the death because I was concerned about keeping Jamal out of the system, that I wanted to return him to his family myself. Okay, so only half of my motives were unmixed. It was enough for Cruz to be sympathetic.

"My oldest daughter, she was fifteen when she got pregnant. They wanted to put her in a foster home so she could give up the baby to be adopted. I told them, no, she is staying with me, and I will take care of my grandbaby. Then the social workers come to my house. They look into everything and ask me questions, like I'm a bad mother because my daughter is pregnant."

Same old story: the do-gooders think they know best. I lifted Jamal off her lap and settled him in the stroller.

"I told them, why don't you go after the boys?" Cruz kept on. "They are the ones responsible for making the babies. I know. I have seven children, because my husband, he doesn't like to wear a condom. I tell my daughter, you be sure your boyfriend takes precautions. It's very important especially now because of AIDS, but still the men won't do it."

"Did your daughter get to keep her baby?" I asked.

"Oh yes." Cruz lifted a photo in a gold frame from the desk. "She made her first communion just last month."

An angel, swathed in white tulle. I smiled wanly.

Then Cruz offered to call the police herself. "Someone has to tell them about poor Marilyn."

"Cruz, maybe you should go upstairs and peek into the room before you call the police, so they'll believe you found her yourself. If you just open the door, you can see the blood on the wall, but you don't have to…"

"Yes, okay." Bless her motherly heart, she winked at me. "You go on and find my little man's *papi*. I'm not saying anything about him to the police."

FIRST THING I DID was hit the pay phone on Broadway and try the 718 number that was written in the diaper bag. No answer, and no answering machine. I let it ring out the full twenty times until the phone cut me off and ate my quarter.

I knew I should call Benno to let him know I had an address for Jamal, and that Jamal and I were off to Staten Island. In my delusion of mental clarity, however, I believed I had it all figured out, that it was something I could handle on my own.

Besides, knowing Benno, he'd either argue me out of the trip or insist on coming along, and I saw no point in getting my husband agitated. Staten Island is terra incognita to most Manhattanites. True son of his borough, Benno had a deep distrust of the city's most Republican enclave. I told myself I'd be back before Benno and Clea even got home, and I'd tell him then.

Jamal's eyes seemed to be closing. The wind pushed an empty plastic bottle over the curb and into the gutter. I thought about the open deck of the Staten Island Ferry. My apartment beckoned. The ebb of endorphins suggested that a nice nap would be just the thing.

I tossed a nickel up and down in my hand, then flipped it. Heads, head for home. Tails, hightail it for the ferry.

"Looks like it's the ferry for us, kid," I told Jamal. A decision is a decision, and having made it, I found I was looking forward to the prospect of a ferry ride, even on a gray December afternoon. It's always good to get off an island—even if you're just going from one to another. Besides, I hadn't walked away from a crime scene just so I could go home and sleep; I had a good reason for what I was doing.

Because if we didn't find his family, I'd have Jamal for another day. And tomorrow, I could bring him to Catholic Charities and request that he be officially placed with us. I thought I had a shot at getting the system to work for me in this situation. Given the shortage of foster-care beds, the fact that we were licensed, and we'd already had him for two days...

Which could be either in our favor or against us, depending on the intelligence and common sense of the person in charge. It was too late by the time a flicker of worry, about whether withholding the presence of a second child in our household might jeopardize Clea's placement, darted across my mind; we were already on the subway.

Even lying in my warm bed ten years later, the memory prodded me up for a solitary cup of coffee with the Christmas tree. I sat on the couch and watched the sparkle of tinsel in the hot air currents rising from the radiator. This day was going to be as sunny as that long-ago afternoon had turned by the time we got out of the subway at South Ferry.

Jamal had perked up as soon as we got on the train and I changed his diaper. I was perfectly content to jolt along underground, with my arm around the baby while he stood on the seat with a chubby hand pressed against the window. He stared out at the moving darkness, and when the lights of each station came up, I felt him press closer against my side, delighted by the flickering lights of the train in the tunnel. If they'd ever impressed me, it was a long-gone sensation.

With a baby on my lap, I gave the other occupants of the car a more than cursory glance. A mixed group of teenagers at the far end, in jeans baggy or tight depending on gender, all in puffy down jackets, gathered around the dominant bass vibrations of a boom box; people reading newspapers and books, others attached by earphone cords to their own personal soundtracks; a woman engaged in the risky business of plying a mascara wand while the train was in motion, using the window as a mirror; a man in work boots and a green coverall asleep on a two-person seat by the door.

Your usual crowd. New Yorkers; they might have flicked me the same glance I'd given them, but no one had anything to say to anyone else.

In the ferry terminal, Jamal cooed up at the pigeons flying in the huge, vaulted space while I risked another quarter on the phone number from the diaper bag. Still no answer, but this time I got my money back.

The crossing was too cold to be out on the open deck. I unbuckled Jamal from the stroller and offered him the bottle I'd brought along. Here we got a few double takes, white woman bottle-feeding black baby, but I didn't pay any attention. Let them look; I was a mother feeding a child, what business was it of theirs?

I felt the memory of Marilyn's body fade as Jamal suckled. There's nothing like a contented baby on your lap to make everything right with the world.

Did it never occur to me that in trying to find the other side of Jamal's family, I might be heading from the fire to the frying pan? That the third person in the room might have been related to Jamal—father, uncle, brother? Of course it did.

I dismissed that line of thought with a disregard for the passions of human nature that now seems absurdly naive for a woman of my age. I reasoned it like this: if the person who killed Marilyn was the same person who had custody of Jamal, then no matter what state of rage or provocation he'd been in, he wouldn't have left Jamal there. A man might be driven to kill the mother of a child he was caring for, but no way would he abandon the child. *Quod erat demonstrandum.*

Stupid, right? I had to have known at the time how misguided I was, didn't I? Maybe. Somewhere.

I've had a soft spot ever since for those women who are so baby-hungry they "borrow" infants they see left unattended for even a few seconds. What you know rationally is not the same as what you know emotionally. That bonding thing—it has nothing to do with blood. I had Jamal, and I wasn't giving him up without a fight.

I justified what I was doing with the pretense that, as an almost-professional social worker, I would be able to assess whatever family situation I found and make the right call for Jamal's future. Naturally, if Jamal's people met my standards, I'd give him back. It was only if they didn't that I'd be forced to use whatever means I could to see that I kept the baby.

The best-case scenario, from my point of view, would be that whoever had custody of Jamal had released him into his mother's care and taken off for Tierra del Fuego. Abandoned on one side, orphaned on the other. In that fantasy, I played the role of Jamal's guardian angel. It would be a stickier situation, probably entailing a court battle, if a reasonable adult had merely allowed Jamal's drug-using mother to have him for an extended, unsupervised visit over the holiday.

I was so wrong-headed and arrogant, it still makes me blush.

In my defense, let me point out that we'd had Clea as a foster child for four years, three months and some-odd days at that point. It had been clear to everyone for most of that time that her mother would never be able to take care of her, and yet the process dragged on. I'd been living with the fear of unbearable loss for a long time, and I was desperate for certainty.

Maybe it was the salt air, or the Manhattan skyline receding behind us; I was suddenly hungry. When Jamal finished the bottle, I bought myself a hot dog with the works—onions, sauerkraut, mustard—and a cola to wash it down. I shared the bun with Jamal, who appeared to want solid food for dessert.

TEN

WHEN WE GOT TO Staten Island, I tried the phone again, with the predictable lack of result. I made an attempt to locate the address on the big map in the terminal but since I had no idea which neighborhood it might be in, I decided to make life easy on myself and take a cab. Staten Island may be the smallest borough but it's still got the population of Wyoming.

Winter Street turned out to be a five-minute cab ride away, in a neighborhood the driver identified for me as New Brighton. Number 303B was the upper half of a duplex on a street of one- and two-family wood houses in various states of disrepair. It was among the better kept, with a new coat of bright blue paint and crisp white trim.

I knew after the first few minutes of no answer that there would be none, but I kept my finger on the buzzer long enough to wake the dead. What it accomplished was to bring the downstairs tenant to his door.

"Yo, lady, no one's home up there." A teenager with a neck like a linebacker, in a bright orange sweatshirt. "And don't start on my bell, either. We're not interested in talking to any Jehovah's."

Personally, I thought I was a little better-dressed than a Witness, but I supposed in that neighborhood, a neatly dressed white woman—

Then he noticed who was in the stroller.

"Hey, that's Jamal! What're you doing with him?" The young man came out onto the porch "You from Child Welfare?"

"No, I'm a friend of Jamal's mother's. She asked me to baby-sit him." Well, it was close enough to the truth.

"So you're looking for Malcolm?"

"Jamal's father," I said, trying to convince the kid I knew what I was talking about.

"His father?" From his tone, I could see that I hadn't gotten it quite right. He was having a hard enough time digesting the situation as it was. My appearance, friend of Marilyn's, here on the doorstep out of the blue...but he definitely knew who the child in my stroller was.

"You better come on inside," he finally said.

I followed him into the front room. Two gold brocade sofas in plastic slipcovers flanked a fake fireplace opposite the true hearth—a thirty-six-inch television in a mahogany cabinet, its top covered with Christmas cards and china figurines. In front of the window, a heavily tinseled Christmas tree sported little colored lights that flashed in a sequence of different patterns, first each solid color, then a ripple from one end to the other, finally a set of multicolored blink-blink-blinks before it started all over again. Jamal was mesmerized.

Good thing, because I was hoping he wouldn't comprehend any of the adult conversation.

"Hey, Ma! Come out here!" The young man headed for the back of the house. He lowered his voice, but not enough so I didn't hear the rest of it. "There's a white lady looking for Malc, and she's got Jamal with her."

That about summed it up.

I perched on the edge of one of the couches and unbuttoned my coat. It was uncomfortably warm in the room. I loosened Jamal's snowsuit and pushed the hood back off his head. The plastic slipcover crackled every time I moved.

I stood when the young man's mother entered the room, and offered her my hand. "I'm sorry to bother you. My name is Anita Servi." Might as well go for the direct approach. "I was hoping to find Jamal's father."

The woman glanced from my face to my hand. I could see

her considering whether or not to ignore it. Manners won out, and she shook.

"Roxanne Conyers. This is my son, Shawn." She was a few inches taller than my five foot two inches, and twice as wide, but I wouldn't call her fat. A solid woman, in dark-green stretch pants and a red sweatshirt with a Christmas scene, glitter-painted tree with rhinestone ornaments and real bits of ribbon on the little packages, her hair short and straightened. No makeup; gold hoops in her ears; a suspicious expression on her face.

I kept up with the disarming patter and put my foot in it. "It was nice of Shawn to invite us in, but I really don't want to take up your time. I just came to see if Jamal's father was home—"

"Jamal's father?" Ms. Conyers interrupted. "Where did you say you were from?"

"I'm sorry, I'm not from anywhere." Why did I keep apologizing? "I know Marilyn, Jamal's mother, but I've never met his father. Malcolm Walker?"

She ignored the implied question. "You're not from Child Welfare?"

I was beginning to think The Question had mutated into a newer and even less pleasant variant.

"No. Believe me, I'm not. I'm a foster parent myself, and I'm trying to keep Jamal out of the system. I thought he might live here with his father." I tried again.

"I don't mean to be rude, ma'am, but you've got some explaining to do before I tell you anything. What did you say your name was?"

"Anita. Anita Servi."

"Well, Miss Anita Servi, you want some coffee?"

I nodded. Since I seemed to be on the receiving end of the interview, I was going to need a shot of caffeine if I had any hope of getting through it intact.

"Go ahead and get that baby out of his things, then we'll sit down and you can tell me what you're doing with him.

Shawn, bring us some coffee out here, and a plate of those cookies from Mrs. Taylor.''

Shawn did as he was told, and so did I. Jamal, freed from the bulky snowsuit, walked himself along the edge of the table until he got to Ms. Conyers.

"And how are we today, Mr. Walker?" She took one of his pudgy hands and shook it.

Jamal crowed back at her and stamped his feet, pleased at the attention. He seemed to recognize her, too, I thought, to be comfortable in this room. I relaxed a little myself, enough to tell Ms. Conyers an abbreviated but still improbable version of how Dolores had delivered Jamal into my care the day before.

Ms. Conyers looked me over. Something about my tale must have met with her approval. She leaned back with a decisive sigh.

"First thing you should know, Malcolm is Jamal's uncle, not his father. And he's Marilyn's brother, not Dolores's."

"But Dolores said she and Marilyn were sisters—" I tried to parse the genealogy.

Ms. Conyers beat me to it. "Marilyn and Malcolm have the same father, different mothers. That's why they have the same last name. Marilyn and Dolores, same mother, different fathers. So there's no blood between Dolores and Malcolm, and no love either."

"Do they know each other?" I was still trying to sort it out.

"Oh, yeah." Shawn answered that one. "Dolores came by sometimes to see Marilyn. Only in the daytime, though, so Malc wouldn't know. He caught her one time, and he kicked her right out on the street. Malc made Marilyn stay with him when she was pregnant, then after Jamal was born Dolores snuck around and got her started using again—"

"Shawn." His mother stopped him. "You get Jamal his package out from under the tree and take him in your room so he can open it."

"Yes, ma'am." The teenager scooped Jamal under one arm and held him like a football, bent again to grab a box wrapped in paper patterned with bearded black Santas and was gone.

"That boy wears me out." Ms. Conyers picked up her coffee mug and held it without taking a sip.

"He seems very well-behaved to me," I said.

"He's got good company manners," she acknowledged, "but fifteen is still fifteen. You have kids of your own?"

"One. A foster child we're trying to adopt. We've had her since birth, and she's four now." I watched the tree blink yellow, green, blue, red, white. "Did Malcolm adopt Jamal?"

"I told him he should, but he didn't want to take Marilyn to court and get guardianship. In spite of what she did, she was his sister, and he wouldn't go against her like that." Ms. Conyers shook her head at the foolishness of anyone who didn't take her advice.

To me, it was hopeful news. In my mind, I hadn't yet crossed over to launching a custody battle, but if I did, I knew Malc's failure to have himself appointed Jamal's legal guardian could be used against him.

"He's a good man, Malcolm Walker, but he always had lousy taste in women. Rented my upstairs six years, and I never saw him bring home one worth the time of day. He has a good job, too, works for the city over in the maintenance yard. Make a fine husband for the right woman, but some men, they can't resist a stray, not even when their hands get bitten. Malc has a talent for picking women who turn on him. Even his own sister."

I wasn't quite following. Ms. Conyers picked up on my puzzlement.

"Never mind." She waved a hand in the air. "When Marilyn showed up with Jamal in her belly, Malc just naturally took her in. Not her no-count sister, though—Shawn had that right. He put Dolores out on her fanny. Marilyn lasted almost a month after Jamal was born before she up and left."

"Marilyn ran away?"

"Left her baby and took six hundred dollars with her."

It was hard to tell which transgression Ms. Conyers was more shocked by.

"Did she come back to visit?"

"Not one time." She exhaled, more in sadness than indignation, and I knew the money was nothing compared to abandoning her baby. "Not until right before Christmas."

I devoutly wished she would tell me already.

"Friday, Malcolm comes home with Jamal after work, and there's Marilyn on the doorstep, wanting to take Jamal with her for a couple days. She convinced Malc she was clean and she had a place in the city where she could keep him. He made her spend the night to prove it. He wasn't going to, but somehow Marilyn always could get Malc to give her what she wanted, and he let her take the baby. It was only supposed to be until tomorrow."

"So is Malcolm at work now?"

She just snorted. I tried again.

"Do you know where he is?"

"Nope. He headed into the city Christmas Eve and I haven't seen him since."

ELEVEN

THERE WAS A COMMOTION on the porch, and then three kids, all under ten, exploded into the room.

"Gramma, Gramma!" The youngest launched himself at Ms. Conyers.

"Easy, child. Where's your mother?" she demanded.

"Parking the car," the tallest said.

Shawn carried in Jamal and set him on the floor. Jamal crawled right for my knees and latched on. When I lifted him onto my lap, he wrapped his arms around my neck. I nuzzled his hair, happy to have his solid weight against my chest.

I felt Shawn and Ms. Conyers both watching me.

"So you don't know when Mr. Walker will be back?" I stood. It was time for us to go.

"Could be anytime now." Ms. Conyers levered herself to stand with me. "Could be tomorrow for all I know. Well, I suppose I'll manage with Jamal until whenever Malc drags himself home."

She said it as though she took it for granted that I'd come to unload Jamal on anyone who'd take him. There was a note of satisfaction in her voice, like she was going to enjoy being imposed on. I was sorry to disappoint her, but I had no intention of parting with Jamal.

The possible significance of the time Malcolm Walker had been away from home was not lost on me, for one thing. Even if he'd had nothing to do with Marilyn's death, I wasn't giving Jamal up until I'd at least met his uncle. I didn't want to get into any unpleasantness with the Conyers, though, so I stayed polite.

"Thank you very much, but it's really not necessary. Jamal's settled in with my family for right now. I'll leave you my address and phone number for Mr. Walker and he can come get Jamal himself when he's ready."

Under cover of Ms. Conyers's grandchildren, I stuffed Jamal back into Clea's old snowsuit. What I really wanted to do was have a look around upstairs, but I couldn't ask without giving Ms. Conyers another opportunity to insist that I leave Jamal with her.

Shawn came inadvertently to my rescue. He pointed to the somewhat girlish kitten appliquéd on the front of the snowsuit. "You want some of Jamal's own clothes for him? I got the keys to Malcolm's place. I could go up and get something."

His mother looked as relieved by the offer as I was. From her point of view, I suppose it was a delaying tactic; the longer I hung around, the more chance there was of Malcolm coming home before I left with Jamal.

Me, I was interested in seeing if there was a pile of bloody clothes on the bathroom floor.

Yeah, right, Anita, like the man's going to kill his sister and leave incriminating evidence lying around his apartment for anyone to find.

ONE THING AT A TIME. I followed Shawn out the door.

The upstairs was smaller than down, with a central hallway, living room and kitchen facing the street, and two bedrooms with a connecting bath in between facing the back. Jamal's was all a child's room should be, a mobile of moon and stars dangling above the crib, a rocking chair in one corner next to a changing table, a plastic laundry basket full of toys. I put Jamal down and headed for the bathroom.

"I'll just be a minute," I told Shawn.

There was a metal hamper at the foot of the tub. I opened

it and lifted out the few items inside. A gray coverall; a handful of socks that smelled like, well, like a workingman's socks; ditto for the undershirts. The underwear I let fall without inspection, but the long-sleeved maroon polo shirt and the green plaid flannel shirt got a closer look. Neither were stained in any way.

I didn't know if I was relieved or disappointed. Part of me wanted to discover that Jamal's uncle was an unfit guardian, while another part wanted the person who'd been taking care of Jamal to be a good man. Evidence, I needed evidence. Whether I'd ever use it or not depended on what it was.

While I was in the bathroom, I used the toilet for its intended purpose. Then I went out the other door and into Malcolm's room.

No clothes dropped anywhere, naturally. The bed was neatly made, with a blue chenille spread that matched the scatter rug in front of the tall mahogany dresser. I opened the closet door, only to find a rack of ironed shirts and pants on hangers, with a neat row of polished shoes lined up on the floor.

So much for obvious signs of unfitness to raise a child; there was nothing in the apartment to suggest that Jamal's uncle was anything other than an exemplary guardian. Relieved, disappointed—either way, all I wanted was to take Jamal home. The irony of the fact that Jamal was already in *his* home totally escaped me.

I picked out a sleeper, two pairs of corduroy pants and some flannel shirts just like Uncle Malc wore. I had a pang of sympathy for the man, wherever he was, not knowing how close he was to losing his nephew. I waved it away by reminding myself of the possibility that he was the same person who might have killed the boy's mother.

Because if Dolores knew that Malcolm was Jamal's guardian, if she knew where he lived, then why hadn't she brought the baby back to Staten Island? Where would he be safer than with his uncle? Unless it was Malcolm who'd gone berserk and slashed Marilyn's throat.

Nevertheless, I found a pad of paper by the phone in the tidy kitchen, and left the information for Malcolm Walker to call and claim his nephew. It was one of the hardest things I've ever had to write.

TWELVE

IT WAS ONLY two blocks to Victory Boulevard, the nearest big street, but cabs are not as easy to hail in the outer boroughs as they are in Manhattan. Fortunately, in Staten Island all bus routes lead to the ferry terminal. We waited on the corner with a tired-looking woman who leaned against an ironing board with a green-striped cover. When the bus came, she folded it up and carried it on with her.

On the ferry, Jamal fell instantly asleep. There seemed to be a lot of small boats tooling around in the harbor, lit up like fireflies in the dusk. I propped my feet up on the edge of the stroller and had a little nap myself.

FULL DARK HAD FALLEN by the time we climbed the stairs from the subway at 110th Street. Midwinter; not even five o'clock, and the streetlights lit up Broadway like noon. The wind had picked up off the river, and it caught the stroller with a hard gust at each cross street.

In spite of the respite of the ferry ride, I was exhausted. Benno came to the door, wrestled in the stroller and folded it for me while I unpeeled Jamal from the snowsuit. He'd been unloading the Christmas dinner leftovers that Catherine had packed for us the day before, and he had a worried expression on his face.

I countered with a smile and a kiss, both of which I sincerely meant. In the regular course of things, it's Benno who walks in the door while I'm making dinner. There aren't many evenings when I'm the one who gets to say "Hi, honey, I'm home."

It didn't do much to unfurrow his brow, though. We had one of those silent marital exchanges, wherein I conveyed my satisfaction at still having Jamal at the end of the day, and Benno expressed his disapproval of my increased attachment to the child. Or maybe I was reading too much into it.

Besides, there was Mr. I-don't-believe-in-using-television-as-a-baby-sitter, allowing Clea to watch a Care Bears video. Leave the man with child care for a day, and see how much he valued a half hour of peace in which to fix supper! Not that I said a word about it, just carried Jamal into Clea's room for a diaper change.

Miss Clea herself didn't so much as look away from the screen when I planted a kiss on her cornrowed head.

"Nice to see you, too," I told her, and set the changed Jamal beside her on the couch. Might as well take advantage of some grown-up time, a commodity that would be in even shorter supply with two kids around than one, and try for a little verbal communication.

Benno transferred turkey, stuffing and gravy to a Pyrex pan. I handled the potatoes, sweet and mashed in separate tinfoil pouches for the oven, and the collards in a saucepan on top of the stove. We let everything take its time reheating while we had a glass of wine at the kitchen table and told our days.

Benno's was less eventful, but since he'd had Clea, he went first. I was relieved to listen, especially since he wasn't complaining; they'd actually had a good time, which was usually how things went when the two of them were together without me. Clea can be quite the talker, and Benno encourages her in a way I don't have time for. The luxuries of being the parent who spends less time on feeding and clothing— or, as Benno would point out, being the parent who works eleven-hour days to pay for the food and the clothes.

I intended to tell the story of my day in reverse chronological order, starting with Staten Island and Jamal's uncle, before I got to finding Marilyn's body, but I never made it that far. Benno shot questions at me: Jamal lives with his uncle? He works for the city? You were in his apartment? The neighbors had no idea where he was or when he'd be back? You left a note? By the time I was done explaining, we'd popped in a second half-hour video for the kids, and that one had finished, too.

Then supper was ready, and it was solid child-time until almost ten. Clea wasn't as easy with Jamal that second night. Good thing I'd brought him pajamas; she didn't want him to wear any more of her things, and as for taking a bath together, forgetaboutit. Her highness ungraciously allowed me to glance at the *Times* while she was in the tub, and expressed her disapproval of the arrangement with an overzealous sinking of toy boats that splashed up onto the paper.

"Hey!" I protested.

"It was a accident, Mama!" Miss Indignant claimed.

"Uh-huh. Have you ever heard of accident prevention? Like when you wear a seat belt?" That was the new big thing, being old enough to ride in a car without a car seat. "Well, you need to fasten your splash belt. That means gentle hands in the water, or else, young woman."

Young woman. That was my mother talking. Three seconds later, an arc of drops splattered across the Metro section. Clea listened about as well as I ever had.

I sighed and folded the paper. I could hear Benno in the kitchen, washing dishes and having a one-way conversation with Jamal. The baby banged around happily with a collection of plastic containers and wooden spoons while Benno chatted to him about the state of the world. No "how about those Jets" sports talk from my husband; he started the discussion by asking Jamal what he thought of the new president.

"Not doing too badly, in my opinion," Benno answered himself. "Of course, he mishandled the health care thing, but at least he tried. What I'm worried about, though, is that he's doing what the Democrats always do, not showing any backbone. Remember when Reagan first got in office, and he fired the air traffic controllers?''

Jamal sent a spoon skittering off the counter and squawked to get Benno's attention.

''Hey, easy with the utensils, kid.''

From the sound of it, Benno retrieved the spoon and Jamal immediately sent it flying again. It was all so normal. I felt like I'd been having a long, convoluted dream and woken to find my family going about life as usual. Except there was Jamal, proof that the day's events were real.

''Anyway, as I was saying, Reagan didn't give a fig what anyone thought, he just did it. Clinton, now, he could have come right out and told the military that they had to let openly gay people in. But no, typical Democrat, he tried to please everyone with this 'don't ask, don't tell' business. You have to take a stand or people will walk all over you.''

''What's so funny, Mama?'' Clea read the grin on my face.

''Oh, I'm just listening to Daddy talk to Jamal about politics, the way he used to talk to you until you got old enough to be bored.''

''I'm not bored!'' Clea said. ''I like to listen to Daddy. I listened to him all day.'' She sent a wave of water sloshing over the side of the tub.

''Okay, Bops, I think you're done playing. Let's have the washcloth and some soap.''

Clea stood for me to wash her. ''Why do we have to keep this baby? I'm tired of him already.''

''Don't you like having a little brother?''

My daughter glared at me. ''No. Maybe if he was a sister, I would.''

Parenthood is a series of challenges. Just when you think you've surmounted one, another pops up. I couldn't wait until we got to dating.

''When you have children, you don't get to choose whether

they're boys or girls." Clea climbed out of the tub and I
wrapped her in the towel. She didn't make any response, and
I realized she was processing this as information. I waited to
see what the eventual question would be, taking my cue from
wherever she wanted the conversation to go.

Of course, Clea knows she's not our biological child. In
the interests of simplicity, we've told her that she's adopted,
and she uses our last name at day care. We've kept her
shielded from the intricacies of the legal situation, however,
seeing no need to share our insecurities with her.

"When you picked me out, did you get to choose?" Clea
finally asked.

These are the moments you both watch for and dread,
when your child looks to you to explain the workings of the
world. It behooves a parent to answer carefully, because how
you present things sets the template for how they approach
everything from tomatoes to sex.

Heavy as she was, I lifted Clea up and carried her out of
the bathroom. "No. Some people who adopt babies ask for
one or the other, but we didn't do that. Dad and I wanted to
be surprised." I set her down on the bed and got out a clean
nightie. "I thought I wanted a boy, but as soon as I saw you,
I knew you were the child for me."

Clea wiggled into the nightgown, then my lap. "But you
still wanted a boy, and that's why you bought Jamal?"

Oy vey is mir. See where honesty gets you?

"No. First, I didn't buy Jamal. I gave his aunt some money
because she said she needed it. She would've wanted me to
take care of Jamal even without the money. Second, I don't
know if we'll be able to keep him. He has—" a mother
somewhere, I was going to say, before I remembered where
exactly Marilyn would be right now: the morgue. "He lives
with his uncle, and I'm trying to find out if he wants Jamal
back," I amended.

Clea shrugged and scrambled off my lap. That's how

quickly a four-year-old is done with serious subjects. "Will you read to me tonight?"

So I went out to see if Benno would give Jamal his bath. The menfolk were sprawled on the living-room floor with the *Times* spread out around them.

"Got him reading the Op-Ed page already?" I asked.

"More like eating it." Benno unwrapped Jamal's fingers from a fistful of newsprint. "Let go, kid, that's brain food not belly food."

I wasn't the only person being won over by the little boy.

Benno made a show of being put upon when I asked him to bathe Jamal, but I knew he didn't mean it. Give my husband his due, when he's home, he more than pulls his weight in the child care department. So there we were: two kids, two parents. An ideal system.

After the bath, though, the usual division of labor reasserted itself. Benno went to bed, and I was left to give Jamal what I hoped would be his last bottle of the night. It was past ten; at Jamal's age, a bottle that late would have seen Clea through the night. I crossed my fingers while he emptied a full eight ounces of formula.

THIRTEEN

NO SUCH LUCK. We were once again sleeping with the door open, and I found my new-mother instincts still in working order. Jamal's first faint cry brought me immediately awake. That, or the need to pee. I tiptoed into the bathroom.

I was hoping the baby would go back to sleep without waking Clea, but after a few minutes of low-level complaint, I gave in. It was more for my sake than Clea's, though. I was awake, and I wanted the feel of that solid body snuggled on my lap.

He was such a good baby. Clea would have been fussing in my arms while the bottle heated. Jamal, a bit of gentle bouncing on my hip was enough to calm him. He watched the pot with a patience not usually associated with infants.

We sat on the couch, in the red glow of the chile lights. I sort of drifted off, into that half zone of night feedings, until a couple of loud sucking sounds announced that Jamal had finished his bottle.

When I brought him back to the crib, Benno came up behind me and wrapped his arms around my waist. There's no cornier moment than parents standing over a sleeping baby, in fact as well as in fiction. Benno being Benno, he had to puncture it.

"I suppose if you only shell out forty bucks for a kid, you've got to expect to wean him off the 2:00 a.m. feeding yourself, huh?"

I jabbed him with an elbow, but I wasn't sorry he'd broken

the spell. We tiptoed out of the bedroom without waking Clea.

"So you think Jamal's going to be with us long enough to learn to sleep through the night?" I tried to make it light.

Benno responded to the undertone of longing I hadn't managed to suppress. "I wish we could keep him, too, Anita, but his uncle will probably call in the morning, and..."

"What if he doesn't? He hasn't shown the least bit of concern about Jamal, letting his drug-addict mother have him. Maybe he's not the best guardian."

"Anita." It was all he needed to say. I knew the ramifications and the pitfalls inherent in what I was thinking as well as he did. The foster care system was beyond reason or rationality, and impossible to trust. Even if Jamal's mother was dead and his uncle deemed an unfit parent, there was no guarantee he'd be placed in our custody.

And Benno didn't even know the whole story of Jamal's parentage. I should have told him right then. I started to, but—

Benno turned me in his arms and kissed me.

"Ready to come to bed?"

I wasn't. I shook my head.

How could I bring the vision of Marilyn's bloody body into the sanctuary of our living room?

Benno ran a finger along my jaw and tilted my chin up. Perceptive as ever, he picked up on the fact that my heart wasn't in it. He didn't say anything, just looked into my eyes for a small moment.

I knew what he was thinking: here we go again with the baby-hunger. My wife, the basket case, cooing over every infant she sees on the street.

He let go of me and went into the kitchen. When he opened the fridge, the light from inside made a halo around his bent head. My husband, the saint.

Benno took two glasses from the dish drainer and gave the jar of leftover eggnog a vigorous shake. Typical man, he neither put the lid back on nor returned the jar to the fridge. Already back then, I'd been married long enough to know there was no point in making an issue of the fact that I'd be the one to clean it up before we went to bed.

When Benno came back to the couch, we clinked our glasses together and ran through a litany of commonplaces: how eggnog always tastes better the second day, and next year Benno should really make it in advance; how nice the tree looked with just the red lights, but maybe next year we'd try all white.

It was so much better than embarking on the conversation we both preferred to avoid.

The one about whether or not to take on another child.

Each of us could have spoken the other's lines, we'd been through it so many times. I skipped lightly through my side of the argument. I wanted a sibling for Clea. Benno and I were both only children, and I wanted her to have the experience of a larger family; I thought it was especially important in the situation so she as a black child wouldn't feel isolated in a white family. The timing was good, since I'd be graduating from school in May and could take a year off, or work part-time. All very practical, right? But the real force that drove me to pursue the issue was beyond reason. Clea was about to start school, and I wasn't done with mothering an infant.

In the silence, without Benno stating his own position, I found myself hearing his views in a way I hadn't before. He worried about being an older parent and maybe not living long enough to see Clea grow up—he's six years older than I am, and both his parents were dead by the time he was twenty-five. Then there was the toll of night feedings, early mornings, increased cooking, cleaning, laundry, the inevitable illnesses and fears and…having two children is more work than having one. Easy for me to say I could take a year off; I wasn't the one already working eleven-hour days. Sure, the foster care money would help, but my student loans would come due, and our expenses would only increase with a second child.

Then I hit the point that had so far stopped me, too—the uncertainty of Clea's adoption. There was still a real possibility that she could be taken away from us. I never allowed myself to venture into what-if territory; I had to believe it would never happen. But to take on a second child, to get attached, to double the risk of loss, the weight of uncertainty?

Benno sighed. From the sound of it, his thoughts had been traveling the same paths as mine, and come to the same impasse.

I meant to tell him about Marilyn. I opened my mouth, and once again Benno tugged me gently away from the precipice. Not that it was hard to do; I wasn't eager to step into territory seeded with land mines. Benno took my empty glass, set it on the floor and slid his hand up under my nightgown. We made love right there on the couch, with our sleeping children a closed door away. It's not only men who think sex solves everything.

FOURTEEN

SOMETIMES IT DOES though, for a while anyway. Tonight wasn't one of those times.

Benno stroked my hair as he addressed the worry I hadn't spoken out loud. "How about this, Anita of my heart. We'll give Jamal's various relatives until noon tomorrow to get in touch with us. If we haven't heard from anyone by then, you can call Catholic Charities and hope Kathy will pull enough strings to have Jamal officially placed with us. She should be able to manage that, shouldn't she?"

I nodded. Once Jamal was officially in the foster care system, the burden would fall on Uncle Malcolm to prove he was worthy of having the child back. I was torn between wanting to use the system in our favor for a change and my reluctance to put Jamal's uncle at its mercy. Waiting until noon seemed like a good compromise, and I said so.

Satisfied that he'd solved the problem, Benno stood, took the empty glasses into the kitchen and proved I didn't know everything by putting the eggnog in the fridge before he went back to bed.

Me, I wasn't quite so sure we'd resolved anything. I pulled on my Lanz of Salzburg nightgown, and the nightmare scenario I'd been keeping at bay returned. What if Jamal had seen his uncle kill his mother?

The hell of it was, if that's what had happened, it meant we had a good shot at keeping Jamal. Who else was there? An aunt on crack, an unknown father?

The floor creaked as I paced. I knew sleep wouldn't come

for me on its own. Never mind eggnog, I poured myself a straight shot of rum. I wondered if there was anything else my middle-of-the-night brain could recall about Marilyn's room. I figured rum would aid the process, you know, use it like a prop, the way actors do to get in character.

Fortified by the liquid fire, I felt ready to look again at Marilyn's body. Flung away, she seemed to me, as if someone had shoved her backward. And all that blood. Whoever had wielded whatever she'd been slashed with would have gotten blood all over himself. The spray had reached Jamal's yellow diaper bag, Dolores's sweatshirt.

Was Dolores wearing Marilyn's down coat because there was blood on her own? Could she have been the slasher? Had she fought with her sister and lashed out in anger, not meaning to kill but to scar?

If you'd asked me whether I'd approached Marilyn's body, whether I'd touched her arm and found it to be cold, I'd have said no. I honestly thought all I'd done was stand in the doorway and stare.

Alone in the night, however, in my own living room with the aroma of balsam rather than blood, I knew that on the nonexistent chance Marilyn was alive, I'd reached down to check her breathing. There was none.

But now I remembered several empty crack vials scattered next to the body, little glass cylinders so small I always wondered how anything could be gotten into them. And a confetti of plastic stoppers, yellow, pink and green.

And there were Marilyn's Salems on the table, along with a red disposable cigarette lighter and a full ashtray. No glass pipe, though. If crack had been smoked, the implement that had been used to do it with was gone.

So who had gotten high that night? Marilyn, with her baby boy in the room? Dolores, while her sister slept in her flowered flannel nightie, and the baby in his crib? Both of them together, to go through that many vials? Probably.

And then brother Malcolm made a surprise visit, found the women high and, enraged, went for Marilyn?

What about the third glass, though? Malcolm had a brotherly drink with the sisters before killing one and frightening the other out into the street with the baby. How likely was that?

Not very. He'd have to have been high himself, and from the looks of his apartment, drugs were not Malcolm's thing. But you never knew, did you? There are functional crack users just like there are functional alcoholics.

Crack. Waster of lives, in more ways than one. The generation of users, the generation of young sellers, the generation of the users' children.

I finished the rum in one gulp. The late-rising moon poured a square of light through the south window. I needed to find Dolores. Until noon, I would look. That was a plan. I unplugged the Christmas tree lights and went to join my husband.

FIFTEEN

A SECOND MORNING of being woken by Jamal in the crib next to her bed put Clea in a less tractable mood than she'd been in the day before. I wasn't feeling any too chipper myself, after the rum-fueled middle-of-the-night events. It took me two cups of coffee before I managed to fill the children with oatmeal.

Lumpy, Clea pointed out. Benno had made an early escape, so chipper from getting lucky on the couch that I wanted to throttle him. Be careful what you wish for, I thought, watching the spread of oatmeal from bowls to bibs to table. Two, two, two children are a lot more to deal with than one.

It was a situation that called for two, two, two aspirins. I settled for three and called Barbara, the building super's wife, my best friend and the mother of a fifteen-year-old on school vacation who I prayed would be happy to earn some money baby-sitting. Which Tabitha was.

"Nail polish," Barbara explained, when Tabitha put her back on the phone. "Eye shadow, eyeliner, mascara, lipstick. I won't pay for it, her father won't let her wear it out of the house, but she's got to have it. I tell George, pick your battles. I don't care if she looks like a tramp, as long as she doesn't act like one."

I wasn't sure I was ready to hear this. If Clea as a teenager was anything like me...

"And in my experience, if you let a girl blow off a little steam with face paint, she's not so likely to need to prove her point by going all the way," Barbara continued. "I just make sure I know where she is and who she's with and the minute she turns sixteen, she'll be on the pill, no matter what George has to say about it.''

Practical parenthood, indeed. My mother got me on birth control at the same age. Little did she know the mare had been out of the barn for some time by then. And little did *I* know that the good luck that hadn't made me a teenage mother would come to seem like bad when I hit my thirties, tried to conceive and couldn't.

I hung up the receiver. One problem taken care of, but finding a sitter was the easy part. Where to find Dolores... The phone rang under my hand.

''What?'' I said, thinking it was Barbara calling back.

''I want to speak to Mrs. Servi, please.'' A Spanish accent.

''That's me.''

''This is Cruz, from The Martha?'' She paused. ''You are the one who came here yesterday with the little boy? Jamal?''

''Yes, that was me,'' I acknowledged.

''I got something to tell you. My son, he helps out here sometimes, he told me he saw Dolores this morning, on 125th Street.''

An answer from the heavens. Cruz's son had spotted Dolores sleeping in a doorway, on the north side of the street between Old Broadway and Amsterdam. He'd recognized her by the down coat, and so I hoped would I.

The M104 carried me north on Broadway. I got off in front of Woolworth's. The window display tempted me to pop in for a pack of colored lights, already marked down to post-Christmas prices. Out of deference to Benno, I refrained. The holiday is hard enough on his Jewish sensibilities, not to mention his innate distaste for tinsel and glitter.

If I'd known that Woolworth's days were numbered—but you don't miss your five-and-dime until it closes. Now the neighborhood is lousy with Rite Aids and Duane Reades, but try to find thread, buttons, jingle bells, knitting yarn, cookie tins, cheap hair whoosies, children's cotton undershirts, Peds—forgetaboutit.

Tuesday after Christmas, there weren't many people on the street. I'd taken a roll of quarters from the laundry money for the panhandlers, planning to distribute them as I went, but I didn't see anyone with a hand out. This was a back-to-work crowd, dressed in winter coats and hats, walking with purpose toward the subway, waiting for a crosstown bus.

The north side of the street was pretty much deserted. A nail place on the corner, not yet open, seemed to be the only going concern on the block. The doorways of the vacant storefronts provided a minimum of shelter for sleeping figures. No one was wrapped in a light-blue down coat, but I paused to study every face that was visible above the improvised coverings. Richest country in the world, city with the single wealthiest zip code in the nation, and look how we treat the least of our citizens. I left four quarters by each sleeper's side, wishing I could have afforded twenty-dollar bills.

When I got to Amsterdam Avenue, I was out four bucks and still no sign of Dolores. Cruz's son's sighting had been at least an hour ago, plenty of time for Dolores to have woken and wandered off who knew where. Probably not far, though.

I stood on the corner and thought. If I were Dolores, where would I go? If I were cold, hungry, in need of coffee, a bathroom, a meal? Charley's Southern Fried Chicken beckoned from the corner across the street. I could see, from where I stood, that no woman resembling Dolores was seated at any of the few tables or the counter.

If I were Dolores, I realized, what I'd be in most need of was a high.

The next thing that occurred to me was that I was only two blocks from the police station. I debated walking in and asking if anyone had seen Dolores. She was easy enough to describe, and I had no fear that they'd encourage me to report her as a missing person. If I were really lucky though, she might have been picked up as a vagrant.

Yeah, right. Picked up for vagrancy in New York City? At that rate, jails would put homeless shelters out of business.

Well, maybe a cop had rousted her from sleeping in a doorway, and would be able to tell me which way she'd gone. Talk about incurable optimism. The proximity to the precinct house appeared to have had no impact on the sleepers in doorways I'd just passed.

Nevertheless, I started up Amsterdam toward 126th. The metal gate on a loading dock across the street had been pulled down almost to the ground, where it was stopped by a bunch of pale-blue fabric. I didn't allow myself to think what it might be, just headed over for a better look.

The bottom three feet of the gate was solid, a spray-painted hash of illegible graffiti tags. Above that was a metal mesh, lighter and easier to roll up. I stuck my face up to the bars and saw what at first I thought was simply an abandoned coat. Yes, Marilyn's down coat, as worn by sister Dolores.

Then it moved.

SIXTEEN

I JUMPED BACK instinctively, thinking, *rats?* Which were what you'd expect to find lurking outside an abandoned warehouse. From inside the gating came a regular thump, thump that echoed my pounding heartbeat. I fought down my primal reaction and went back for another look.

This time I saw a blue-jeaned leg, and the foot in a grubby running shoe. I dropped to a crouch and slid my gloved hands under the edge of the gate. It took all the effort I could put into my back muscles to budge the thing. Once it started moving, however, the gate shot up as far as I could stand and hold it.

The figure in the coat scrambled out and curled into a ball, like a porcupine protecting its soft underbelly.

"Dolores?" I asked.

At the sound of her name, she pushed herself to her knees.

I let go of the heavy metal gate in order to help her. It slammed down with a crash that startled both of us. Dolores started to stand, then doubled over and collapsed against me.

I lowered us both to the sidewalk. I sat with my back to the metal wall, Dolores practically in my lap. Looking over her shoulder, I could see that the front of her coat was stained dark red. No, bright red.

Dolores had her hands pressed against her side. Her breathing was rapid, shallow.

So was mine. I took a few deep breaths. I needed to process what I observed. Bleeding. Stabbed? Shot? Help!

I put my hands over Dolores's, stanching a wound I

couldn't see and had no desire to expose for better evaluation. I touched my cheek against hers. From what I could tell, her body temperature was neither cold with shock nor hot with fever. A good sign.

A drift of goose down settled around us. The sleeves of the coat had been slashed to ribbons.

"I'm okay." Dolores spoke.

"Okay?" I wanted to shake her. I shifted her position slightly, without letting up my compression on the wound, so I could look at her face. "You're not exactly okay, Dolores."

"Yeah, I'll be all right with a few stitches. The coat made it so the knife only stuck me once. I acted like I was dead, and he stuffed me in there. I'da been outta there by now if I coulda got that damn gate up." She stopped for breath.

I gauged the distance to Charley's Southern. Half a block, not even. If someone came out the door, I'd yell for help. No one did. Cars sped past on Broadway. Across the street, pedestrian traffic moved right along.

I aimed a shout in that direction anyway. "Hey! Help! Over here!"

Dolores tried to squirm away from me. "What're you doing? He'll hear you."

"Who?" I tightened my grip and shouted for help again.

No one paid the slightest attention to us. Not that there was anyone around; the windows across the way were bricked shut, as were the ones in the building behind us. Dolores didn't answer.

"You might as well tell me. I found Marilyn's body yesterday."

She shivered in my arms.

"Franklin," she whispered. That was it.

"Franklin stabbed you?"

Dolores nodded.

"And Marilyn?"

She nodded again.

"Who is he?" I had to ask the obvious question before I jumped to conclusions.

"Man I know."

That told me a lot. "Is he Jamal's father?"

"How should I know?"

Full of information, Dolores was. I didn't believe her, and I made a tsking sound to let her know.

"No, really. Probably not even Marilyn knew who started Jamal. At one time, she told Franklin the baby was his, but he thought she was two-timing him and he beat on her pretty good. That's when she went to live with Malcolm. She told him some story about the baby's father was a married man."

Well, in terms of Jamal's custody, either drug dealer, married, or unknown were hopeful possibilities.

"How do you know Franklin?" I needed to keep her talking until someone walked by and I could holler for help.

"Marilyn used to go with him. Hadn't seen him since she got clean, and I had to go and..."

Her skin was ashy pale, and now there was sweat on her forehead.

Shock. Delayed, but still dangerous. No one within hailing distance.

"Dolores. I'm going to leave you for a minute and go call an ambulance."

"No." One hand came out from under mine and clutched my wrist. "I can't go to no hospital. He'll find me."

I might've been a street-naive white woman, but I knew better than to believe her. What Dolores meant was that in the hospital she wouldn't be able to score. Not only that, but they'd do what they could to find her a spot in a rehab program.

The question was, if I left her alone, would she manage to crawl away and finish bleeding to death before I got back?

SEVENTEEN

"FIRE! Fire! Help, fire!" I gave it all I had.

Dolores moaned and struggled.

Two men came out of the chicken place and looked our way.

"Help us, please," I called out to them. "We need an ambulance."

"What do you mean, *we?*" Dolores muttered.

I didn't know if she meant it to be funny or not, but it brought home the anomaly of the situation. White woman cradling black woman on the sidewalk on a deserted street in Harlem, early on a cold December morning, one of them bleeding, the other yelling "fire." At least we weren't in a crowded theater, I thought.

The men appeared to consult with each other, some silent communication. They were a matched pair, elderly but not decrepit, in camel hair overcoats and fedoras with feathers in their bands. One of them nodded and ducked back into the diner.

The other tucked his scarf tighter around his neck and headed our way. He stopped a cautious ten feet away. "Somebody hurt?" he asked.

"No, we practicing the Kama Sutra," Dolores snapped.

Shut me right up, laughing.

The man shrugged. "You need you an amalance or not?" It was a slow Southern voice, with pronunciation to match.

"Yes," I said. "She's been stabbed."

"All right, then." He stood there and nodded at us for a moment before he turned back to the diner.

I thought Dolores was going to give me an argument. I forestalled her with a question.

"What was Franklin doing at Marilyn's on Christmas Eve?"

"It was my fault. I was looking for Franklin so's I could score before I went over there. I found him down the block here, and he saw I had a package all wrapped up for Jamal so he decided he wanted to see Marilyn's baby. Made me give him the address, said he wanted to bring her some Christmas cheer."

I felt the shakes come and go in Dolores's body.

"So what happened?"

"It was late already when he showed up. We were all sleeping. Franklin wanted to wake the baby up so he could see what Santa brung him. Marilyn, she didn't want him to. Franklin made so much noise, baby woke up anyway. He sure liked that truck!" She closed her eyes, and her face relaxed into a smile. It didn't last long.

"Next thing you know, Franklin's lighting up. Marilyn been clean a couple months, but soon as she smelled that smoke…" I felt Dolores shrug. "Pipe got lit a few times. We all feeling pretty good, drinking Bacardi. Damn if I know what set him off." Dolores shivered. I made sure she was pressing tight to the wound, then reached to pull the coat over her legs and settle the hood around her head.

Once you've been addicted…a situation I'd never been in, so I wasn't prepared to sit in judgment on someone who had. "Where was Jamal while you all were partying?"

"He fell asleep on the bed with his arms around that truck. I just got up to put him back in the crib when Franklin shouts 'Bitch!' and Marilyn says 'Don't you touch me.' I pick up the baby and I see Marilyn has a knife out, Franklin backed up against the wall."

I kept watch on the corner of 126th, expecting the police

to show up any second. Two blocks from the station house, if the men in camel hair coats had actually called 911, how long could it take them to respond?

"Franklin grabbed her wrist that's holding the knife, and he slapped Marilyn in the face. She went down, and he snatched her back up again by her nightgown so he could hit her some more. Then she dropped the knife, and Franklin went for her with that." Dolores's voice was almost a whisper.

"What were they fighting about?"

She shook her head. "Something with Jamal. Franklin started in on was the baby his or not, and Marilyn wouldn't tell him. She said Jamal was in a good situation with her brother and she wasn't gonna mess that up. All I know for sure is, when I saw Franklin had the knife, I grabbed up the baby and got the hell out of there."

Now the trembling didn't stop.

I rocked her in my arms. "It's okay, it's all going to be okay. You did the right thing."

We heard sirens from way down Amsterdam. I wondered if it was our ambulance or someone else's.

"I was going to bring him to Malc, but I was afraid Franklin would come after us. He knew where Marilyn used to stay, over on Staten Island. Then I saw you, and..."

Uh-huh, I thought. And I took the baby off your hands and gave you money for crack. Look where it got you.

Dolores looked up at me, her eyes as defensive as if I'd spoken out loud. "Yeah, okay, so I'm a addict, but I'm not stupid. I made sure Jamal was safe, didn't I?"

"Sure you did," I soothed. "And now you have to tell the police—" who were still nowhere to be seen "—so they can get Franklin off the street. Then you'll be safe."

Dolores made no response to this. Her eyes were closed, her face blanched and beaded with sweat.

I could see the ambulance now, siren wailing in frustration

as it tried to cross Broadway against the light and got no mercy from the traffic.

And two cops, ambling down 126th, who to their credit broke into a heavy trot at the sight of us.

EIGHTEEN

I PUT UP a good fight but neither the police nor the paramedics would allow me in the ambulance. I ran the gamut from pleading to curses and ended with tears. By the time I'd run out of strategies, the doors were closing.

One of the EMTs dropped me a crumb. "We're taking your friend to Saint Luke's Hospital. You can see her there."

"Soon as we're done with you." The men in blue had no such comfort on offer.

While they'd been ignoring me, I'd done some thinking about the explanation I was going to have to give. I decided I'd tell as much as I could while minimizing Jamal's presence in the whole affair. It was a long story, especially after I'd been through it three times. First for the uniforms on the spot, then two detectives and a lieutenant back at the station.

They all had the same reactions in the same places. Skeptical amusement at me giving Dolores money so I could "baby-sit" for her nephew. Angry disapproval that I'd found Marilyn's body and left the scene without reporting it. Outright disbelief carried them along to Staten Island with me, and sustained them right up through my going to look for Dolores on my own this morning.

Benno, I knew, would react in much the same way when he heard the full story. By the time I got through the first telling, I'd figured out the best way to minimize the trouble I was in. I played the irrational female, acting on emotional instinct. Hey, if a stereotype works for you, I say take ad-

vantage of those dumb enough to fall for it. And given my
state of mind, the role wasn't much of a stretch.

It wouldn't be so easy to convince my husband.

If the cops ever let me go home to him.

They weren't arresting me, but they weren't releasing me,
either. I managed to wrangle a phone call to check on the
kids, and found Benno back at the apartment. Malcolm Walker had called, spoken to Tabitha, who then called Benno,
who was now home waiting for Jamal's uncle. The thought
of Jamal leaving—of Jamal leaving without my having a
chance to say goodbye—was enough to put me in real hys-
terics.

It's never wise to challenge the guardians of law and order,
especially when you're on their turf. I also knew that they
couldn't stop me from leaving. I put down the phone and
stood. "I have to get home to my family."

"Sounded to me like your husband had things under control there, Mrs. Servi." This from the detective in the starched
white shirt with the rolled-up sleeves. The radiators in the
small room where they'd stashed me were on the overactive
side; gave a new meaning to sweating a suspect.

"I need to go home to my family." My story and I'm
sticking to it. The broken-record technique; don't get drawn
into an argument, just repeat the same statement over and
over.

"Well, ma'am, there are just a few things we still need to
clear up." This from the other detective, an older man also
without a jacket, his white shirt in considerably less pristine
condition than his counterpart's.

"I'll be happy to talk to you again later, but right now I'm
leaving. You have my address, so you know where to find
me." Nothing like a good cliché.

I put on my coat and headed for the door.

That got them out of their chairs and precipitated a flurry
of rolling down sleeves and shrugging on jackets.

"Hang on a minute, miss, we'll give you a lift," the older one offered.

Miss? Like hell.

"I'm perfectly capable of taking the bus."

The man gave his partner a "Women, what're ya gonna do about 'em?" roll of the eyes. But I was done with the act and determined to get home. I was out the main door and on the street before they caught up to me.

Starched shirt dangled a set of car keys. "It'll be much quicker if we drive you."

I was in a hurry, and good-cop had a point. The thought of parting with Jamal hit me again, a sharp pain.

He slid a supporting hand under my elbow. "Come on, Ms. Servi. You've helped us, now let us help you. We're heading over to the hospital to talk to this Dolores anyway, and it'll be our pleasure to drop you at your place."

"Thank you." I allowed him to usher me into the back seat of an unmarked car. If I was going to yield, might as well do it with grace.

WHEN I WALKED IN, Benno and Mr. Walker were drinking coffee and staring at a plate of Christmas cookies while Clea helped Jamal piece together a wooden puzzle. It was obvious that the two men had run out of things to say and were waiting for me. I wasn't anxious to go through it again, but I knew that with a third party present, Benno would go easier on me.

They let me have a few minutes in the bathroom to wash up. Benno fixed me an essential cup of coffee, which I used as a delaying tactic. I needed to frame the story a bit more gently for this particular audience.

The dead woman's half brother, Malcolm Walker, was a tall man with a sturdy build, clean-shaven nut-brown skin and no gray in his hair. He wore a button-collared shirt under a maroon wool V-neck sweater. There was an ironed crease in his jeans.

A suitable guardian for a boy child, from his appearance. Behavior, though, there was still that. Malcolm Walker had placed Jamal in his mother's care, and look what happened.

On the living room floor, Jamal picked up puzzle pieces and tried to fit them into their places. He was too young for the task, and Clea guided his hand. Each time he got one, Jamal chortled his pleasure.

This is what Clea needs, I thought. She was made to be a big sister. I glanced up at Benno. He was also watching the children, and I thought I could read longing on his face. And Benno, Benno needs a son. As for longing, I hadn't yearned for a baby like this since Clea was an infant. I wanted Jamal to stay with us. I wanted a bigger family. I wanted—

Mr. Walker cleared his throat. "I thank you, Mrs. Servi, you and your husband, for all you've done for my nephew. If you wouldn't mind just telling me...?"

I blushed. I wanted this man's child.

There was a mother-voice inside me, as possessive as a tigress, that wasn't going to let go of this little boy until I was convinced he'd be in good hands. Now I was wishing I *had* called in Child Welfare.

Jamal crawled over to the table and pulled himself to standing at his uncle's knee. He had a wooden T-Rex clutched in his fist. The man made it growl for the child, who laughed and plopped down on his butt.

I was instantly ashamed of what I'd been thinking.

"Yes, of course," I said. "Would you call me Anita? I've been getting 'Mrs. Servi'd' all morning by the police."

"Malcolm, then." He offered a hand across the table, and we shook.

"The police?" Benno prompted me.

For the police, I'd tried to minimize my overall involvement, to paint myself as a bystander drawn into events that had nothing to do with me. In this telling, I kept the focus on Jamal, and my concern for his safety. I didn't gloss over my desire to keep him, though, in case it turned out that

Uncle Malcolm was not all that eager to continue being his full-time guardian.

Neither man was pleased by this version. Malcolm bristled protectively, and Benno was embarrassed by my proprietary air. I started out thinking I had nothing to lose by revealing how attached I was to the child, but by the time I finished, I could tell that there was no way Malcolm Walker was going to invite an overinvolved white lady to play any kind of role in his nephew's life. Grateful, sure, but he didn't owe me a place in Jamal's future.

AND IN THE YEARS SINCE, he hasn't provided so much as a toehold. I sent a gift the next Christmas, but what hopes I had for a reunion were disappointed. No invitations to birthday parties, no school photo, not even a thank-you note.

The one thing Jamal's brief time as a member of our family brought with it was an end to the debate over whether or not to take in another child. The sense of loss even Clea felt after Jamal went home with his uncle served as a catalyst for Benno and me to reach a decision. Until Clea's adoption was finalized, neither of us felt we could risk the pain of getting attached to another child whom we might not be able to adopt.

We hadn't known, then, that it would be another seven years before we were legally a family. Would it have made a difference if we'd been sure that the adoption would eventually go through? I don't know.

I had to live each court date as it came. By the time the process played itself out, it was too late for another child; some seasons simply pass you by. In my forties, to start with an infant again? Benno pushing seventy when the child started college?

Meanwhile, I'm left to conjure up the person Jamal is becoming. I wonder how Malcolm Walker explained his mother's death, and if the story included the time Jamal spent with us. I wonder what's become of the wary expression in Jamal's eyes, braced for the unexpected already at the age of a year. I hope it hasn't developed into his uncle's edgy distrust of white people, that Jamal will use his cautiousness to distinguish good people from bad, rather than black from white.

Most of all, I hope someday Jamal will ring my buzzer and I can see for myself.

THE GOLD BAND
by Michael Jahn

In memory of Vivian Lebetkin

ONE

A Christmas Goose

ON A COLD Tuesday, December 23, with the wind snapping in off the Hudson and raising the collars of the young men walking their Jack Russell terriers and rustling the restaurant menus in their mahogany holders alongside the doors of the fancy places on Hudson Street in the West Village, Captain Bill Donovan of the NYPD had gone out to buy a goose.

He had just moved into his house a month or two earlier, having left his apartment on the Upper West Side to his grown son and moved downtown to enjoy—or, in some cases for an old man-of-the-people like him, tolerate—the fruits of having married a wealthy woman. Marcy and he were planning to celebrate by treating their five-year-old, Daniel, to a traditional Christmas dinner of goose with fruit stuffing and other trimmings. It had fallen to the captain to buy the bird, which should not have been a difficult task given that their town house was on the outskirts of Manhattan's historic Gansevoort Meat Market district.

But the wind was up and bitter, and the shadows had grown long and Donovan's old suede jacket, veteran of more than twenty West Side winters, was clearly overwhelmed by the first season in the age of *El Niño* that was actually cold. While trudging past the new and exotic restaurants peopled with young men and women who looked like and perhaps were models, his eyes fell upon a small joint with a redbrick facade, a name, The Emerald I'll, that amused him and a neon sign reading Kaliber, that being the nonalcoholic beer made by Guinness and favored by Donovan in the decade and a half since he bade goodbye to the harder stuff. He went inside.

Donovan felt the hot blast of a fireplace, the smell of a good brandy, and then he saw, behind the bar tending to a goodly dozen of patrons, an old and white-bearded face that he knew well from years past.

"Oh, jeez," Donovan swore, spun and walked out.

That was not to be the end of it. For out of the bar and into the wind came two men, burly men dressed for work in the cold. One grabbed Donovan by the arm and said, "Hey, wait."

"What?" the captain said, looking down at the hand holding him back.

"The gentleman inside has asked us to escort you inside to share with him some cheer of the season," a lyrical Irish voice rang out.

"Tell him that the mere sight of him makes me feel like it's a hot day in hell," Donovan said.

"Be a sport," the other one said in a voice that said Bronx.

Donovan sighed and let the two men do as they had been asked.

Once back inside he heard, "If it ain't Bill Donovan." George Kohler extended a hand across the bar.

"It ain't," Donovan said, shaking the hand nonetheless. "You've abducted the wrong man."

"Merry Christmas," Kohler said.

And to the two men he said, "This is my old friend and the man who once supported the liquor distribution industry on Upper Broadway, Bill Donovan."

"Paul O'Neill," the Irish one said.

"Tom Drozak," said the other.

Donovan pumped their hands, said "How ya doing?" and got the usual responses.

Then he added, "George and I go back long enough for

me to know him well, which is why I turned and walked out when I saw him.''

Kohler made a gesture not quite in keeping with the cheer of the season.

''Do your friends know who they've kidnapped?'' Donovan asked.

''Bill is a captain in the NYPD,'' Kohler told them, his face offering up a wicked grin.

''Oh, Christ,'' O'Neill said.

''Sorry, man,'' added Drozak.

Donovan told them not to worry.

''And not only is he a captain in the NYPD,'' Kohler continued, ''he is the captain who caught that Afghan thug in Coney Island the summer before last.''

As O'Neill and Drozak offered awed congratulations and thanks, Donovan said to Kohler, ''Actually, it was an Afghan *rug* and you're wrong again.''

''What'll you have?'' Kohler growled.

''A Kaliber, what do you think?''

Donovan took a stool between O'Neill and a young couple who may or may not have been models. The fire crackled a dozen feet away in a redbrick fireplace built into a similar wall that was lined with tables for two. The jukebox played the Chieftains.

''In light of the weather you should have a real drink,'' Kohler said.

''Homey don't do that,'' Donovan replied.

''*Still?*''

''Fifteen years,'' the captain said proudly.

''And you've *never* had an actual drink, not in the, what is it, three years, since we last talked?''

''I have a ceremonial glass of wine when Marcy's mom hosts Passover,'' Donovan said. ''And I had a sip of vodka last summer after catching the Afghan rug you were talking about,'' Donovan said. ''But it was only to prove the absolutists wrong.''

"Those being the doctors who say that alcoholics should never have a drink," Kohler said.

"I'll have a sip of Absolutist right now," Drozak said, pushing a five-dollar bill across the board and waiting while a shot of vodka was produced.

"I don't think of myself as being an alcoholic," Donovan said. "On the other hand, I also refuse to believe I'm over fifty."

"You don't look it," Drozak said, and O'Neill concurred.

Donovan thanked them. "Having a five-year-old helps," he added.

"How is Danny?" Kohler asked.

"Fine. Happy as a lark."

"And still…and still…you know?"

"Not walking. No, he still doesn't walk. I'm working on it. Me and the doctors. A different one every day, or so it seems. That's what I spend most of my time doing these days. I'm good at understanding things and finding people, as I think you know."

"Detecting," O'Neill said.

"I'm trying to find a cure for him. Anyway, I found Daniel a motorized wheelchair for Christmas," Donovan said.

"How do you spend all that time helping your boy and still be a cop?" Drozak asked.

Taking a sip of Kaliber and nodding appreciatively at Kohler, Donovan said, "I've pulled back a little."

"You?" Kohler exclaimed. "Never."

"After the rug thing, the commissioner offered me a special arrangement. So I could spend more time helping Daniel, I became chief, sort of emeritus, of the department. I keep my shield and gun, exercise loose supervision, but only show up in person when needed. I'm a figurehead."

"They pay you for this?" Kohler asked.

"Only in a sense," Donovan said. "My salary is donated to the Police Widows and Orphans of 9/11 Fund."

"And who's running Special Investigations day to day?" Kohler asked. "That bozo from Brooklyn?"

"Brian Moskowitz just made lieutenant," Donovan said proudly.

"Does that mean he has to stop wearing the T-shirts with four-letter words on them?" Kohler asked.

"Yeah, but he still bench presses 350, so be careful what you call him. You got anything to eat around here?"

Scowling, Kohler produced a black platter that held a jar of WisPride cheddar surrounded by three rings of Ritz crackers. The three men dug in, dipping crackers in cheese, munching and licking off fingers like little boys sharing buttered popcorn.

"Ritz crackers and I have a long history together," Donovan said. "I used to spend summer Sundays at my aunt's place on Long Island, sitting on the lawn in an Adirondack chair, eating Ritz crackers, drinking rum and Coke, and watching the river flow."

"What river is that?" Kohler asked.

"In the metaphoric sense," Donovan replied. Then he added, "Do you guys know if I can get a goose around here?"

"Turn around and bend over," Kohler said.

Grumbling, Donovan said, "Marcy and I want to cook a traditional goose Christmas dinner. Something simple, you know—caviar on toast points, Dom Pérignon, fish soup…sole, of course, vegetable tart, roast goose with chestnut puree, carrots, peas, fresh winter asparagus…"

Kohler had leaned against the backbar during the recitation of the menu. He hooked one thumb in the weight belt he used to ease the strain that his immense belly put on his back, and said, "Pass the freakin' crackers, would ya?"

Donovan passed the freakin' crackers, then said, "I need to buy a goose. That's what I was out looking for when I stumbled over this place and its delightful barkeep."

Laughing, O'Neill said, "Speak of the devil." And he

slipped off his stool and pulled open his jacket to reveal a bloodstained T-shirt reading Gansevoort Live Poultry Market.

"You're kidding me," Donovan said.

"It was fate that brought us together. The market is my place. Tom here is one of the half-dozen bums who work for me."

Drozak nodded, a bit drunkenly, Donovan thought, and opened *his* jacket to display a similar shirt. Then he sat back and resumed what Donovan took to be his nervous habit, wringing his hands, one of which was bandaged rather crudely from the palm to the topmost knuckle.

"Clearly I came to the right place," Donovan said.

"Only problem is, I closed up an hour ago," O'Neill said, looking at his watch. "And once I've locked the place up, I don't open it again until the next business day. My ironclad rule.

"At two in the afternoon on December 23, you closed up?"

"I'm never open the day before Christmas. I got a lot of my own cooking to do, so I lock up on the twenty-third and the place stays locked up tight until the twenty-sixth or twenty-seventh. I make enough good money during the year that I can take a few days at Christmas. So this is it. I brought the boys here for a drink. After that we're off."

Donovan looked around, and finally O'Neill directed his attention to the back room, where four men were playing pool, smoking great clouds of white and flirting with a young woman who bore the suggestion of readily adaptable morality. All the men wore Gansevoort Live Poultry Market T-shirts.

"Those guys are more athletic than us," O'Neill said.

"So I see," Donovan replied.

"Come to think of it, I'm tired and got to get home," Drozak said.

"Where's home?" Donovan asked.

"Bronx," the man replied, zipping his jacket back up.

"Where Bronx?"

"Fordham Road."

"That's a long ride," Donovan noted.

"I got to get going," Drozak said.

"You're the most pussy-whipped man I ever saw," O'Neill said with a smile.

"I love my wife," Drozak replied, draining the little bit of Absolut remaining in his glass and sliding off the stool. He moved a bit stiffly, as a man might while trying to hide his drunkenness.

"They were married on Christmas," O'Neill said. "It's a special day for them, even more than usual."

"Take care of yourself," Donovan said.

"Merry Christmas, Tom," O'Neill said, reaching to pump the man's hand.

"Yeah, from me, too," Kohler said.

"Happy holidays, boss," Drozak said. Then he straightened his jacket and headed for the door, his gait purposeful and measured.

"I hope he makes it," Donovan said.

"Ah, Tom is a good soul," O'Neill said. "So he drinks a bit too much. There are worse things. As for being whipped, you ought to see his wife. What a looker!"

Kohler had gone off to service other customers, leaving Donovan grateful to have avoided another burst of revelations about his own past relationship with demon rum. He said, "So how can I convince you to open your market and get me a goose?"

O'Neill checked his watch. "I don't have to be home for two or three hours, so let's do it now," he said.

"You don't mind?" Donovan asked.

"Nah. You're the guy who nailed that Afghan whatever-he-was. I remember reading about it in the papers, but I forgot the details."

"Me, too," Donovan replied, making it clear that he didn't want to talk about *that*, either.

"Let me say goodbye to the boys," O'Neill said. He got off his stool, left a five-dollar bill on the bar as tip and walked out back.

Donovan did the same and followed the man, out of idle curiosity...to see the back room, for he was always on the lookout for good places to entertain the horde under his sometimes guidance at the Department of Special Investigations.

The pool table was new and well balanced. The jukebox was nearby and, upon casual inspection, contained a great deal of Irish and Scottish music including several rare bagpipes CDs. Seven or eight two-person tables occupied one wall, facing off against four booths that were upholstered in red and shone like holly berries in the glow of assorted neon beer signs.

O'Neill's men stopped playing pool when he came over. They greeted him with handshakes and obvious warmth, and even accepted the boss's new acquaintance. Now that the room checked out well enough to be under consideration as the venue for Brian Moskowitz's upcoming birthday party, the captain sought mainly to keep O'Neill focused on goose. It was so easy for a man to lose his focus during the Christmas season, especially when standing amid co-workers in a cozy bar.

After being introduced, Donovan got three smiles. One man, a dark little fellow with nervous eyes and a bit of a tremor in his left hand, kept his eyes averted.

The captain filed that observation in a small recess of his skull, and when O'Neill was done saying goodbye clapped him on the back and steered him out of the bar, pausing just long enough to offer Merry Christmas thoughts to the surly, white-haired barkeep and accept the "Yeah, same to you" reply.

The shadows were an hour longer than when Donovan had stepped into the Emerald I'll, and the wind was even crueler.

Raising his collar and watching O'Neill do the same, Donovan said, "Do we have far to go?"

"Fourteenth and Washington," the man replied.

"Not too bad," Donovan replied, and set off with O'Neill on the four-and-a-half-block jaunt.

TWO

"It's not good to wake up the night watchman," Donovan said idly.

INEXTRICABLY LINKED to Manhattan's working waterfront of centuries past, Gansevoort Market is a five-sided area of twenty-five or thirty blocks hard on the Hudson River between the West Village part of Greenwich Village and Chelsea. It was built on the site and took the name of Fort Gansevoort, a military citadel built to defend New York during the War of 1812. The fort was named for Peter Gansevoort, a Revolutionary War hero and grandfather of Herman Melville, who toiled there for two decades as an inspector for the Department of Docks, during which he lived briefly in the brownstone that a century and a half later would become the property of the Donovan family. After the Civil War and following some judicious use of landfill, the region had become a bustling market and commercial center, with commercial docks, a yard for the Hudson River Railroad, ox-drawn wagons carrying produce grown on Long Island and in New Jersey, and, rising in the middle of the twentieth century, the Gansevoort Meat Market. When Donovan and O'Neill fought the wind over the thickly cobblestoned streets beneath the black and rusting frames of old elevated New York Central Railroad tracks and decrepit pedestrian bridges, Gansevoort Market was another bit of New York history that some wanted to preserve, others planned to demolish in favor of shops. The battle raged between the two sides.

Wanting only a goose, Donovan thought not of the battle or very much of the history shining off each granite lintel and fancy cornice. So when he followed O'Neill up to the front of the Gansevoort Live Poultry Market he focused on the bird, trying to conjure recipes in his head, ignoring the *size* of the place or how the roll-up security gate rumbled when pushed skyward.

"The lights are on timers," O'Neill said, explaining why the inside shone like afternoon in a barnyard. "It's a good idea to keep the birds on their normal daily cycles."

"Right up to their last one, right," Donovan said.

"Yeah."

The front of the warehouse-size market included two freezer cases flanking a Formica sales counter that ran about twenty feet from side to side. The dual cash registers shared space with racks of dried ostrich meat, spices both dried and fresh, and sauces of every kind. Packages of rice and pasta designed for poultry dishes ran up against a rack of cookbooks offering "1,001 ways to cook a chicken" and like topics. In the freezer cases were rock-solid packets of chicken, duck, goose, turkey and ostrich patties alongside soup stock, French Fries, and every imaginable sort of frozen dish made of or complementing poultry.

"This has got to be the place," Donovan said, inhaling a scent part basil, part freezer.

"We're the biggest live poultry market in Manhattan," O'Neill said. "And we only sell to legit buyers, if you know what I mean."

Donovan knew what he meant. "No voodoo supplies go out of here, right?"

"Not so much as a buffalo wing. We're too close to Wall Street for there to be a lot of witchcraft."

In a case twenty years earlier, Donovan dealt with voodoo ceremonies performed before dawn in Riverside Park. They typically included sacrificed chickens. The supplier in that case was in Harlem.

"At least not of the kind that involves animal sacrifice," the captain replied.

O'Neill nodded, then continued the tour. "Out back there's the slaughter and preparation area, where the guys you met this afternoon work. Behind that is what I call 'the coop.' Want to see it?"

Donovan did, and let himself be led through the preparation area…all stainless steel, he noted on the way through, with no hint of antique wooden chopping blocks or anything at all that might harbor germs. What O'Neill called "the coop" was the back of the warehouse, accounting for perhaps eighty percent of it. There were five rows of floor-to-ceiling cages stretching off to the building's horizon.

The scent of basil and freezer was replaced by the odor of poop and feathers. But before Donovan got to ponder it, the general murmur of birds in cages was replaced by a cackling shriek that itself gave way to a warehouse-wide cacophony from regular hens plus ducks, geese, turkeys, pheasants and twin showcase peacocks.

"Guinea hens make great watch birds," Donovan said.

"Very good," O'Neill replied.

"They set off the rest of the flock."

"How does a New York cop know about guinea hens?" O'Neill asked.

"When I was a teenager, my parents shipped me off to my aunt's place in the country every summer. She lived in the caretaker's cottage on an old estate. They kept guinea hens, ducks, geese and turkey. I can remember lying there in bed fast asleep and a fox or raccoon would try to sneak up on the henhouse."

"And the guinea hens would scare the shit out of the critter…."

"And blast me out of bed," Donovan continued.

"Oh, they can do *that*, all right. Here in the city they mainly wake up the night watchman next door at the beef distributor."

"It's not good to wake up the night watchman," Donovan said idly.

"Wrong. The son of a bitch *should* stay awake, considering all the break-ins we have had around here in the past few weeks."

"Robberies?"

"Middle of the night. Smash a window and get in and steal stuff. Some of the other meat guys have set up video cameras hoping to catch the bastard. Can you help?"

"Was there a break-in last night?" Donovan asked.

"Not so's you'd notice," O'Neill replied. "The guinea hens must have spotted a rat. We've passed all our inspections, but, this *is* a meat market, it *is* right by the river, and...you know."

"I don't know what I can do to help," Donovan said. "My specialty is homicide, but if you like I can call up the local robbery detectives and call their attention to the fact that I now live in the neighborhood and am paying attention."

"That would be great," O'Neill replied.

When the racket from the guinea hens died to silence, he led the captain down one of the aisles, to the end of the warehouse and back. There were White Plymouth Rock, White Cornish, Rock Cornish and New Hampshire Red chickens; Muscovey and Pekin ducks; and African, Embden and White Chinese geese. All were in cages roughly six feet square and, to Donovan's eye, not too happy about the matter.

The captain eyeballed the four geese. "These would be them," he said.

"You don't know anything about geese, do you?" O'Neill asked.

"Not a damn thing. Beyond a couple of recipes, of course."

"These are Embden geese. A pretty common variety. Yours is already prepared and up front, unless you want me to pick one of these and..."

"No, thanks," Donovan said. "I used to watch my uncle do that, and I don't want to see it again."

"Thank God," O'Neill replied. "I got to get home."

"We all got to get home for the holidays," the captain replied.

"I still got a couple geese prepared that didn't sell."

"What's wrong with them?" Donovan asked, ever the suspicious New Yorker.

"Nothing. It's just that not that many people want goose for Christmas," O'Neill said.

"Turkey has taken over, eh?" the captain said.

"You bet. People have turkey for every holiday these days. Why did you pick goose? Is this a Christmas tradition in your family?"

"We have no particular tradition, other than a Star of David atop the tree."

"Who's Jewish?" O'Neill asked.

"My wife is Jewish and African-American," Donovan reported. "It's my job to place the Star of David atop the tree."

"At Hanukkah do you hang Christmas tree balls on the menorah?"

"Not a bad idea," the captain replied, making a mental note to suggest it during a light moment at the family dinner, which the Donovans were hosting on Christmas Eve in their new home.

Donovan followed the market owner back to the front of the establishment, where soon was produced a fine, fifteen-pound goose—trussed with assorted stuff that Donovan didn't care to know the details of, stuffed inside.

"Will one do?" O'Neill asked.

"I was told to get just one," Donovan replied.

"How many you got coming over?"

Donovan ticked off the guest list on his fingers: "Marcy, me, Daniel, Marcy's mom and dad, my cousin, my grown son, my mom. How many is that? Six?"

"Eight," O'Neill replied. "Too many for one bird."

"Most of my family members are dieting," Donovan said. "One goose will do fine."

"You got it," O'Neill replied.

Donovan laid a fifty-dollar bill on the counter and, following the captain's refusal of the bird as a gift, O'Neill made change.

"You got a recipe?" he asked.

"My wife does. Cooking ain't what I do best. My specialty is egg sandwiches and home fries."

"Mine, too. Hey, look, this is a quality goose, killed and trussed up right here this morning. It's easy to cook, even for a guy who normally does home fries. My bird will give you a good holiday. Merry Christmas to you, Captain."

"Merry Christmas to you, too," Donovan replied, and watched as the bird was put into a plastic bag that itself went into a plastic shopping bag.

Soon Donovan was back on the street. He walked O'Neill to his car, a white Lincoln with a vintage about a decade in the past. There was a tinge in the air, and the wind off the river carried with it the scent of snow.

"Is it supposed to snow?" O'Neill asked.

"An inch by midnight," Donovan replied.

"I better get going home."

"Where's home?" Donovan asked.

"Rockville Centre," the man replied.

"Drive safely," Donovan said.

As he was about to turn away, O'Neill reached inside his coat and from his shirt pocket produced a business card. He handed it over, saying, "You got a problem cooking that beauty, you call me at home. The number is on the lower left."

"Thanks," Donovan replied, handing over one of *his* cards and pausing to write on it his home phone number and address. "If the local cops can't help with those robberies, give me a call."

"See you around," O'Neill said as Donovan waved and

headed off away from the cold and the river, his feet making clomping sounds on the soccer-ball-size cobblestones of Gansevoort Market.

THE SNOW FELL relentlessly from about seven in the evening, a bit faster and harder than expected, producing the promised inch by 11:00 p.m. and three inches by daybreak on December 24. Donovan awoke to the heavy scraping sound made by the New York City Department of Sanitation plows as they made their noisy way down the street, and the much lighter, rhythmic scraping of aluminum hand shovels clearing the sidewalk. There also was the smell of fresh coffee and thyme wafting up the elevator shaft from the ground floor. Then there was the sound of the elevator rumbling up and, following that, the clang of a bronze gate swinging open, pushed tentatively by a tiny hand. Donovan rolled out of bed, stretched, yawned and rolled his eyes.

His small arms straining from a year's worth of wheeling himself around, Daniel slid into his parents' bedroom with a slight whoosh of rubber tire on parquet floor. He was dressed for the day before Christmas in a blue-and-red Gap polo shirt and jeans, and his bright, dark-brown eyes glistened in the light pouring through the window from the snow outside.

"Time to get up, Daddy," he said.

"Good morning, slugger," Donovan said, reaching his arms out to let the boy wheel himself into his father's hug.

"Mommy wants you to help cook."

"Mommy knows that I like to help. But I'm helpless when it comes to cooking."

"She said to take your shower and come down," Daniel insisted.

Donovan said that he would do as he was told. Then he asked, "How are you doing with that elevator gate?"

"I can do it good now," Daniel said proudly.

"You can do it *well*. I thought I heard you getting it open faster."

"Yeah!"

"You do it better than I do. I'm going in the shower."

"I'll go tell Mommy to make your coffee," Daniel said.

When Donovan appeared in the kitchen half an hour later dressed for the day in a navy-blue polo shirt and brown corduroys, he saw the sort of scene unimaginable during his many years living—if that's what one would call it—as a hard-drinking, eccentric bachelor and brilliant but loose-cannon cop who once kept a snapping turtle in one of the bathtubs of his rambling, Upper West Side apartment. The kitchen scene might have been painted by Norman Rockwell, had not the mother been multiracial and the precious little boy been confined to a wheelchair by a mystery illness that his father had rearranged his life and career to conquer.

Marcy had a red-and-green holly bush patterned apron over her leotard top and peasant skirt, and was slicing celery at the counter. Mary sat at the kitchen island—a massive, French provincial butcher table bought during one of Marcy's weekend antiquing trips upstate—having tea and toast. And Daniel had his chair up alongside his mom and held a bunch of thyme, waiting for the moment to hand it over.

The boy looked around when Donovan arrived.

"Daddy's here," Daniel announced.

"God bless all here," Donovan proclaimed, taking a line from *The Quiet Man*, long the only John Wayne movie he could tolerate.

"Honey," Marcy said, "just because we're making some Irish side dishes doesn't mean that you have to do Irish shtick all day."

"Yes, it does, I think," Mary said, adding, "Good morning, William, and Merry Christmas Eve."

"And the same to you," he replied, smiling as she reached across the table to switch on *Morning Edition* for him.

"Hi, honey," Marcy said.

"Hey," he replied, easing up behind her and planting a

kiss on the side of her neck while patting her gently on the bottom.

"Mmm," she said, tilting her head toward his and giving him a little nuzzle.

"Daddy," Daniel said and reached out to be hugged.

The counters on both sides of the sink were crowded with ingredients variously chopped, diced, sliced, or crumbled and waiting to be cooked into the Christmas goose meal. There was butter, onions, celery, day-old whole-wheat bread, thyme, salt, pepper, eggs, carrots, bay leaves, and flour.

A large stockpot simmered atop the stove, the perfume of butter enriching the smell of coffee and the sight of snow still falling outside the French doors leading to the garden.

Donovan poured himself a mug of coffee—Maxwell House Lite, consisting of half decaf, half regular coffee, and added cream and sugar. Then he went to the garden door and opened it, stepping outside long enough to feel the snow on his cheeks. Then as the coffee steamed the air above the white-robed garden, he ducked back inside.

"Honey, would you help me out here?" Marcy said.

"Sure," he replied, moving back alongside her and giving her another pat on the bottom.

"Stir the butter, would you?"

She handed him a wooden spatula and moved to one side to begin chopping a large onion. He began stirring the butter as she chopped away next to him.

"What's on the agenda today?" Donovan asked.

"We're going to cook the goose… I'm having trouble getting those words out of my mouth…this morning, put it aside and nuke it this evening to heat it up after the family gets here."

"Makes sense," he agreed.

"That will give Mary and me time to straighten up the house and Daniel and you time to go out and buy a tree. Santa is coming, you know."

"Yeah!" the boy exclaimed.

"But first we have to put together the rest of the meal," Marcy said.

"Which is…"

"Christmas pudding, among other things."

"Christmas pudding," he replied blankly.

"You *are* Irish, aren't you?"

"Half," Donovan replied. "So I'll take a halfhearted guess…plum pudding."

"That was close," she replied. "But try dried fruit, spices…"

"Plum pudding," Donovan said.

"Held together with suet," she said.

He gave her a sharp look. "Suet? Did you take it off the tree in the garden? The chickadees must be pissed."

He looked in that direction, but saw only snow and the ghost of coffee steam on the glass.

"I substituted," she replied.

"What substitutes for suet? A hockey puck? Chicken fat? What does your grandmother call chicken fat, *schwartz?*"

"*Schmaltz,*" Marcy replied, a trace of exasperation in her voice.

"*Schmaltz* liquor," Donovan suggested.

"I use Crisco," she replied. "Keep stirring the butter, hon."

"Crisco."

"You don't eat a *lot* of Christmas pudding. So we have to mix the ingredients, give the pudding a ceremonial good-luck stir… Daniel will do that…"

"I'll do it," Daniel said, trying to drive his chair between his parents.

Donovan moved over and, when his son wheeled himself up, patted him on the head.

"…and after the stir, we boil the pudding for a couple of hours," Marcy said.

"I think the butter is ready," Donovan said.

Marcy walked around behind her husband, gave *him* a pat on the butt and peered into the pot.

"It's ready," she said, and poured in a bowl of chopped onion.

Donovan snapped his head back. "Whoa," he said.

"You'll love this when it's done."

"Assuming I survive. Where did you get the recipe?"

"I used to run a restaurant, remember?" Marcy said.

"Which never served goose."

"I got it off the Web. Let me stir the pot. You get me the rest of the ingredients. They're all ready over there."

She nodded at the batch of materials she was preparing when Donovan had come downstairs.

"What are we making?" Donovan asked.

"Stuffing."

"Okay. What else?"

"We'll also have bread sauce. That's made from bread crumbs, milk, onion and cloves. And I'm going to make trifle."

"Whazzat?" Donovan asked suspiciously, using the snappish New York accent usually reserved for unnerving suspects.

"A sweet dessert," Marcy replied quickly, perhaps sensing where he was going conversationally.

"It's not cow guts?" he asked.

"That's *tripe*. William, how could you know so much about the universe and be stuck at the bacon-cheeseburger level when it comes to food?"

Mary giggled and excused herself.

"I know about alfalfa sprouts," he protested. "I like my bacon cheeseburger to sit on a bed of them."

Marcy made a face. She continued, saying, "It's *Christmas*, William. Be nice. Anyway, trifle is made…at least *I'm* making it, and this is a 250-year-old recipe, from biscuits, red wine…as much as it takes to soak the biscuits through, whipped cream, sugar, lemon juice, and white wine. Served with walnuts.''

"Red *and* white wine?" he asked.

She nodded. "You'll survive that, too. Remember, you *must* prove the absolutists wrong."

"I nearly did yesterday afternoon. I forgot to tell you. Guess who's tending bar at this Irish joint on Hudson?"

"No," she replied.

"The same."

George Kohler had been part cook and part bartender at Marcy's Home Cooking on Broadway on the Upper West Side. When she closed the place to go back to Columbia Law, and the restaurant became a Starbucks, Kohler claimed to welcome the six months' unemployment as being the vacation he long deserved. But Donovan wondered if he wasn't resentful.

"He seemed grumpy," Donovan said.

"Imagine that."

"What are we making beyond stuffing and Tribble?"

"Trifle!" she exclaimed.

"What else?" he asked.

"The usual…potatoes, carrots, peas, winter asparagus, gravy."

"Yesterday you said something about caviar on toast points," Donovan said.

"Too ostentatious," she replied. "I reconsidered."

"Good," Donovan agreed.

"And, of course, a choice of cranberry sauce and chestnut puree. I bought the puree at Balducci's. Honey, pass me the celery, please."

He did as he was told. The sliced stalks slid into the pot and soon were cooked crisp yet tender. With Donovan and his son handing over the ingredients one by one, into the pot went day-old whole wheat bread pieces, thyme, salt and pepper. A while later and following removal from the heat and addition of eggs and water, Marcy took the pot off the fire and set it atop a slice of cork at the far end of the counter.

"Is the goose done, Mommy?" Daniel asked.

"No, honey. Just the stuffing. Daddy has to get the goose ready."

"Can I do it?" the boy asked.

"Not this time," she said. Then, winking, added, "You know that, in New York City, Daddy is in charge of cadavers."

Spoke, she hoped, over her son's head.

"What's a cadaver, Daddy?" Daniel asked.

"This," Donovan replied, plucking the bird out of its plastic bag, rinsing it and then dropping it onto the gleaming steel rack that sat in the bottom of the black enamel roasting pan.

"Daniel, Daddy is a cop," Marcy said. "He looks into cadavers. Mommy is a lawyer. She tells him what he can and cannot do about them."

"Oh," said the boy.

"Thank you for delineating our roles so well," Donovan grunted.

Smiling, Marcy reached over Daniel and touched Donovan on the arm.

The captain reached into the body cavity of the goose and removed the small plastic bag containing the neck and giblets. He handed it to his wife, who put it into a bowl. Then Donovan lifted the bird to let the excess liquid drain out.

It was then that he heard a clink, a ringing of metal, a bit like a quarter being dropped into a pot, only more musical.

"What's that?" Marcy asked.

"I think the ghost of the goose tossed a grenade," Donovan said.

"Maybe this is the goose that laid the golden egg," Daniel suggested.

"No deal, slugger. I got that when I married your mom." Marcy laughed.

"But while we're all on the subject of marriage, look what the goose gave us."

He reached into the roasting pan and picked up a small, glittering object. "Not a golden egg," he said, "a golden ring."

He held a man's wedding band up to catch the morning light, then rinsed it off in cold water and did it again.

THREE

"Geese don't have crops, no matter what you may have read," Donovan replied.

THE RING GLITTERED, all the more so from just having been fished from the innards of a holiday meal and washed off. It appeared to be relieved, Donovan thought.

"A wedding ring?" Marcy asked.

"Yeah. Weird."

"In the goose?"

"Well, the roasting pan didn't lay it," Donovan said. "And I've got *my* ring."

He showed her, waving his hand around so she could be assured that it would never leave his finger.

"And I've got mine," she replied, doing the same as him.

"I want a ring, too," Daniel said.

"In time, Daniel," Marcy told him.

Donovan put down the ring long enough to wash and dry his hands. Then he picked it up again and walked over to look at it in the natural light streaming in from the garden.

"The ring didn't come from this house," he said. "I only took the bird out of the bag just now."

Marcy walked around Daniel to get to the sink and finished what her husband had been doing with the bird.

"It has two linked hearts engraved on the inside," he said. "Nothing else."

"No initials?"

He shook his head. "Just two hearts. I don't suppose that Mary...."

"Honey," Marcy said, "if Mary had a wedding band, church bells would be ringing from here to Tipperary."

He smiled.

"And we'd be out of a nanny," she added.

"Could the goose have *swallowed* it?" Donovan wondered.

"Doubt it," Marcy replied as she spooned the stuffing into the rinsed goose.

"No, of course not. It would be in the giblet bag, or wherever the stomach has gone, and I really don't want to know where that is."

"If the goose swallowed the ring," Marcy said, "wouldn't it wind up in the crop?"

"Geese don't have crops, no matter what you may have read," Donovan replied. "Besides, geese don't swallow hard objects. I'm pretty sure that their main diet consists of suburban golf courses."

"Different kind of geese, I think."

"I'll call O'Neill, the goose guy, later and ask if he knows what the story is," Donovan said.

"William, it's Christmas Eve...."

"Not until sundown."

"You can't work today," she insisted.

"I'm not *working*," he replied. "Only curious."

Donovan's thought process was interrupted by the doorbell, which rang forcefully and caused him to check his watch.

"He's early," Donovan said.

"Who's at the door, Daddy?" Daniel asked.

"Santa."

"Santa! But he doesn't come until after we're asleep!"

"Sometimes Santa has to make two trips," Marcy explained.

"Especially when he has something that's too big to fit down the chimney," Donovan added.

"Is it for me?" the boy asked excitedly, suddenly able to overcome the difficulty of pushing his chair away from the counter, and executing a pretty good ninety-degree turn to point toward the door to the dining room.

Followed by the little boy, Donovan walked through the dining room and into the front hall, where Mary had just pulled open the front door.

Lieutenant Brian Moskowitz stood there, the tassel of his red-and-white Santa cap flopping over his NYPD parka, one hand resting on an immense box. The container was several feet long and high but not quite as wide. A huge red ribbon was taped to the red-and-green-striped wrapping paper.

"God bless all in this house on this fine Christmas Eve," he announced in a pointedly phony brogue.

"Merry Christmas, Brian," Mary said, standing on tiptoe to give him a hug and a kiss.

"Same to you. Where's the boss?"

"Captain Donovan will…"

She fell silent when Donovan slipped up behind her and said, "Thanks, Mary."

As she went back upstairs, Mosko mockingly mouthed the words "Captain Donovan will see you now."

"Hey, that's my name and rank, *Lieutenant* Moskowitz," Donovan said.

"Yo, bro," Mosko said. "Ho, ho, ho. Help me carry this freakin' box inside."

"Whatever," Donovan said. He squeezed by the beefy Mosko, who, no matter the promotion and the somewhat improved manner of dress, still pumped iron, to get out the door to assess the size of the package.

"It's Uncle Brian!" Daniel exclaimed, rolling up, his arms straining at the wheels.

"Hiya, kid. Ho, ho, and all that."

Mosko bent far over and kissed him atop the head.

"You're not Santa!"

"He's coming later," Mosko replied. "I'm one of the freakin' elves. Roll out of the way while your dad and I get this box inside."

"Is that for me?"

"You got to ask the big boss man," Mosko said, rejoining Donovan on the stoop.

"Daddy!"

"Just a minute," Donovan said.

Then he turned his attention to Mosko and said, "It's narrow enough to just fit in the door. How did you get it in such a narrow box?"

"Some assembly is required," Mosko explained.

"Oh, great. Something else to do today."

"Not to worry, m'man. I brought tools and, being as the Moskowitz family Christmas dinner is tomorrow, not today, I have nothing to do except play elf. So I'll call Uncle Stanley, who is waiting around the corner in the truck and tell him I'm gonna hang here for a while and he can go home."

"He can come in."

"Nah, he won't want to. He's got to take a couple gross of plastic dinnerware and two dozen ceramic reindeer to a store in Jersey. I'll tell you what, I'll lift the back of this box. You get your fingers under the front and guide it inside."

That was fine with Donovan, who exchanged places with Mosko and did as he was told. Soon the box was inside the door, which shut on the snowy scene outside.

"Is that for me?" Daniel asked again.

"Yes, it is, Daniel," Marcy replied, coming down the hall wiping her hands on her apron. "Merry Christmas, Brian."

His eyes billowed at the sight of her in the cuddly domestic apron. "Well, if it ain't Pam Grier doing one of her famous kitchen scenes," he said.

Marcy gave him a withering smile.

"Merry Whatever to you, too," Mosko continued. "How's the goose I heard so much about in the past week doing?"

"The goose is cooked," Marcy said. "Well, it's cooking…just went in the oven."

Donovan squatted alongside his son and said, "Daniel, this present is so special that we thought you would like to have it on Christmas Eve."

"Can I open it now?"

"Sure. For one thing, you will need it later on when we go over to the meat market to buy a tree."

"They sell trees there, too?" Marcy asked.

"You can buy anything. And you can steal quite a bit, too, from what I hear. Come on, everyone, let's carry Daniel's present into the living room."

With Mosko doing most of the real lifting as usual, the family carried the big box into the living room, where space had been made for the tree and presents in front of the big bay window where the room projected out slightly over Kinderhook Street. They sat on the floor around the box, and Mary came in with coffee and crumb cake. Daniel burst into tears of joy when he got the wrapping off to find himself staring at a shiny new, motorized wheelchair.

"It's got an engine," Donovan said proudly. "It has batteries like we have in the van, and it has a stick that's like a driving wheel. You steer it with the stick."

"I can drive it! Like a car?"

"Not on the street, honey," Marcy said.

"Don't know about that, Mrs. D.," Mosko said. "The kid's got a 5.2-liter engine, double overhead cams and racing suspension in this beast. He could blast all the way to CBGBs before you could say 'Ramones.'"

"My son is *never* going to a punk rock club," Marcy sniffed.

"Don't touch that dial," Mosko replied.

Donovan grinned, but only angling his head so Marcy couldn't see.

"Can I drive it *now?*" the boy asked.

"We have to finish putting it together, son," Donovan said.

"I'll go get my tools," Daniel said.

With just enough difficulty to underscore the need for a motorized chair, he turned and headed back down the hall, toward the elevator.

"Hey," his father called after him.

"What?" Daniel asked, stopping.

"What do you say?"

"Thank you, Uncle Brian," Daniel said, without turning.

"Anyone else?" Marcy asked.

"Thank you, Mommy and Daddy and Aunt Mary," he said and then rolled off again.

"Kids," Mosko said.

He picked up the coat he had left on the floor and pulled from one pocket a soft leather pouch containing a ratchet set. Then he began working on the chair, joined shortly by Daniel, who rolled up with his plastic tool set. The two men and the boy spent the next hour around the new chair, which at last expanded to its full width. When the controls were hooked up, Daniel—proudly doing as much as he could by himself—swung over to the new chair, which he had already announced would be called The Beast.

Another hour passed, and Daniel had mastered the basics of moving forward and back and, to a lesser extent, turning to either side. Following his promise to avoid destruction and Mary's vow to keep him from so doing, Donovan and Mosko went into the kitchen for a snack and to watch the bird come out of the oven.

The smell of roast goose filled the room, and heat frosted the windows. Another pot of coffee was in the final stages of brewing, and as Mosko reached for another piece of crumb cake, Marcy gave him a small slice of goose off the tip of the carving knife to taste.

"Try this," she said.

"Is goose kosher?" he asked.

"As if you care," she replied.

He bit the piece off the knife, and said, "Cool."

"That's it? Cool?"

"Very cool," he replied, then added, "It needs salt."

Marcy shrugged and offered a piece to her husband, delivered in the same manner.

Donovan reached for the salt, and as his fingers closed around the shaker he knocked the gold band off the shelf. It hit the countertop with a ring, then rolled off and onto the floor, making another ring.

"Dammit," Donovan said.

"Whazzat?" Mosko asked, reaching down to pick it up.

"Try it without the salt," Marcy snapped.

"Yes, dear," he replied, and did as he was told. Then he smiled and said, "It's good...really good."

"*Now* you can put salt on it," Marcy added.

He did so, then said, "Nothing you cook can be improved upon."

She took a playful slap at his face. He ducked it.

Mosko held the ring up to the light and said, "Who lost his wedding ring?"

"The goose," Donovan said.

"Say again."

"That fell out of the goose."

"Like out of a box of Cracker Jack?" Mosko asked.

"Yeah, exactly like that," Donovan said.

"Well, that's weird," Mosko said.

"Ain't it just."

"Maybe the goose ate it. Those birds will eat anything."

"We went through that before," Donovan said.

"If that were the case, the ring would be in the giblet bag," Marcy said.

"My Uncle Stanley had too many giblets the other day," Mosko said.

"That's *gimlets*," Marcy said. Then she added, "Would

you stop infecting my husband with this Marx Brothers shit you spout all day and night?''

Mosko waggled his eyebrows, Groucho-style, and pretended to waggle a cigar.

''Somebody could have stashed the ring in the goose to hide it,'' Marcy said.

''Who?'' Donovan asked.

''I don't know…the thief,'' she said.

''This would have to be some kind of expensive ring for someone to steal it and hide it in a *goose*,'' Mosko said.

''And it doesn't look it,'' Donovan said.

''It looks like a plain wedding band,'' Mosko said. ''Apart from the two hearts.''

''They don't look like anything special,'' Donovan said.

''They were to *somebody*,'' Marcy said.

''I don't get this,'' Mosko said. ''A guy steals a very expensive ring that happens to be cunningly disguised as a four-hundred-buck wedding ring. Then he stashes it in a goose. How does he plan to get it back?''

''Maybe he doesn't want to get it back,'' Donovan said. ''Maybe the thief stuck it there to get rid of it.''

''Like if he was about to be caught,'' Marcy said.

''By who?'' Mosko asked. ''The poultry police?''

She shrugged.

''It's like tossing it into a Dumpster as he runs down the street eluding capture,'' Mosko said.

''Stuffing it in a goose as you run down the street is a little harder,'' Donovan maintained.

''Then someone sells the bird to a cop?'' Mosko replied. ''I must be missing some marbles, 'cause I can't figure out how all that makes sense.''

''It's got to make sense to someone,'' Marcy said.

''This is New York,'' Donovan said. ''This is not only New York, this is Greenwich Village. Not everything has to make sense. In fact, in this neck of the woods making sense is considered bourgeois.''

Marcy sighed, put down the carving knife, then went about covering the goose with foil and putting it in a secure corner of the counter. As she did so, she said, "You boys worry about this. I have to make trifle."

Mosko's eyes lit up, and he put on his Groucho look again and said, "Say, you're gonna make a—"

"Out!" she commanded. "Out of my kitchen!"

Donovan took the ring from his friend and, waving him to follow, went out into the dining room. "What are you doing the rest of the day?" Donovan asked.

Mosko tossed his hands up. "Not much. In my mom's Christmas, the men aren't allowed to touch the food, except to eat it, of course. And that we do a lot of."

FOUR

"Think of pheasants with polka dots."

"TELL ME AGAIN how this bird got into your life," Mosko said, plopping into the leather chair that faced Donovan's desk and hoisting his feet onto it.

"There's a big poultry place in the Gansevoort Meat Market," the captain explained. "Since no one in your family sells dead birds, to my knowledge, I went over there yesterday in search of a goose."

"Why not a turkey, like an American?"

"We wanted something different," Donovan snapped.

"So you walked over there in the snow."

"It wasn't snowing yet, only threatening. First I stopped in at this place, the Emerald I'll, to sit for a minute and rest."

"A likely story," Mosko said.

"And ran into George Kohler. He was behind the bar. Remember him?

Mosko nodded, saying, "I also remember that case of poison ivy I got last summer at Orchard Beach."

"At the bar was this guy Paul O'Neill, who it turned out owns the poultry market. He took me over there even though he had closed for the holiday. He opened up for me and sold me the goose you saw before. An Embden."

"Whazzat?"

"The model of goose," Donovan explained.

"Oh."

"I took it home in its plastic bag, stuffed it in the fridge and only opened it this morning when Marcy was about to stuff it. When I pulled the giblet bag out, the ring fell out.''

"Lemme see it again," Mosko said.

Donovan handed over the ring.

"It's a damn ordinary wedding band," Mosko said after a moment's reinspection. "But I guess it could have special meaning to someone."

"O'Neill told me there's been a bunch of break-ins at the Gansevoort Meat Market in general," Donovan said. "His place escaped so far."

"These robberies are just lately?"

"Last couple of weeks," Donovan replied, nodding. "I promised the guy I would call up the local robbery cops and light a fire under their butts. Anyway, I guess what could have happened is that the thief killed some poor slob and stole his ring...and was afraid to be caught with it while breaking into the poultry place."

"Did an alarm go off in the market the night before you bought the goose?" Mosko asked.

"I think that O'Neill would have mentioned it," Donovan replied. "But I'm sure of one thing—the guinea hens went off."

"Oh...o*kay*," Mosko replied.

"Guinea hens are from West Africa originally," Donovan said. "Think of pheasants with polka dots. They're famous for raising holy hell when there's an intruder. They make good watch birds."

"O'Neill has a flock of 'em?"

"Yeah."

"The perp breaks in, the birds freak out, the guy thinks the cops are going to nail him and quickly gets rid of something he doesn't want to be caught with," Mosko said.

"It's entirely possible," Donovan said.

"But why didn't he come back in the morning when the store opened and try to buy every goose?"

"Maybe he did," Donovan said. "For some reason, it escaped my mind to ask O'Neill if a customer came in that morning and tried to corner the goose market.''

"How many geese can a store *sell* in New York City?" Mosko asked.

Donovan shrugged. He began picking through the papers atop his desk. One pile, about six inches deep and arranged more or less neatly, concerned current cases. Most prominent among them was that of an apparent serial killer who had struck several times in the South Bronx not far from Hunts Point Market. The proximity to Yankee Stadium had resulted in a great deal of pressure from the mayor's office to catch the perp fast…or at least before the baseball season home opener. Pressure notwithstanding, the case had lain fallow over the previous week, as if in celebration of the holidays, a key witness having gone home to the Dominican Republic for Christmas.

A second pile of papers, an inch deeper than the first, concerned Donovan's new house, including such perils of home ownership as maintenance contracts, contractor's invoices and taxes.

The third stack of papers, taller than the others, related to Donovan's relentless search for a cure for whatever paralyzed his son's legs.

When he didn't find what he was looking for atop his desk, Donovan pulled open the top drawer and stared into it balefully for a time, but without touching anything. The impression he gave was that the drawer contained a black hole from which fingers, carelessly inserted, might never emerge.

"If you're looking for the latest forensics report from Hunts Point, I'll have it for you right after Christmas," Mosko said.

"O'Neill gave me his card," Donovan said. "I lost it."

"I'm not surprised," Mosko said. "Looking at your desk, I wonder how you manage to keep so much stuff in your head."

"I do it to avoid putting it on the desk," Donovan replied.

"Maybe the card jumped onto the floor and ran and hid," Mosko said, bending and pretending to peer under the desk.

"I'm sure I put it in my wallet," the captain said, pulling his wallet from his pocket and laying it on the desk. He stared at it for a moment.

"Afraid of looking in there, too?" Mosko asked.

Donovan shook his head. "I did already. Twice. I must have thrown out O'Neill's card by mistake."

Mosko stretched and said, "I do believe this is a sign from God that you and me should go up to the...what did you say that place was called?"

"The Emerald I'll."

"Yeah, that place. We should go up there and have a drink and do what we can to make George Kohler's life miserable."

"As he has done for us so many times over the years," Donovan replied.

He returned his wallet to his pocket and had just stood when the doorbell rang.

"Who's that?" Mosko asked.

"Uncle Stanley, maybe."

"Nah. He's on his way home from Jersey—" Mosko pronounced it *Joisey,* of course "—by now."

They couldn't see the front door from Donovan's study, only the rich wood-paneled hall as Mary walked briskly to the door, all the while looking anxiously over her shoulder at the giggling little boy pursuing her with his not-so-carefully steered wheelchair.

Smiling, Mosko said, "The First Armored Division just blew by in pursuit of whatever fate awaits it."

"I'm afraid this is only the first of many chase scenes we can expect around here," Donovan said.

Then they heard Mary and a man talking and, after a moment, she stuck her head in the door to the study and said, "A Paul O'Neill is here to see you."

Donovan and Mosko exchanged glances, and then Mosko said, "Obviously he came to help you find the card."

"Obviously," Donovan agreed.

The two of them got up and followed Mary down the hall to the front door, where their visitor was admiring Daniel's new chair. The boy looked up at the man, unsure of what to say and, thus, silent.

"Hey, Paul," Donovan said.

"Hi, Bill," O'Neill replied. "Is it okay to call you that?"

"Why not? You meet a guy in a bar and it's hard to be too formal. Say hello to Brian Moskowitz."

"Yo, babe," Mosko said, clasping O'Neill's hand just hard enough, in that way that cops often do, to tell a man who was the likely winner should a conflict arise.

"Hi," O'Neill replied, a bit uncertainly. It was then that Donovan noticed the long lines around the man's eyes and the general look of someone for whom sleep was a distant memory.

"Brian and I work together," Donovan said.

"I sort of got that impression. Look, I'm sorry to bust in on you."

"No problem," Donovan replied. "I was just going to call you anyway.

"You *were?*" O'Neill asked, surprised.

"The captain got a prize outta your goose," Mosko said.

"I found this," Donovan said.

He held up the ring so O'Neill could see it.

"A wedding ring," the man replied.

"I found it in the goose," Donovan said.

The man's brow furrowed. "*In* the goose? That's weird. You mean, like, in the stomach?"

Donovan shook his head. "No, just rattling around in the cavity."

"Inside the giblet bag?"

"No. It fell out after the giblet bag came out. When I lifted the bird to drain the goo."

O'Neill took the ring and scrutinized it, holding it up to the light.

Then the store owner shrugged and said, "A wedding ring. I got one, so finder's keepers." And he tossed it into the air, where Donovan snatched it.

"You don't care?" Mosko asked.

"Hey, I only *sell* these birds, not raise them. I only know so much about them, and that doesn't include the weird shit they might eat."

"The ring wasn't in the stomach," Donovan said.

"It could have fallen out and the butcher not noticed," O'Neill said. "My guys are good at killing and preparing fowl, but they work fast at this time of year, and I don't know how much attention they give to every bit of intestine."

"Well, if it doesn't bother you…" Donovan said.

"As long as it doesn't bother *you*," O'Neill said. "I mean, at least you didn't break a tooth on it."

"I was just curious," Donovan said, pocketing the ring.

"I'll put a sign up on the bulletin board after the holidays, and if anyone claims it I'll give you a call."

"Fine with me," Donovan replied.

The captain wasn't sure, but thought that O'Neill might have been eager to change the subject. At any rate, that was what he did, looking down at Daniel and his new chariot and saying, "I see Santa brought a new wheelchair."

"This is Santa here," Donovan said, patting Mosko on the arm.

"How do you like it?" the man asked Daniel.

When the boy took too long to respond, Donovan prompted him, "Tell Mr. O'Neill if you like the chair."

"Yeah," the boy said.

Perhaps also sensing a need to change the direction of conversation, or just reflecting an old-fashioned tendency to whisk the children away from the grown-ups, Mary jumped into the conversation. She said to the boy, "Mr. Man, let's show the gentleman how fast you can go."

"Yeah!" Daniel said again, and whipped the chair into a hard left.

"Where are you from in Ireland?" O'Neill called after her.

"Roscommon," she answered over her shoulder. "And your family?"

"Dublin."

"Nobody's perfect," Mary replied, and continued down the hall with Daniel pursuing.

"Whoa," Mosko said as the boy clipped his foot as he started off in pursuit of his nanny, then careened off the wall.

"I think he's getting the idea," Donovan said as his son, laughing and giggling, disappeared down the hall.

"Do a wheelie, kid," Mosko called out.

"Didn't he just climb aboard that thing?" O'Neill asked.

Donovan nodded.

"He's picking it up fast."

"He's very smart and learns things quickly," the proud dad said.

"Imagine Einstein with a four-speed," Mosko said.

"Danny also is pretty good on a computer."

Donovan focused his attention back on the visitor and said, "I guess you had a break-in last night."

O'Neill raised his eyebrows. "How'd you know that?" he asked.

"What the captain is saying is that he assumed you didn't beam into the neighborhood for the wassail," Mosko said.

O'Neill looked from one detective to the other, then nodded. "I guess my number came up," he said. "The guys— the other meat market owners—told me that it would happen."

"How long after you and I left the store did the break-in occur?" Donovan asked.

"About one in the morning."

"After all the other markets closed and everyone went home," Donovan replied.

"Yeah. And about an hour after the cleanup crews left," O'Neill said. "Only the night watchmen were left."

"And the security cameras," the captain said.

"That's right."

"Did you have one?" Mosko asked.

O'Neill shook his head. "I promised myself one for Christmas," he replied.

"Too bad you're not Jewish," Mosko replied. "Hanukkah came two weeks ago."

O'Neill nodded. "I should have thought of that."

"Did a suspicious figure turn up on any of the other security cameras?" Mosko asked.

"The cops are checking on it," O'Neill said.

"Did the guinea hens wake up the night watchman?" Donovan asked.

Mosko gave him a peculiar look.

"Nope," O'Neill said.

"Was anything taken?" Mosko asked.

The store owner shook his head again. "Not that I could tell."

"How do you know there was a break-in?" Mosko asked.

"I have a silent alarm that rings at a security company," O'Neill said. "They sent a car over and found that one window had been jimmied. But it took them half an hour to get there, and in that time the thief was in and out."

"Half an hour?" Mosko asked.

"About that," O'Neill replied. "They said they were short-staffed due to the holiday."

"How much you paying them?"

"Nothing...*now*."

Donovan shoved his hands into his pockets and said, "Well, I see nothing but dead ends here. The goose ate the ring and that's that. The thief broke in but stole nothing."

"Time to send out for some wassail and forget the whole thing," Mosko said.

"But despite the lack of damage, the episode is bothering you," Donovan said to O'Neill.

"Yeah, but I don't know why," O'Neill said.

"It's bothering me, too," the captain admitted.

"I don't have anything better to do," Mosko added.

FIVE

A scrawny needle from a tree dying wretchedly slow along-side the Vince Lombardi Rest Area off the New Jersey Turn-pike

THE STREETS GLISTENED with new snow, and the sun that had just come out gleamed brightly enough off it to make the men shade their eyes with their hands. As the two detectives accompanied O'Neill to his store, they walked through a pic-ture-postcard scene that lacked only horse-drawn sleighs and the sound of jingling bells. Children puffed up in down and wool until they looked like designer penguins laughed in the snow while their fathers pushed aluminum shovels along sidewalks. A lumbering snowplow plied the avenue as, on the tree-lined side streets, cars were smoothed over into glim-mering white lumps that might have been white-blanketed haystacks in a wintry Vermont pasture. Out on the river, ice floes drifted casually with the outbound tide. A red Moran tug pushing a coal barge was the solitary traffic in the winter-narrowed shipping channel. Clouds of white puffed from its stack in the frosty air.

On the corner of Gansevoort, a truck with Canadian mark-ings sat beside a nearly block-long display of Christmas trees. A man and a boy—his son, from the cut of their jaws and nearly identical brown parkas—tended a kerosene heater and one of those tree-bagging machines that struck Donovan as being spawned of a wood chipper and a crab trap. The older man held a red enamel coffee mug that steamed deliciously in frosty air scented by Norwegian fir needles and French roast.

"Wait a minute guys, okay?" Donovan said to his walking companions.

"What's up?" Mosko asked.

"Got to reserve a tree."

"Aren't you and Mario Andretti doing it together later on?"

"He'll help me haul it home," Donovan said. "I'm buying a tree now 'cause I want to make sure I get a good one. If he wants a different one, I'll switch."

"Is his chair gonna be able to go in the snow?" O'Neill asked.

"I had it fit with snow tires," Donovan replied.

The man laughed.

"Tires with knobby treads," Donovan explained. "All-terrain, kind of like they put on mountain bikes."

"The kid has to keep up with his dad," Mosko added.

"I have a feeling that Danny and I are going to be putting on a lot of mileage together."

"The captain plans to take the kid with him on cases," Mosko said.

Donovan nodded, telling his friend, "He can help me on those days when you're too busy *managing your department.*"

"What have I gotten myself into with this lieutenant thing?" Mosko moaned.

"I need a nice, full tree for a high ceiling," Donovan said to the older of the two people, who had put his coffee cup atop the kerosene heater and walked over.

"If you will follow me," the man replied, betraying a robust French accent.

"Quebec?" Donovan asked.

"Yes. How do you know?"

Donovan pointed at the man's large flatbed truck, parked just beyond the trees and not quite obscuring the view of the side of the Gansevoort Live Poultry Market. It bore Quebec plates.

"My son and I drive down every season," the man added.

Then he showed the captain half a dozen Christmas trees that were lined up against the high chain-link fence that separated the sidewalk from the poultry mart's back storage yard of snowed-over empty cages and pallets of miscellaneous items. Even though the fence was a ten-footer, one of the trees towered above it.

"How high is your ceiling?" O'Neill asked.

"Ever been in Saint Pat's?" Mosko asked.

"Yeah, yeah," Donovan said, separating the majestic tree from the one next to it by squeezing between them. Then he held up the big tree. It was marvelous—twelve feet tall at the very least and perfectly conical, with no empty spots.

"This is the finest I have," the Canadian said.

"It's a beauty," Donovan replied. "I'll take it."

"That will be a hundred dollars," the man said, as Mosko looked away, restraining himself from dispensing too much guff.

Donovan handed over two fifty-dollar bills. Then as the man took the tree and was about to bag it, Donovan said, "Hold this for me, okay? I want to come here later with my boy and get it then."

"What's the name?"

"Bill and Danny," Donovan replied.

The Canadian scribbled a note on the back of a parking ticket and affixed the same to a branch, using a length of twist tie.

"How old is your boy?" he asked.

"Five."

"Five going on MIT," Mosko added, apparently having exhausted his ability to remain silent.

"Well, I'll be glad to hold the tree for you," the man replied. "Is there anything else I can get you today? A wreath for the door?"

"Gotta have a wreath for the door," Mosko said.

"I'll let Danny pick that out," Donovan said, and began edging away from the display of Christmas greenery.

"Two wreaths," Mosko said. "One for the front door. One for the *garden* door..." He gave that word a sharp edge. "And how about a third for the *terrace* door?"

Donovan glared at him and Mosko turned away again, this time smiling. So doing, he found himself staring in the direction of the back of the truck, and when the Canadian's attention had gone elsewhere, Donovan tapped Mosko on the arm and motioned for him to make a note of the license-plate number.

Mosko nodded in agreement.

When the man turned back, it was to stare at the captain's shield.

"Oh," he said.

"I just want to ask..."

"About the robbery last night?"

"About that," Donovan replied.

"Another policemen already asked."

"Like there are grades of Christmas trees, there are grades of policemen," Mosko said.

"What did you tell him?" Donovan asked.

"That my son and I didn't see or hear anything," the man replied.

"I didn't get your name."

"James Le Bec." He obliged by spelling it. "My son is George."

"Bill Donovan and Brian Moskowitz of the Special Investigations division," Donovan said.

"Hiya," Mosko said, then drifting off to make a call on his cell phone.

"You know Paul O'Neill, right?" Donovan said.

"Yeah, he does," the poultry man replied, frowning slightly.

Le Bec didn't reply, and didn't smile.

"You guys got a problem?" Donovan asked. "What is it, the fence?"

"Yeah. I don't get anything out of his leaning trees on my fence," O'Neill said.

"I increase customer traffic," Le Bec argued.

"I haven't sold so much as an egg because you brought someone in," O'Neill returned. "And I got nothing to say about him using the sidewalk."

"It's a public sidewalk open to everyone," Le Bec said.

"To every American citizen it is," O'Neill replied.

"I come here every year...."

"To take our money and give back nothing," O'Neill insisted.

"Okay, guys," Donovan said.

"And I keep asking him to stop leaning trees on my fence and he keeps doing it," O'Neill said.

"Where would you suggest I put them?" the Canadian asked.

O'Neill wound up and said, "Why don't you...?"

Donovan interrupted, saying, "So, Mr. Le Bec, you didn't see or hear anything unusual last night?"

"Correct. However, I don't take notice of what goes on around his store and didn't see anyone go in and out after you two left."

"How late were you here?"

"We shut down at ten and finished cleaning up by eleven."

"What then?" Donovan asked.

"I went to get a sandwich and a beer," Le Bec replied.

"Where?"

"Hog Heaven."

"The biker bar," Donovan said.

"The sort-of biker bar," O'Neill added.

"Why do you say that?" Donovan asked. "I'm new to the neighborhood."

"The customers mostly seem to be lawyers driving twenty-thousand-dollar Harleys,'' O'Neill replied. ''They like to rev up outside and then go in and talk trash with the tattooed barmaid.''

Donovan said that he understood, it being Manhattan and all.

''And your son went with you?''

''Nope. Too young. He stayed and watched TV. I brought a cheeseburger back for him.''

''Back to where?'' Donovan asked.

''To the truck. It has an extended cab. He sleeps in the back. I sleep on the seat. For a couple of weeks every year, we can deal with it.'' Then he added, ''I guess being a New Yorker you don't know that much about trucks.''

''Beyond suffering through a Burt Reynolds movie one time, no,'' Donovan replied. ''What time did you get back from the bar?''

''Midnight.''

''How can you be sure?''

''I like to keep to a schedule, so I checked my watch,'' Le Bec said. ''Is that any help?''

Donovan told the man that it was. ''You'll be even more helpful if you tell me you heard a flock of birds yowling,'' Donovan added.

''Birds?''

''Guinea hens. They raise the roof when there's an intruder.''

''No,'' the man said emphatically. ''But then, I sleep like a rock.''

''I heard them,'' a voice said.

It was the son, who unnoticed by the others had finished with a customer and crept up, his own enamel coffee cup in hand and making a small cloud.

Le Bec made the introductions. When O'Neill's name came up, the boy's face froze harder than the ice crystals on the chain-link fence.

''What did you hear and when?'' Donovan asked.

"I heard guinea fowl, like you said," the boy replied, looking at Donovan only.

"You have heard them before?" his father asked.

"In the summer before last, when I stayed at the farm."

"My brother has the tree farm where I get these trees," Le Bec explained. "He also keeps chicken and other birds. Me, I know nothing about raising birds."

"I know not to stand beneath them when they're in trees," Donovan said.

"And me also," Le Bec replied.

"When did you hear them last night?"

"It was at one o'clock."

"You're sure?"

"Yes," he said emphatically. "I have a small TV in the truck. I was watching it after lying down and my father had fallen asleep in the front. I heard the sound after my show ended at one."

"What were you watching?" the captain asked idly.

"*Farscape*. It was weird."

"Which, the birds or the show?" Mosko asked, returning and sticking his cell phone back in its belt holder.

"Both," Donovan said. Then to the boy he added, "Tell me about the sound."

"First there was one outburst that lasted two or three minutes," the boy said. "Then nothing for twenty minutes or half an hour. Then the birds did it again, but only for a minute the second time. A little after, the police came."

"And you didn't hear anything else?" Donovan asked.

"No."

"Did you go over and see what was happening?" Mosko asked.

"Why should I?" the boy replied.

"No reason," Donovan said.

"Did you stay in the truck the whole night?" Mosko asked.

"The whole night," the boy said.

"Both of you?"

"Yes," was the reply.

"Where did you go to the can?" Mosko asked.

"We have a portable toilet in the back of the truck," Le Bec said.

"So you *did* get out of the front of the truck," Donovan said.

"No," both Le Becs replied.

"You held it all night?"

"We only sleep five hours," the father said.

"We're up at six in the morning," the son added.

"Okay, guys, thank you for your help," Donovan said. "I'll be back in a couple of hours with my son to pick up the tree."

"And the wreaths," Mosko added.

"And them," Donovan said.

"Three. One for each door."

Sighing, Donovan walked away from the display of trees, the others following. When he passed the truck with the Canadian plates and reached the gated facade of the poultry mart, Mosko said, "They're both dirty."

"I knew it," O'Neill said, flashing an I-told-you-so look.

"The old man is a major scofflaw," Mosko continued. "You saw him use a parking ticket to write notes on?"

Donovan had noticed.

"Well, that's about the kindest thing he does with them. He owes over seven thousand dollars for the past six or seven Christmas seasons."

Looking increasingly pleased with himself, as if the break-in was worth it to prove his point, O'Neill added, "He comes here every year and takes and repays the city by taking some more."

"Any outstanding warrants on this grinch?" Donovan asked.

Mosko shook his head. "No, but the kid's a different story."

"Tell me."

"George has a pretty big history for an eighteen-year-old."

"Drugs?" Donovan asked.

"Yeah. Two pot possessions and—"

"You know I don't care about that, except that it explains why he likes *Farscape*," the captain said.

"—and one shoplifting. He's currently on probation for the shoplifting."

"What did he steal?" Donovan asked.

"It doesn't say," Mosko said. "But the dollar figure doesn't matter. It's the thought that counts."

"How did the two of them get into the country?" O'Neill asked.

"What American border guard looks that closely at a father-and-son team hauling a truckload of Christmas trees?" Mosko said.

"The border guy probably eyeballed the driver's license and let 'em pass," Donovan added.

"Even after 9/11?" O'Neill asked.

"No way you'd mistake those square-jawed Caucs for Muslim fundamentalist terrorists," Donovan said.

"You shouldn't let Le Bec get away with being a big-time scofflaw," O'Neill said, as he took the keys to his shop out of his coat pocket.

"I knew the bum was a thief when he hit you for a hundred for that tree," Mosko said. "Wanna bust 'em?"

"Not until Daniel and I pick up our tree. *And* wreaths, and enough already about the number of doors I own."

Mosko smiled mischievously.

O'Neill unlocked the padlocks that secured both sides of his slightly rusting steel security gate and rolled it up, making a metal racket that caused two tree oglers down the block to look over.

"Those two Canadians could have been the ones who broke into my place," he said.

"That would be pretty stupid, wouldn't it?" Donovan said.

"The guy—the kid, anyway—has a record of theft and goes and breaks into the place next to where he's camped out in his truck and is a likely suspect."

"I wouldn't rule it out," Mosko said. "That kid looks like he has the IQ of a pine needle…and not one from a hundred-buck tree at that."

"A scrawny needle from a tree dying wretchedly slow alongside the Vince Lombardi Rest Area off the New Jersey Turnpike," Donovan said. "Did the cops who came last night look for footprints in the snow?"

"They said somebody walked all the way up the alley on the west side of the building right up to the window that was broken into," O'Neill replied.

"I don't suppose they took evidence…photos and all," Mosko said.

"You're a dreamer," Donovan said. "For a break-in where no one was hurt and, so it seems, nothing stolen?"

"Not so much as a feather was taken that I can see," O'Neill said. "The cops who came said that the main thrust of the whole deal was to piss off the birds. But the real main worry I got is that if this was a robbery and the insurance company gets ahold of last night's police report, my rates will triple and I'll have to close up."

"Let's see what we can do about this whole thing," Donovan said.

He paused to brush some fir needles off his pants, shoes and out of his cuffs. Eight or nine of them fell in a halo around his feet.

Mosko stared down at it. "Got 'em all?" he asked.

"I think so," Donovan said.

"He thinks so," Mosko said to the frosty air.

"Let's go," Donovan said.

He followed O'Neill into the store and watched while the man disabled the alarm, which was encased in white plastic dotted with buttons and lights and set in the wall to the left of a freezer. Donovan's eyes skittered from the glittering display to a clump of frozen emu patties, then back.

"Tell me again when the alarm went off," he asked.

"Just about twenty after one. But security didn't get here until almost one-fifty. Did I tell you I fired their sorry asses?"

"They called the cops who called you," Mosko said.

"Yeah. That's about all the security company did. I could pay a homeless guy ten bucks a week to sleep out back and drop a dime when the joint is broken into."

"Ten bucks plus all the chicken fingers he can eat," Mosko added.

"Again, when did the cops get here?" Donovan asked, closing his eyes while making mental calculations.

"Five minutes after the security guys," O'Neill replied. "About five to two."

"And you got here?" Donovan asked.

"A quarter to three."

"That's pretty good time from Rockville Centre," Donovan replied.

"At that time of night going into Christmas Eve?" Mosko asked.

The captain said, "I need to know when three things occurred—the guinea hens screamed the first time, the alarm went off, and the guinea hens screamed the second time. I think that was the order of occurrence."

"From what I can tell, the hens first sounded off at one," O'Neill responded. "The alarm went off at one-twenty, which is right about when the hens screamed for the second time. The cops came at five to two, five minutes after the lame private security guys."

"Interesting," Donovan said.

"Why?" O'Neill asked.

"Because either the thief couldn't get in at first and was stuck outside for twenty minutes after the hens went off the first time before trying again," Mosko said.

"...or the thief *got in* and was inside for twenty minutes

despite the guinea hens making a fuss yowling when he came and left,'' Donovan said. ''In either case, he wasn't afraid of the noise they made. I mean, the first time I was sleeping over at my aunt's house in the country and a fox tried to get into the henhouse in the middle of the night, the guinea hens made a racket like you couldn't believe. Imagine a Mariah Carey song played at 78 rpm.''

O'Neill winced. ''My daughter is into her,'' he added. Then he said, *''kids.''*

''I jumped so high I hit my head on the ceiling,'' Donovan added. ''The dent is still there, right next to the holes from the thumbtacks where my cousin hung his balsa wood model planes.''

''The window where the intruder got in is out back,'' O'Neill said, and flicked a switch that filled the back of the market with light. In response, the seemingly arenaful of birds began to cackle nervously. The guinea hens were silent at first, as if the commotion of their fellow fowl was warning enough. But then the three men walked down the aisle off the right aisle, which ran between rows of cages that stretched all the way to the back of the mart, and got too close to the guinea hen cage. The round little speckled birds set off their ear-splitting screech.

''Shut the hell up,'' Donovan snapped.

''Sounds like the number one local pulling into South Ferry,'' Mosko said.

''This is the window,'' O'Neill said, after the birds settled down.

SIX

"They get that damned whiff of freedom and just go wild,"
Mosko said.

HE TOSSED HIS HEAD in the direction of a two-by-three-foot
casement-type window set in the concrete wall about five feet
off the ground.

"Did the cops look at it?" Donovan asked.

"Sort of."

Donovan peered at the window, leaning his head into the
little space where it fit into the wall. Then he traced his finger
around the outline, but without touching. And then he looked
around.

When the captain stepped back, Mosko replaced him at
inspecting the window and its setting.

"Can I see this from the outside?" Donovan asked.

"Sure. Out the back door. The other cops did that, too."

O'Neill led the way out the back door, a windowless gray
steel portal through the otherwise featureless concrete-slab
wall. When he pushed it open, the door scraped off the thin
layer of snow that had fallen atop the many footsteps left
from the night before. Those footprints made a path curving
off to the right and around to the side of the building. Other
footsteps tracked around the whole of the backyard, around
the spare cages and other stuff, tracked everywhere, even to
that side where the chain-link fence supported the small forest
of Christmas trees on the sidewalk side.

"It looks like the other guys sure got around last night," Mosko said.

"And trampled everything with their hobnailed boots," Donovan added.

"They went everywhere," O'Neill added.

Donovan started around the corner into the narrow alley onto which the windows looked, retracing the snow prints of the many feet that slogged along before him.

Looking down and around, Mosko said, "Hey, Bill. The local cops missed one or two spots where they could have stomped evidence. I think we ought to tell them about it."

"Yeah."

They got to the outside of the window. It clearly was the point of entry, for every available bit of snow beneath and around it was packed as hard as ice by footprints. And whatever snow had fallen on the window ledge was scraped away.

Both detectives looked down at the snow and around it, and Mosko stooped to pick up and inspect several handfuls of snow from around the base of the window.

"Our colleagues didn't take the whole evidence thing too seriously," Donovan said.

O'Neill pointed at the outside of the window and said, "It looked like it might have been pushed in when the guy came in and then pulled back in place after he left. When I looked at this window the last time, the window was closed smack against the frame. But when I got here after the break-in, the window was open an inch, just like this."

"Are you sure you didn't leave it this way?" Mosko asked.

"I'm sure. I know because the alarm on this window is broken. You see the metal tape?"

"There's a break in it?" Donovan asked, referring to the half-inch-wide electrical conducting tape that ran around the inside of the glass and, by way of an electrical gizmo, to a wire that led, he surmised, to the white plastic alarm box in the front of the store.

"There's a short of some kind," O'Neill continued. "This goes back a few weeks when somebody hit it with a broom while cleaning up. I tried to program the alarm box to ignore signals from this window, but can't get it right. As things stand, if you open the window, no alarm. But if you close the window, the alarm goes off. Go figure."

"What do you do?" Donovan asked.

"We stay away from this window," O'Neill replied. "Not that there's reason to open a window anyway. It only gets the birds riled up."

"They get that damned whiff of freedom and just go wild," Mosko said.

"Something like that," the store owner agreed.

Donovan said, "The thief or would-be thief could have pushed open the window and slid in and then, on the way out, tried to pull it all the way shut but couldn't because his fingers got in the way. He could have tried to close it to exactly the spot it was before, but blew it. Did the cops look for fingerprints?"

O'Neill laughed. Then he added, "There were only two uniformed cops, and they just kind of walked around."

"There should be fingerprints on the inside of the top of the window where he pulled it shut," Mosko said.

"Assuming the guy didn't wear gloves," Donovan added. "Is Bonaci doing anything today?"

"Who's that?" O'Neill asked.

"Our forensics guru," Donovan replied.

"He's off," Mosko replied.

"Wouldn't this guru be going last-minute Christmas shopping?" O'Neill asked.

Donovan shook his head. "Not likely. Bonaci is so organized I'll bet he did all his Christmas shopping by Easter. Brian, ask him to drop by."

Lowering his voice, as if O'Neill, standing three feet away, couldn't hear, Mosko said, "You know, it's one thing for you and I to mess around on Christmas Eve. But if we ask

Howard to come here in the three-quarter-million forensics van, my budget is gonna take a hit."

"*Your* budget?" Donovan said, smiling. "I guess I better get used to hearing that. Well, you're a good manager who always keeps cost in mind. You can justify the expense on the grounds that the guy breaking in here could be the same guy we're after at Hunts Point Market."

"Think it's possible?" Mosko asked.

"It will do for an excuse. Ask Howard to drop by."

"Tell him he gets a free goose," O'Neill added.

"I don't think that phrasing it that way will be much of an enticement," Donovan said. "How about offering him a turkey? Howard's got a huge family."

"You got it. In fact, it's turkeys all around."

"Sounds like the crowd I used to hang with," Donovan said. "Okay, Howard will check for prints and any other evidence that may catch his eye. Let's look at the rest of the windows. Do *they* have active alarms?"

"They're all active," the store owner replied as he led the two detectives past the three other windows on the west side of the building, then allowed them inspection time. The four windows on the east side of the building all faced the sidewalk and were in clear line of sight with the tree guys. So Donovan ignored them for the time being and walked across the backyard to where the Christmas trees rested against the fence.

There were footprints there, too, seemingly hundreds of them, running the length of the fence up to where it abutted the neighboring building, which housed a sausage wholesaler. Donovan walked up to where his tree stood against the fence, the scribbled-upon parking ticket visible through the chain links and the branches.

Donovan squatted and sifted through the snow in much the same way Mosko had done earlier beneath the window.

"I got pine and other needles here," Donovan said. "Squashed down by the feet of our esteemed colleagues."

"I expect them along the fence line," Mosko said. "That's where the trees are leaning, much to Paul's annoyance."

"You got that right," O'Neill added.

"And you know what else?" Mosko continued. "If the needles are falling off already and it's only Christmas Eve, the tree that you paid way too much for is a no-good tree."

"My tree isn't shedding, only its neighbors," Donovan insisted. "Did you see needles under the window?"

Mosko shook his head.

Donovan continued, saying, "That doesn't mean that the kid couldn't have climbed the fence and broken into the store. It only means that he didn't shed any needles in the process. Which I consider unlikely, given the flock of them I dispensed outside the market door."

After giving the chain links an especially close look, Mosko leaned back on his heels and gave the fence a sharp kick. As it rang and vibrated, startling the Le Becs and a passel of shoppers, most of the snow that had clung to the topsides of the links shook off. It fell atop the snow already on the ground, leaving a line of tiny white mounds running ten feet in both directions.

"None of that was there before," Donovan said.

"I'm not sure what that proves," Mosko said. "It snowed all night. If anyone came over the fence at or about one in the morning, any snow evidence similar to what I just did would long since have been snowed under."

"My gut tells me that no one came over this fence last night," Donovan said.

"The only other access to the window that was broken into is up the alley," O'Neill said.

"Show me," Donovan said.

The store owner led them back up the alley, past the windows they inspected before, to an iron gate that appeared to have been hung during the administration of Calvin Coolidge. Many layers of cheap black paint covered as many layers of rust that had crept across the three-quarter-inch-wide struts, giving the overall impression of charbroiled lizard skin. A padlock of somewhat more recent vintage secured a galvanized iron chain to a post bolted into the brick wall of the adjacent beef wholesaler.

The gate was but six feet high, and though topped with six inches worth of slightly spiked iron, looked easily scaleable.

"How long do you think it would take you to get over that?" Donovan asked Mosko.

Mosko scrutinized the gate, shook the bars and noted the powdered brick that tumbled from the spots where the post was bolted into the brick.

"No need. I could kick the whole thing down," he replied.

"Barring that."

"It's easier than climbing over," Mosko replied.

"No one did, so give me an estimate that doesn't include devastation," Donovan said.

Mosko stepped back, looked at the gate for a moment, then said, "Two steps, foot in the crossbar, three seconds and I'm over the top."

"That's how it happened then," Donovan said. "Maybe the miscreant couldn't do it as fast as Brian, but that's what he did.

"I think you're right," Mosko replied.

The captain cast his eyes through the gate and downward onto the freshly shoveled sidewalk and said, "Any prints that might have been out there are long gone. I wonder if the cops who came last night at least wrote down if they saw any."

"I'll get a copy of the report," Mosko said.

"The perp went over the fence, down the alley and more or less straight to the window that he broke in through," Donovan concluded. "Now, how did he know which window? For one thing, the alarm tape looks like it's older than this gate."

Donovan gave the thing a rap with the side of his hand.

"You know when you inspect the plumbing—take a leak—at any bean wagon in the borough, for as long as it takes you got to stare at the filthy window beyond which is the alley?'' Donovan continued. ''There's always alarm tape, and the condition it's in makes it look like flypaper. Nobody in the world thinks the shit works. Anyway, the tape on the window back there—'' he nodded in the appropriate direction ''—fools nobody. The alarm doesn't work. At least not how it's supposed to. That's the window I would break into.''

''The perp did and the alarm didn't go off then,'' Mosko said.

''But the birds did. That didn't stop the intruder. He went inside and took...what?''

''There's nothing missing,'' O'Neill said.

''Can you look again?'' Donovan asked.

The three men went back inside the market. O'Neill turned on the systems at the front counter and in his office. Donovan and Mosko wandered around, peering at this and poking at that, gathering impressions.

Finally the market owner caught up with them as the two detectives were scrutinizing the twin rows of gleaming stainless-steel butcher tables that took up the greater part of the meat preparation area.

''There's nothing gone,'' O'Neill said.

''You're sure?'' Donovan asked.

''My cash drawers are locked up and untouched. The wall safe in my office hasn't been robbed. All the equipment seems to be here. There's nothing gone. Even the CD player in my office is still there—and it's one that cost me a hundred and fifty bucks at Circuit City. The disk is still in it.''

''What disk would that be?'' Donovan asked idly, leaning forward to inspect a narrow shelf set into the wall over the largest table.

''Mariah Carey,'' O'Neill replied. ''That shelf is where the men put their personal stuff...watches and all that...when they're working.''

''Mariah Carey is the reason the player wasn't stolen,'' Mosko said.

"The disk belongs to my daughter," O'Neill said hastily. "She was in here the other day working on her homework. She told me that disk covers up the sound of chickens being slaughtered."

"Mariah Carey *sounds like* chickens being slaughtered," Donovan said. "Doubtless one shriekfest cancels out another. It's a little-known principle of Newtonian physics. Did you check absolutely everything when you were making sure that nothing was stolen?"

O'Neill nodded. "Whoever broke in last night was here twenty minutes and didn't take a goddamn thing."

"No birds were snatched?" Mosko asked.

"*That* I can't tell you without doing inventory, but it sure don't look like it."

"How do you do inventory at a place like this?" Donovan asked.

"On the computer," O'Neill replied.

"Did you check the computer when you checked everything else?" Donovan asked. "I don't mean did you use the computer to check inventory? I meant, did you notice if the computer was tampered with?"

O'Neill shook his head.

"Please do it," Donovan said.

"Lemme help," Mosko said, turning to follow the man back to his office.

"When my colleague here isn't pumping iron he's working the mother board," Donovan said.

When the two of them came back five or ten minutes later, Mosko said, "It doesn't look like the PC has been used since yesterday in the a.m. Hey, Bill, even if you couldn't do a quick inventory, I don't see some thief breaking in here, stealing a chicken and taking it home on the subway."

"Stranger shit hath plied the underground in this burg," Donovan replied. "Paul, do you keep anything in the PC or in your office that someone would want to steal?"

"Like what?" the man asked.

"Business records, confidential information, that sort of thing."

"Names of city inspectors you had to pay off," Mosko added.

"Anything that might be of value to someone," Donovan said.

O'Neill replied that he couldn't think of anything. "And I don't have any enemies," he added.

"Other than a couple thousand doomed hens," Donovan said.

"Yeah, I would guess."

"I was looking at these shelves," Donovan said, redirecting O'Neill's attention to the seven- or eight-inch metal shelves that ran the length of the butcher tables. They held a variety of items—pens, notepads, scissors, trussing cord, boxes of wide rubber bands imprinted with the store name and phone number, and miscellaneous small items. Donovan could see that there were seven workstations, each with its own stool, and three personalized with family and other photos. One had three snapshots—of a young white couple first by themselves, looking lovestruck and beaming with newfound joy, then with a pink-clad baby. The shelf above another workstation had photos of a Latino family, a large one with sons and daughters and in-laws galore surrounding a seventyish couple. The shelf and wall above the third workstation was plastered with photos, clipped from various magazines, of Britney Spears.

"I guess that each guy has his own workstation," Donovan said.

"The dressers, yeah," O'Neill replied.

"That would be the guys who dress the chickens and other birds," Donovan said.

O'Neill nodded. "We do the slaughtering in the big area just behind."

"On the killing floor," Donovan said.

"I just call it the slaughtering area."

"I was thinking of an old blues song. Who are the dressers?"

"Asa Williams, Juan Estevez and Tom Drozak."

"Tom is the guy I met in the bar," Donovan said.

"He's a real good guy," O'Neill added.

Donovan peered at the photo of the man and his wife, then noted, "She really *is* stunning, like you said yesterday."

"Yeah," O'Neill said, "and the problem is that being married to Heidi Klum you kind of worry about crossing her and having her run off with someone who...who..."

"Does something a bit more income-generating than dressing chickens," Donovan said.

O'Neill nodded. "It's all I can do to pay my guys ten dollars an hour, you know what I mean."

"How long have they been married?" Mosko asked.

"I guess five or six years."

"And his daughter?" Donovan asked.

"She's two now, I think. Why do you ask?"

"No reason," Donovan said. Then he added, "They look like a happy couple."

"Tom says they are," O'Neill said. "As for him, I would think he's happy just to be out and on the straight and narrow."

Donovan and Mosko exchanged looks, then returned their attention to O'Neill.

"Whoosh," Mosko said.

"Whoosh?" O'Neill replied.

"The sound of something going right past Bill and me earlier in this conversation," Mosko replied.

"I don't understand."

"You said he was out," Donovan said. "Out of where?"

"Coxsackie Correctional Institute," O'Neill said. "Three years now."

He was careful to pronounce the name of the Upstate New York medium-security prison accurately—Co-sacky.

"What was he in for?" Mosko asked.

"Breaking and entering," O'Neill replied.

"Whoosh," Donovan said.

SEVEN

"What we have here is a failure to communicate."

"WHAT DID HE break into?" Mosko asked.

"Three Circuit City stores in Westchester and Putnam counties. He took CD players and sold them on the corner of the Grand Concourse."

"Where on the Grand Concourse?" Mosko asked suspiciously.

"Way downtown, I'm pretty sure."

"Like near Hunts Point Market?" Mosko asked.

"Yeah, come to think of it, around there," O'Neill replied.

Groaning audibly, Donovan said, "And you didn't think this information was somehow pertinent to today's topic of conversation?"

"What, that Tom has a record? Jeez, he's clean now, real clean. Actually a Boy Scout, fawning over that wife of his and worrying about doing anything to piss her off. In all, Tom is grateful, very grateful, to me for giving him a job. So are Asa and Juan."

Donovan and Mosko exchanged a look of astonishment such as men display upon learning that the shaking ground that leveled the garage was but the *early* part of the earth-quake.

"Do you hear an echo in here?" Mosko asked his captain.

"Absolutely," Donovan replied.

Then he said to O'Neill, "What we have here is a failure

to communicate. Are you telling us that you run a hiring program for ex-cons?''

"Um, yeah, sure I do.''

"And you didn't think this worth mentioning?'' Donovan asked. "I mean, in the context of an investigation—even if that's just Brian and me dueling the dogs of boredom on the day before Christmas—into a break-in?''

"I trust my guys with my life,'' O'Neill replied, his lips tightening into a show of resolution. "They're *friends of mine,* and, anyway, nobody is good enough an actor to seem that on-the-track and sincere and still be a bum.''

"George Burns said, 'the most important thing in life is sincerity…if you can fake that, you've got it made,'" Donovan stated.

Mosko added, simply, "Ted Bundy.''

"I understand your understanding for the right of former offenders to lead honest and straight lives without flatfoots like us annoying them with our suspicions,'' Donovan said.

"But if you want your crime solved, we gotta check what they were doing last night,'' Mosko added.

"They will understand and expect it,'' Donovan said.

"Not Tom,'' O'Neill said.

"Why not?'' Donovan asked, leaning forward to give the shelf above Drozak's workstation a closer look.

"He's a very proud man. He's *proud* of the fact he's on the straight and narrow. He's *proud* of having a beautiful wife, a great family and having bought a small house, the first time he ever lived in a place he owned. He wouldn't do anything to jeopardize all that.''

"Oh,'' Donovan said.

"Besides, his wife would kill him if he screwed up.''

"She looks like a puffball,'' Donovan said, picking up the family photo and holding it up to the light.

"Looks can be deceiving,'' O'Neill said. "She's one of

the reasons he stays on the straight and narrow. You saw how he was in a hurry to get home yesterday? They're in love."

"And he wouldn't do anything to hurt her," Donovan said.

Nodding, the store owner repeated himself, saying, "She would kill him."

"My wife would kill me, too," Donovan said. "And is eminently qualified to do it."

"She's a black belt in kung fu," Mosko said.

"More dangerously, she's a lawyer," Donovan said.

The captain turned the photo over several times before returning it to its place on the shelf and leaning in to scrutinize the shelf itself. He peered into a waste basket below Drozak's workstation. Then he repeated the procedure at the other workstations. When he was done, he said, "You keep a very clean work environment."

"It's scrubbed at the end of every day and all the trash is thrown out before we close. We got to do it," O'Neill replied proudly.

"Because of city inspectors?" Mosko asked, going around and repeating Donovan's inspection.

"Because of salmonella and E coli," O'Neill said. "If by some accident we get a piece of contaminated meat in here, we got to make sure we kill all the bacteria. Or else a customer could get infected and—"

"And all of a sudden you're on the front page of the tabloids with a headline reading 'Killer Hens'," Donovan said.

"'Deadly Duckies'," Mosko added.

"You got it," O'Neill agreed.

"Ever have that problem?" Donovan asked.

"What problem? Been in the papers? You got to be kidding."

"Have you had trouble with disease or inspections?" the captain asked.

"Not in the past three years," O'Neill replied after a brief pause.

"What happened four years ago?" Mosko asked.

Looking down at the immaculate tile floor, O'Neill said, "A batch of bad hens came through."

"Flew into town, scaring the horses, shooting up the saloon," Mosko added.

O'Neill was not amused. "A supplier in Kansas City sold us a bad batch. A couple of people got sick. There was a small item in the back of *The News* but no big story. I settled out of court, but my insurance rates went way up."

"Which is one reason you're a little gun shy now," Donovan added.

O'Neill nodded, a bit embarrassed, perhaps. Then his resolve rebounded and he said, "That episode also is why I'm so careful about cleanliness now. One of the reasons I hired Tom, Asa and Juan is that I believe in giving a guy a second chance. After all, I got another chance after the salmonella thing. But another reason is that they're *clean*. And also I have this one-strike-and-you're-fired rule. One breach of cleanliness…one fuckup of *any kind*. And you're out."

"Do you scrub everything every night?" Donovan asked.

"Every inch, using bactericidal soap and Lysol," O'Neill said.

"Including the workstations?" Mosko asked.

Bobbing his head, the store owner said, "Counters, floor, stools, walls, shelves."

"Yeah, I see," Mosko said, adding, "Who does the scrubbing?"

"Tom. It's his specialty. The guy is a clean freak. He scrubs everything just before we close up."

"The world needs people like that," Donovan said.

"I wish I had one at the unit," Mosko added. "The way

things are now, forget about clean. I'm lucky if they shovel out the crud.''

''I assume you keep inspection records,'' Donovan said.

''On the computer,'' O'Neill replied. ''I got to show them to the inspectors or else I'm in deep trouble.''

''Would you check and see if they're okay?''

O'Neill seemed surprised by the request, but agreed to comply. ''Okay, but I checked the computer before. So did Brian.''

''Humor me,'' Donovan said. ''First tell me about Asa and Juan.''

''Juan is a hard-working guy. Very friendly, too.''

''What was he in the slammer for?'' Mosko asked.

''Receiving stolen property. He worked in a chop shop.''

''Where Honda Accords were reduced to their component parts and redistributed,'' Donovan said.

''I guess,'' O'Neill replied.

''Where was the place?'' Mosko asked.

''Long Island City.''

''Wonder of wonders,'' Mosko said.

''Where did Juan serve his time?'' Donovan asked.

''Coxsackie. Same as Tom and Asa. They were buddies in the joint. Tom came first and then he brought in the other two. It's a state program.''

''And Asa? What did he steal?''

''Nothing. He was in for aggravated assault.''

''On who and when?'' Mosko asked.

''A bartender in the South Bronx. Ever want to kick the shit out of a bartender?''

''Only about two hundred times,'' Donovan said.

''Same bartender each time,'' Mosko added.

''Anybody I know?'' O'Neill asked with a smile.

''Could be,'' Donovan said. ''Where in the South Bronx?''

''Near Hunts Point Market,'' O'Neill said. Apparently noting their reaction, he added, "You seem to be interested in Hunts Point."

"We have a current case there," Donovan replied.

"So you just take in strays, is that it?" Mosko said.

"Like I said, I believe in giving a guy a second chance. In return, I get loyal employees. These guys *love* me and wouldn't do anything to hurt me."

"Are you sure?" Donovan asked.

"I would bet my life on it. And they would bet their lives on it. Like I said, one strike and they're out. Which in their cases means having their paroles revoked."

"There have been no arguments?" Donovan asked. "Nothing to cause one of 'em to get mad at you?"

"Nothing important," O'Neill said.

"With all due respect, can we be the judge of that?" Mosko said.

"You know, we've had words. I get on their cases about keeping the work environment even cleaner than they would naturally. Like I said, salmonella. They don't always see eye to eye with me. They don't like the one-strike-and-you're-out rule. Asa and Juan in particular. Like I said, we've had words. But it's all in the family."

"Cons can get a little touchy when pissed off," Mosko replied. "And one of yours has a record of assault."

"There's *nothing* here to steal except birds," O'Neill replied. "And they can have all they want. All they have to do is ask."

"Did you ever bribe a city official?" Donovan asked.

O'Neill looked surprised, was speechless for a moment, then said "No" while looking down at the floor tiles.

Having read the hesitation as the prelude to a lie, Donovan said, "Look, Brian and I are only interested in murder. You smoke a joint, you visit a hooker, you bribe an inspector, frankly, my friend, if it ain't layin' in the gutter bleeding…"

"We don't give a rat's ass," Mosko said.

O'Neill smiled a cautious sort of smile and said, quietly, "There may have been one or two things."

"Aren't there always," Donovan replied.

"I got this cousin Sammy," Mosko added, "who used to be a big-shot lawyer in Queens. One time he had to bribe a city official to get this huge contract. The bribe was fifty grand. So there was my cousin taking fifty grand off his taxes as a business expense."

O'Neill snickered.

"Look, Sammy enjoyed his year and a half at Danbury...."

"Minimum security slammer," Donovan added, just in case O'Neill hadn't heard of the place.

"Two good things happened. He got out of a marriage that sucked anyway, and he learned metalworking. Now Sammy's happily living the life of a sculptor."

"Aided in part by the couple mil he moved offshore before the gavel fell. Which reminds me, tell him about the gavel," Donovan said.

"Sammy's most famous sculpture is a twelve-foot-high bronze gavel," Mosko said proudly. "It decorates the plaza in front of the Queens County Courthouse, where he did most of his trial work and also was sentenced. Ain't America grand?"

"He got a second chance," O'Neill said.

"In a sense," Donovan replied. "The moral of this story is that a little crime can lead to a pleasant sort of lifestyle modification."

The captain used one of his tones of voice where people who didn't know him well found themselves hard-pressed to determine if he was serious or not.

"There *were* one or two bribes," O'Neill admitted.

"Did you keep records that someone with a beef against

you could use to get you—and the inspectors you bribed, of course—in trouble?'' Donovan asked.

O'Neill nodded.

"Where?" Mosko asked.

"On the PC."

"Nobody turned on that PC during the time frame we're discussing," Mosko said.

"I burned a CD," O'Neill admitted.

"Oh, you *burned a CD*," Donovan said.

"I was afraid that someone might take the info off my hard drive. So I burned a CD and left it, unmarked, in with the rest."

"So you saved your data in a form that's easy to steal," Donovan said. "Good thinking. How'd a guy who runs a meat plant learn how to burn CDs?"

"How do you think? My daughter taught me."

"Go get the disk," Mosko said.

O'Neill walked off to do as he was told. When he was gone, Donovan waved a hand in the direction of the shelves and said, "Let's get Howard to go over these shelves."

"Okay. Looking for what?"

"The owner of these prints," Donovan replied. He pointed out a handful of finger smudges on and around Tom Drozak's workstation. The smudges were on both the top of the shelf, the top of the stainless-steel counter, in the sink around the drain and on the frame surrounding the photo of his family.

"They belong to Drozak," Mosko said. "It's a nobrainer."

Donovan shook his head. "There are no prints at the other workstations."

"Drozak was the one who cleaned up."

"Yeah, he's a clean freak," Donovan said. "He cleaned up everyone else's places so well you can't see prints. You can't see *anything*. Well, *I* can't. Marcy can glance at the kitchen counter and find smudges that I couldn't find using a scanning electron microscope."

"My wife can do that, too," Mosko said, a trace of chagrin in his voice.

"Anyway, Drozak cleaned up but left his own work area with prints all over it. Actually, I was wrong about that. There are no prints on the faucet. So either he never touched it or he wiped it off. But he cleaned up the other guys' prints."

"Maybe he can see everyone else's dirt but not his own," Mosko offered. "My wife says I'm like that. She says 'You got no problem scoopin' up other people's messes but leave your own crap all over.'"

"I hear you," Donovan said.

"One good thing—since these guys are all ex-cons, Howard will have no problem getting fingerprint records."

The captain tossed up his hands, and Mosko began looking idly around the area. He crouched and looked under the workbenches, and in the grout separating the floor tiles and then examined the racks of knives, poultry scissors and other tools.

"I don't know what the hell we're looking for, Bill," he said finally. "Why don't we leave this all to Howard and go to the Emerald I'll and ruin George Kohler's holiday?"

"An outstanding suggestion," Donovan replied, yawning and stretching.

It was then that they heard O'Neill swearing. Then they heard a door slam and, quickly, approaching footsteps.

"What's up?" Donovan asked O'Neill as the man burst, red-faced and tensed up, into the area.

"The CD is gone," he exclaimed. "Someone stole it!"

"Now we're getting somewhere," Mosko said.

"I could be ruined!" O'Neill wailed. "I could *go to jail!*"

"For what?" Mosko asked, then added, "It always helps the investigators to know what the crime actually *is.*"

"Are you sure the CD is missing?" Donovan asked.

"Of course I'm sure. I left it on my desk right next to my Civil War disk series."

Donovan asked him to explain.

"I'm a Civil War buff," the man replied. "A month ago I bought the entire history of the Civil War on CDs. Pictures and all. I love this stuff and look at it whenever things are slow."

"I'm partial to the Napoleonic Wars myself, especially Trafalgar," Donovan said.

"I kept my accounting CD in there with my Civil War set and my daughter's CDs. I figured nobody would find it."

"*Wrong,*" Mosko said.

"Who knew it was there?" Donovan asked.

"Tom, Asa and Juan, I guess. They're the ones who have been in my office the most. I let them use my PC to check the scores of ball games. You know, the major leagues, the NFL, the NBA."

"Curiouser and curiouser," Donovan said, smiling slightly.

"Let's see the scene of the theft," Mosko said, waving his hand to urge O'Neill away from the bird-dressing area to the office.

That room was a small thing set behind the front counter. The door was small and covered on the outside with a rack holding pamphlets offering recipes of all sorts for the various forms of fowl on sale. At that moment, Christmas recipes and the colors red and green predominated.

"This room ain't too easy to find," Mosko said.

"I like it that way," the store owner replied. "I like it hidden from prying eyes and also cozy. I hide in there sometimes. And my daughter does her homework in there every so often. Like, when she's been in the city shopping and is waiting for me to close up and drive her home."

He pulled open the door and led the two detectives into a windowless room barely large enough for a junky metal desk and three metal folding chairs. But a large monitor sat atop the desk, a rack of CDs alongside. The disks were wedged between the base of the monitor and a concrete-block wall that had been covered with enough layers of heavy white paint for the surface to serve as a scratch pad for phone numbers. Donovan scrutinized several of them.

O'Neill stepped behind the desk and stabbed a finger at the CDs.

"See…gone," he said, as if the other men could discern the absence of the disk merely by scanning the pack of plastic-framed disks from a distance.

"When did you see it last?" Mosko asked.

"The day before yesterday," O'Neill replied.

Donovan leaned over the desk and looked more closely. In addition to the Civil War series and a copy of Microsoft Office were disks by pop stars such as Ricky Martin, ★NSYNC, Shakira and Alicia Keyes.

Mosko joined him, saying, "Marcy looks like Alicia Keyes."

"Marcy is taller and can't sing," Donovan said.

"Your wife is very striking," O'Neill said.

"Especially in kung fu mode," Mosko added.

"I think these music disks must belong to your daughter," Donovan said.

"Oh, not mine, and that's for sure," O'Neill said quickly.

"Where exactly was your accounting disk?" Mosko asked.

"Separating Ricky Martin and Shakira."

"As unnecessary as that may seem," Donovan said.

"She shares these records with all her friends," O'Neill added.

"We need for Howard to look for prints on Ricky Martin and Shakira," Mosko said.

Donovan nodded, asking O'Neill, "Who would you expect to have touched these CDs?"

"Just Alana and me."

"When was she here last?" Donovan asked.

"Yesterday."

"Whoever took the accounting disk had to have touched the others," Mosko said.

"How was it marked?" Donovan asked.

"It wasn't," O'Neill replied. "It was just there by itself."

"Okay," Donovan said. "We'll check it. Brian, how is Howard doing getting here?"

Mosko took out his cell phone and punched some numbers. A moment later he said into the instrument, "Who *is* this? It's Harvey Keitel, who the hell do you think? When are you getting here?"

Donovan smiled.

"Ten or twenty minutes," Mosko replied after he shut off the phone.

"Howard is a good boy," Donovan replied.

Then to O'Neill he said, "Paul, here's what I'd like to do. Get on the phone and ask Asa, Juan and Tom to come down to the Emerald I'll this afternoon."

"On Christmas Eve?"

"Tell them a story. Offer them something. Did you give them Christmas bonuses this year?"

The store owner shook his head. "I was going to give them all one hundred dollars each—what I normally give—but then there's this recession."

"I hear you," Donovan said. "But I want you to decide if keeping your insurance rates low is worth three hundred dollars."

"Of course it is," O'Neill replied. "If the insurance goes up, we're talking eight thousand."

"Consider the three hundred an investment. Call the guys

up and tell them you found the money, but they gotta come in and get it. Toss in paying for some booze, WisPride cheese and Ritz crackers, and we'll have a party. I'm pretty sure I can prove that no thief broke into your store last night.''

"You can?'' O'Neill asked with nervous enthusiasm.

"You can count on the captain,'' Mosko said.

Donovan checked his watch and said, "Have them get to the bar around two. In the meantime, Brian and I are gonna go back to my place, collect my kid and introduce him to the joys of playing pinball in a warm saloon and picking out a Christmas tree on a frosty sidewalk in New York City. Then we'll meet you on the corner. I'll call and tell you when.''

O'Neill asked what he should do in the interim, and Donovan told him to wait and let Bonaci into the market.

"You guys better come back,'' O'Neill said.

"I also have to invite the kid,'' Donovan said.

"Your kid?''

"No, George Le Bec, the Canadian petty thief.''

"It's my party,'' O'Neill objected. "No way.''

"You want to know what happened last night, don't you?'' Donovan asked.

"Yeah,'' the store owner grumbled.

Mosko said, "As they used to say in the captain's time, 'Go with the flow.' ''

"The 'captain's time?' '' Donovan said indignantly. "The *'captain's time?'* ''

"I meant, like, yesterday,'' Mosko said, smiling.

"Uh-huh,'' Donovan replied.

Then to O'Neill, he added "Get some eggnog. We'll have a little celebration.''

"And some music,'' Mosko said. "You got a CD player. Can we use it at the bar in case the jukebox sucks?''

O'Neill said that they could. "The guys listen to the Spanish station all day,'' he added.

"What do you have to play other than Ricky Martin and Shakira, which to me sounds like a kind of Japanese beer?"

"My daughter listens to ★NSYNC."

"I'm not listening to In the Sink, despite the obvious relevance to the location of the fingerprints," Donovan said.

"They're guys who sing," O'Neill added.

"Or so the story goes," Donovan said. "Let me bring a couple of disks from home."

"If my daughter had decent taste it would be different. But all she listens to is this junk. She even makes copies for her friends…burns CDs both here and at home. She clutters up my hard drive. I yell at her, but what good does it do?"

"Is she gonna be in the neighborhood this afternoon?" Mosko asked.

O'Neill nodded. "She's going to FAO Schwarz to pick up a last-minute present for my nephew. Then she's gonna meet me here to get driven home for the holiday."

"Invite her, too," Donovan said.

"The more the merrier," Mosko added.

"As long as she doesn't bring her music," Donovan added.

EIGHT

Just a little sweet story

"IS THIS THE BEST possible test of his ability to take the chair out on the sidewalk?" Marcy asked, looking askance at the unfolding scene.

Donovan was buttoning up his son's navy-blue peacoat and adjusting his cap prior to venturing out onto Kinderhook Street for the boy's first outdoors jaunt using the new chair.

Mary stood back a bit, her role having been preempted to some extent by the doting dad. This dad, however, looked hardly ordinary. For one thing, he looked ready for urban combat, wearing torn old jeans, his ageless, famous suede jacket and a United States Army Rangers backpack given to him as a present for his role in the 9/11 investigation. In it was stashed a stack of CDs. The disks shared space with the boy's water bottle, a Tupperware container of French Fries and the emergency medical kit that went everywhere with the boy. Looped over Donovan's shoulder was enough rope to hog-tie a hurricane.

"Are you sure you have enough stuff?" Marcy asked, handing her husband a folded old blanket.

"One can never have too many tools when taking one's son into the wild to chop down a tree," he said grandly.

Mary giggled as she slipped Daniel's insulated lunch box—the container holding *approved* food—into the carryall on the back of his chair. She told the boy, "Now, Mr. Man, you have your milk and your mush and an apple if you need one. Not too much of the food your father brings for you.''

"Yes, Aunt Mary," he replied, looking as pleased as could be both by all the attention and his first foray outside the house in his new chair. Donovan beamed over his son's clear joy at this grand adventure with his dad.

"You ready, slugger?" Mosko asked.

Daniel nodded.

Marcy had begun arranging fresh flowers in a vase on the marble-topped table alongside the front door. "You boys be careful out there," she said.

"We venture forth into the unknown," Donovan said.

"If you remember, pick up a box of confectioner's sugar," she said.

"Gotcha," the captain said as he pushed open the door.

Excited, Daniel drove forward into what had become an eye-hurting sunny Christmas Eve afternoon. While the snow on the branches of the trees lining Kinderhook Street hadn't entirely melted, it was hanging in gobs that every so often detached and fell onto the scraped and salted sidewalk or the unwary stroller.

As Donovan predicted, the way was smooth enough. Only at the intersection with the avenue did the boy need help. There, snow banks tossed up by passing plows made little mountain ranges that required adult assistance. Donovan and Mosko lifted the boy, chair and all, over these, while he made jet airplane noises. Before long the trio had made it up the avenue and across the street to the Emerald I'll.

The bar glowed with the Christmas lights that George Kohler had draped, doubtless with a great deal of huffing and puffing, onto a small tree inside the window. Donovan pondered what he knew had to have been a four-hour marathon of shots, beer, curses, intentions good and bad, broken balls and insults dispensed as freely as Budweiser that inevitably accompanied the display of holiday cheer.

"Wait here while I make reservations for later," he said.

"Can I go in?" Daniel asked.

"You can, but only with me, until you get to be bigger."

"You always tell me I'm a big boy," he protested.

"You have to be bigger to go in there," Donovan said. "You have to be bigger still to stay out."

"I don't understand, Daddy."

"I'll explain one day. Today you'll come in with Uncle Brian and me, after the three of us pick up a tree and solve a crime."

"Can I help solve a crime?" the boy asked, true excitement flashing across his pink cheeks.

"I'm counting on you," Donovan replied.

"Did someone get hurt?" Daniel asked.

"Not this time. But a man went into a building where he wasn't supposed to. We have to find out who that man is."

"Is it wrong to go into someplace you're not supposed to?"

"Sometimes, son," Donovan replied.

"You mean like I can't go near the furnace?"

"Like that," Donovan said, then excused himself and ducked into the bar.

There he found George Kohler slumped atop the stool he had positioned for himself at one end of the bar. The Santa hat did nothing to offset the grinchlike expression. Donovan's entrance failed to help. In fact, upon seeing the captain, the bartender growled, "Oh, shit," and brought a slender glass of draft beer to his lips.

"And a very Merry Christmas to you, too, sir," Donovan said.

"This is twice in two days you've been in here. Whaddya

want? You don't drink and you're married, so it can't be for booze and women."

"I came for your charming company," the captain said, smiling.

"Get lost," Kohler snarled.

"Why'd you have your two henchmen drag me in here yesterday if you're gonna sit there with the personality of an arthritic crocodile? And after all I've done for you over the years."

"Like what?" Kohler snapped.

"I got you the job at Marcy's Home Cooking," Donovan replied.

"Which your wife closed and sold out to Starbucks, putting me out of work."

"I also came and visited you when you were tending bar at the Hotsy Totsy Club." That was Legs Diamond's old hangout, recently reborn as part of the cleanup of Times Square.

"And one of my best customers was impaled on a cross-bow arrow," Kohler said.

"Not my fault," Donovan replied. "And they're called bolts, not arrows."

"Well, bolt the hell out of here," Kohler growled, finishing the beer in his glass and licking the foam off his gray mustache.

"Okay, I'm gone," Donovan said, turning toward the door.

"Where are you going so fast?" Kohler asked.

Donovan sighed and half turned back to his old friend. "You know, I have time for many things at this most wonderful time of year, but not for this."

"Merry Christmas, Bill," Kohler said, smiling.

"I'll be back in a couple of hours. I want to reserve a table for six or seven and the pinball machine."

"You got it," Kohler said as the captain disappeared out the door.

Out on the sidewalk, Mosko looked at Donovan's expression, which said, *I just survived another encounter with Kohler,* and asked, "How is Mr. Personality today?"

"The usual."

"Great. I can't wait to spend time with him. Let's go get the tree."

"Yeah," Daniel added.

The Christmas tree expedition continued uptown and reached the grove of freshly cut evergreens propped against the fence that belonged to the Gansevoort Live Poultry Market.

The elder Le Bec was off with a young couple, arguing, his gestures wild.

Donovan wondered what they were saying, then lost interest in the matter and sought out the son. He was alone down the row of trees, wedged between two Norwegian spruce, facing the fence.

"The kid's taking a whiz," Mosko said. "Good thing you already got your tree and it isn't one of those."

"Yeah," Donovan agreed.

He led the way to where his proud tree stood out from and above the rest and showed it to Daniel.

"This is the best one," Donovan said. "Do you like it?"

"Yeah! It's bigger than last year."

"Last year we were in the apartment," Donovan said.

"And this year you got the Elysée Palace," Mosko added.

Donovan gave him a Kohlerish scowl.

"Can we take it now, Daddy?" Daniel asked.

"You bet."

"I want to carry it."

Laughing gently so as not to seem dismissive, Donovan said, "It's a bit big, son. We'll have the man wrap it, and then after we're done at the market I'll put a rope on it and you can drag it behind your chair.''

"Okay!''

"With a little help,'' the captain told Mosko quietly.

Donovan reached in between the branches, grabbed the trunk and pulled the tree up to the vertical. The branches sprang out to their full width, prompting Daniel to shake his hands in glee.

George Le Bec then emerged from the trees and walked quickly down to Donovan and party. The young man adjusted his clothes as he walked, sending a small shower of pine and fir needles onto the snow-covered sidewalk.

"Watering the flowers?'' Mosko asked.

Momentarily caught off guard, the boy stammered "I—I wasn't…I mean, I was making sure that the trees weren't leaning too hard on Mr. O'Neill's fence.''

"Oh,'' Donovan said.

"Do you want me to bag the tree?'' the young man asked.

"Sure,'' Donovan said.

Le Bec took the tree and, hugging it to his chest, carried it halfway down the row of timber to where a tree-bagging machine sat alongside the kerosene heater.

It took amazing agility and years of practice, Donovan was sure, to so easily rotate a twelve-foot Christmas tree and shove it through the gigantic metal basket, open on both ends, that left the tree wrapped in plastic mesh.

"Amazing gadget,'' Donovan said.

"It keeps the branches from breaking on the way home,'' the young man said. "Do you want it on top of your…?''

He looked around for Donovan's car and, seeing none, tossed up his hands.

"When we're ready to go home, we'll tow it,'' Donovan said.

He took the coil of rope off his shoulder and trussed the

tree by the base of the trunk. He left tow ends of rope dangling—one to tie the base of the tree to the back of the chair, and the other for use in surreptitious pulling.

Then he stood the tree up again, preparatory to carrying it to the front of the poultry market. Donovan reached out with a toe and gently tapped the tree-bagger.

"What would happen if a man was pushed through that thing?"

"He'd be in the bag," the young Le Bec said with a laugh.

"I've bagged guys for crawling though tight spaces," Mosko added.

Perhaps unsure of what the detectives meant and definitely caught off guard again, the young man simply looked blank and turned away. Then he asked, "Didn't you want a wreath, too?"

"Three," Mosko said.

The young man produced three from a pile of them. They were two feet across each and trimmed with holly's red berries and green leaves.

"Sixty dollars," he said.

Donovan handed over three twenties. "Father Christmas here will carry them," he said, indicating Mosko.

"Do you play pinball?" Donovan asked.

"Sure. Why?"

"I want you to come to a Christmas party we're having at two at the Emerald I'll a couple blocks down Hudson."

"Why me?"

"You can help clear up some things about last night," Donovan explained. "And there's a vintage Kiss pinball machine that must be seen to be believed."

"Can I say 'no'?" the young man asked.

"Sure, if you want us to think you were the one who broke into the store last night," Donovan said.

"You got a history of that, kid," Mosko said.

"That was years ago."

"This is now," Mosko said. "Come to the party and play pinball like a good boy."

"I'm underage."

"You can have Coke," Donovan said.

"Okay, if my dad says I can," the young man said, adding a shrug as a way to show he was nonchalant about being suspected of breaking and entering.

"See ya," Mosko said, hefting the stack of wreaths and starting off down the block toward the store entrance. Carrying the tree, Donovan followed while Daniel drove along, holding his end of the rope.

When the trio was out of earshot, Donovan asked his son, "Do you think he wants to come to the party?"

"Yeah," Daniel replied.

"Are you sure? You know that you're my little lie detector."

"Yeah. He liked when you asked him."

"I think so, too," Donovan replied.

"When are we gonna hook the tree up to my chair, Daddy?"

"Soon, right after we go to the goose store and talk to Uncle Howard. There's his van."

Daniel smiled at the sight of the Special Investigations forensics van, which was parked against the curbside snow bank in front of the market. The word *van* was a misnomer, for the vehicle was as big as a medium-size truck and bristled with communications antennae. It also hummed with the sound of its own electrical generator, installed to power the miniature but complete lab inside.

Donovan set the tree against the side of the van and slid open the side door. He stuck his head inside and called out "Yo, Howard! What's happening?"

"Merry Christmas, boss," the man replied.

Like Mosko, Howard Bonaci was a Donovan veteran who began with him at the West Side Major Crimes Unit and followed him to the citywide Department of Special Investigations when he made captain and was given its helm. The three-quarter-million-dollar van was part of the incentive package offered the forensics genius.

Donovan lifted his son out of his chair, carried him inside the van and helped him onto a chair alongside Bonaci.

"Merry Christmas, Danny," the man said.

"Merry Christmas, Uncle Howard," the boy replied.

"Are you ready to go to work?"

"Yes!" the boy replied with evident excitement.

"Hit Enter," Bonaci said, tapping the smallest of the three keyboards that were mounted at varying angles at his console.

Daniel did so. The small monitor placed partway up the wall burst into life with a vastly enlarged image of a fingerprint. Varying text surrounded it.

"A print!" Daniel said.

"You got it."

"Is that from a bad man, Uncle Howard?"

"That's what we're going to find out," Bonaci said.

"That print is from Drozak, isn't it?" Donovan said, crouching between his son and the forensics chief.

"You got it, boss. The man himself. He cleaned up everything in the freakin' place but his own prints."

"Which were all over the place," Donovan said.

"You said it. Except on the window. Only smudges on the window."

"What about the two other hoods?" Mosko asked.

Bonaci shook his head. "I pulled their prints out of the files, and the only place I found 'em in the market environment was on the snapshots and pictures decorating their work stations."

"Drozak cleaned up the others," Donovan said.

"No shit," Bonaci replied. "This guy cleaned up like his life depended on it. There was nothing anywhere 'cept for his own prints all over his sink and around there. There *was* a hefty dose of alkyl dimethyl benzyl ammonium saccharinate and ethanol."

"I *knew it,*" Mosko said.

"Illuminate," Donovan said.

"Lysol."

"In and around the sink," the captain said.

Bonaci nodded. "There and on the wad of paper towel in the trash can below."

"The last thing Drozak does before closing time is empty that can," Mosko said.

"And so he did," Donovan replied.

"As for the stack of CDs in the office, there are two sets of prints, and only two sets of prints—belonging to O'Neill and his daughter. At least I presume the latter. O'Neill let me take *his* and showed me a CD…who or what is a Beyonce?"

"A Beyonce is a séance that's on hold," Donovan replied.

"I thought that," Bonaci said, continuing. "Anyway, he showed me a CD that his offspring just bought. Only one set of prints were on it—hers."

"And on the PC?" Mosko asked.

"The two of 'em, father and daughter. And the three other guys."

"One other thing," Bonaci said.

"Yeah?" Mosko prompted.

"I checked with the boys in the Bronx like you asked me to. And Drozak, Williams and Estevez were in their respective homes last night, more or less. Want details?"

"First the 'more or less,'" Donovan replied.

"Estevez went out for an hour," Bonaci said. "This was around ten, and he came back with a six-pack and four lottery tickets."

"Seems like a reasonable thing for a man to do in the evening," Donovan said.

"The wife attests to it."

"What about Williams?"

"His wife alibis him except for the period from eleven-thirty to about two," Bonaci said.

"Explain."

"He says he went to the local bar and shot some pool, then picked up a Genoa salami and a bottle of Grey Poupon mustard and went home. The wife was asleep by then and can't verify the return time."

"Does Grey Poupon go with Genoa salami?" Donovan asked, yawning.

"What do the guys at the local bar say?" Mosko asked.

"Our boys in the Bronx are still trying to track 'em down," Bonaci replied.

"Does Drozak's alibi hold?" Donovan asked.

Nodding, Bonaci said "His wife says the two of them went to bed around nine…"

"Love is a wonderful thing," Mosko said.

"And that he didn't budge…"

Continuing Mosko's thought, Donovan said, "In theory."

"…until morning. But she's a heavy sleeper," Bonaci said.

"So the three of them have only so-so alibis," Mosko said.

"Like I told you, it was 'more or less.'"

Donovan unwound himself from the crouch he had been in and placed a hand on his son's shoulder. Then he said, "Daniel, what do you think? Would you have stayed in bed all last night?"

Daniel shook his head. "No, Daddy. Remember, I wanted to go see the snow. But Mommy wouldn't let me."

"I would have wanted to go out and see the snow, too," Donovan added.

Then he stretched, expelled a burst of air, and said, "Our

work here is almost done. Howard, would you do me a favor and test the snow at the spot where the boy who sells trees took a leak a short time ago? Brian will show you where.''

"What am I looking for?''

"Round up the usual substances,'' Donovan replied.

Then he returned his attention to his son and said, "Time for you to haul the tree to the bar and then home.''

"Do you know who the bad guy is, Daddy?'' Daniel asked, the fire of adoration in his big eyes as he looked up at his father.

Donovan smiled warmly and said, "There's no bad guy today, son, just a little sweet story. After all, it's Christmas.''

DONOVAN HAD NO IDEA how George Kohler laid his growling hands on Christmas carols, but they poured from the jukebox with the momentum of a new red sled hurling down the slope. The back room of Emerald I'll was decorated with wreaths, holly branches and a snowy white Christmas tree that gleamed brightly enough to make holiday revelers disregard the fact it was plastic. To complete the festive holiday feeling, a long table was covered with a white paper tablecloth that was printed with tiny red Santas frolicking with reindeer atop snowy, evergreen-studded slopes.

Daniel had dragged the family's own Christmas tree all the way down the avenue from the side street upon which sat the meat market, garnering many smiles from pedestrians charmed by the sight of a boy in a wheelchair towing an immense tree. If he could tell that his father and "uncle" were helping surreptitiously, Daniel politely gave no indication of the fact. Once the tree reached the bar, Donovan and Mosko stood it upright next to the door and went inside, following Daniel's chair.

O'Neill sat at the head of the table, surrounded by his entourage. His daughter, a quietly beautiful Irish girl with wavy light-brown hair and a witchy smile, sat to his right, stirring a nonalcoholic drink that looked tropical. It was of a purple color with a faint yellow something swirling in it. Donovan wondered how much abuse she had endured from Kohler to get it, but then decided that Mr. Shots-and-Beer had turned benevolent at long last, shown also by the decorated back room. The three poultry trussers sat in a row to his left, looking half grateful at the unexpected and sudden Christmas bonus and half afraid of what was meant by the police presence. Across from them and next to Alana O'Neill was Howard Bonaci, who had locked the van and joined the party. The young Le Bec sat off from the rest, angled so that he couldn't make eye contact with O'Neill.

"Season's greetings and salutations," Donovan said grandly, urging his son to the other end of the table and to the chairless place that awaited him.

All present exchanged hellos and introductions. As Donovan took a seat at the head of the table at the other end from O'Neill, he noticed Alana staring at Mosko. The sergeant-turned-lieutenant had that effect on women, who nearly always were captivated either by the size of the muscles or his powerful presence, sometimes both.

Kohler appeared, bearing two pitchers of beer. He deposited one at either end of the table, then eyeballed Daniel and said, after a few seconds' pondering, "I remember you when you were a little kid."

"Hi," Daniel said brightly.

"I remember being shocked when your mom and dad decided that the world needed another Donovan. Well, everyone's entitled to an opinion. Welcome to my bar, kid. If you're anything like your dad this will be the beginning of a long association."

Daniel smiled and looked away.

"I dig the chair," Kohler added.

"Are you done?" Donovan asked.

"Yeah. Whaddya want, a virgin Mary?"

"A bottle of Kaliber, of course. Now get the hell outta here and let me work."

"I Windexed the Kiss pinball machine for the kid," Kohler said as he shuffled back to the front of the bar.

Daniel looked up at his father and asked quietly, "Daddy, why is that man unhappy?"

"I've been trying to figure that out for twenty years," Donovan replied, touching his son on the arm. "But he's a good man. Pay no attention to what he says. After all, he cleaned the pinball machine for you."

Daniel nodded, then smiled brightly and said, "Can I have a Coke?"

"And a Coke!" Donovan shouted to the retreating figure of Kohler, and was rewarded with an elevated middle finger.

After beer was poured and snacks distributed and ten or fifteen minutes' worth of small talk, most of it about the football playoffs, endured, Donovan got everyone's attention by clinking his beer bottle with a spoon. The others looked at him, O'Neill's three helpers with a look of mild dread.

"First of all, to everyone a merry Christmas," Donovan said, standing. "That said, and so we all can get home to *enjoy* Christmas, I have some business to attend to. As some of you know, I'm Bill Donovan, a captain in the New York Police Department and adviser to the Department of Special Investigations. My esteemed colleague here, Lieutenant Brian Moskowitz, heads that department and, from time to time, lets me assist him with cases."

Mosko smiled and sipped at his beer.

Donovan continued. "Now, along with your unexpected holiday bonuses—and congratulations, by the way—comes the news that someone broke into the Gansevoort Live Poultry Market last night."

The three men, and Alana, looked down into their laps. O'Neill watched the reactions, as did the two detectives and Daniel.

"A break-in at the market can mess with all your lives, I think you know," Donovan continued. "It can raise insurance rates, and that could play havoc with profitability. I know that you all want the market to continue to succeed, especially the three here—" Donovan cast an eye on the trio of poultry dressers "—for whom this job represents the best way of staying far away from the Coxsackie Correctional Institute. Did I pronounce that correctly?"

"Yeah, that was okay," Asa Williams replied.

Donovan felt the man was warming to the idea of cops being present.

"Now, let's be straight on one thing. Lieutenant Moskowitz and I don't give a flying—"

Donovan then remembered that his young son was present.

"Don't *care at all* that you guys were in jail. Some of history's most admirable figures spent time in the can. So you won't be discriminated against because of that. However, you *are* likely suspects and, like I said, no one wants to have it on record that a crime occurred last night at the market. But someone *did* go in through a back window.... You guys know the one where the burglar alarm doesn't work?"

All three nodded.

"That alarm hasn't worked in a while," Drozak said, raising a still-bandaged hand.

"I think you meant, 'never worked *right*'," Donovan said. "Anyway, I'm sorry to see that your hand hasn't healed, Tom."

Drozak looked at his bandaged hand, then moved it back to his lap.

"It's okay," he said in a low voice.

"I never like to see men in pain," Donovan said. "Any chance you got that while carving my goose?"

"Could have," Drozak said.

"We cut ourselves all the time," Estevez said.

"I'll bet," the captain said.

"What did the guy steal?" Estevez asked.

"We don't know," Donovan replied. "The only thing that seems to be missing is a CD—a compact disk—taken from Paul's office. There were confidential business records on that disk. They could cause a certain amount of trouble…"

"A *lot* of trouble," Mosko added.

"For Paul, if they got into the wrong hands," Donovan said. "Since I'm pretty sure that no one here wants bad things to happen to Paul and the market, let's go over a few items to see what happened last night."

"First thing is your alibis for 1:00 a.m.," Mosko said.

"Asa, your wife says you were home till eleven-thirty, after which you say you went up to the corner bar and shot pool until two."

"That's about right," Williams said.

"Disregarding the question of whether a parolee is allowed to shoot pool in local bars, that seems a pretty normal thing for a guy to do on a holiday evening," Donovan said. "And it's exactly what you did. We checked. You're a pretty mean man with a cue, my friend."

"I won me ten bucks," Williams said proudly.

"One of several facts we won't trouble your parole officer with," Donovan added. "Another being that while you're a good pool player, you were up against guys who couldn't tell a clock from a kangaroo. They were all in the bag and none of 'em could remember exactly when you left."

"Dumb bastards," Williams snarled.

"Probably true," Donovan continued. "In any event, you

had time to hop on a train and get here by 1:00 a.m., which is about when the event in question occurred.''

Williams downed some beer and muttered to himself, looking down and shaking his head.

Donovan turned his attention to Estevez. ''You were home with the little lady last night,'' the captain said. ''That's except for the time you went out for beer and lottery tickets. Did you win anything?''

''The drawing is Thursday,'' Estevez said.

''Oh. Never bought a lottery ticket…''

''He doesn't have to,'' Mosko added.

Donovan gave him a look. Then he continued, saying, ''You got home around eleven, but your wife is hazy on the time she fell asleep. Could have been twelve. Could have been twelve-thirty. So your alibi is a little weak-kneed. And as for *you*,'' the captain said to Drozak, ''you and your wife hit the sack around nine. Which I suppose means you hit it with a hammer. I love to hear about good relationships.''

''We're in love,'' Drozak replied.

''But unfortunately for your alibi she's a heavy sleeper, and as such has no idea what you might have done afterward. So you could have grabbed a downtown train and done it.''

''Done *what?*'' Williams asked.

''Come in through that window we talked about,'' Donovan said.

''And stolen what?'' Estevez asked.

''Actually, stolen nothing. Not a damn thing was taken. Not so much as a pheasant's egg. Paul, you *do* have pheasants, don't you?''

''We have everything,'' O'Neill said. ''But what about the CD with my business records on it?''

Smiling, Donovan looked at Alana and said, ''Well?''

''Well what?'' she asked, startled and jumping slightly in her seat.

"Where's the disk?" Donovan asked.

"What disk?"

"The one you took from your father's desk. Remember, the unlabeled disk he left between Ricky Martin and Shakira?"

She looked down, then up again. What had been a look of defiance turned to charm and light, the basic teenage girl I'm-naughty-but-I'm-cute look.

"Oh, *that* disk," Alana said. "I thought it was blank, you know, like I could burn a copy of the new Shakira album for my friend Lisa. So I took it home to do that and I found out that was Daddy's business stuff."

"Where is it now?" O'Neill asked.

"In my room with my other disks," she said. "What's the fuss?"

"Your father kept things on it that could be embarrassing if they got out," Donovan said.

"You mean, like porn?" She giggled.

"Alana!" O'Neill said.

"I was just kidding," she replied, giggling some more.

"Business records," Donovan said.

"Oh. I don't care about his chicken stuff."

"Give me the disk the second we get home," O'Neill snapped.

"Yes, Daddy."

"So much for the great compact disk caper," Mosko said.

Nodding, Donovan said, "Now, that leaves us with young Le Bec here. Those of you who haven't met him may know him as one of the Canadian fellows selling Christmas trees on the edge of the market."

There was a small chorus of "Hi's." O'Neill's voice was not among them. *He* had turned away to avoid eye contact, and instead was glaring at his daughter.

Continuing, Donovan said, "Now, George here was perhaps the closest to the scene of the supposed crime. While his father slept in the front seat of their tree-hauling flatbed truck, he was lying in back watching *Farscape* and... Howard, what was he doing?''

''Smoking a joint,'' Bonaci replied. ''His urine showed traces of marijuana.''

Shocked, embarrassed, and panicked, George stammered ''I—I didn't...I mean, you're wrong....''

''Shut up, kid,'' Mosko said.

Tapping his own chest, Donovan repeated an old mantra. ''See this *S* on my chest, son? It stands for 'Should I care?' Frankly, watching *Farscape* does lend itself to having a few tokes of Bolivian Time Warp, or so I hear out there on the streets and sidewalks of New York.''

''Secondhand,'' Mosko added.

''The point of all this being that you are an unreliable witness as to what did or didn't happen last night,'' Donovan said.

''I—I did pretty much what you said, sir,'' the boy replied. ''Do you really mean that you don't care?''

Donovan shrugged. ''Did you see or hear anything?''

''No. Like I told you. I was watching TV.''

Addressing the crowd, the captain said, ''That clears up another piece of this puzzle.''

''So *who* broke into my store last night?'' O'Neill demanded.

Donovan gave Drozak a look, accusing yet kindly. Then the captain said, ''Tom...are you sure that your hand is okay?''

Startled, Drozak jumped. Then he lifted his bandaged hand, holding it up to the light before resting it, like a robin with a broken wing, on the Santa tablecloth.

''Um...yeah,'' he said.

"I'd like to see the cut," Donovan said. "Please take the bandage off."

Drozak's face went white and he sucked in his breath.

"Take it off," Donovan said.

"It—it'll get infected," the man protested.

"I brought first aid," Donovan said, reaching into the carryall on the back of Daniel's chair and producing a plastic bag containing sterile bandages and a tube of bacitracin.

"Whip out your palm," Mosko snarled.

Nearly sweating, Drozak did as he was told. When the bandage was unwound, he looked away at the wall, studiously refusing to look at his hand.

"Hold it up to the light," Donovan said.

The man complied, and as he did a look of resignation came over him. There was no cut, nothing at all.

"*Tom,*" O'Neill said, looking at his employee and friend. "What gives? You told me you cut yourself."

Donovan reached across the table, took Drozak's hand, pulled it into a beam of light from one of the minispotlights and said, "Tom didn't cut himself. He made that story up while looking desperately for an object he put on the shelf above his work station yesterday and then lost. This is an object that would get him into a huge amount of trouble with his wife should she find out it was missing. Especially on Christmas, the anniversary of their marriage."

Drozak looked astonished when Donovan stood, reached into his pants pocket and produced the gold band.

"Your wedding ring," Donovan said. "It fell off the shelf and into the inners of the goose you were trussing up. This is the goose that found its way to my kitchen, where your ring fell out while I was preparing it for a walk down the aisle to the dinner table."

Drozak looked grateful enough to cry. "Can I have it back?" he asked.

"Sure," Donovan said, handing it over to a man who put it on his finger so fast that tracking the motion was nearly impossible.

"You took the ring off to work...."

"I don't allow the men to wear jewelry while working," O'Neill added. "Rings and other stuff like that could harbor bacteria that then could get into the meat, make customers sick, and result in my losing my shirt and all these guys their jobs."

"So Tom took off the ring and put it on the shelf next to the picture of his beloved wife."

"I always do," Drozak added.

"But while he was working it fell off and into the body cavity of the bird he was dressing. At closing time, he noticed it was missing. But the market was closing early and insistently, and Tom didn't have time to find the ring. So he quickly bandaged his hand so his wife couldn't see that the ring was missing, concocted a story about cutting himself and went home. He came back after she fell asleep, let himself in through that window and conducted a more thorough search."

Drozak bobbed his head.

"He still couldn't find the ring, which by that time was in my refrigerator, and was so panicked that he left fingerprints over his work station. Normally, he would leave this area spotless."

Again Drozak nodded.

"Not knowing what he would do, Tom went home."

"Tom, why didn't you tell me?" O'Neill said.

"I was afraid you would fire me," Drozak said, sounding like a little boy who was fessing up to one malfeasance or another. "I didn't want to go back in the joint."

"I would *never* do that," O'Neill said, reaching out and

grabbing Drozak's hand and squeezing it. "I would forgive you, just as I forgive my daughter for stealing my disk."

He gave her a look that implied that forgiveness was but a concept.

"Now forgive her for liking Mariah Carey," Donovan said.

"Can't do it," O'Neill said.

"Good man," the captain replied.

Again the girl giggled.

Donovan stood, waved his bottle of Kaliber high in the air and proclaimed, "The false alarm about a break-in at the Gansevoort Live Poultry Market is solved. There was no break-in and no reason to trouble the insurance company with that misinformation."

"Thank God," O'Neill said.

"There was but an attempted ring rescue, which has now been concluded successfully. So if we're all done with business, let's have a party."

Amid a racket of congratulations and applause, Donovan sat back down and took a slug of beer. He thought for a moment, then turned to young Le Bec and said, "I'm all for tolerance and international cooperation and all that, but since 9/11 my tolerance for foreign foul-ups has faltered. Your father owes the City of New York seven thousand dollars. Tell him to pay up or clear out."

"I can call the boys about the scofflaw thing right now," Mosko said, brandishing his cell phone as if it were a grenade.

"Get outta town by sundown," Donovan snapped.

The boy turned pale, finished his soda and left.

"I always wanted to say that," Donovan added.

O'Neill flashed a broad grin.

"Can we play pinball now, Daddy?" Daniel asked.

"Absolutely," the captain replied. Then he added, "I used

to play a pretty mean pinball myself. Did I ever tell you those stories?''

''Can we play pinball?'' Daniel asked.

Donovan smiled and said, ''Sure.''

''And then take the tree home?''

''Yep.''

''And trim it?''

Donovan nodded.

''And eat the goose?''

''I'm hungry, too,'' Donovan said, and got up to go off in search of crackers and cheese.

REUNIONS CAN BE MURDER

A CHARLIE PARKER MYSTERY

Connie Shelton

When an octogenarian goes missing, his obnoxious daughter pesters Charlie Parker to find him. Charlie follows the eccentric old man's trail to a ghost town—site of a gold rush, a bitter scandal and now a corpse.

Charlie discovers Willie was looking to strike it rich by claiming a legendary fortune. Determined to link Willie's path with her suspicions of illegal drug doings in the deserted town, Charlie sets out across the searing desert toward the mountains, prepared for anything...except murder.

**"Charlie is slick, appealing, and nobody's fool—
just what readers want in an amateur sleuth."
—*Booklist* on *Memories Can Be Murder***

Available November 2003 at your favorite retail outlet.

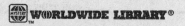

MYSTERY ™ **WORLDWIDE LIBRARY®**   WCS475

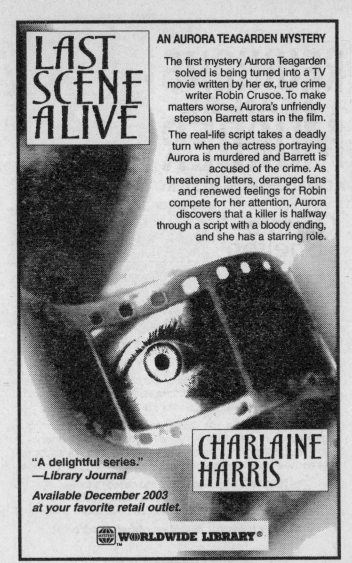

Take 2 books and a surprise gift FREE!

SPECIAL LIMITED-TIME OFFER

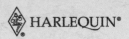

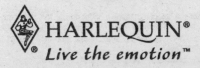

crazy LOVE

A BUBBA MABRY MYSTERY
STEVE BREWER

Bubba Mabry is hired to find out who had an affair with a millionaire's late wife. The answer comes quickly, but typically, it all goes south when the guilty paramour is murdered.

Bubba doggedly pursues the secrets that lie at the heart of Albuquerque's most exclusive residential community and the cranky rich women who live there. And learns that love is like P.I. work: once burned, twice stupid, three times…you're dead.

"Steve Brewer exhibits his usual comic flair…."
—Publishers Weekly

Available December 2003 at your favorite retail outlet.

SINS OUT OF SCHOOL

A DOROTHY MARTIN MYSTERY

You can't deprive Dorothy Martin of
Thanksgiving dinner, even in merry
old England. But Dorothy gets a
serving of trouble when she fills in
for a missing teacher at the local
school—and the woman is now
the prime suspect in the murder
of her husband.

The victim's death was really a
blessing for his wife and daughter—
but did one of them kill him? The
answer leads Dorothy to secrets
and lies, and into the cold heart
of an evil man, and the surprising
face of a killer.

Jeanne M. Dams

"Fans of the English cozy will put
the kettle on, snuggle under a lap
rug, and sigh contentedly...."
—*Kirkus Reviews*

*Available November 2003
at your favorite retail outlet.*

WJD474